Cry of the Peacock

Juliet Dymoke

PIATKUS

Copyright © 1992 by Juliet Dymoke

First published in Great Britain in 1992 by
Judy Piatkus (Publishers) Ltd of
5 Windmill Street, London W1

**The moral right of the author
has been asserted**

*A catalogue record for this book is available
from the British Library*

ISBN 0–7499–0140–3

Phototypeset in 11/12pt Times by
Phoenix Photosetting, Chatham, Kent
Printed and bound in Great Britain by
Biddles Ltd, Guildford and King's Lynn

*For my nephew Michael,
for Hazel and their family*

Chapter 1

The silence of the dank and dreary January morning, broken only by the soft footfalls of the burial party, was suddenly shattered by the raucous shriek of a peacock. The Hollanders' peacocks occasionally wandered out of the grounds, seeming to like the churchyard wall, and one of them perched there now, spreading its great fan of feathers. It cried out again, disturbing not only the mourners but a young horse being put through his paces in the snowy field beyond.

There was a swift and violent disruption to the interment, the thunder of hooves as the black stallion, terrified and out of hand, leapt the wall and plunged up the path. Head tossing, eyes wild, he scattered the mourners to either side. One lady stumbled and was held up by her husband; another gentleman cried out, "Are you mad, sir? Can't you see –" but his reproof was drowned by the horse's drumming hooves and the furious shouts of the rider. He was wrenching at the reins, concentrating on keeping his seat as the animal reared and plunged.

"Damn your blood," he bellowed. "Hold, curse you, hold."

The stallion's eyes rolled in terror and Obadiah Smith, groom for many years at Hollanders House, leapt forward, endeavouring to catch the reins, but the horse was too maddened to heed his clutching hands. Sir Thomas's man of business attempted the same thing and was sent headlong into a yew tree.

Maeve, who had been following her sister Mary, was forced to jump aside, stumbling against a crooked tombstone. She held on to it to steady herself and had a brief glimpse of the rider, a big man in a mulberry coat, his face red with rage and exertion as he struggled to control the maddened animal. His tall black beaver hat flew off, landing almost at her feet as he thundered past, his horse sending snow flying to spatter her dress. She cared nothing for that – she hated black – but she felt a swift anger and a strong desire to kick his hat after him.

The burial party had broken up in some disarray. Maeve's twin Mary, gave an involuntary cry and clutched at the arm of her husband, William; several gentlemen stepped forward, and Lionel Hollander, nearest to the path, had swept his terrified young sister up into his arms and carried her out of danger.

And then it was all over, horse and rider gone, pelting out of the gate where only a short while ago the funeral cortège had passed in. There were murmurs among the gathered mourners, whispers of incredulity that such a thing could happen, before everyone began to collect themselves and reassemble.

The Vicar had gone to his sister-in-law and had said something quietly to her, but she stood rigidly, her eyes blazing with anger rather than fear or grief. He waited until there was quiet and the bearers able slowly to lower the coffin into the deep hole dug to receive it, the grave-diggers standing respectfully at a distance, waiting to complete their work. Sure now that no one was hurt, and in a voice only slightly shaken, he brought out the last words: "Ashes to ashes, dust to dust . . ." and cast some earth on his brother's coffin.

The widow, a clod of Hollanders soil in her hand, threw it down so that it fell on the brass plate, bearing the name Thomas George Hollander. Only then did she show the strain it had all been, the toll the ghastly interruption had taken; she swayed on her feet and her two sons came, one on each side, to support her.

Maeve turned impulsively to her. "How awful. Dear Aunt Isabel, I'm so sorry."

"It was outrageous," Lionel agreed. "Mama, are you all right?"

She braced herself, as she had always done in times of crisis. "Of course," she said in a low voice. "But I shall make it my business to find out who that - that desecrater was."

"I've not seen him before," William said, and the Vicar turned back to add, "He is not to my knowledge one of my parishioners. To ride through the graveyard like that! He seemed quite unable to control his horse."

"It must have been the peacock that frightened him," Maeve suggested. "I saw it on the wall a moment before. It was old Solomon."

"Whatever the reason, I've a poor opinion of the rider as a horseman," the Reverend Martin Hollander, brother of the dead man, went on. "Someone might have been killed. Nell, my dearest, let me take your arm."

They moved off, but the widow paused for one last moment, glancing back at the deep hole in the earth. Memories flooded her mind and heart. After misunderstandings and unhappiness in the early years of their arranged marriage, miraculously she and Tom had fallen deeply in love and the last twelve years had made up for all the rest. Now he was gone, a victim of Marsh fever and inflammation of the lungs, so Dr Sergeant had said, when she had hoped for many more years together, and she let a small bunch of snowdrops fall on the coffin.

Maeve raised her head and stole a glance at her aunt. Isabel, Lady Hollander, was tall for a woman, handsome rather than pretty, a masterful lady. Her rich dark hair was still abundant, her figure upright, and though she was very pale she shed no tears, keeping firm control over her emotions. Maeve wondered that she did not weep, but she remembered once that her aunt had said, "We should keep our tears for the bedroom, my dear." Certainly a strong lady, Aunt Isabel. Maeve saw now that she was looking over their heads towards the distance and the wide flat acres of Romney Marsh.

The village, the church and Hollanders House were built just in Sussex, close to the border with Kent, on part of the ridge of hills that sloped away to the Marsh, murky and misty on this dreary day, the distance shrouded, sheep like white ghosts moving in the pastures below. She loved it as her aunt did, though her mother had never cared for it and seldom went there except to drive by the road to New Romney or on rare occasions to Hythe. Several farms below belonged to the estate of Hollanders, and Roger Watts of Becketts and his brother David Watts of Top Farm had been two of those who had borne their master's body from his house to this part of the churchyard where Hollanders had always been laid.

Maeve's sister, married to Sir Thomas's youngest son, stood by her side, weeping quietly and clinging to her William's arm – gentle-hearted Mary who could never keep her emotions back – while Lionel, the second son, stood beside his mother. He was, as his father had once been, a naval officer and very like him, tall and fair and blue-eyed. He had fortunately been at his home in Portsmouth, on leave while the sloop he was to command was in for a refit, and had come at once on hearing how ill his father was. Unable to bring his wife who was within days of having their second child, he was as anxious for her as for his widowed mother.

Maeve could not keep back a deep sigh. It was Freddy who was wanted here, Freddy the eldest, now Sir Frederick and owner of Hollanders, Freddy whom she loved, and had loved all her life.

Ten years ago in 1815 Freddy had persuaded his father to let him leave Eton and join the Army. It had to be the cavalry for Freddy, like his mother, had a passion for horses and Sir Thomas purchased him a commission in the 12th Light Dragoons. Aged 16 he had fought at Waterloo in Major General Vandeleur's brigade and distinguished himself by his enthusiasm and ability. Over the years he had proved a first-class officer and recently been given his majority, but the 12th had gone to India and she had not seen him for eight long years. Perhaps now, at last, he might come home. When his mother's letter reached him and he learned that he was master of Hollanders in his father's place, surely he would manage to return, even if only on leave until he had decided what to do.

Now tears did sting her eyes. She longed for him to come, to take her in his arms, tell her he loved her as she loved him. When he had gone abroad he had been barely eighteen, she only sixteen, but in a brief moment alone in the parlour at Hollanders he had taken her hand and said, "Wait for me, Mauve. I'll come back, you'll see, and then – " But then they were interrupted and when a little later he kissed all the ladies of the family goodbye, he had pressed his lips to her cheek and murmured, "Darling Maeve." That was the sum of what had happened between them but she had lived on it through all the years since.

It was sad that he had not been here to hear the short eulogy given by his Uncle Martin, a few moments ago. The Vicar had been Uncle Martin to her too throughout her child-hood but when at last, after years of devoted waiting, he had married her widowed mother, she and Mary had gradually come to call him Papa. In the fine old church with its Saxon foundations and Norman arches Martin Hollander had spoken of his brother's sterling qualities, the strength of character that had borne him through all difficulties, of his goodness to the poor in the district – no one ever came to Thomas Hollander or asked for help in vain – and of his years as a Jurat on Rye's town council and one year as Mayor. His youngest and adopted child, fourteen-year-old Ellen, broke into sobbing, burying her face in her brother Lionel's blue uniform coat.

But Martin spoke too, deep with sorrow as this loss was, of thankfulness for such a life, of peace and of going home to eternal joy, his final words of "the sure and certain hope" that all Christians had.

Thinking now of the last dark days of illness and of her husband's quiet serenity Lady Hollander's face contracted and Lionel, leaving Ellen to William and Mary, put his arm about her.

"Come, Mama," he said gently, "you will take cold if you stand out here any longer." And in response she straightened, gave him a brief smile and walked away with him.

"She's so brave," Maeve whispered to her mother, who reached out for her black-gloved hand.

"She has always been strong." Nell gave a deep sigh. "When we were young she lost her brother – which of course was why your Uncle Tom came here as the heir – then her father, Sir Frederick, died and some years later she lost a little daughter. A very great friend too who – " Suddenly recollecting herself Nell Hollander broke off, about to reveal something that was never, nor should be, spoken of in that context. "She has known a great deal of sorrow."

Maeve was suddenly curious and began, "Who . . .?" but

her mother went on, "It is a great comfort, though, to know that she thought her dearest Tom the best husband in the world, as your stepfather is to me."

At Hollanders House there was a large array of funeral meats laid out in the long dining room. Isabel had herself well in hand again and moved among her guests as they arrived and were warmed with a welcoming glass of hot punch. The elderly butler, Fletcher, was in charge of this, his face lined with sorrow, while his wife, who was the housekeeper, was directing the maids in the final arrangements for the meal.

Sir Edward Dering, white-haired and with an aged face scored with wrinkles, was there with his family for he had been a close friend of Lady Hollander's father, while Roddy Rokeby, a companion of Isabel's youth and now one of the Lords of the Marsh in his father's place, had brought his wife and daughter and his two young sons; Dr Sergeant had come, and the Mayor of Rye, and numerous gentry from all over this part of Sussex and across the Kentish border by horse and carriage to pay their respects to a man who had been liked and admired and who had done so much good in the district. Tom's friend from his naval days and Freddy's godfather was also among the mourners and staying in the house. Captain Frank Sinclair had never married and considered the family at Hollanders his own; Tom had been his friend since they were boys of fourteen, roughing it together on their first ship, and Isabel was grateful to have him here at her side while she moved among her guests.

The talk was at first, inevitably, of the unpleasant interruption to the service and Sir Edward remarked, as if he had brought out an original idea, of which he was generally short, that the rude fellow must be a stranger.

"Certainly no one we know would have done such a thing," Lord Rokeby said indignantly. "He must be a guest somewhere in the district." His fourteen-year-old son murmured to his younger brother, "Well, it jollied things up no end," and his father, whose hearing was acute, cast a freezing look towards him.

"I suppose in fairness one should say it could hardly have been intentional," Nell said gently. She was still a pretty woman, with dainty English looks, her soft brown hair only lightly turning grey. It was the great sorrow of her life that she had not given a child to her second husband, but he was devoted to her twin girls and in many ways the unmarried Maeve was his right hand in the parish. The twins were not identical, Mary more resembling her mother while Maeve had the Irish looks of their disreputable father, Donavon Dacre – dark hair, almost black, firmly curling, and very blue eyes with a milky skin. She could have been married several times, Nell thought on a sigh, one or two of her suitors being most eligible young men, but she had refused them all and Nell knew why only too well. Perhaps now, however, the new baronet would come home. He was much needed.

Maeve was finding the whole thing wearisome and wondered that her Aunt Isabel could bear it so well, glad when the last guest had gone, after what seemed to her a very long time, and the family could sit down to a quiet dinner together.

They talked of everyday things in a desultory manner until Martin, quite deliberately, began to speak of his brother, Captain Sinclair joining in to reminisce about the battle off Cape St Vincent during which Tom had been badly injured in the chest and which left him too with a permanently stiff leg, causing the end of his naval career. Isabel recalled the wedding trip she and Tom had made to visit his mother at Porchester in the days when French prisoners of war were housed in the huge old castle there.

"That's where you got the little carved ship you keep on the table in your room, isn't it?" Mary said, and her aunt smiled. "It was the first gift your uncle ever bought me, carved by one of the prisoners. Oh, I was a hoyden then, I used to say the most dreadful things."

"Did you really, Mama?" Ellen opened her eyes wide. "What fun. Do tell us some." For a moment with the resilience of youth she had pushed aside the grieving of the day. But though Isabel Hollander smiled at the eager girl, she shook her head. "I think perhaps not today." Ellen flushed with the awkwardness of her age and Isabel reached for her hand. "One day I shall have a lot to tell you. Frank, pray take a little more beef."

The tension despite the quiet reproof had however eased a little, all of them thankful to speak openly of the dead man, his empty chair showing a house without a master. None of them had eaten much and soon the ladies withdrew to the parlour, Isabel pausing to instruct Fletcher to have the remains of the funeral meats distributed among the tenants and labourers on the estate. The two brothers retired to their father's study to discuss what was to be done on the morrow and when Mr Biggs, their attorney and man of business, should be summoned from Rye for the reading of the will.

"The sooner the better," was Lionel's comment. "It is no good waiting in hopes that Freddy might be on his way. He had best come home, of course, though I'm sure you can run this place from Moon's End till he does."

"Of course I can," William agreed. He was a rather stolid young man who had never wanted to do anything but care for the land and the small estate his father had bought for him, Moon's End, which had once belonged to the late and unlamented Donavon Dacre, his wife's father. He had an overmastering love for the countryside, and the Marsh in particular, as his mother had. Giving his brother a slight smile, he added, "You don't think Mama capable of looking after the affairs of Hollanders House? She's always been a part of it."

"I know that, but it is quite another matter to lay it all on her just now. I know Papa always kept everything very much at his fingertips and although Mama may say she can manage everything, she is not so young now. You will have a great deal to do, being in two places at once."

"How long can you stay?" William asked.

"I really ought to leave by the end of the week. Madeleine was so near her time when I came up that I may not get back before the child is born. Your infants thrive?"

"Yes, indeed. Little Fred is all over the place now and leads Annie quite a dance while Isabel is nearly six months old and, thank God, very healthy."

Lionel stretched out his long legs. "When Freddy comes back, as things are now, do you think he'll sell out?"

"Leave the Army?" William drew his brows together and leaned forward to fill his brother's glass. "It's always been what he wanted to do. I wonder if he'll come back a regular Nabob?"

Lionel grinned. "I wouldn't be at all surprised. He's been in India a good number of years."

William stirred uneasily. "It must be a very strange place. Do you remember, Li, how he got into trouble for trying on the cocked hat belonging to the Commander of the Military in Sussex, Sir James something or other?"

"Oh, yes, old Pulteney. How annoyed Papa was. It was the day all those great men came to discuss the cutting of the canal. Fancy you remembering – you couldn't have been more than three."

"It's odd to think that once the canal wasn't there at the foot of our hill. Do you remember we first went out in a boat on it after Waterloo, when there weren't any more scares that Boney might come?"

The brothers were relishing this brief time together, even though the occasion was fraught with sorrow. Lionel was by nature a silent man and when he was not at sea lived with his wife in Portsmouth, seldom coming home, but this chance to talk to one of his brothers was a rare treat and he relaxed, going on to say, "But to go back to Freddy . . . of course Biggs has everything in hand and Mama is here, but Papa never approved of absentee landlords – though God knows there are enough of them."

"I know. He used to say a man should know what's going on under his own roof."

"I remember that too." Lionel gazed into the fire. "How we're all going to miss him. Hollanders doesn't seem the same without him. Poor mama, she bears up so well."

"She is very brave," William agreed. Being the nearest to home it was he who had lived all these years as his father's companion and assistant, and he thought that apart from his mother only he knew the range of his father's qualities and would miss him the most. After a while he said, "I've always thought that Freddy will marry Maeve when he comes home. Mary thinks so too."

"And she knows Maeve better than anyone." Lionel glanced across at his brother. "Is that why Maeve has never married?"

"I'm sure of it. She's had the chance more than once. Roger Uttley – you won't have known him, his father bought an estate Hawkhurst way – was after her last year, and Damian Havers was constantly here at one time, desperate to have her." William got up. "It will be good to have Freddy home."

"You think he'll come?"

"Oh, yes," William said, "I'm sure of it. Now I must take Mary home. She'll be very tired."

In the parlour the twins' mother was offering to stay the night if she could be useful, but Isabel said briskly, "Nonsense, my dear Nell. I am perfectly all right, and I have Lionel here and Ellen for company. But first Lionel must take you and Maeve home."

Cloaks were brought and Nell accepted her nephew's arm, her husband and Captain Sinclair having gone off an hour before to look at a book of naval battles that Martin, a great reader, had recently bought. Lionel walked between the two ladies, thinking of what he and William had discussed, and when his aunt Nell asked how soon he thought they might expect to hear from Freddy hazarded a guess that it would be summer before they could receive any response to his mother's letter, written in December.

"So long," Maeve said on a sigh. "Dear Uncle Tom buried today and Freddy won't know of it for such a long time."

"And I shall be off the coast of Africa by then," Lionel finished. "That's the worst thing about being at sea, not knowing how the family are going on."

He kissed Maeve's cheek, bidding her goodnight, and it occurred to him that William might be right.

The vicarage was quite small compared to the grandeur of Hollanders House which had high ceilings and long corridors, cold even in the height of summer. At the vicarage there seemed to be as many draughts, but they were easier to try to block out; it had been Maeve's home since she was fourteen.

When she entered the hall, she saw the beaver hat hanging from one of the pegs in the entrance. Presumably her stepfather had, out of the kindness of his heart, seen it on his return through the churchyard and brought it back. She would not have bothered. It remained there, a reminder of a horrid day.

Upstairs in her bedroom she sat down in her low chair by the hearth and stared into the flames. From a box on the table she had taken Freddy's last letter, more than six months old now, opening it on her knee. He was not like Lionel who was always more fluent on paper than in speech. Freddy wrote spasmodically, though she sent him regular long letters full of family doings. She had hoped for a letter at Christmas, but it had not come, only one for his parents to send all good cheer, adding that he wished he could be at the annual Twelfth Night party, and she thought sadly that it was then she had seen Uncle Tom beginning to look really ill, taking to his bed soon after. She had read the letter many times since and its cheerfulness seemed poignant seeing that he was not aware of anything being wrong at Hollanders.

He wrote of a sortie into the wild country where there had been trouble, described the wedding of their Colonel's daughter to one of his fellow officers, and also an entertainment given by a local Maharajah; a world away from quiet Sussex, Maeve thought, immersed in sights and sounds of which she knew nothing.

Oh, it was hard to be a woman and left at home. One Hollander during the Civil War nearly two centuries ago had dressed as a man and served in a Cavalier regiment for almost a year before she was discovered. Such a thing, Maeve reflected sadly, would not be possible these days, but if she could have got to India somehow, she would have gone.

How would he be when he did come home? Her heart ached to know if he still loved her – or had it been only a boy and girl affair, meaning nothing as the years passed and they both grew to adulthood?

Only for her nothing had changed, simply deepened into the feelings of a woman very much in love. If he didn't come – or worse still, if he came and no longer cared for her except as a cousin and childhood friend – what should she do?

She gave a little shiver, despite the warmth. Oh, she didn't want to be permanently just "the Vicarage daughter", doing good in the parish. No, much as she enjoyed going out with her stepfather on his calls, riding on the Marsh with him where he was greatly respected for the kind and generous man he was, she did not want that to be the purpose of her life. She wanted to marry Freddy, have his children, and one day be mistress of Hollanders.

She saw him in her mind – laughing, cheerful as always, his dark brown eyes so like his mother's in their bright alertness, his dark curling hair unruly. And at the end of this fraught, exhausting day she gave in to the indulgence of a few tears. For the tiresome, upsetting and, in her opinion, incompetent horseman, she had no further thought.

Chapter 2

A few days later, in the manner of country places, the talk had gone round the villages and Martin came in to say he had been told that the rider of the runaway horse was the new owner of Welford Park, Sir Ralph Digby. No one seemed to know much about him except that he appeared to have a great deal of money for he had brought an army of local workmen in to Welford, which was making him popular at this time of year, as well as paperers and painters from London. The whole place had been sadly neglected and it was hoped that once the refurbishing was done he would employ a great many Sussex folk, both outdoor and indoor staff, to maintain it.

"Your father nearly bought it once," Nell said reflectively to Maeve when they were in the stillroom. "But it was one of his schemes that came to nothing."

Maeve nodded. She remembered only too well the days in the cramped little house in Rye when she and Mary had hoped they would one day move back to a rebuilt Moon's End or a new home. She had learned then that her father's word was not to be trusted. It was so odd that her sister should now be back on the land he had once owned in a new Moon's End, bought after his death and rebuilt by Sir Thomas for his third son.

"Is Welford a big place?" she asked.

"Yes, very large. It was used to belong to Sir Harry Vernon but after he died it only had tenants, and no one really cared for it. It sounds as if the new owner is going to restore it, which will be a very good thing – except that we didn't get much of an impression of him last week, did we? Shall we take out that jar of peaches for dinner and one of Papa's favourite chutney?"

Nothing more was said of the new arrival in the district, Welford being some six miles away to the north, until late one morning when the three of them were in the parlour, Martin reading the latest copy of *The Times* while his wife and step-daughter were finishing a dress and bonnet for a poor child in the village. In answer to a knock on the door their footman came in to inform his master that Sir Ralph Digby of Welford Park requested a word with him.

Martin raised his eyebrows and glanced at his wife. Then he said, "Pray show him in, Barlow."

Sir Ralph entered with a purposeful walk. He was above average height, a well-built man in his mid-thirties, with sandy hair cut short and brushed upwards in the fashion of the day. Maeve recognised him at once as the rider of the runaway stallion, even if she had not known by now who he was, and she looked at him with active dislike. The main feature of his unexceptionable face was his eyes. They were wide-set, of a very pale piercing blue and most striking. When they met hers they became suddenly alert, flickered over her face and then away as he bowed.

"May I present my wife," Martin said, "and my step-daughter, Miss Dacre."

The visitor greeted the two ladies. "Ma'am – Miss Dacre – I hope you will forgive the interruption of a call, I can see you are employed." He had a rather grating voice and once more his eyes swept over Maeve so that she felt distinctly uncomfortable and thought him somewhat ill-mannered.

But he turned immediately back to Martin and went on, "It is very good of you to receive me, sir." He had come in a mood of boredom to pay a tiresome visit and apologise for what was not entirely his fault. He hated boredom and he hated apologising, but whatever Maeve might think, good manners overlaid the boredom even though his tone was stiff. It did occur to him, however, that the presence of an extremely pretty girl might make the whole business less tedious. "I am afraid," he went on, "I am that unfortunate man who so unforgivably upset the burial you were conducting the other day. I hope it was not one that touched you too closely."

As if that would make it any less heinous, Maeve thought indignantly, and glanced at her stepfather.

Martin, however, merely said quietly, "It was that of my brother," and seeing the consternation on the visitor's face added, "Pray sit down, Sir Ralph. I am quite sure it was entirely an accident."

Sir Ralph took the chair and the olive branch. "I am, I assure you, much put out by the whole episode. I had only bought the horse the day before and he had not learned who was master – which he has now, by God!"

There was a little silence. The harshness of his voice matched the words and Nell laid down her sewing. To her mind such language was not for her drawing room.

Martin's eyebrows had twitched, but he merely said, "A young horse can be very wilful until broke."

Sir Ralph inclined his head. "You are generous, sir, but that's small excuse. I thought I could manage him better than that. It was the damn' – the wretched peacock screeching and fanning its tail, you see. Almost under the animal's feet too and he was off over the wall before I could hold him."

"I'm afraid the peacocks do stray into my churchyard," the Vicar said with a slight smile, and Maeve added, "They come from Hollanders House. You will have seen it as you rode in."

"That big place with the old watch tower? Medieval, I should think?"

"The tower, yes," Martin said. "The house is Tudor. By the way we have your hat. We've only recently learned whose it is and I'm afraid it is still hanging in our hall. But I am forgetting my manners. You will take a glass of wine with us, or sherry perhaps?"

The visitor murmured that it was good of them to have rescued the hat and opted for sherry. After the first sip he looked appreciative so that Martin wondered in some amusement if he was surprised to find so good a sherry in a modest vicarage. It had come from his brother's cellar at Hollanders, for Tom had insisted on keeping him supplied. The memory brought a deep involuntary sigh, but he turned from his own thoughts to add, "It is my sister-in-law you should really be speaking to. My brother was her husband, Sir Thomas Hollander."

Sir Ralph took another sip of sherry. It was at least something to have a good wine to help him get through this tiresome business. "I do realise I should have addressed my apology to the widow," he said, "but I hesitated to intrude on her grief. I thought that if I called on you, you would be obliging enough to pass on my sincere regrets." He felt even more uncomfortable now that he knew the personal relationships involved, and guilty that he had not bothered to find out all this before, being too involved in his own affairs at Welford Park. But he was not entirely unfeeling and was somewhat taken aback to learn the rank of the man whose obsequies he had so rudely interrupted.

"But now I know – " he nearly said 'who you all are' but kept back the words and merely went on " – that Lady Hollander is so close a neighbour, I shall beg permission to call on her later on when she is receiving visitors."

"I'm sure that would be appreciated," Nell said in her quiet way, but Maeve had caught the repressed inflection in his voice and her dislike of him grew.

To smooth over the moment Martin asked if he was a Sussex man, and if not, how he came to hear of Welford.

For the first time Sir Ralph smiled and crossed his booted feet. He felt a little more at ease, the awkward moments over, and he thought the Vicar seemed a very good sort of man. As for the girl – he let his smile extend to her, but received no response other than a disinterested look down her well-shaped nose. He almost laughed. Little minx!

"I have a house in London where my mother and I have been living," he explained, "My father came from Devon – the Digbys are a Devonshire family – but my mother is North Country-born. We had a great, lumbering, singularly ugly house near Durham which my grandfather built, so that it had not even the attraction of antiquity, and what with the riots and rick-burning of the labourers up there I decided to get rid of it once and for all. We've not lived in it for years, above a month or two when necessary, as the climate there does not suit my mother's health. I was on the look-out for a suitable country place, and when my man of business heard of Welford I came down to view it. I saw its possibilities and bought it at the end of December."

"We know of it." Martin said and refilled his glass. "My wife used to visit there when she was a child."

"Indeed?" Sir Ralph turned to her. "Perhaps it was not so shabby then?"

Nell smiled. "I don't know. Children don't notice these things. We were more concerned with primrosing, or playing games in the shrubbery and collecting mulberries off that great tree in the circular lawn."

"I'm afraid I've had it taken down. It was old and wild and unsightly."

"Oh dear. But things one remembers from childhood so often change or are gone when one goes back. I understand Sir Harry Vernon had let everything deteriorate in his last years and tenants seldom look after property as they should. I am glad Welford has a new owner who will care for it."

He smiled at the pretty speech. "I hope, Mrs Hollander, that when I have things in order and my mother has arrived, you will do her the kindness of calling on her. I suppose it will be in April or early May."

"I should be delighted to," Nell agreed, the annoyance of his first intrusion into their lives forgotten. "When she is settled, my daughter and I will come over. I have another daughter, Maeve's twin, who is married to Sir Thomas Hollander's youngest son and they live near Wittersham. I'm sure she would like to come with us and show your mother a real Sussex welcome at her home."

"Thank you," he said with more warmth than he had yet shown. "She will know no one in the county and would be very glad to receive visitors. I will, if I may, write to you when we are settled in."

"You must come to dinner," Martin said, "and let us show you we have taken no offence at what I am sure was totally unintentional. And by midsummer my sister-in-law would maybe join us."

"You are very generous, sir," Ralph Digby said without any of the hauteur of his earlier talk. "I am trying to familiarise myself with this part of the country which is quite new to me." He glanced at Maeve, wondering if that stiff back would unbend a little. "I suppose you know the area well, Miss Dacre?"

Obliged to give him a civil answer, she said, "Yes, very well, having lived here all my life. Down below us is Romney Marsh. We love it, but it is a queer place, very lonely, and strangers easily get lost. There's a great deal of damp and rain and mist at this time of year. Probably you would not care for it at all."

"I must admit that when I looked down from the hill that day nothing attracted me to explore it further."

"It is different in the summer," she said defensively.

"But still mainly farms and sheep?" he queried.

"And fine churches," Martin broke in. "I made a study of them when I first came here. You must let us show them to you. My wife doesn't much care for riding, but I, if I'm free, or my daughter here would be delighted to show you our treasures."

"You must see the Martello Towers," Nell put in. "Such odd things."

"They were supposed to keep Napoleon away," Maeve said, "but nowadays they don't even deter strangers from coming on to the Marsh." There was an edge to her voice which surprised Martin and he steered the conversation into a more promising channel.

"Not their purpose, of course. People are beginning to think them a waste of public money. There's one at Dymchurch occasionally shown to visitors. We must ride down there some time."

But Sir Ralph, while answering politely, had given Maeve an appreciative glance as if he liked to cross swords. "You enjoy riding, Miss Dacre?"

It was Martin who answered. "Oh, she's a capital horsewoman and a good hand with the ribbons too. She often drives me in my curricle when I've calls to make."

The guest continued to stare across at her. "An accomplishment indeed. I look forward to riding with you."

"Perhaps," she said coolly. "I have very little free time."

"But you just said you liked to ride. I'll have to persuade you to spare a little of that occupied time for me. After all," he added with a smile, "it's a Christian precept to be kind to strangers, isn't it?"

Before she could answer Martin asked quietly if Sir Ralph had yet been to Rye.

18

"Once," he said with a rueful smile," to buy that horse. He's been a brute but I hope he'll justify my guineas. I mean to set up a good stable."

"Do you need some advice on local horse fairs or a groom? We could no doubt recommend – " Martin was beginning, but Sir Ralph shook his head.

"I am considered in general a good judge of horseflesh and shall no doubt go to Tattersall's to set myself up. As to grooms, I shall bring my own down."

"Well," Maeve did not meet his look, "I hope the black stallion lives up to your expectations. He will need a skilled hand to break him."

"I am seldom wrong in such matters," he retorted, and Nell felt suddenly sorry for him. She could not think why Maeve had answered him in such a manner. He *was* a stranger within their gates, and on an impulse she said, "We have taken to having a light meal about this time now that we eat dinner so much later. Would you care to join us, Sir Ralph?"

Without the slightest hesitation he accepted. It had already occurred to him that life might not be so dreary in this unknown county after all. To be away from London, from his boon companions, from boxing and fencing, racing and congenial evenings; from his particular friend George FitzClarence, to say nothing of separation from the arms of his latest mistress – though that liaison had begun to pall – had been unappealing to say the least. However, seldom as he showed it, his affection for his mother ran very deep and this whole project was for her sake. Mrs Hollander and certainly Lady Isabel would be genteel people for his mother to visit, and as for this girl – to find her in a country vicarage might be some compensation.

The arrogance of this thought did not cross his mind. His swift glances in her direction had taken in her poise, the shape of her head, her dark curly hair simply but prettily dressed, the turn of that long slender neck, beautiful shoulders too, no doubt, which he might see when she was dressed for the evening and not in a plain gown of blue cloth with muslin set into the low cut bodice and reaching up to make a little frill about that neck. He appreciated female beauty, seeing the cream of it at court in London, at Royal Lodge in Windsor, or the Pavilion in Brighton, but this vicarage girl had a natural elegance that would not be out of place at any of those venues. She would pay for dressing too. He imagined her in a ball gown and then brought his thoughts sharply to order as they rose to go to the table, hiding a smile as he thought of what some of his racier friends would say at the idea of him sitting down in this homely vicarage to a luncheon of excellent soup, a large ham, fresh baked bread and locally made cheese.

Martin, determined to keep the conversation away from horses, drew him out to talk of London and he entertained them with tales from court and of the people that frequented it. He asked if they had been to Brighton. Only the Vicar had and then only to pass through, so Sir Ralph gave them a description of that extraordinary, lavish and oriental building that the King had raised for himself in the days when he was 'Prinny', the Prince Regent of England, and his father, the late King George III, old and ill and suffering bouts of madness.

"It was finished near three years ago," he concluded, "but his Majesty complains now that Brighton is no longer the peaceful little place it was. People are flocking there and there are a great many houses going up. It is considered good for the health to take the sea air and even indulge in sea-bathing."

Maeve listened in silence. Clearly he moved in the highest circles and there was something in his assured manner that irritated her. But her mother and stepfather were obviously enjoying his company, finding his talk witty and amusing, and when his horse was finally brought to the front door Martin went out on to the steps to speed him on his way. The drive was in full view of the parlour window and Maeve and her mother watched their guest mount up.

"What an interesting and amiable man," was Nell's comment. "It will be very pleasant to meet his mother and exchange visits. But I am surprised at you, my dear. Why were you so rude to him?"

Observing him settle well in the saddle, gathering the reins into strong hands and holding the restive horse, Maeve thought she saw marks on the flank from excessive use of the spur. "He seemed to be full of himself, and in need of a put down."

"It was not quite the thing for you to take upon yourself," Nell said with rare severity. "He must have remarked your rudeness."

"I am sorry, Mama," but she spoke absently, her eyes on the departing guest, and as he disappeared out of the gate she added, "And I think he's likely to be a bruising rider. I'm sorry for that poor beast."

The winter weeks after the funeral were quiet. Maeve was occupied with her usual activities and in this weather there was a great deal to do to ease the lot of the poor in the village. The harsh Corn Laws, putting up the price of bread, caused a great deal of hardship; there was always unemployment in the winter and she hated to see hungry children staring up at her with vacant eyes. Her mother made up packages of bread and beef and Maeve and her stepfather took them to needy folk. Martin had made himself much loved around the parish and further afield on the Marsh. She thought some of the local clergy put on him, often sending messages asking him to do extra duty when he had enough of his own. His very willingness encouraged them and it made her angry on his behalf, though he always laughed and told her his shoulders were broad. But neither was he a soft man and he had no time for men who whined that they could not get work and asked for Parish Relief when there were jobs available which they were too lazy to take.

This winter it was particularly cold, the ice hard on ponds and water butts, and February came and went with thick snow, the lookers on the Marsh keeping fires going in their huts so that when the ewes dropped their lambs any sickly ones could be carried in to shelter and fed on warmed milk. Nothing more was seen of the newcomer and Martin heard from the Vicar of Peasmarsh that he had returned to London.

One afternoon Maeve wrapped herself in a thick cloak with a fur-lined hood, put pattens on her feet, and walked across to Hollanders House to visit her aunt. Passing between the tall frost-encrusted trees of the avenue she was enjoying the crisp fresh air, the pale winter sunshine. The snow crackled under her feet and occasionally a slither of it fell from a branch. There would be great fires at Hollanders to try to warm the old house but it was a hard task and, as she well remembered, in the long dining room, however hot the fire, she had often been half frozen when she happened to be at the far end of the table. The house had always seemed to her to be permanent, dependable, and she had looked on it as a safe and secure place where she and her mother and Mary had found a haven, a welcome when things went wrong, as they had all too often when her father was alive. She loved it with all the more passion for the secret longing, the hope deferred over so many years, that one day she might, as Freddy's wife, be mistress of it.

Turning the bend in the drive to the circular gravel entrance she saw smoke curling from half a dozen chimneys, only the old watch tower looking cold and deserted. She hurried up the steps as Hinton, who had observed her coming, opened the door for her and relieved her of her cloak and gloves. As she stepped out of her pattens he said that her ladyship was not in the large drawing room but in the library, smaller and always more easily heated. Hinton was a solidly built man in his forties who had been Sir Thomas's valet for many years and was staying on, taking some of the work off the ageing butler's shoulders and prepared, should the new baronet require it, to serve him in the same capacity as he had his late father.

Entering the parlour Maeve found her aunt sitting by the hearth, her writing desk on her knee. She looked up and smiled at her visitor.

"How nice to see you, dearest. Come to the fire, that's right. What a cold cheek to kiss. Hinton will be bringing something to warm you. Such a sensible man, he never needs telling what one would like."

Maeve took the chair opposite. She loved this book-lined room. Over the wide stone mantelpiece hung a portrait of Lady Hollander's father, the previous Sir Frederick, painted in London by George Romney. She didn't remember him but he appeared to be a jolly sort of man and Freddy had a great look of him. Opposite, between two bookcases, hung the picture she loved – Sir Thomas in riding dress, brown coat, fawn breeches, and black boots with tan cuffs. Under one arm he had a hunting gun and Rigger, his retriever, sat at his feet looking expectantly up at him. They had all laughed at this for the artist had caught Rigger's usual expression when he was waiting to be taken out hunting. Now however he was old and lay here in front of the fire, only a slight twitch of the tail showing that he knew the visitor.

Maeve bent down to caress the silky head. "Dear old fellow. Are you writing to Freddy, Aunt Isabel?"

"No, dear, to Lionel's wife. She will need a little cheering up with Lionel gone for at least two years. I'm sure I should have hated it if your uncle had stayed in the Navy. It's such a good thing her mother has gone to stay with her now that she has another baby to care for. Your uncle would be so pleased that they have called him Frank after Captain Sinclair and asked him to be godfather. It is such a shame that your uncle cannot have the pleasure of watching our grandchildren grow up, he would so have enjoyed having them to stay here."

Isabel paused, remembering, her eyes dark with grief. To be separated by death after twenty-seven years together was very hard, like a wrenching apart of her whole being. But death had to be accepted and what was left to her now, what Tom himself would have wished, was for her to try to be what he had been to their family, their friends and Hollanders.

She gazed out of the window at the white garden, the snow lying untrampled. It was impossible today to see into the distance where the Marsh lay, her beloved Marsh. When she was able to go down there again would it still fill her with that curious satisfaction it had always given her? She had taken grief there before.

And then, never one to indulge in self-pity, she brought her attention back to the girl opposite her whose cheeks were still pink from the walk in the cold crisp air. Really, she was pretty! How long, Isabel wondered, would the child go on waiting for her absent eldest son? "Have you had a letter from Freddy lately?" she asked.

Maeve shook her head on a little sigh. "Not since September. It's a long time, but he isn't the best of correspondents, is he?"

Isabel smiled. "No, Freddy always has to be 'doing', not

sitting down for anything except his dinner. Lionel is the one for letter-writing, but of course they are dependent for reaching us on passing ships on their way home."

Maeve returned the smile. "But they are like a journal when they do come, so full of interesting things. I loved the diary he kept, that Madeleine sent us to read last year, about all the exotic birds and flowers he saw in the East. And his drawings are quite beautiful."

"He may not have so much time now that he is captain of his own ship," her aunt said. "But I was going to write to Freddy next. I do wonder if – "

"If he might come home soon?" Maeve finished. "When will he get the letter you wrote to him after Uncle Tom was taken ill?"

"Not yet, I'm afraid. It does take so long." Isabel gave a deep sigh. Was that warm colour in the girl's cheeks only from the fire after her walk in the snow? "But I think when he knows his father is gone and Hollanders is his he may consider his position in a different light."

"And leave the army?" Maeve asked the same question that was on the minds of the heir's brothers.

"I've no idea, my love. He's had ten years of it, but since Waterloo he's seen very little action, nothing but a few skirmishes with rebel tribesman, or so he says. Well, we shall have to wait and see. Your uncle's death had put a different complexion on everything, though I can manage very well and with William only a few miles away at Moon's End, I know I have help on hand should I need it." Isabel paused, looking at the girl gazing pensively into the fire. "You've waited so long and so patiently," she said at last. "I wonder if it is right. You will be – what is it – twenty-four in April?"

"Yes." Maeve gave a rueful laugh. "Quite the old maid. I suppose I shall have to put on a white cap and act the spinster."

"Hardly that just yet, my dear, but I don't like to see you wasting your youth –"

"When my sister is so happily married with two babies?" Maeve added. "I trust the Monarchs are well?" The family nickname for William and Mary had become a familiarity since their wedding for obvious historical reasons. She added,

"I've not see them for a while because of the snow."

"Yes, there's nothing amiss at Moon's End. William was here yesterday for a while. Fred has a cold but it's on the mend, and so far he has not given it to his little sister. But I was going to say, darling, that you could have been wed several times over. I always liked young Damian Havers."

"He was pleasant enough." Maeve agreed, as if he was hardly worth mentioning, "but you know, dear Auntie, that I've never cared for anyone except Freddy. Only sometimes I wonder – I'm afraid that – " she paused and Isabel finished the sentence for her.

"That when he does come, he may be changed?" Maeve nodded and her aunt went on, "I've known for a long time that that has been at the back of your mind. You were both so young when he went. Does he ever say – no, I'll not pry, but he has grown into a man now, with years in the Army away from us all in a far distant strange country. He is bound to come home changed in some ways."

There was a knock and Hinton came in bearing two steaming silver mugs of mulled wine. "Thank you, Hinton," Lady Hollander said, and Maeve added, "That will warm me after my walk."

"Yes, miss, and Mrs Fletcher wants to know if there will be an extra cover for luncheon?"

Maeve glanced at her aunt who said, "Yes, dear, do stay."

"Then I will. Thank you, Hinton."

He bowed and went out, leaving them to sip their wine.

"By the way," Isabel said, "I've had a very civil letter from Sir Ralph Digby. What did you think of him when he called?"

"He was civil, as you say, but I thought him too uppish by half, though at luncheon he made himself very entertaining. He got on well with Papa."

"And you?"

"I must admit I didn't care for his manner – or the way he handled that black horse."

Isabel smiled. "I'm afraid you and I judge people by the same standards. Well, he says he hopes I will receive him if he brings his mother to call on me when they arrive at Welford, which will not be till early summer. Very considerately expressed. I shall be interested to see what he does with the place."

"So Mama says. He means to keep a large stable apparently which will interest Freddy when – " And then, dismissing Sir Ralph, she reverted to the topic filling her mind. "I'd never think of you as prying, Aunt Isabel. You know that. Freddy's letters have always been – just as one might expect from him. He's often said he wished I could see some of the sights of India, the temples and palaces and processions and elephants. Those lengths of silk he sent us two years ago made up into beautiful dresses, didn't they?"

"Yes, indeed, it was fortunate that his friend Captain Ingles was coming home and sent them down to us. Whether I shall wear mine again, I doubt."

"Oh, don't say that. Don't stay in black for always. Uncle Tom wouldn't like that. You know he never cared for black, and nor do I."

Tom's widow gave a half laugh, half sigh. "No, he didn't, did he? He used to say it didn't suit my colouring." Under her black lace cap her dark hair was only slightly tinged with grey, and she had the warm complexion that suited brighter colours so well.

Freddy was so like her, Maeve thought. She finished her wine and then said, "But in answer to your question, no, Freddy's never written anything to me about – about marriage."

"Perhaps he has felt you ought to be free, with him so far away?"

"I don't know, perhaps, and yet he has always seemed to take if for granted that we shall go on doing everything together when his regiment is posted home. That's why – "

"Why you have waited for him?" Isabel gave her an affectionate smile. "I hope he will appreciate such faithfulness."

"I love him, Aunt Isabel."

"I know, my darling," Isabel reached out and took her hand. "You are just the wife I want for him. Well, perhaps we'll get a letter soon."

They ate their lunch cosily at a table drawn near the fire. Ellen came running down from her morning lessons to join them and enliven them with her chatter. She had always looked on the twins as her elder sisters and after the meal persuaded Maeve into a game of Chinese Checkers. She was a bright pretty girl with a mass of flaxen fair hair, and no one even remembered now that she had been adopted by Sir Thomas and his wife when she was very young, her own father apparently a relative of his. She was simply the daughter of the house and to Maeve a young cousin of whom she was very fond.

The afternoon was waning when Maeve finally walked home through the crunching snow. The sun was a red ball, sinking in a glory of colour behind the old church tower, and she stood for a few minutes, watching the sunset, thinking of Freddy in the hot climate he had described and how in one letter he said he longed for a crisp snowy day in Sussex. But she was aware of unease. He may have been longing for home but how would he be when he did see it again? Aunt Isabel was right, eight years would have turned the boy into a man, a man who had experienced life, a world apart from Hollanders and this corner of England.

There was no answer to this question. Memories of her father beset her, that wild Irishman Donavon Dacre. When she was a very small girl, he was handsome, careless, his cravat generally undone, his hair never looking brushed, setting her on her first pony, and how she had loved him. Then after the fire that had destroyed the old Moon's End and burned her grandmother to death, he had utterly changed. He had sent her mother and herself and Mary to Rye and lived himself in one small habitable part of the servant's quarters with only one old retainer, scarcely ever visiting them. He was nearly always drunk and turned to crime to try and mend his fortune. He became increasingly violent, almost unhinged by his hatred of Tom Hollander, until the day when he actually tried to murder her uncle and was shot himself in the affray. She remembered that funeral and the misery of it. It had all made a deep impression on her, far more so than on the less introspective Mary who seemed to have put the past far behind her, content with her William and her babies. Maeve, however, had never been able entirely to dismiss it from her mind – it showed so clearly how a man could change into something quite unrecognisable.

After that appalling affair she and Mary moved with their mother back to Hollanders and life became much brighter for them. Then her mother had married Martin Hollander and they had gone to live in the Vicarage from whose windows they could still see the great bulk of Hollanders House. It was the happiest thing that could have happened to them, Maeve thought, as she walked up the path by the old yew tree.

Her mother was in the hall as she came in. "Oh, there you are, my love. I do hope you've not taken cold?"

"Not a bit. It's a lovely day for a walk. Aunt Isabel sends her love."

Nell pointed to a salver on the hall table. "Look there, Maeve."

Her face lit. "Oh! it *is* from him." She gave her mother a radiant smile and ran up to her room. There she sank down on the floor by the fire and broke the seal with eager fingers. But it was disappointingly brief. He was sorry he had not written before but they had marched up into the hill country where it was cooler to give some newly arrived reinforcements a taste of service in India and he'd been too busy to write. Dear Freddy, she thought, happy as always to be active. He had only just returned and was off to dine at the Governor-General's house. He hoped all was well at home and everyone in good health. His love to them all and he remained her affectionate cousin, Frederick Thomas Hollander.

She laid it down, aware of tears pricking her eyes. Seldom given to weeping, she brushed them away impatiently. But it gave her a bitter sense of disatisfaction. Not one personal word for her, nothing remotely resembling a love letter. In his early days away he had often said how he missed her and longed for them to be together again, but over the years these sentiments had been expressed less and less. She would have to face it. He *had* changed.

Leaning her head on her hand she stared blindly down at the irregular writing – Freddy was never tidy, unlike Lionel whose script was a joy to read. Was Aunt Isabel right? Had he changed, forgotten a childhood affection, while she had remained the same? No, not the same, for she loved him now as a woman, not as a child, the years of his absence only endearing him to her the more. But was she in love with a dream?

The hurt suddenly became too much. Perhaps she should

have taken Damian Havers after all and would now have babies to fill her arms and her heart. She was a foolish woman to waste her life on a man who, when he returned, might not want her after all. Springing up, she went to the wash basin and splashed her face with cold water, drying it on a towel. She would not indulge in such weakness again, and if she was to be a spinster, so be it.

When Sir Frederick came home she would not throw herself into his arms, no indeed. And yet, as she went down the stairs to the parlour, she imagined him coming in through the front door, looking up at her with his old smile, his arms held wide, and what else would she do but throw herself into them?

Chapter 3

"I plan a rose garden there," Lady Digby pointed to where a gardener was already lifting the turf, "in a circle, you see, with perhaps a stone basin and a fountain in the centre."

"And arches for climbing roses?" Mary suggested. "We have done that at Moon's End. Perhaps you would care to drive over and see how we have arranged them. They make a very pretty prospect."

"I should like that very much. Moon's End? What an odd name." Lady Digby was past sixty, an upright lady with a great deal of white hair, elegantly dressed. She never wore anything but black, but her dress had been made by a couturier in Bond Street; she walked with a silver-topped ebony cane and her pallor seemed to bear out what her son had said about her health. "There's so much still to do," she went on. "The garden has been very much neglected, hardly any bulbs in it, but I plan to have plenty of daffodils planted ready for next spring. And perhaps a parterre there, so very attractive."

For a time she and Mary talked gardening while Ellen wandered happily in the straggling shrubbery where another outdoor man was struggling to deal with two bushes that had become inextricably entwined. Maeve walked beside them, wishing she could have gone to the stables with the men, Sir Ralph inviting the Vicar and William to view the new buildings, the first project he had turned his hand to, which, she thought, showed a good sense of priority. She would have liked to see the horses he had brought down from London, from Tattersall's no doubt, but as this was their first visit it might come about later. She tried to look really interested in the discussion as to where would be the best place for a cherry tree.

Lady Digby's companion, a middle-aged spinster by the odd name of Miss Mufferton, walked beside Maeve.

"I suspect," Miss Mufferton was saying, "that you are not as keen a gardener as your sister." A lock of brown hair escaped her bonnet and she pushed it inside, her softly lined face wearing a quizzical expression. Her dress was plain but well cut and her slippers of soft kid.

"No, I'm afraid I'm not," Maeve answered. "I like to arrange flowers, but leave the growing to someone else. The garden is my mother's hobby. I'm sorry she wasn't well today, she would have enjoyed seeing the garden. Of course she remembers it as it was in Sir Harry Vernon's day when it was quite a show-piece." Some chairs had been set on the grass under a spreading cedar and they sat down together. "Have you been with Lady Digby long?" she asked.

"Oh, goodness, yes. Twenty years or more. We are connected by marriage."

"Then you must have known Sir Ralph's home – near Durham, I think he said."

"Yes, indeed. Not a beautiful house like this." They both glanced in the direction of the fine stone building, the old mullions having yielded to sash windows, pillars rising two floors by the entrance at the front, and at the back here a series of low windows and a stone terrace with large pots full of wallflowers, their scent carrying on the breeze.

"Mockford Place was built by Sir Ralph's maternal grandfather. The house was always cold, the wind seemed to find every crack. I never liked it. And of course Sir Ralph was seldom there after –" Miss Mufferton broke of hastily and Maeve wondered what she had been about to say. "Well, he never liked it and much preferred to be in London."

"From what he told us he is often at court?"

"He has a great many friends there and is an intimate of the King's circle. It began really when he served in the Peninsula."

"He was in the army?" Maeve's attention was instantly caught. Freddy had been too young to have been in the

Peninsula campaign, but perhaps they had both been at Waterloo.

"Oh, yes." her companion went on. "When he was quite a boy he went out to Spain with his regiment. He went right through until 1814. Then there was some trouble," she waved her hand vaguely, "so he sold out. His sister married about that time and he felt he should be more at home as his father was very ill."

"I didn't know he had a sister."

"Yes, indeed, Lady Selena Hillingdon. She is in Dublin at the moment where Lord Hillingdon has a government post. She hopes to be home later this summer. But to go back to Sir Ralph – his father died about then, so he bought a London house and we have enjoyed many seasons there. I was glad he got rid of that great place in the north. In London he could entertain his friends. When he was in Spain he met George FitzClarence, the Duke of Clarence's son, you know."

"Oh? I don't think I quite recollect – "

"The Duke is the King's third brother, William. He has no children by his Duchess, such an admirable woman and so well liked, but a great many I have to say by Mrs Jordan, the actress, and Colonel FitzClarence is the eldest. A charming man, and quite adored by his soldiers, so Ralph says. They became the closest of friends and I'm sure the Colonel and his lady will be down here this summer. She is Mary Wyndham, the Earl of Egremont's daughter," she lowered her voice, "not born in wedlock, you know, but then neither was Colonel FitzClarence so it made no odds. No one minds in the least when they are such quality. Sir Ralph is so pleased to have a place near enough to London where he can entertain." Miss Mufferton paused to draw breath and smiled at her in a rather condescending manner. "No doubt you live very quiet in your village. I can see I shall have lots of interesting tales to tell you, and no doubt we will provide you with more society than you are used to."

Maeve, still trying to take in all this information, was suddenly irritated by this garrulous woman who made it seem as if the family at Welford would be conferring great favours on the local gentry. Pardonably annoyed, she said, "We have some very pleasant associations around here. My late uncle,

Sir Thomas Hollander, entertained a great deal. The Duke of Wellington comes occasionally now he is Lord Warden of the Cinque Ports and last year he brought General Sir John and Lady Colborne. The General was here years ago when everyone thought Napoleon was going to invade us – though I was too young to remember that."

Miss Mufferton looked surprised, for Sir Ralph had merely spoken of the Vicarage family, not having met any others during his winter visit with its unhappy mishap, and Maeve had to suppress a smile. The woman was a snob, she thought, basking in the status of her employer, while Lady Digby appeared to have a natural dignity that needed no such pretensions. Maeve was glad when she and Mary rejoined them, and she was rescued from Miss Mufferton's sole company.

"The prospect of that gentle slope and the distant trees lends itself to a better design." Lady Digby waved a hand towards the long sweep of lawn. "I wish we had Mr Lancelot Brown to lay it out for us. You remember, Mufti, his work at Blenheim. I wonder if –"

"My dear," Miss Mufferton broke in, "he's been dead for many years."

"Oh, has he?" Lady Digby looked disconcerted for a moment. "One forgets, but of course I knew that. I merely meant he would have known what to do. His work was very striking at Petworth too, and at Kew. You remember we went there with Colonel FitzClarence?"

"Do you not think we should go in?" her companion suggested. "The ladies have not even taken their bonnets off yet, as we came straight out, and I'm certain they would enjoy a cup of tea."

"Very well. Don't fuss, Mufti. I don't need my shawl, it's very warm."

"Just round your shoulders, perhaps?"

"I do not wish for it." Lady Digby rose, pushing the shawl back into Miss Mufferton's hands, and led the way across the grass. Maeve followed with Mary and they exchanged amused glances, suspecting that such verbal duals might be frequent.

The house inside was equally magnificent. The hall was very large with white pillars, a heavily stuccoed ceiling and a fine Adam staircase rising to two floors above. Doors of Spanish mahogany led off it and as the gentlemen joined them Sir Ralph took them on a tour of the ground floor rooms. The dining room had a long oak table, large enough to seat fifty people; there was a fine billiard room with a new table and a library where Sir Harry Vernon's books still remained, augmented by Sir Ralph's own, so that the shelving was extensive. To Maeve it seemed that he had indeed done everything in excellent taste. She couldn't help exclaiming over two Stubbs paintings of racehorses that hung on either side of the hearth, and Sir Ralph said, "Racing is one of my abiding interests, Miss Dacre."

They moved into the great salon with its wallpaper of cream and claret coloured stripes, with claret brocade curtains. There were gilt chairs and elegant settees, a Boule escritoire, a fine Ormulu clock, and over the mantelpiece a large portrait of Lady Digby as a young bride. On another wall was a landscape by the artist Turner.

Maeve admired it and Lady Digby said. "We have met him many times at Petworth House. He has his own studio there." She patted the seat next to her, and said in a pleasant tone but one that, Maeve guessed, was unused to encountering any argument, "Miss Dacre, pray take the seat next to me."

Maeve obeyed and the butler served the tea while a housemaid passed round a silver tray of delectables. The talk was general, of the unsettled state of the country, and the sagging government of Lord Liverpool.

"I'm afraid our Foreign Secretary, Mr Canning, and the Duke of Wellington don't get on at all. The Beau should have stayed a soldier, seeing he was the best our country has ever had," Sir Ralph said drily.

"The Duke can be extremely witty and his talk is always to the point," Lady Digby remarked. "Of course he is part of the Cottage Clique, and Canning hates that."

"The Cottage Clique? Who are they?" William asked.

"The King's particular friends, Mr Hollander; the Duke of Clarence of course and his eldest son Colonel FitzClarence; Count Lieven, the Russian Ambassador and his wife, Princess Dorothea – such a pretty woman but a meddler – oh, and one or two others who gather at the Royal Lodge at

Windsor. Mr Canning is jealous, and that's the long and short of it."

"He works hard," her son admitted, "but I must confess I find him a tiresome fellow at the dinner table."

"If we could get a government who can do something about the bad state of the country it would be very much to the point," William said. "Of course, we land-owners must get a fair return from our land but I think eighty shillings a quarter for wheat excessive. The Corn Laws have brought great hardship to the working man."

"We thought that after Napoleon was beaten everything would be so much better, but the politicians have not served us well," Maeve said coolly. "Perhaps if Mr Canning is inclined to work rather than spend his time at Windsor, it is all to the good."

Lady Digby gave her a surprised look, but Sir Ralph's mouth twitched and it was Martin who added hastily, "Even though we live in the country, my daughter and I make a point of studying the political news in the paper. We see a great deal of the suffering that comes from lack of employment and high prices." And wondering if such talk was becoming tedious to his hostess, he asked her if she was finding Sussex, and Welford in particular, to her liking. She answered that she liked the place very well and thought the country very pretty compared to the north. "Especially now that the country up there is being disfigured by this new railway to go between Darlington and Stockton. I believe it will be opened this summer. Such a dreadful idea." Lady Digby gave a little shudder. "What lady would wish to travel in a coal truck when she might be sitting in comfort in her own carriage?"

Ralph laughed. "I'm quite sure, my dear mother, that a railway carriage for people will be a little more comfortable than a coal truck."

"Well, nothing would induce me to go in one. What do you think, Miss Dacre?"

"I know nothing about them, ma'am," Maeve said. "We don't have such things here."

And her step-father added. "I doubt very much if we ever shall. It would quite ruin the countryside."

Later when Ralph and the Vicar were discussing hunting

and William issuing an invitation to shoot at Moon's End, Lady Digby turned to Maeve and said. "I like a young woman who has some opinions of her own. But then you are not a shy miss just out of the schoolroom, are you?" And before Maeve could answer she went on, "Tell me about yourself. Do you like to read or paint, do you play the piano? What kind of fancy work do you do? I cannot do any nowadays, because of this wretched rheumatism." She held up her gnarled fingers. "So tiresome. My son tells me you like to ride and that sometimes you drive a curricle. When I was young I used to take the ribbons in a perch-phaeton, a rather dangerous carriage for a lady really though I never cared for that, and my father encouraged me. When we were in London I used to drive in Hyde Park where one meets everyone, a most pleasant occupation, but I don't suppose you know London, Miss Dacre?"

"I've been once with my aunt and sister for her bridal clothes."

"Ah, well, you would have been busy with that and not riding in the Park, I expect. No doubt you find occupation of some sort in your village?"

Maeve was to discover that Lady Digby had the disconcerting habit of asking a number of questions and then leading off on another tack by which time one had forgotten the first question. And that she had no intention of giving offence by her in-born sense of superiority. "To live in a vicarage is a busy life," Maeve said. "My step-father believes a clergyman should do more than preach a sermon on Sunday and he does a great deal of good anywhere where there is any sort of hardship. I often drive him out, and as far as possible I like to ride each day."

Her hostess nodded. "Ah, my son will like that."

Maeve wondered why it should matter whether he liked it or not and was beginning to feel it was time that they went home when Lady Digby, from whom Ralph had got his piercing eyes, turned her gaze on her and added, "My son is going up for the Ascot races next week. Would you care to spend a day with me?" And as Maeve hesitated, more from surprise than anything else, she laughed and tapped her hand. "Come, take pity on a stranger, unless you would find a day with an old lady too tedious?"

"No, indeed, ma'am, I shall be honoured," Maeve said politely, not sure just how far she wanted the acquaintance between the two families to proceed. However, it was settled for Thursday and shortly after bonnets and gloves were called for and they took their leave, Lady Digby saying to Mary that she looked forward to further meetings and Miss Mufferton smiling amiably. Obviously the family had passed muster, Maeve was somewhat amused to reflect as she tied her bonnet ribbons.

Sir Ralph stood briefly beside her on the steps as the carriage was brought round. "This is an excellent thing for my mother," he said. "I heard you say you would spend a day with her and I must express my appreciation. She does like to have congenial friends about her and she has obviously taken to you, Miss Dacre."

Somewhat embarrassed, she said stiffly, "It will be a pleasure. I shall look forward to it."

As they came to the bottom step, while William was handing his wife into the carriage, Sir Ralph added, "I wonder if you would care to ride with me? You did promise to show me Romney Marsh."

She hadn't exactly done that, Maeve thought. In fact she seemed to remember she had told him he would not like it, but he was continuing, "May I give myself the pleasure of calling for you one day when I come back from the races?"

"I don't think my step-father would object," she answered, but kept her tone cool. "He may very well like to accompany us. He is quite an authority on the Marsh churches." She took a quick glance at his face and noticed again that twitch of the mouth which was apparently one of his characteristics. She had been clumsy there and realised she had to deal with a man who had his wits about him. Very much aware of this, she said, "I am sorry I have not yet seen your stables."

He nodded. "I thought you would have preferred to see them than sit with the ladies. I'm afraid Mufti does rather go on."

"A little," Maeve said, and could not help returning his smile, "but indeed I enjoyed talking to your mother. I think we share many interests. Among other things she told me she liked Sir Walter Scott's novels, and so do I."

"Do you indeed? When I am at home I often read from one of them in the evening – she likes to be read to."

She nearly burst out laughing. The idea of Sir Ralph, after Miss Mufferton's description of his occupations in London, sitting down quietly to read to his mother, seemed quite incongruous. Her expression must have betrayed her for he said, "I assure you I get a great deal of enjoyment out of it. It is one of the least boring of domestic obligations."

His sarcasm annoyed her, but there was nothing further she could say, and she accepted his hand to mount into the carriage.

"Well," the Vicar said as they drove home, "we are fortunate to have such pleasant people arrived in the county. I am sure your mother, William, will enjoy meeting them in due course."

"I doubt if we shall see much of Sir Ralph," Maeve said sharply. "From what I heard his preference is for London life."

"Really?" William raised his eyebrows. "When we talked in the stables I got the impression that he meant to spend most of the summer here. He says London is dead in July and August."

"At any rate," Mary added, "I'm sure, as you say, Papa, that Aunt Isabel will like Lady Digby. Certainly there's no lack of conversation with her."

They laughed but Maeve added, "It is a pity we have to listen to that companion as well. I thought her garrulous and verging on the vulgar in her talk of all the high-up persons the Digbys mix with."

"Don't be waspish, Maeve," the Vicar said.

"Oh dear, was I? But you'll admit, Mary," she appealed to her sister, "she was tiresome, wasn't she?"

"I doubt if there's any harm in her," Mary said in a kindly way, and her stepfather added, "It is the position that poor relations often find themselves in and it can't be easy. I remember Lady Vernon's companion – it is a sort of effort to make their mark."

Mary went on to talk of how well the house had been decorated and filled with elegant furniture, much of which had been brought from London, and William said he would like to try the billiard table. There appeared to be wholehearted approval of the new connection, but Maeve was silent for the rest of the journey. She rather wished Sir Ralph had never galloped through the churchyard and into their lives.

The day with Lady Digby passed off better than she expected, though it had its awkward moments. She drove over in the curricle rather than riding, for she did not want to spend the day in her habit. The Vicarage groom, Joseph Smith, Obadiah's eldest son, accompanied her and as it was fine and warm she enjoyed, as always, handling the curricle.

Joe occasionally said, "Mind that hole, miss," or "We're coming to the sharp bend," just to show he was watching over her. He was a good lad, not much younger than herself, and she liked him; certainly Obadiah, notably the best hand with horses in this part of Sussex, had trained him well. She smiled at him and said, "Yes, Joe, I'll mind."

When she was shown into the great drawing room she was glad she had chosen to wear her new dress of sprigged blue silk with a muslin over-skirt of white, little puffed sleeves, and a thin shawl of white cashmere draped around her shoulders, for Lady Digby immediately looked her over and even before a greeting said. "What a charming dress, my dear." Miss Mufferton was there and over luncheon indulged in her usual flow of chatter until occasionally silenced by Lady Digby with such remarks as, "We know that, Mufti," and more often, "Yes, you've already told us that." Maeve began to feel rather sorry for the companion, remembering her stepfather's remark in the carriage going home from their last visit. After the meal Miss Mufferton excused herself and disappeared.

"She's a good soul," her ladyship said dismissively as she and Maeve settled themselves in chairs by the open windows. A gentle breeze stirred the curtains and the view was very pleasing on this summer afternoon. "But a little wearying at times," she went on. "I told her to go off for her rest after luncheon so that we could have a talk together." She turned a little to look full at her guest. "I received yesterday a kind note from Lady Hollander inviting us to call at Hollander's House. Tell me about it."

"It is very fine," Maeve said warmly, "Tudor brick and more than forty rooms. Mary and I counted them once when we were children and got into trouble for going into the maids' rooms at the top. It only had two floors at first but my aunt's grandfather added another. The view from the top is wonderful, looking right down over Romney Marsh."

"It must be. It's an unusual name, for the house and the owners as well."

"I suppose it is. You see, the first one came from Holland in the sixteenth century. He was escaping from religious persecution and was a merchant, with two ships of his own. He made a great deal of money and bought the land on the ridge so that his house would have a fine prospect." Maeve smiled. "The local people couldn't pronounce his name which was Van Schleningen so they called him the Hollander and he adopted it. In the reign of James I he did some service for the King and was made a baronet. There's a portrait of him on the stairs, in a ruff and doublet. He was very handsome."

She became aware that the penetrating blue stare she was coming to expect from both mother and son was bent on her, and looked back with equal candour.

After a moment Lady Digby said, "I can see a visit to Hollanders House will be of great interest. At the moment, however, it is you who intrigue me. You are, I think, the younger Mrs Hollander's twin? Yes, I thought so. So you are not a young girl – yet you have chosen not to marry. I can't believe you've not had offers, you're certainly pretty enough and with more than enough accomplishments to attract young gentlemen."

To her annoyance Maeve felt her cheeks warm with colour and with some dignity retorted, "I think, ma'am, that is a private matter."

Her hostess was not in the least put out, having a preference for plain speaking. "Perhaps it is, but don't be getting on your high horse, my dear. I am old enough to indulge my curiosity when I am interested in someone. I like you, Miss Dacre. If I go to London for part of next winter, would you care to spend a few weeks with me? I would like to bring you forward."

The offer took Maeve's breath away, especially after her

refusal to be drawn on the matter of suitors. "You are very kind," she said at last, but could not resist adding impishly, "Do you look to find me a husband?"

Lady Digby laughed. "I might well. Oh, I can see we shall have a very entertaining time together."

"You hardly know me, ma'am."

"I see enough," her hostess answered cryptically. "No doubt we shall get to know each other better during the summer. We will talk of London later. It would be enjoyable to go shopping together in Bond Street, wouldn't it?"

And Maeve was woman enough to agree that it would. Her Uncle Tom had settled an ample dowry on both herself and Mary when their father died and it was wisely invested so that she now enjoyed an income from it, of which she spent very little. She would have money in her pocket and could draw on Hoare's bank for her needs. The prospect was undoubtedly pleasing.

Then, with the sudden change of subject that she was getting used to, Lady Digby asked if she played the piano, and on receiving an affirmative answer begged her to try out the magnificent new instrument Sir Ralph had brought down from London.

"I used to play myself once, and rather well even if I do say so, but alas my fingers are too stiff now. And I'm afraid Mufti over-estimates her own efforts."

Thankfully aware she herself played reasonably well, Maeve sat down at the piano which she had been hoping to try, and began with a simple tune, a country dance, and then played a Bach jig. When she had finished her hostess nodded approvingly. "You play well, child. Who taught you?"

"My aunt employs a music teacher from Lewes to come once a month to teach her daughter Ellen, and Mary and I shared the lessons. It is one of my great pleasures," Maeve finished warmly.

"I can see it is. When my father brought me to London for my first season he engaged one of the best masters for me. How I enjoyed it."

"Do you like London, Ma'am?"

"Oh, it is the hub of the world," Lady Digby told her. "All good society is there. I was fortunate enough to be present ten years ago after the battle of Waterloo when the Tsar of Russia, the King of Prussia – so stiff and correct – and the French King, Louis, all came for the celebrations. I remember the Tsar and his sister were at Pultney's Hotel and the French King at Grillon's. We dined there one night. He was very affable, but enormously fat, rather like our Prinny is now. I actually danced with the Tsar at Carlton House. My husband had been on a diplomatic mission to his court years before. He remembered and was very gallant to an elderly lady. It made me feel quite young again." She went on with several anecdotes of her youth and how she had refused Sir John Digby three times before she had been induced to accept him. "He was very wealthy and my parents thought it a good thing for me. And then it all turned out so well. He grew into an admirable man and his death left me greatly saddened."

"It was like that with my aunt and uncle," Maeve said impulsively. "She told me their marriage was arranged but they grew to love each other so very much."

"Parents are generally wiser than an inexperienced girl and can best see what would suit," Lady Digby added drily. "I sometimes wonder if Selena regards Hillingdon in the same light. I hope you will meet her soon."

"I hope so too, ma'am," Maeve said politely.

At the end of the visit she thanked Lady Digby very much for her hospitality and was pressed to come again. Accepting, she realised how much she had enjoyed the elderly lady's exhilarating company – she might be crippled by rheumatism but her mind was alert, perceptive, and Maeve had the feeling that little passed her by.

As she prepared to leave Lady Digby said, "Maeve is an unusual name. Where does it come from?"

"It's Irish, ma'am. My grandmother came from the north of Ireland, so my father was half Irish and very Irish in looks and temperament, I believe, though I was young enough when he died only to have thought about him as my father."

"He must have been young. Was he taken with a sudden illness?"

"One could say so, ma'am." And with the arrival of the butler with her bonnet and gloves, Maeve thankfully made her escape.

Reaching the Vicarage in time for dinner she walked into the parlour to find her aunt and Ellen there with her mother, and it was Ellen who jumped up and ran to give her an impulsive hug.

"Oh, Maeve, he's coming, as we hoped. My dearest brother! Isn't it wonderful?"

Maeve stood still in her embrace, colour flooding her face. Half afraid to believe it, she looked across at her aunt.

"Yes, dearest," Lady Hollander said. "Such good news. He is very distressed of course at losing his dear father, and he writes that he has given the future a great deal of thought. He has decided to sell out and come back to Hollanders, he feels it is his duty. And the dear boy adds that is his wish as well. I am so very pleased."

Maeve gave Ellen another hug, and then disentangling herself, came over to kiss her aunt. "I can hardly believe it after all this time." Though she did not know it her eyes were shining, her whole face alight, a little smile curving her mouth. "Does he say when?"

Isabel shook her head. "No, he says rather cryptically that he has things to settle, the most important of which he hopes will please me. I'm not sure what he means."

"Perhaps he is going to bring home an elephant." Ellen suggested, hardly able to keep still in her excitement.

Amid the general laughter, the talk and the dinner afterward, happier than any had been since Sir Thomas's death, Maeve felt as if she were walking in a dream. The years between, the long wait were nearly over, and though she knew the voyage could take several months it was possible he would arrive some time in September. In her joy she pushed aside all anxiety, and when the visitors left threw her arms about her aunt. For a moment they clung to each other.

"Oh, my dear," Isabel said at last, "only a little longer."

Later, alone with his wife in their bedroom, Marting Hollander said, "I don't know why, but I am uneasy. Perhaps another letter will come for Maeve herself, but there was no message for her, no enclosure in Isabel's."

Nell turned from the dressing table, and taking off her long satin toilette robe slipped into bed beside him. "I noticed that and wondered if it occurred to her in her moment of joy. Do you think he's changed, that he's forgotten her? No, of course he couldn't have done that, but – "

"But is he looking at her now only with the affection one might have for one's relatives, a cousin with whom he shared things in his childhood?"

"If it is only that – poor Maeve. It has gone very deep with her."

"Exactly. He can't help but have changed, as indeed she has," Martin pointed out. He blew out the candle on the table beside him and put his arm about Nell so that they lay close together as they always did. They had come to marriage late, having loved in vain for many years, and in a busy life their moments alone together were to be treasured. "I have been troubled in my mind about this for some time," he went on. "She has never swerved in her loyalty to him, but you know, my love, I rather wish she had."

Nell was startled. "Do you? Somehow, like everyone else, I always took it for granted, as she did, that he would come home to marry her – he knows she has not wed anyone else – but I didn't think it would be so long."

"That is what worries me. It has been too long. I fear, I greatly fear, Maeve is going to be hurt. But perhaps when they see each other again, all will come right." He paused and added, "Or maybe they will both realise they are different people."

"Martin! Don't you want them to be wed?"

"If it is for their happiness, yes. But I've often thought, as the years went by, he could have written to ask her to come out and marry him. It would have been fraught with difficulties, I know, and I'm not sure either you or I would have wanted that, but he never did, did he?"

Nell had to admit he was right, and she began to fear for her daughter, amid all the rejoicing, and almost to dread the homecoming. But it had to be settled sooner or later. Maeve must not be allowed to waste her love, her young life, and not to know the happiness Mary had.

She talked it over, in private, with Isabel in the morning, but all her sister said was, "You worry too much, Nell. We all know Freddy, and why should the man, at heart, be so different from the boy? He will still be the dear fellow we all love and I for one look forward to the day he comes down the aisle of St Mary's with Maeve on his arm."

"I hope you are right," Nell said, but with a great deal less confidence.

Chapter 4

Maeve dressed with care for her ride with Sir Ralph Digby in black habit, white blouse with lace spilling over at neck and cuffs, and a tall hat with a scarf of yellow gauze floating from it. Papa was right, of course. She could not shut herself away for months until Freddy came, and because she liked Lady Digby so much, she could not be rude to her son. Looking at her reflection in the mirror she suddenly raised her arms in an access of joy. Freddy was coming, might even be on board ship. Soon it would be with him that she was riding on the Marsh, and though she did not know it her face was radiant as she went downstairs. Sir Ralph was waiting in the hall and looked up as she came, standing quite still. Then he took her outstretched hand and wished her good day.

They rode down the lane past Hollanders, Sir Ralph saying he was looking forward to seeing the house when Lady Hollander would be receiving callers again. He asked the history of the old tower, and then coming down to the bridge exclaimed on the canal and the engineering feat that it was.

"It was made by the Royal Staff Corps," Maeve said, "and a friend of my aunt and uncle, a Major Irvine, had a great deal to do with it. He was killed at Corunna at the same time as Sir John Moore. His aunt lived in the village, but she died last year. The Staff Corps is still stationed at Hythe in the new barracks. Miss Mufferton told me last week that you were in the Army."

"For a while," he said, unsmiling. "When the Duke of Wellington went out there after the débàcle at Corunna, I joined the 10th Hussars. It was where I met my friend, George FitzClarence."

He elaborated no further and after a moment she said, "My cousin, Sir Frederick, has been serving in India, but he's coming home now that Hollanders is his."

Her companion made some conventional remark, but he in his turn was wondering whether this piece of news was what had put that glow in her face.

They cantered on along the Military Road towards Rye and at Scots Float crossed the Rother to take the New Romney road. It was a warm day, a breeze coming off the water.

"You will get a better impression of the Marsh than when you saw it in January," she said. "It's a fine prospect on a day like this."

He took in the view, the wide acres, the sturdy Marsh sheep, the old churches and few farms, the lonely lookers' huts. "I think I prefer the more wooded land where Welford is," he said at last, and thinking that a diet of too many Marsh churches would bore him, she took him only to Snargate, explaining how it had been used in the height of the smuggling days to store kegs of brandy and tea, tobacco and silks and laces. "All done up in oilskins," she said, "so that they could be dropped on a rope into the sea at a moments notice if a Revenue cutter came by or a Navy vessel, and then hauled up later."

"Is there still much smuggling?"

"Nothing like the old days, or so my aunt says. It was very bad at one time, the coast here is so flat and around Dungeness so deserted that it lends itself to the trade. But since the taxes were reduced, there's not so much profit in it. We had an affray here between the Free Traders, as they call themselves, and the customs officers a few years ago, but I've heard of nothing since – though I'm sure it still goes on in a small way."

"I suppose a good many folk benefitted from it," he said in some amusement.

"Oh, yes," she laughed across at him, "Aunt Isabel's father had his brandy regularly left in the old tower, and tea for his sister, but my Uncle Tom who succeeded him was a Justice of the Peace and very much against it. A good number of his farm workers were involved at one time but he managed to put a stop to most of it."

As they came out of the church, she added, "Uncle Tom told me the story, against himself, of how when he first came to Hollanders as a young naval lieutenant he got lost and asked his way in the Red Lion over there. The men drinking in the taproom had smuggling tools on the table and thought he was a spy so they knocked him to the floor and sat on him! Luckily my aunt arrived and rescued him. She knew them all and was more than a match for them."

"What a way to meet one's future wife," he said. "I imagine Lady Hollander to be a formidable lady."

"Oh, she is indeed, but really the kindest soul. Only she doesn't put up with nonsense."

"I shall have to mind my manners when I visit Hollanders House," he said lightly. "I fear I was somewhat on edge when I first called at the Vicarage."

"Well, it was difficult for you," Maeve said, and he gave her a quick smile.

They cantered on up the road towards Appledore, enjoying the ride. After a while he said, "That's a fine mare you have. What have you called her?"

"Blanche. I like a grey."

"Is she not a trifle heavy for you?"

"Oh, no," Maeve said, "I can handle her."

"And I believe you can handle a curricle competently too. My mother watched you drive away last week."

"I enjoy it," she told him. "To be out and free – I'm like my aunt in that."

"Very independent for a lady," he remarked. "You remind me of Lady Hester Stanhope. You've heard of her travels?"

"I've read her book, and how I've envied her. But I'm afraid my sole adventures are on the Marsh, jumping dykes and scattering sheep."

"Like Don Quixote tilting at windmills," he said. "Yet I think you have that sort of spirit. She chose not to marry but to live an independent sort of life, though it is thought that she would have married Sir John Moore if he had come back from Corunna. At least that was the talk at the time." He paused for a moment and then said calmly, "Have you too chosen not to have a husband?" She looked at him in astonishment, and as if to explain himself he went on, "Your twin is obviously happily married to Mr Hollander and with, I gather, two children. Now to my mind you are the prettier and I wonder, is there a dearth of presentable young men in the district?"

Maeve gave him a straight look. "As for Mary, she is a much nicer person than I am, so you should not judge by outward appearances. And your mother, in slightly different words, asked me the same question."

"And what answer did you give her?"

"That it was my own affair."

"Did you, by God! I wonder how she took that?"

"She said I was quite right and that she liked me for it."

"And what answer will you give me?"

The same, sir," she said with her chin tilted, "except that I consider your question impertinent. What may be asked between an older lady and a younger one is not acceptable between a lady and a gentleman."

He threw back his head and laughed. "Well, you don't mince your words. I can't imagine your sister giving such a set-down. Am I to consider myself snubbed?"

"You laid yourself open to it, Sir Ralph."

"I suppose I did." He became serious again. "But I would have liked an answer."

Maeve allowed herself a smile. "It is a sad world, sir. We seldom get all we would like."

"Now you are rubbing salt in the wound," he told her, but it was clear from his expression that he enjoyed the verbal match. Privately he thought her twin's gentle nature admirably suited to the, to him, eminently worthy but somewhat dull William, and much preferred this girl's spirited refusal to be drawn. "Am I to get no more than that?"

"No," she answered. "You should not have asked such a question." Touching Blanche's flanks with her heels, she cantered off.

He caught up with her and shot her a sidelong look. "Relent," he said, "forgive my impertinence. It was only because, like my esteemed parent, I would like to know you better. And let me say she does not take easily to making new friends – and I mean friends, not mere acquaintances, and none that I know of as young as you."

She did relent at that. "She is very kind," she said in a

softened voice, "and I find her company very pleasant indeed."

"I know why," he answered. "You can sharpen your wits on each other."

"Well," Maeve said, "since I am put down as a forthright person, I might ask exactly the same of you."

To her surprise the smile was wiped from his face. "Then I regret I must follow your example and make the same answer."

There was something so grim about his face that she was startled and paused for a moment before she answered. "I don't think either of us should have spoken of this. After all, we are only recently acquainted." And she added lightly, "Shall we agree to keep our own counsels?"

"Willingly," he said, as if the word was forced out of him. But he turned to give her a wry smile. "You will have to forgive us. I'm afraid we are maybe too outspoken. My sister is the same, sometimes with disastrous consequences as she moves in diplomatic circles."

"To be honest," she answered, "I prefer people to speak their minds."

"Then we are agreed, I can see why my mother has taken to you."

She inclined her head at the compliment, but it was less a politely conventional one than a statement of fact. Changing the subject she pointed out to him that they had come in a circle back to the canal, and cantering once more along the Military road they reached the vicarage half an hour before dinner. Joe came to lift Maeve down but Sir Ralph was before him and took her down himself.

"I enjoyed our ride." he said, "I hope we can do it again soon. I've not seen a Martello Tower yet."

She made a half promise and led him into the house where, leaving him to be entertained by her stepfather, she went upstairs to change, thinking that Sir Ralph might become something of a nuisance, especially when Freddy was back.

However, as the summer weeks went by the two families spent a great deal of time together. Isabel emerged in part from her mourning, though she said the time had not yet come for her to remove her black, and driving over to

Welford with Nell pronounced Lady Digby to be a sensible woman with good conversation. She had nothing but praise for what Sir Ralph had done to the place, though she regretted the loss of the mulberry tree, and certainly Lady Digby's fondness for Maeve won her approval. She gave a small dinner party – it could not be more until the full year was up – but Sir Ralph brought his mother and Miss Mufferton, Lord and Lady Rokeby were present, as her oldest friends, the Monarchs and the Vicarage party making up the number.

Afterwards Isabel said to Maeve, "I do understand your friendship with Lady Digby. When I was young I had the same sort of relationship with old Lady Rokeby – you wouldn't remember her. I missed her so much when she died. Now there was a formidable woman!"

Maeve laughed and said she found Sir Ralph's mother daunting at first, but her kindness had been exceptional. "She invited me to go to London next year, 'to bring me forward', as she called it, but of course now I shan't go."

"Perhaps you and Freddy will go together. It would be nice to have patrons in London. Only that might not be quite what she meant."

"No," Maeve agreed, "I don't think it was." And they exchanged smiles of understanding.

Other visits followed, William and Mary gave several dinner parties to introduce the Digbys to local gentry, William trying to save his mother too much too soon in that line. But Isabel Hollander was fast recovering her natural vigour and she was quite sure her beloved Tom would not want her to sit in widow's weeds with the blinds down for too long. She began riding again; the Hollander ladies, as she, Ellen and Maeve were called, to be seen once more in the lanes and on the Marsh. Sir Ralph went shooting with William and found him less dull when they got on to topics of country life. He discovered that William had written and illustrated a book on Marsh flora and rode down to Rye to order a copy.

For Maeve it was a very pleasant way of passing the time until the arrival of a ship from India. Her friend Elizabeth Rokeby, Lord Rokeby's eldest girl, remarked that with the arrival of the Digbys and Sir Frederick's return there was more excitement than they had had for a long time.

At the height of the summer the Digbys invited a large number of their friends to spend about ten days at Welford Park. London was dead at this time of year, Sir Ralph told Maeve, and society given to moving from one country house to another among their friends. After this, he and his mother were going to Petworth.

"A magnificent house," he said, "and the Earl of Egremont, Lady FitzClarence's father, has made a fine collection of pictures and china and works of art."

"Your mother told me that Mr Turner often works there."

"Yes, Lord Egremont has been his patron since he began and one is amazed at the pictures that come out of that chaotic room. There's a large park, very pleasant for riding. I wish you could see the place."

"That's hardly likely," she answered. They were walking in the Vicarage garden where she was cutting roses for the house.

She had learned more about him now – that he had enjoyed boxing when he was younger and occasionally went to a fencing school in London, "to keep myself trim", he said. Racing seemed to be a passion with him for he went to Doncaster, Ascot and Newmarket, was a member of the Jockey Club, and apparently owned a horse stabled and trained on the Newbury Downs. He was also, he told her, looking forward to the hunting season. As for his friends, they seemed legion, despite his sometimes abrupt, sometimes harsh manner.

But this morning he was at his most courteous. Carrying her basket, he went on, "The Earl is not coming to Welford next week. He's getting on in years and seldom leaves Petworth now, but Colonel FitzClarence and his wife will be with us. George has just been appointed Lieutenant-colonel of the Coldstream Guards. He's mighty pleased at that, soldiering has been his life. He had the most amazing adventures coming home from India."

Maeve's attention left the roses abruptly. "He was in India?"

"After he left the 10th, yes. He was aide-de-camp to the Marquis of Hastings who was Governor General and Commander-in-Chief at the time. There was a campaign against the Mahrattas in '16 and when peace was arranged, George was sent home by land with the duplicates of the treaty, in case of mishap to the originals which went by sea. He wrote an account of his adventures which was published about six years ago, a fascinating story."

"I wonder, Sir Ralph, do you have a copy you could lend me? I'm interested in anything to do with India."

"Of course," he said, "your cousin is out there, isn't he?"

"Yes," she answered, and turned to cut a red rose of particularly beautiful shape.

"May I keep this one?" He took it from her hand.

She shrugged. "If you wish." And when he had put it carefully into his coat, was aware she had sounded ungracious. To turn the talk away from roses she asked when his visitors were coming.

"In about a fortnight. I hope you will all come over to join us. When I have some entertainments arranged, I will send an invitation."

"I'm sure it will be very pleasant." she said, and led him in through the long doors into the parlour.

The first event at Welford that the Hollanders attended, even Isabel persuaded by Lady Digby, was an expedition by carriage to see Bodiam Castle and picnic by the moat. Servants went ahead in a wagon with everything necessary, the company following in open carriages. Introductions had been made in the courtyard but there were so many well-dressed ladies and gentlemen that Maeve found it hard to take in all the names, though she was attracted at once by the tall, dark and very good-looking George FitzClarence. He had the build of his father, the Duke of Clarence, but in colouring and features resembled his mother, Mrs Jordan. His wife Mary was both pretty and charming, and when they had shaken hands, he said, "Dig – Sir Ralph –, has told me a great deal about you, Miss Dacre." to which she answered, "And he has told me a great deal about you, sir."

"When two young fellows go through such battles as Badajoz and Salamanca and Vittoria together, it makes a bond," he said with a broad smile. "I was only sorry we weren't at Waterloo."

"Oh? Somehow I always think every officer I meet must

have been at Waterloo, but I see that it's quite naive of me."

"I'm afraid a great many of our best Pensinsula troops had been shipped off to America during the year of peace, and of course there was, as always, a considerable army in India." He did not enlarge further as there was a move to enter the assembled vehicles. Instead he said, "May we capture you for our carriage, Miss Dacre?"

She accepted and sat beside Lady Mary, the Colonel joined by a shy man, a Mr Wyndham, who was apparently one of Lord Egremont's numerous relations. The sun was warm but not too hot and the sky clear, with no likelihood of rain. For a while the talk was of India. Maeve explained her interest in that country and Colonel FitzClarence proved himself a great raconteur. She said she had been promised his book by Sir Ralph, and the Colonel looked pleased.

"I am working on an account of Sir John Moore's Peninsula campaign at the moment, for the United Service Magazine, and have had cause to check a few details with Sir John Colborne who was his Military Secretary." He paused and added, "As you are interested in India, Miss Dacre, you might care to know that a number of gentlemen and myself founded last year the Royal Asiatic Society and hope to produce papers from time to time. I will see that Sir Ralph has copies so that he can pass them on to you."

She thanked him, mentioning that she had met Colonel Colborne when he had visited the area. The journey passed pleasantly as Maeve listened, intrigued, to this intelligent man. But in the lane leading to the castle she did wonder why he and Sir Ralph had not gone with their regiment to the campaign of Waterloo. She wished she could have asked, but thought he might consider it impertinent.

The conversation turned on admiring the magnificent ruin of Bodiam set in its moat, calm and peaceful on this summer day, and Maeve was able to entertain them with its history. The party was very cheerful, enjoying the prospect and the walk round the fine old building. There was a lot of coquettish laughter and teasing among the younger guests, one of the Seftons' daughters chased round an oak tree by a young gentleman and pretending to reject his advances. Ellen looked a little startled but Maeve whispered that she thought high society freer in its ways than they were used to.

The picnic was elegantly arranged and served by Sir Ralph's butler and a couple of footmen. Chairs had been brought for the older folk, but Maeve sat on a rug with other young ladies and enjoyed herself, Lady Sefton complimenting her on her pale yellow dress and matching bonnet. She found herself sitting by Lady Augusta Millbanke, a strident young woman with a hooting laugh, aptly called Gusty by her friends, but likeable and entertaining.

In the afternoon they toured the castle, crossing the moat by the footbridge into the castle courtyard, and she found herself beside a middle-aged man with amiable features whom she had noticed at the picnic bustling about, chatting to everyone. He told her his name was Thomas Creevey and that he had two stepdaughters, one about her age, though his wife had sadly been taken from him. He then proceeded to ask her all about her family. He nodded knowledgeably and said he was sure he had heard Lord Sefton's father speak many years ago of Sir Frederick Hollander. They had been fellow members of White's Club, as far as he remembered.

"The present Lord Sefton is my friend and patron," he explained. "I am a lawyer by trade, Miss Dacre, and have been a member of Parliament, and Lord Sefton has kindly brought me into society. He is that gentleman over there, in the blue coat, talking to King Jog."

"King who?" she asked and he laughed.

"King Jog. Actually he is Lord Lambton, but he once remarked that he thought he could jog along on forty thousand a year, and so he has been King Jog ever since."

She was amused and he entertained her with various tales and gossip for the rest of the walk. She put him down as a likeable busy-body, naming for her all the members of the party with a potted version of their families and status. Later, back at Welford when she was preparing to go home, Sir Ralph walked to the carriage with her.

"I've hardly had a word with you all day," he said. "I saw Creevey monopolising you at Bodiam."

"He was being very informative."

"I'm sure he was," he said drily. "He is the most appalling

gossip. You had better guard your secrets when you are with him, Miss Dacre."

"So I thought," she answered, without reflecting, and then added a little awkwardly, "Oh dear, I didn't mean to be rude. He said nothing out of order, I promise you."

"Just as well. You can't turn round in society without tripping over him, and yet there is no real harm in him. In fact, he has a genuine liking for people and he can certainly be relied on to keep the company entertained if the slightest *ennui* creeps in. But I can't imagine you have any terrible secrets to hide."

They had reached the line of carriages and she made no reply to that remark. Really, sometimes he talked to her as if they were on terms of greater intimacy than she liked. On the drive home she was able to be quite informative about the guests and Lady Hollander said quietly, "I wish your uncle had been here. How he would have enjoyed organising an entertainment for them all at Hollanders."

"When Freddy comes –" Maeve began, and then stopped. She realised she had actually not thought about Freddy for a whole day and she felt oddly guilty.

On the last evening of the house party, Sir Ralph gave a ball, inviting all the Hollanders, as well as most of the local gentry with whom he had become acquainted since his arrival. Isabel insisted on ordering new dresses to be made for both Maeve and Ellen. Ellen's was of a simple design for a young girl, white with a blue sash, while Maeve's, though also white silk, was decorated with pink gauze rosebuds, a few of them woven into an ornament for her hair.

"You look lovely, my dear," Martin said as she came down the stair carrying white gloves and a fan as it was a warm evening, "quite the equal of any lady there, I'm sure," And Nell whispered, "Freddy must see you in this dress, dearest."

The ball was not to commence until ten o'clock and the summer dusk had fallen when their carriage arrived in the circular drive, Ellen beside herself with excitement. She was just fifteen and it was her first ball. Lanterns had been strung in the trees near the house, candlelight showed in all the windows, and as they came up the steps to the great doors, thrown wide, Sir Ralph was there to greet them. He pressed

Maeve's hand warmly, his pale eyes sweeping over her in his usual manner, taking in the gown, all the more elegant for its simplicity. For her part Maeve thought him looking most distinguished in a green satin coat, white satin breeches and silk stockings. His mother was in her customary black, a somewhat out-dated turban with feathers on her head. The rooms were crowded, dancing was already beginning, and Maeve found herself claimed for the first dance by Lord Rokeby whom she had known all her life.

"Isn't this splendid?" he said. "I never imagined the old place could come alive again like this."

She agreed that it was, and a little later danced with her one-time suitor Damian Havers, who had recently married Sir Edward Dering's granddaughter.

"You look beautiful," he said to her, with the familiarity of an ex-suitor. "I suppose it is still Freddy with you?"

"Of course," she laughed up at him. "And I can see you are very happy with your choice. I watched you dancing with your bride. Marianne seems such a charming girl, and so pretty."

He was pleased. "She is," he agreed earnestly. "And I saw you dancing with our host. I've not had much talk with him. What do you think of him?"

"He can be extremely agreeable," she said with a shrug, "but I think he has a temper. He rides well. He's certainly making a place for himself in the county."

"My father had a run-in with him concerning the boundaries of Brockett's Wood," Damian told her. "He says it's a case of 'new man, old acres'!"

She laughed at that but said, "I hope it's been settled amicably. I always thought Brockett's was on your land?"

"Oh, yes, mostly, but not the part of it cut off by the stream – you know where I mean?"

She nodded. "I remember when we paddled in it once looking for sticklebacks and I was scolded for getting my dress wet. Is your father here? I don't see him."

"He has the gout – and perhaps a fit of pique as well. But the matter of Brockett's Woods has been settled without too much fur flying." He glanced down at his partner. "When do you expect dear old Freddy home?"

"Soon," she said, "soon."

Later, dancing with Sir Ralph who, very correctly had led out every lady in the room, he said in a low voice and a very different tone to Damian's light remark, "There is no one here to touch you for beauty, Miss Dacre."

"You are very kind but not very truthful," she retorted. "I think Miss Dulverton is quite stunning."

"If you like Greek statues," he agreed, and she could not help smiling.

"That was most unkind, but I've learned to expect such remarks from you."

"I wish you to learn more about me," he said abruptly, and then as the dance came to an end she was claimed by Mr Creevey for a country measure. Her mind on what Sir Ralph had said, she asked her companion for a glass of lemonade and a few minutes later they were sitting on two gilt chairs set in an alcove.

Mr Creevey was chatting as usual, this time telling her how Lord Melbourne and his wife Lady Caroline Lamb had agreed to live separately. "So sad," he said, "both such splendid people in their own ways, but dear Lady Caro was always wild. I remember once, I think it was at her mother's country place – Lady Bessborough you know, the Duchess of Devonshire's sister – she put on trousers and went riding bareback round the park with Lord Byron. That was a scandalous business. She has not been the same since he died."

"You seem to know a great deal about what goes on in the world," she said, and then on an impulse, taking advantage of the moment, she added, "Mr Creevey, I wonder if –"

He smiled down at her. "I keep my eyes and ears open, my dear. What is it you wish to know?"

"It came up in conversation the other day that Sir Ralph and Colonel FitzClarence both left their regiment, the 10th Hussars, I think, about the same time and weren't present at Waterloo. I don't know why but I got the impression that something unusual happened."

Mr Creevey was delighted. There was nothing he enjoyed more than to be asked to relate a tale with a little spice of some sort in it. He settled himself comfortably and gave her a conspiratorial smile. "Ah, I thought you might be a little interested in our host, as I can see he is in you."

To her annoyance, she flushed. "I assure you it is no such thing. As far as he is concerned, I'm sure I don't know."

He gave her an impish look. "Don't be coy, child. I'm old enough to be your father."

"I'm not." She was beginning to rise, but he patted her hand and went on, "Yet you would still like an answer to your question, eh?"

"I don't think I should have asked. It's no concern of mine."

He was still holding on to her hand so that she was obliged to remain sitting beside him. "Do stay awhile, my dear child. If you hadn't wanted to know you wouldn't have asked, so let me tell you all about it. It's a very entertaining tale."

Cross with herself for being ruled by her own curiosity and aware that she could not, as she wished, free herself and walk away without giving offence and maybe drawing notice on herself, she remained seated and tried to appear slightly bored. "Very well, sir, if you wish."

Mr Creevey began with some relish. "It was a pretty reprehensible affair at the time. Sir Ralph and Colonel FitzClarence had fought together through the whole Peninsula War, in fact the Colonel was badly wounded at Toulouse and probably owes his life to Sir Ralph who managed to get him out of a dangerous corner. Their colonel made a sorry mess of this affair and when the 10th returned during the peace of 1814, when you remember Napoleon was held on the island of Elba, he was charged with incapacity and misconduct on the field."

"How shocking," she said. "It can't be often that such a thing happens."

"No, indeed. He was eventually tried by court martial at Whitehall in October of that year and the charges proved, at least in part. Sir Ralph and FitzClarence were among the officers called as witnesses, but as it was believed that all the officers of the regiment had combined against their colonel – which they had, for he was a very poor sort of commander – they were, to my mind most unjustly, removed to other regiments as a warning against insubordination."

"That sounds very unfair."

"So it was," he agreed, but added with some amusement,

"They were nicknamed 'the Elegant Extracts' after that because they were sent to different regiments. George FitzClarence went to the 24th Light Dragoons."

"And Sir Ralph?"

"Well, he was apparently very angry at the injustice of it and sent in his papers in a huff." Mr Creevey laughed heartily. "But I believe," he added more seriously, "that he had troubles at home. His father was very ill and we did not see him in London for some time. I believe it was about then that he lost his wife, poor fellow. That must have been about ten years ago. His sister, Lady Hillingdon, was married by then, so he brought his mother to London and never went back to their place in Durham, except I think to arrange the sale."

Maeve listened in surprised silence. Having no idea that their host had ever been married, she couldn't resist a glance across at him as he circled the floor with Lady Sefton. It seemed there was a great deal she did not know about him. His mother had never spoken of it. And then she remembered that Miss Mufferton had been about to explain, on their first meeting, why Sir Ralph hated Mockford Hall but had bitten back the words. It was, to say the least, very odd.

Just then Mr Creevey was called away to settle a discussion and she excused herself, going to sit beside Lady Digby.

Though she told herself she was not really interested, a natural curiosity made her want to ask for enlightenment, but it would have been excessively impertinent. Lady Digby said she was glad to see Miss Dacre enjoying herself.

"I expect you will all dance into the small hours," she said. "I did when I was young, but I think I will retire now. Come along, Mufti." And with obvious reluctance Miss Mufferton was removed from a scene she was enjoying, Maeve watching her go with some amusement.

Later, dancing with her again, Sir Ralph said rather abruptly, "I saw you having another long conversation with Creevey. I suppose he was full of gossip as usual. Was I included in it?"

She wanted to retort that she wondered why he was conceited enough to think he would be, but it would be the silly sort of remark she so hated in some coquettish girls, so instead she said lightly, "Well, you told me you wished me to know more of you."

"But not from Creevey, by God! What was it all about?"

"He told me about – what was it – the 'Elegant Extracts.'"

"Oh, that business. It's long forgotten, though at the time I thought we were very shabbily treated."

She looked up at him as they turned in the waltz, thinking how well he danced. "Did you regret leaving the Army?"

"Very much. I did it in a fit of temper which I regretted later, though I believe it was justified. Afterwards there was no question of my buying into another regiment when Napoleon escaped. I wished I could have done, but I was too involved at home."

"Mr Creevey said your father was very ill at that time."

"Yes, he died a few days before Waterloo. Anything else?"

"Nothing of any moment," she began, and then not being given to prevaricating, she added, "He did say you were married shortly afterwards."

"Nothing of any moment." he echoed, his grip on her hand tightening. "Good God, do you think *that* of no moment?"

The wretched colour ran into her face. "I didn't mean to imply any such thing. Forgive me, Sir Ralph. Is there some reason Mr Creevey should not have spoken of it? As you have never mentioned a wife, nor has your mother, I was a little surprised, that's all."

"I'm sure you were," he said sarcastically. "How you must have enjoyed that piece of gossip. But I didn't take you for a tittle-tattle."

"I'm not," she retorted, stung. He had never spoken to her in such a tone. "It only came out in casual conversation."

"Casual! Did you think it so?"

"No. At least – it was not meant – oh dear, I see I have given offence, Sir Ralph."

His face was dark with annoyance, her poor fingers half crushed by his, and she was thankful that just then the music ceased. In the confusion of couples leaving the floor, he held out his arm, without enlightening her, and led her back to her mother. Then he bowed and left them.

"You look very hot," Nell said. "It is warm in here. Perhaps you've got overheated with so much dancing. I don't believe you've sat down at all."

For once impatient, Maeve said, "Oh, Mama, don't fuss. You know I can dance all night."

"Did Sir Ralph say anything to upset you? Neither of you looked as if you were enjoying yourselves just now."

"I don't think I like him very much," Maeve said sharply, and not answering her mother's question she excused herself and went to join her sister who was chatting to Lady Rokeby and her sixteen-year-old daughter Elizabeth.

Seething with annoyance at both Sir Ralph and herself, the rest of the evening was spoilt. She did not speak to him again for he didn't seek her out and later in the bustle of departure it was Lord Sefton who handed her to the Vicarage carriage. She heard a few days later that the whole party had moved on to Petworth House and was not sure whether to be glad or sorry. She tried to stifle her curiosity but questions bothered her. Why had none of them ever spoken of his wife? Why had he been so angry?

She was sure she did not care – not with the imminent prospect of Freddy's return. Nevertheless, it niggled her. She hated unanswered questions.

Chapter 5

Some weeks later, when the sun was hot, drying the grass on the Marsh, the watercourses brackish and yellow-green with weed, breeding malaria, when the sheep were being dipped against liver-fluke and harvesting beginning, poppies scarlet among the corn at Top Farm, the Hollanders began to look for the arrival of the new baronet. Deciding he must have a home-coming present Maeve, accompanied by Obadiah, went down to Rye to choose a new saddle for him and selected one of the very best leather, ordering it to be sent up to the Vicarage. Then she and Obadiah walked down to the market where there might be some horses of quality for sale, her aunt having asked her to look out for a new mount for Freddy. They were inspecting a likely mare, Obadiah running his hands down the forelegs, when she heard a voice bid her good day.

Turning, she saw Sir Ralph, immaculately dressed in riding clothes, his top boots shining as always. He had removed his hat and stood looking down at her. "Are you thinking of buying this beast?"

"Not for myself. It's a commission for my aunt, for her son when he comes home."

His brow twitched slightly, but he walked round the mare before the horse-trader ran her up and down. "A nice action," was his comment. "She has a good eye and sound wind – a little wilful, I think, but that can be channelled into giving a spirited ride."

"I doubt if you would ever choose a mount that didn't give a spirited ride," Maeve said, smiling up at him, hoping their altercation at the ball was forgotten. "What do you think, Obadiah?" And to Sir Ralph, she added, "Smith here has been at Hollanders as head groom for more years then we can count. We rely very much on his judgement when it comes to horses. Isn't that so, Obadiah?"

He straightened. "I hope so, Miss Maeve. Good day, Sir Ralph. She has a likely look, I'm thinking." He fondled the mare's nose and looked at her teeth. "Healthy enough, I'd say, and deep in the girth, as I always look for."

"I agree with you. I've a mind to her myself if you don't take her."

"You are too late, sir," Maeve said gaily, envisaging Freddy on the mare's back with the new saddle under him. She sent Obadiah with a purse to settle the sale and then take the horse on a leading rein up to Hollanders.

Sir Ralph asked if she was going to the livery stable and on hearing that Blanche was there, held out his arm and they walked together. "I didn't know you were back," she said. "I hope you all had a pleasant visit to Petworth."

"Very," he answered. "But I must admit I would have liked you to be among the guests. Unfortunately I'm not here for very long, just to settle my mother in again. I've to be in London at the end of the week to attend a parade of the Coldstreams that George is organising. There's to be a dinner afterwards given by the Duke of Clarence which I promised to attend, though London is damnably hot at this time of year. By the way, I bought a horse from Lord Egremont while I was at Petworth."

She laughed and said, "You will have to extend your stables." She had long since had the opportunity to inspect them.

"Well, I had to turn off the roan, he was short of wind. But you are quite right. My stables are full and I took on another groom yesterday. He was hanging about the livery looking for work and seemed to have his wits about him."

"Oh, who was that?"

"A young fellow called Jacob Hatch." He saw her expression change. "Do you know something against him?"

Rather sharply she said, "We did offer to assist you in choosing staff when you first came here."

"I've been accustomed to selecting my own," he retorted, "kindly though I'm sure you meant it. Why should I not employ Hatch? I thought he seemed to have good hands with a horse."

"So he has, and he's reliable – at least with horses."

"Are you implying he's not in other ways?"

She gave a little shrug, her eyes on the street ahead. "He doesn't have the best of reputations – a thought wild, I'm told."

"Well, if he doesn't behave himself, he'll be dismissed at once. The odd thing is I have a feeling that I've seen him before, yet I'm sure that's not so. Be that as it may, I'll give him a trial. He's at Welford now and my head groom will keep an eye on him."

She inclined her head. "And of course you know your own affairs best. But I could not but warn you."

"Thank you," he said. "I'll bear it in mind."

His tone was terse and there was a moment's silence as they waited for a coach to pass before crossing the road. Then she said, "I think you were very angry with me at the ball, Sir Ralph. Believe me, I did not wish to offend you."

At once he put his other hand over hers. "I'm sure you didn't. I think it is I who should ask your pardon for my ill-temper. Whatever questions you were asking, I'm certain they were kindly meant. And I'm really quite fond of old Creevey, though he can be too busy at times."

"I couldn't help but be glad he told me that you saved Colonel FitzClarence's life at Toulouse."

He shrugged that away. "It was no more than any man there would have done. I just happened to be nearest to him, that was all. As for my – " he paused as if it was an effort to speak of it, " – my marriage, I intended to tell you of it in my own good time."

"Really, Sir Ralph, there was not the least need." She kept her voice cool and removed her hand. Why should he think it should concern her at all? But he evidently did and she regretted that imperceptibly such a situation had arisen.

However all he said was, "When the right moment comes I will explain. Forgive me if I say nothing further in the middle of Rye on market day."

They had reached the livery stable and as Sir Ralph's new mare was brought out she was glad to leave the too intimate subject and to ask if the animal was well paced.

"I'm trying her out today. Come with me and see. Have you time to divert a little before you go home?"

Glad for Lady Digby's sake that there should be no bad feeling between them, she agreed and asked him if he had been to Winchelsea yet. When he shook his head they set off across the bridge over the River Brede. At a comfortable trot they covered the two miles, talking horseflesh amiably, and rode up the hill on which the town was built. She told him about the French raids in the fourteenth century that had burned the old town and how it had been rebuilt on a grid pattern. After showing him the church and the court house she said, "I know a short cut across country to Welford where we can get a long gallop. Would you care for it?"

"Willingly," he answered. "I like the feel of this girl, and I'd like to try her at a hedge or two."

"I know just the place." Maeve led the way off the road, down what was barely a lane and then into open country. The horses bounded across the turf at a good gallop, Maeve with her eyes sparkling, for such moments were the joy of her days. With the breeze in her face she laughed across at him and queried, "That hedge?"

He grinned back and set off towards the lowest part of the hedgerow, clearing it easily. But, partly out of a desire to go one better, she misjudged the height. Blanche caught one rear hoof, struggled vainly to get clear, and then came down heavily on the far side. Maeve was thrown clear and lay momentarily stunned.

Then she opened her eyes, shook her head a little and became aware of Sir Ralph on one knee beside her. He had flung himself out of his saddle and was putting one arm about her shoulders, lifting her to set his brandy flask to her lips. He said sharply, "Here, drink some of this." But she pushed his hand away.

"Good gracious, I don't want brandy. I've taken a tumble before now."

"You crazy girl," he said, his anger rising now that he knew she was seemingly unhurt. "Why in hell did you take the highest part of that hedge instead of going over where I did?"

His harsh words, contradicting the concern in his face, shook her, "I've jumped here many times," she retorted, "though not for a while. I suppose the wretched hawthorn has grown." She began to struggle to her feet, but a little uncertainly so that she was forced to lean on his arm for support. "I'm all right now." she steadied herself, letting go as soon as possible.

"You were lucky the mare didn't roll on you," he said scathingly. "You'd have got no more than you deserved for your recklessness."

The truth of this didn't make it any more palatable. Gritting her teeth she said, "I'm quite ready to go on."

"I daresay. But after a fall like that it would be excessively foolish to go careering across the fields. We'll go back to the road."

"Nonsense." She turned to look at her mare who was on her feet, blowing a little. "As Blanche seems to be all right – I'm no tame rider, Sir Ralph."

"I didn't think you were," he said drily. "but I was considering your horse."

"Wretch!" Now that the episode was over with no ill consequences, she gave a shaky laugh and this response had the effect of dissipating his anger. He walked round Blanche, ran his hands down her legs and then straightened.

"No harm that I can see," he said.

"Then pray help me up, Sir Ralph."

"Very well, but we'll go back by the road at a sober pace."

She regarded him with a steely look. "I think you underestimate me, sir."

"No, I don't," he retorted, "by God, I don't, but I'm counting on you having one particle of common sense."

"I assure you I can take you to Welford without encountering any more high hedges. Your hands, if you please."

He shrugged. "It was not I who came a cropper, you know." But he cupped his hands and threw her up.

They rode in comparative silence until at a gate which he leaned down to open for her, she said, "I'll leave you here, Sir Ralph, as our ways part."

"You will not," he said more calmly. "You forget, you have

sent your groom home and I will have you driven back in our carriage. Blanche can run behind. I think she's had enough for today." And as he saw her hesitate he added, "I'm right, aren't I?"

She shrugged but submitted, still feeling a trifle shaken despite her assurance to the contrary. At Welford there had to be explanations, to Lady Digby's consternation, but she accepted Maeve's cheerful assurance that she and her horse were recovering fast. Miss Mufferton pressed her hand and fussed and was told not to be silly. "Miss Dacre is made of the right stuff," Ralph's mother said firmly. "I've had many a fall in my time." She insisted, however, on her taking a cup of tea before she left.

Sir Ralph took her out to the carriage which Jacob Hatch had been ordered to put to. He was holding the horses, and touching his hat, glanced to Maeve. "You all right, missy? I 'eard as 'ow you took a tumble."

Before she could answer, Sir Ralph said sharply, "Be off to your work, Hatch. It is not your place to speak to my guests in that familiar manner."

Hatch gave Maeve a cheeky grin and ambled off, and Ralph said irritably, "I begin to think you were right about that fellow. He's too uppish by half."

Maeve paused, her foot on the step. "I've known the family all my life. They live on the Marsh."

"That doesn't excuse familiarity. If he steps out of line again he can go."

She got into the carriage in no mood to explain about Jacob Hatch and was driven away. Glad of the solitude she leaned against the cushions, taking herself very much to task, both as to Blanche's welfare and for appearing careless in Sir Ralph's eyes. She had not admitted it but she had a stiff and bruised knee.

Sir Ralph went back into the drawing room and gave his mother a pointed look. She turned at once to her companion and without beating about the bush said, "Off you go, Mufti. I want a word with Sir Ralph." And when she had gone, used to such blunt dismissals, Lady Digby turned to her son. "Well, my dear, what is on your mind? Miss Dacre?"

He stood with his shoulders against the mantelshelf, his arms folded. "Yes."

"And not just because of her mishap, eh? Well, I am not surprised, and you know how much I have taken to her. I like a girl with spirit who can take a knock or two and not be missish."

A smile twisted his mouth. "She's certainly not that." And then with the smile gone he added, "But when I saw her lying there – "

"I see." She gave her son a long searching look. "And what is your intention, pray?"

"I mean to offer for her."

"Then why the glum face? Do you doubt her response?"

"I've no particular reason to think she might take me."

Lady Digby shrugged aside the idea that any girl might refuse her son. "But none either to think she would not. I presume you have not yet told her about Alice?"

He stirred restlessly. "No, I haven't, though Creevey let slip to her that I'd been married."

"Dear me, how tiresome he can be. I wonder what she thought of that?"

"I don't know. I was annoyed when I found out."

"Naturally," she said. "You would have preferred to tell her yourself. But, you know, I wonder if there is not some secret there too. Twenty-four, and with so much about her, a lively mind as well, and still unwed."

"I've wondered too," he agreed. "I asked her and was firmly put in my place."

"So you should have been. That was hardly wise."

"No," he agreed, "but wisdom has not been a predominant quality in either Selena or myself."

Lady Digby smiled. "Perhaps not, but all may yet turn out well. I never thought, after Alice, that you would look at a chit of seventeen. This young woman may suit you very well, and it's time and more that you took another wife. But it's more than that, isn't it?"

"Yes."

"Well, my dear boy, you deserve some good fortune. It would be nice to set up a Digby dynasty here and become part of the county. But if you will take my advice, go slowly with her."

"Why do you say that?"

She clasped her hands on her stick and rose. "My instinct in such matters tells me so. There must be much about her that we don't yet know. And you must tell her at least a little about Alice, not necessarily the whole – but that is up to you. If she is the girl I think she is, it will not sway her decision in the least."

"I hope not," he said. "By God, I hope not."

Martin Hollander had an orderly mind and Saturday morning was the time when he composed the words he would preach before his congregation on the morrow, folk as varied as Sir Edward Dering and his numerous family, Lord Rokeby and his tenants and farmers, stable hands and labourers. It was a task on which he expended much effort, for he did not, as some clergy did, take his sermons out of a collection between the covers of a book, but laboured over them with considerable care.

The house was quiet this morning. His wife had gone into the village to visit a parishioner, Maeve was riding on the Marsh with his sister-in-law and Ellen, and when there was a knock on the door he let out a little sigh. Somebody wanting something, he supposed, but he wished they wouldn't want it on a Saturday morning.

A few minutes later his footman came in to announce, "Sir Ralph Digby, sir. I've shown him into the parlour."

"Quite right," Martin said. Sir Ralph had become too regular a visitor to be left standing in the hall. He laid down his pen with some regret, but perhaps once the visitor learned he was the only person at home, he would take himself off again. "And bring in some sherry."

He crossed the hall, and in the parlour held out his hand. "Good morning, Sir Ralph. If you are looking for my daughter she is out, riding with her aunt, and my wife is not home either."

"So your man told me, Mr Hollander. But it is you I wish to see."

"Then pray sit down." He paused as Barlow came in bearing a tray. "Let me offer you a glass of sherry."

When they were alone again, seated opposite each other, it seemed to the Vicar that his visitor was restless, picking up his glass and setting it down again and disinclined to say why he had come. Martin began to have a strong suspicion, but he merely said, "How may I serve you, sir?"

Ralph got up suddenly and stood facing him, hands behind his back. "I have come, sir, to ask your permission to address Miss Dacre."

So he was right! Poor fellow, Martin thought, he was doomed to disappointment. But he merely said, "My daughter is her own mistress, Sir Ralph and as you must know, past the age when consent would be necessary."

"I am aware of that, but I thought it only proper to speak to you first."

"Quite right, and very good of you. Do pray sit down again and enjoy your sherry. You are no unfledged lad to have to stand in front of me."

With a faint smile Ralph complied. "I am nearly thirty-five, and past the first flush of youth." Then he added seriously, "But there is something I must tell you. I don't know if Miss Dacre mentioned that I had been married before?"

"Yes, she did, but only that, no more."

"No," Ralph answered, "so I understand. Unfortunately it came out in a conversation she had with one of my more voluble guests. I wanted to tell her myself, but the right moment had not come before she heard it elsewhere."

"You are a widower, then?"

"Yes," Ralph answered, his voice even harsher than usual. "And I must tell you the circumstances."

"You need not if you don't wish to, if it is too painful. I'm sure you have nothing dishonourable to disclose to me."

Ralph turned restlessly, not answering this, though it was hardly a question. He went on, "It might explain some things – why I haven't taken another bride in all the years between, why we got rid of the house in Durham. Though there were other reasons for that too. You see," he looked beyond his host to a very dull painting of a duck, "Alice and I married very young. I was barely twenty, she was eighteen, and we were very much in love. Our parents approved as it was a suitable match with advantages on both sides. Ten months later my wife gave birth to our son. The baby was sickly. He died the next afternoon and my wife that night."

"My dear sir," Martin said, shocked. "We had no idea, of course. It must have been a great grief to you."

Ralph raised a taut face. Even after so many years it was clear that speaking of it was difficult. "I must tell you, sir, something of how she died."

Martin made a deprecatory gesture. "I assure you, you need not, if you don't wish to."

"I believe I should. You see, there was a tragic accident, a fall down the stairs, a short while before the child was due, which caused premature labour. The details have never been talked of outside the family, and if you will not be offended, I had rather not go into it all, even now."

"Of course not," Martin assured him. "But do you wish my daughter to know all this?"

"No, I think not. I don't want her to take me out of pity."

Poor fellow, Martin thought, she's not going to take you at all, and he felt a great liking for Sir Ralph, for his straightforward manner, half wishing the marriage was possible. He had misgivings, as he had told his wife, about Maeve's expectation of marrying Freddy on his return. "What do you wish me to say to her?" he asked gently.

"Just that my wife and son died when we were both very young. I might tell her more later, but not now – only I felt you should know."

"Thank you for your confidence," Martin said. "I can see why you hated the house after that."

"I never really lived in it again. I never could go up those stairs without seeing . . ." he broke off.

"That is understandable. I hope Welford Park will be a new and happier home for you."

Some warmth crept into Ralph's face. "It will be if she will accept me."

Martin wished his last words back, having received these confidences without being able to disabuse him of that idea. Carefully, he said, "I feel I ought to warn you, though, not to get your hopes up. She has refused several suitors."

Ralph got up suddenly and stood facing him again. "Is it because of one person – her cousin in India?"

Martin rose too. He was not entirely surprised by the question. "It may be, Sir Ralph. But he has been away a very long time. They were little more than children then and a childhood romance may not bear the light of adulthood."

"I see I have small chance." Ralph's face was set in rigid lines. "But be so kind as to lay my suit before her. And believe me, Mr Hollander, when I say it would be my purpose in life to endeavour to make Maeve happy."

"I'm quite sure it would, Sir Ralph. If she did accept you I would consider her fortunate."

"Would you indeed? That's uncommon good of you, sir." Ralph paused. From the first he had observed Martin Hollander to be above the far too common stamp of cleric, the "hunting parson" who spent his time in society and left his duties to a poorly paid curate. "If I have your approval –"

"This is entirely between you and me," Martin broke in. "I have frankly never thought, though the rest of the family take it for granted, that Sir Frederick may necessarily prove the best husband for her, nor indeed that he may come home with that in mind. There have been signs – but this is mere conjecture on my part. All I can do is to pass on your offer to her and beg her to wait a little while, to take time to consider, at least until Sir Frederick comes home. And I think the fact that you and I have discussed this aspect of it should remain a private matter between us."

"You are quite right, sir. I shall mention it to no one. I go to Newmarket tomorrow to join the Seftons and some others, but I expect to be back in two or three weeks." Ralph held out his hand. "Thank you for listening to me so patiently."

Martin smiled and gave his hand a warm shake. "Listening is one of the most important functions of the clergy, Sir Ralph, to my mind anyway. I am more sorry than I can say – for the young man you were, anyway. I hope it is all behind you."

Ralph straightened his shoulders. "I believe so – now. But I have taken up enough of your time. Goodbye, Mr Hollander." Then at the door he paused and added, "Only one never quite forgets, does one?"

"No," Martin agreed. "Maeve has never quite forgotten the tragedy of her father. Do you know about that?"

"Miss Dacre has mentioned him, but my mother told me he died when she was a child. Of a sudden illness, I believe."

"That is not entirely true," Martin said. "I think perhaps you should know the truth, sir. We had better sit down again." And he related to Sir Ralph an unvarnished account of Donavon Dacre's unhappy life and violent death. "It was no easy thing for children of thirteen to put aside." he finished, "though I believe Mary managed it better than Maeve, but then she had William. They cared for each other from a very early age, but Maeve, you see, is of a different temperament."

Ralph sat quite still, digesting this. Then he said, "It is strange, isn't it, that we should both have tragedies in our past? As if – " he broke off and Martin pitied him. He could imagine what Sir Ralph had been about to say and for a moment was tempted not to prolong the affair, to tell him at once that Maeve would not consider him, but he could not do it. It was for her to answer, though he had no doubt of what her response should be. And yet – and yet, his instinct that all would not be as she imagined remained with him. He was extremely fond of Freddy, but that made no difference at all. Furthermore, he had come to like this man. Sir Ralph might be a hard-riding, sometimes harsh-spoken man of the world, wealthy, involved with court life, and Martin could hardly imagine him to have been a celibate since his wife died – and yet he had a lively mind, appreciated books and music and good conversation. There was much to commend him, much, he thought, that would appeal to Maeve if her head and heart were not filled with Freddy.

He showed his visitor out, promising to speak to her as soon as she came in, and then returned to his study. But he did not return to his sermon. Instead, he sat for a long time staring down at his clasped hands.

"But it's quite ridiculous," Maeve said in some indignation, an hour later. She had been down on the Marsh, riding with her aunt. They had called on the Rokebys and spent an enjoyable hour there with Roddy and his wife, Elizabeth and Ellen with their heads together as always, and she had come in with her cheeks glowing, only to be irritated by Sir Ralph's tiresome proposal. "Papa, you should have told him at once that I would not accept him."

"My dear, how could I?" Martin said. "He would have thought it very odd if I had. I could only agree to pass it on to you. He deserved that courtesy."

"I suppose so." Maeve was wandering up and down the room. "Oh, it is so tiresome. Now it will affect our relations with them and I do so enjoy visiting Lady Digby. I wish he hadn't made the offer."

"I thought it was coming," Martin said. "Didn't you?"

"No – yes – I don't know. I suppose I suspected, though I thought he must have had plenty of choice among London society. I hoped he might have had more sense than to set his mind on me."

"He seems to me to have a great deal of sense and taste too to ask for our darling girl." Martin smiled at her. "And I like him very well. If it were not for Freddy, I would be glad to see you wed to him."

She stared at him. "Would you really? He's bad-tempered, speaks his mind too freely – oh, I suppose you will say he has his good side, but indeed, Papa, it's not to be thought of, is it? Thank goodness he's gone away for a while."

"It seems to me that you two have a great deal in common."

"Papa! You can't mean you actually want me to – oh, it's too absurd! Freddy will be here any day, and then . . ." She broke off and put her hand to her mouth to stem a little sob of annoyance, her nerves fraught with the waiting. "Papa, Papa, I wouldn't say this to anyone else, but though I long for him to come, I'm – I'm half afraid."

He came to her and put his arms about her. "My darling, I didn't mean to upset you, and I can understand how your feelings must be torn this way and that. And patience is very hard to come by at your age. There's the uncertainty too. But we mustn't be unkind to Sir Ralph. I believe the poor fellow to be very much in earnest, and he's not a young man to get over this easily, though I fear he may have to. Perhaps by the time he returns Freddy will be here and then everything will be settled." Yet Martin regretted those words. He wanted to prepare her for the situation not resolving itself quite as she hoped and expected, but he could not bring himself to say more.

"Yes, Papa." Maeve managed a smile and kissed his cheek.

"You did just what is right. But I wouldn't accept Sir Ralph anyway. Where's Mama?"

"Gone to the village to see Mr Forster's wife."

"Then I think I'll go and talk to Aunt Isabel and leave you to get on with your sermon. You haven't finished it, have you?"

Martin glanced down at the paper, a sentence broken off, half completed. "No, I haven't. It's been a morning of interruptions. Off you go, and give your aunt my love."

She walked across to Hollanders House and found Isabel still in the gravel drive with Obadiah Smith. "Can I talk to you, Aunt Isabel?"

"Of course, my dear. Thank you, Obadiah. See to that matter of the stable roof, will you? Come alone, Maeve." They were up the steps, Hinton holding the great door open, when the sound of a carriage made them turn. "It's probably Mary and William," Lady Hollander added. "Dear me, I'd forgotten they were coming for luncheon, and here am I not even changed."

"It's not their carriage," Maeve said. "It's a post chaise. Oh! Look, Aunt Isabel!" Some instinct rooted her to the spot, her heart leaping, Sir Ralph's proposal and her talk with her step-father all forgotten.

A hand opened the door, a familiar signet ring on one finger, and before the step could be let down Freddy had leapt out and was up the steps three at a time.

"Mama! Maeve! Oh, this is splendid – both of you here! Darling Mama, oh, what can I say?" He had her in his arms and was kissing her over and over again. "If only Papa was here – " His voice broke and for a moment he struggled with sudden tears. Then he turned to Maeve, threw an arm round her, kissing her cheek, holding them both.

"Freddy, Freddy!" His mother was breathless. "Oh, my dear – we didn't know."

The years rolled away. Maeve leaned against him, half suffocated with ecstatic joy. This was still Freddy, warm, impetuous, loving. And yet, it was not the young Freddy. This was a man, more thickset than the boy who had left, broad shouldered and sturdy, his skin browned by the sun, his dark hair more orderly than it had once been.

Ellen, hearing the commotion, had come running out of the house, crying, "Oh, Freddy! Oh my dear, dear brother!" And he gathered her too into his arms.

"Why, it's Ellen. I'd hardly have known you, you've grown up from that little girl I left behind."

Then in a moment he released them all saying, "But wait," and bounded down the steps again.

Maeve saw then that there was someone else in the coach. The post boy had let the step down and an elegant foot emerged. Freddy was handing out a lady, dressed all in white except for a black ribbon tying her bonnet.

He held her hand and at the bottom of the step looked up at the three women in riding habits. "Just as I remembered you at least," he said, laughing. "Mama – Maeve – Ellen – this is Angela, my wife."

Chapter 6

The shock was so great that for a moment no one on the step moved, only Ellen cried out "Oh!" and clasped her hands together. For Maeve the world seemed to go black and yellow, a spasm seized her stomach and her mouth went dry. In sudden dizziness she clutched her aunt's arm, her only thought: I mustn't cry – I mustn't faint.

Lady Hollander was also shocked. Shaken out of her normal calm, she murmured, "Oh, good God!"

Just then, fortunately, there was a diversion as the Moon's End carriage swept into the drive and William almost fell out of it. The brothers clasped hands and then hugged each other, William exclaiming, "Freddy, by all that's holy! Home at last, eh?"

Mary followed, astonishment on her face, unable to hold back a swift glance at her sister. What she saw there horrified her, for every vestige of colour had drained from Maeve's face, leaving a white mask. Then she was being kissed in her turn. Freddy seemed to be the only one at ease, joy at this return bubbling over, but as he took his wife's hand to bring her up to his mother, even he could not but see the consternation on their faces.

"Mama! You all look amazed. Never tell me – didn't you get my letter?"

"No, no," Isabel said hastily. "We've heard nothing for a long time."

"But we wrote, we sent a letter before we left."

Isabel gathered her bewildered forces, her feelings indescribable. Much as she rejoiced in seeing her first-born again, she could not help being aware of the rigid figure by her side. How could he? How could he do this to Maeve? But she thrust this thought away, not looking at her niece but holding out her hands to the stranger she must now call daughter. She saw that Angela was very unusual – hair a pale silky yellow showing under her bonnet, yet with a golden brown skin that did not usually go with it, her eyes a deep brown. She was a little taller than Freddy, with a lovely figure if a trifle thin, and she seemed to have a natural grace of movement.

A proud smile hovered about Freddy's mouth as he said, "Angela, this is my dearest mother. She'll be a mother to you now, won't you, Mama?"

"Of course," Isabel said, and tried to put some warmth into her voice. "Welcome to Hollanders House, my dear."

"Thank you, ma'am," Angela said politely, but when Isabel kissed her, she sensed no response. How could there be? They were strangers.

Under cover of all the greetings, numbed and sick, Maeve dredged up every ounce of courage and control as Freddy turned to her and said, "I want you two to be friends." She managed to smile and say, "How do you do?" while Angela merely inclined her head.

Is he quite insensitive? Isabel wondered. Doesn't he *know*? But wishing with all her heart Maeve had not been present at this arrival, that she could have been told privately at the Vicarage, she had to take charge of the situation. She swept everyone into the house, telling Freddy to take Angela into the drawing room and indicating that William and Mary should follow while she gave necessary orders to the servants. Maeve caught her arm, her fingers digging into her aunt's flesh so that later there was a bruise.

"Please, say nothing to him about – about what we hoped," she whispered. "*please*, Aunt Isabel, *nothing* – don't let him know."

All right, my darling, of course I won't," Isabel said at once in a low voice. "At the moment I'm too amazed to think straight. Ah, Hinton, you'd better have the baggage taken up to the west wing rooms, and send one of the maids up to prepare them. Bring wine for us all and tell Mrs Budge there will be two extra covers for luncheon." She gave Maeve a swift kiss, whispering, "You needn't come in now, go home and tell your mother and father." She hurried into the drawing room and Mary, waiting by the open door, came back to catch her sister's hand and hold it tightly.

"Oh, Maeve, I'm so sorry. This is awful. I can't believe it. We all thought, didn't we – "

Through stiffened lips, Maeve said, "Don't – don't say any more. Why should he still have thought of me, out there all these years? She – she's very beautiful, isn't she?"

"Not like you." Mary was instantly partisan. "I can hardly bear to look at her."

"Don't think like that," Maeve said again. "He – he's still our – " She could not bring out the name. "But I can't go in there yet. Aunt Isabel says I need not. I'm going home – say I'm taking news to the Vicarage."

She fled, out by the courtyard door. Obadiah, wreathed in smiles, called out to her how good it was to have the young master home, but she didn't pause, hurrying along the path, breaking into a run, anything to get away, to put distance between herself and that room where the new arrivals were being welcomed. But after a few moments she was forced to pause by a tree, leaning against it to try to control the shuddering that shook her. She could not go into the Vicarage just yet. It was as if she was in the middle of a hideous nightmare and would, must, awake soon. If only it was yesterday when there was hope and joyful anticipation! How often had she imagined the homecoming, envisaged Freddy walking towards her, his arms wide open, claiming her as his wife. "Freddy," she whispered, her cheek against the rough bark, "my love, my darling, how could you do this to me when I've loved you for so long?" And the man who had come home in the place of the boy seemed even more handsome, even more desirable. Her misery was so unbearable that all she wanted was the sanctuary of her own room, where she could lie on the bed and cry and let out this awful threat of rising hysteria that could only find relief in total release.

But she had to go into the house first, face them, tell her mother and dear Papa, explain to them, bear their sympathy. The awfulness of it made her feel very sick and she stood still, drawing deep breaths. And then a squirrel appeared and began to hop about among the early fallen leaves, looking for nuts. His tail was bushy and curving prettily as he found something edible, holding it between his paws to nibble at it. He kept his distance from the figure by the tree, though now and then he looked up at her, his eyes bright. Contact with the little creature somehow occupied her attention, her mind shying away from the enormity of what had happened, and when he put his little head on one side she wished she could pick him up and hold him, expend her shattered love on him. Only the moment he saw her move, he scampered away.

But he had calmed her in an odd way. She brushed away the leaves clinging to her riding habit and began to walk slowly home, hoping against hope that everyone was out.

Her stepfather, however, was in the hall as she came in. He took one look at her face and then brought her quickly into his study. "My dear child, what on earth has happened? Your aunt?"

"No, no –" How to bring out the words, how to say it?

He brought her a glass of wine from a small table. "Sit down and drink this. Then tell me."

She found her knees were shaking and she obeyed, gulping down the claret. Then she said baldly, "Freddy is home."

"Freddy! But that's wonderful." And then he saw that it was not wonderful at all. "Tell me," he repeated.

She forced out the words. "He – he has brought home a – a – wife." And then all her control broke. The glass fell from her hand to smash on the polished wood of the floor, and as with a swift exclamation he sat down beside her, she threw herself into his arms. "Papa! Papa, how am I to bear it? I never thought – never imagined he could – oh, to see him – and her – together, and he was laughing – so proud, so happy." And she broke into wild weeping.

He let the storm wear itself out, found a large handkerchief and put it into her hand. There was no satisfaction in having been proved right. At last he said, "What can I say to you, my dear child? I can give you little comfort just now, but you know the worst hurts pass. They soften with time."

"I can't feel that now." Exhausted, she leaned against him, "I was so sure, so sure."

He talked to her quitely, his wisdom full of sympathy but

without encouraging self-pity, and though Maeve found it hard to take in at this moment, phrases came back to her afterwards.

A moment later he was saying, "Ah, here's your dear mother. Nell, my love, there's good news and bad."

His wife was as shaken as the rest had been and plumped down on her knees by her stricken daughter, her reaction the same – relief that Freddy was safely home, but consternation that no letter had prepared them all for the circumstances of it.

"I can't believe it," she kept murmuring. "Oh, my darling child, that he should inflict this on you!" Angry tears filled her eyes as her husband said gravely, "I think we have all been living in a fool's paradise."

Maeve got to her feet. Through stiffened lips, her own weeping spent, she said, "Don't cry, Mama. I'm all right now – really. It's done and I must make the best of it. Papa is right. It was a dream built on nothing." She gathered up her discarded hat and gloves and added, "I think I'll go up to my room now and change."

When she had gone her mother turned to Martin. "She is so brave. I don't know how he could do such a thing to her – without warning. It's cruel. I can't think of another word for it."

"Maeve says that he did write to his mother about this girl but Isabel never got the letter, and you know, my dear, Freddy never in so many words wrote of marriage, never told her that they would marry when he came back, never asked her to go out to him. It's quite clear that he, with all the busyness of his new life, never saw the matter as she did."

"But before he left there was an understanding, you know there was."

"Yes," he agreed, "but only think how young they were. He was a mere lad embarking on an absorbing career. We should none of us have let Maeve build so much into a few tenuous words when she was barely out of the schoolroom."

Nell gave a deep sigh. "The poor child – and yet, she's not a child now. She's a woman grown and as such she's suffering this dreadful shock. Do you think I should go up to her?"

"No," he said gently. "I believe she would be better alone for a while."

Upstairs Maeve was thankful for the solitude. She got out of her riding habit and lay on her bed in her petticoat, staring at the ceiling. No more tears came, only a sensation of being drained, exhausted, drowning in a depth of misery such as she had never known. The long afternoon passed. There seemed to be nothing to think about, no future, no plans, a dull life in a country vicarage that had once seemed full and pleasing because of her ultimate purpose. Now those years were over, seeming utterly wasted.

Her hands clenched on the quilt, a delicate embroidered affair made long ago by a Hollander lady at the time of the Civil War, a present to her from her aunt. Oh God, how was she to bear this, how ever to appear normal again, to dine and ride and visit with all the family, even be friends with this strange girl who was Freddy's wife? But she refused the onset of tears. She would never again weep over Freddy. Tomorrow she would have to face a changed life, but for now nature was kind. She drifted into sleep and did not move until her mother came in as dusk was falling.

Maeve stirred and sat up, pushing her disordered hair from her face as her mother sat down on the bed beside her.

"You've had a sleep, my darling? That's good. Here is a note just come over from your Aunt Isabel. Can you see to read it?"

Maeve nodded and took it. Isabel wrote that she did not think it a good idea to inflict too many of the family on Angela at once. William and Mary had gone home but would come back for dinner tomorrow and Isabel begged the Vicarage party to join them. For her dear Maeve she sent her love and she was to come or not as she wished.

"You can see what she means," Nell said. "You need not go until you feel you can bear it."

Maeve laid down the letter. Outside, the last of the autumn sunset was fading from the sky, the summer garden below all but gone, only a few Michaelmas daisies left. Today's breeze had dropped and it was very still. A last bird winged its way across to the trees and was gone.

From somewhere deep within and out of the shock, the shattered hopes, the awareness of having been put aside, another preferred to her, something rose in her – hurt pride perhaps, an innate courage, above all a refusal to be an object of pity. She got off the bed and going to the basin poured water, washing her face and hands, the very coldness of it banishing the lethargy of the last hours.

"Certainly I'll go," she said. "I won't have them all pitying me, Mama, I won't. No one will ever see, outside this house, what he's done to me."

Nell gazed at her daughter, seeing the shadowed eyes, the lack of colour in her face. "Can you do it, dearest? When you see him –"

"I can," she said, "I will, I must!"

"But it need not be yet," Nell broke in, aching with pity for her. "You could go to Madeleine for a while. I'm sure she would welcome your company with Lionel away for so long."

"Run away?" Maeve looked at herself in the mirror. "I think not, Mama. I have to see them sooner or later."

"It would give you time to conquer your feelings, compose yourself."

Maeve turned away from the mirror, her eyes glittering oddly, her mother thought. "I am quite composed now, thank you, Mama" She gave her a quick kiss. "Shouldn't you be changing for dinner? It must be getting late."

And by that Nell understood that the matter was closed to further discussion.

"Quite right," Martin said in their bedroom a few minutes later. "Nothing will be served by going over and over it, it would only distress her the more. Let the matter lie. She has to make a new beginning and all we can do is support her in any way we can." And probably he, at their quiet dinner table, at which Maeve ate practically nothing, was the only one who gave a thought to Sir Ralph Digby, waiting for his answer.

In the morning Isabel herself walked over to the Vicarage and found her sister and brother-in-law alone in the parlour.

"Well!" she said. "They are settled into the rooms Tom and I had when we were first married. I've left them to themselves for the morning. Freddy plans to show her the estate and drive her down on the Marsh. I need not tell you both how horrified I am. All our plans come to nothing!"

"I'm afraid they were ours," Martin said, "Not Freddy's. He looks well and happy, Isabel."

"Oh, he is, and it's wonderful to have the darling boy home at last, but I never expected this, I never thought otherwise but that he was planning to come home one day and marry Maeve."

"Nor did I," Nell agreed. "Do you know how it came about?"

"He told me something of it at breakfast this morning, Angela had hers in bed. She is apparently the daughter of an East India Company man who married an Indian, a Rajput lady of high caste, I understand. They died in that cholera outbreak that Freddy mentioned in his letter about Christmas time last year. Angela had no English relations out there and refused to go to her Indian ones – they insisted on her mother being buried according to their strange customs and quite spurned the poor girl, having never approved of the marriage. She stayed for a while with a widowed English lady in Calcutta where Freddy was at the time and he told me he fell in love with her the first time he saw her. But unattached ladies are apparently in very short supply and she was besieged by suitors. When he finally got my letter about his father and felt he should come home to take his place at Hollanders, she agreed to marry him and travel to England with him."

"It sounds as if the prospect of a baronet with a good estate settled her mind," Nell said, and Martin raised his eyebrows. "Well, I'm sorry," she added unrepentantly, "but it is my daughter who is so hurt."

"I know, dearest," Isabel's sympathy was swift, "and you know how I feel about that. In fact I'm haunted by how much of it is my fault. I encouraged Maeve, I wanted her for my daughter too. With William married to Mary it would have been so perfect. How is she?"

Martin said, "I think she got over the worst yesterday. She is calm and determined to accept it without any fuss. She went out a while ago on an errand for me to Appledore. I thought the ride and the solitude would be good for her."

"Quite right," Isabel said. "She is like me in that respect. But poor darling child, I could only imagine yesterday what she was going through."

"And what do you make of Freddy's wife?" Martin asked.

"Though I suppose it is too soon to say a great deal."

"I don't know," Isabel answered frankly. "So far I must admit I haven't warmed to her. She seems to be very reserved, and wary of me, which is understandable. Oh dear, I am now the Dowager Lady Hollander. Isn't that dreadful?"

Nell looked suddenly aghast. "Does that mean – "

"That she is the new mistress of Hollanders House?" Isabel gave her a faint smile. "In correct terms, yes. But can you imagine me stepping aside and leaving the whole place in charge of a girl who has only just set foot in the country? She would have no notion how to go on, of that I'm sure. No, no, everything must be left as usual for the time being. Freddy as much as said so at breakfast – poor boy, he was trying to be so tactful. He will need me."

Nell, much as she loved Isabel and despite her criticism of the girl, was faintly sorry for Angela. As long as Isabel was at Hollanders, no one else would take the reins. If it had been Maeve, how different that position would have been! "She's an unusual looking girl," she commented, "and beautiful in a compelling way."

"Even so, I am not sure I can quite see why Freddy fell in love with her," his mother said. "She is beautiful of course, but very thin. I must not make any judgements yet but indeed I must try to love her as a new daughter for his sake. Time will tell. You are all coming to dinner tonight? What about Maeve? I did say in my note –"

"She won't hear of not coming," Nell said in a troubled voice. "I did suggest she went to Madeleine for a visit but she won't hear of that either."

"She has great strength of character," Martin put in, "More than any of us realised, perhaps."

"Yes," Isabel agreed. "I find the disappointment hard to bear and how much more must she! I wish I could understand it. I promised her yesterday I would not even mention the subject to Freddy, not speak of our dashed hopes, so I must not, but it was very hard at breakfast when he said he was looking forward to a long chat with her and a ride round their old haunts. It's clear he sees her only as a friend, almost a sister really, with whom he once shared his youth. I should have perceived this in his letters, but I suppose one doesn't see what one doesn't want to see."

"We none of us did," Nell said sadly, and then added, "No, I'm wrong. You felt all along that things might not turn out as we hoped, didn't you, Martin?"

"Perhaps," He agreed, "but I would have been happy to have been proved wrong."

Isabel rose. "Well, I must go. Give Maeve my dearest love and say –" she paused, for once lost for words.

Nell walked with her to the door. "Maeve knows exactly what you would say to her, Isabel."

The family gathered in the long dining room that night to welcome its new member, and if one or two there found conversation difficult, Freddy kept it flowing with his lively talk. He was full of the pleasure of being home once more, bringing out treasured memories and laughing over anecdotes, looking round for corroboration.

"Do you remember, Mama – I'm sure you don't, William – when all those military men came and I got into trouble with Papa for trying on one of the cocked hats? And do you remember how we used to play in the tower?" He glanced at his wife. "I showed you that this morning."

"A very old place," she said, "and so cold."

"Angela finds everything cold here." He gave her a swift smile. "I'm sure you do remember going up those rickety old stairs, William, on Major Irvine's back?"

"Of course I remember that," his brother agreed, and their mother added, "I'm sure none of you boys will ever forget the Major." Nor I, she thought, the treasured memory of that old love long buried. "How I wish Lionel could have been here tonight to enjoy your home-coming and add his own recollections."

The brothers started off on school-days until at last she said, "All these reminiscences must be very tiresome for Angela. My dear, do tell us something of your life in India. I'm afraid we are shockingly ignorant and have only had Freddy's letters to teach us."

Angela crumpled bread between thin fingers. "It seemed quite ordinary to me. I've known nothing else, you see. My

Papa had been in the Company since he was eighteen, so I was born in Calcutta."

Freddy took up the conversation, explaining the position of the East India Company, adding, "Wait until you see the things we have brought home. The carter should be here in a day or two. We've brought all sorts of ornaments and china and beautiful Indian silver and all sorts of curios. And Angela has chosen silks for all you ladies."

"How lovely," Ellen exclaimed. She was gazing with something like hero-worship at this newly-arrived brother whom she had not seen since she was very small; so handsome, she thought, and full of life, and with so many stories to tell. "Do go on, Freddy."

He laughed, "It will take weeks to tell it all, and there's so much I want to know. My goodness, how you two Monarchs have changed. To see you married what is it – four years?"

"And ridiculously young," Martin put in, smiling. "As far as I recall, Freddy, your brother never so much as asked my permission to steal our Mary."

Mary was laughing. "Oh Papa. We knew each other so well it hardly seemed necessary – we just sort of slipped into making arrangements."

"And if I had and you had refused," William put in with unwonted spirit. "I'd have carried her off and married her out of hand."

"Would you indeed? You do surprise me William."

William grinned back at him. "I'm very sure I don't, sir."

Freddy was revelling in all this family talk. "And now you're a father with babies. I'm looking forward to seeing them and being a real godfather instead of by proxy."

"Fred would not thank you for calling him a baby, for he's three now."

"We'll drive over and see them tomorrow." Freddy promised. "I've brought a present for my namesake and I want to see what you've done to Moon's End. The Monarchs of Moon's End, eh? Perhaps tomorrow, Angela?"

She inclined her head. "But why do you call your brother and Mrs Hollander the Monarchs?"

"William and Mary," he said, laughing, and then, seeing her blank face, explained that King William and Queen Mary had been on the English Throne over 100 years ago, adding to the assembled company, "Never having been to England, Angela never learned much English history, did you, my love? But we'll amend that as we go about, won't we?"

Maeve sat in her place and listened. She had taken trouble to look her best this evening, a small act of defiance and pride, and Freddy had taken her hand, saying unashamedly, "By Jove, you look lovely tonight, Maeve."

Which was exactly what she meant him to think. But she had command of herself now and she joined in the talk in a lively manner, supplying her own memories and then talking of the busy social life they had had since the arrival of the new owners of Welford Park. "You will like Sir Ralph," she told Freddy. "The ball he gave this summer was quite spectacular. He and his mother have recently been guests of Lord Egremont at Petworth House, but he is gone to London at the moment. We danced till two in the morning at that ball. I met a gentleman by the name of Mr Creevey who, I swear, knows everyone of note. He told me some most entertaining anecdotes which had me laughing half the evening."

But to Isabel and to her parents there seemed to be a kind of brittle brilliance about her tonight, as if she was determined to outshine Angela, and after a while Isabel said quietly to her new daughter-in-law, "I'm afraid we are a rather overwhelming family, my dear, and being reunited after so long. there is so much for all of us to say. Pray forgive us."

"Yes, ma'm," Angela said. "I supposed it must be so."

"I warned her," Freddy smiled at her and laid his hand briefly over hers on the white cloth. "I told her what you would all be like."

Yet even under the circumstances Isabel detected a lack of animation in the girl and wondered if the journey had lowered her health. Freddy had said she had been very sea-sick, expressing the hope that good Sussex food and Sussex air would benefit her.

"It's wonderful to have English beef again," he said now with relish. "I can tell you I got heartily sick of endless curry. But I expect Angela will miss it, won't you, my love? We will have to get Jamila to show Cook how to make it."

They had brought an Indian maid with them, a woman who had been with Angela since she was a small girl, a dark plump woman in Indian dress with sleek black hair tied at the back. Isabel had asked Hinton just before dinner how the servants were taking to this new addition to their ranks.

"With some curiosity, my lady," he said, "But I believe she will not find us unfriendly." He was delighted that the new master had shaken him warmly by the hand last night and said, "Of course you'll look after me as you did my father, won't you Hinton?" And he had replied, "It's what I was hoping, Sir Frederick."

"I'm sorry dear old Fletcher's gone, "Freddy was saying, "and Mrs Fletcher too. It was good of you to let them have Rose Cottage, Mama. I'll go to see them soon. If I keep Hinton busy, we'll need someone else as butler."

"Yes, I thought of that," Isabel agreed. "We'll have to settle various matters concerning the servants."

"There'll be so much to do," Freddy said, his eyes sparkling for a moment, but more gravely he added, "I shall try to do it all as well as dear Papa did." He looked down from his place at the head of the table, sitting there for the first time. "I'm glad I've got you all to help me."

William said, "Did you mind leaving the army? Li wondered if you'd try for some sort of transfer back here, the Guards perhaps?"

"What? Be a Hyde Park soldier after the Hussars? No fear," he dismissed the idea. "All parades and polish. No, I've had ten years of it, and Angela and I decided it would be best for us to settle here."

"We've recently met the Duke of Clarence's son, Colonel George FitzClarence," Maeve told him. "He's just been appointed Captain and Lieutenant-Colonel of the Coldstream Guards." Her voice was light and cheerful but under the table her hands were gripped together for a moment. It was hard to see him sitting with Angela on his right. It should have been her place – hers! But the moment passed and she took up her knife and fork again.

"Oh, I've heard of him, of course," Freddy said in answer. "They thought very highly of him in India, I can tell you. I've not met him because he was gone before I arrived."

"We think him an excellent fellow." William put in, and Maeve added, "It's a thousand pities he can't be his father's heir and maybe come to the throne one day. It was reported in *The Times* this morning that the Duke of York is in very poor health and if he should die the Duke of Clarence would become Heir Presumptive."

Angela opened her eyes wide. "But why can this colonel not succeed his father?"

Such subjects had never been considered indelicate at the Hollanders table under the previous Sir Frederick's rule and his daughter had no inhibitions on that score either, so she explained to Angela the rules of succession, that neither the King nor any of his brothers had a legitimate heir, except for the Duke of Cambridge's little girl, the Princess Victoria. As Cambridge was younger than the Duke of Clarences, it was considered a great pity that George FitzClarence was his illegitimate son by an actress.

Angela merely said, "Oh, I see," and pushed her half-finished plate of beef aside.

"What a great deal we have to learn about people in England now," Freddy remarked, "Where's Sir John Colborne? Does anyone know? I must try to see him."

"Difficult at the moment," his brother told him. "It was in the *Gazette* that he's just been made Lieutenant-Governor of Guernsey. I take the *Gazette* as I like to know of appointments, especially of any officers we know of. By the way, you're home just in time for the Harvest supper. We've taken to having a combined one with Moon's End and Hollanders folk together."

"Where do you set it up?" Freddy asked.

"At Top Farm in the large barn." The talk flowed on, Freddy delighting in all the news, and it was a long time before the ladies retired upstairs to the small parlour Isabel favoured. On the way up Mary caught hold of her sister's hand.

"Maeve dearest, are you all right?"

"Of course I am," she said rather sharply. "Please don't keep harping on it."

"I'm sorry, I didn't mean to upset you."

"You haven't. But I don't wish to discuss something that's over and done with."

Mary looked a little crushed, for they had always shared everything, but she understood well enough and didn't broach the subject again until a day when Maeve herself spoke of it.

Isabel, dispensing tea, was thankful when the evening was finally over. Thereafter, she thought, it would be easier, but whether she would ever win this strange girl's confidence she didn't know. Angela answered almost every subject with a monosyllable, leaving her mother-in-law somewhat perplexed.

A week passed and she began to understand something. Angela's very quiteness, her circumstances in India, coupled with her astonishing looks, seemed to be what the cheerfully extrovert Freddy needed. He fussed over her, considered her first in everything – if he had treated Maeve in this way, Isabel realised, she would have had enough of it very quickly. But her heart was sore for the unhappiness Maeve was hiding so well, and at what must be such a cost. It was doubtful if, just now, the poor child could see all this. And perhaps Freddy would have been different with her. But such speculations were fruitless and Isabel could only set herself to learn to love his choice – which was far from easy.

Maeve herself only knew she had to live one hour at a time to keep herself in hand. She shut everyone out of her confidence except occasionally her stepfather – they had always contrived as far as possible to keep difficulties or troubles from Nell, because of her indifferent health, and now when her daughter assured her that she had put the past behind her, Nell was only too glad to believe it.

Maeve occupied herself with exceptional busyness about the parish or riding down on the Marsh, where she could hide her unhappiness as, unknown to her, long ago her Aunt Isabel had done before her. The wide acres, the flocks of sheep wandering eerily in the autumn mists, all the familiar farms and churches, were something to hold on to, something known and cherished.

One afternoon as she returned in the dusk she found Freddy in the stableyard in the act of mounting his own horse. He had been to see his Uncle Martin on some business and he paused to say, "Why don't we ride together? Angela doesn't care for riding and prefers to go out in a carriage. Mama is taking her and Ellen to Rye shopping tomorrow, we could go then."

He was looking at her with great affection, as at an old friend newly discovered, and a great longing rose in her.

"I can't," she said swiftly in a harsher tone than she meant to use, but a solitary hour with Freddy was a test she could not take. "I am already engaged."

There was bewilderment in his face. "Engaged? All day?" He paused and added, "You spoke then as if I was a stranger."

"I think perhaps you are," she said and left him, crossing the yard to enter the house and close the door behind her.

Chapter 7

The harvest supper two nights later served to introduce the new master of Hollanders to all his tenants. The barn at Top Farm was swept and decorated with great sheaves of corn, long trestle tables set up with benches for the labourers. Maids with heavy jugs of ale filled tankards and an ox was roasted in the yard outside. There were large round cheeses and loaves of freshly baked bread, butter and rosy apples, bowls of frumenty and jars of pickles.

Freddy moved about the barn greeting men and women he remembered, and speaking to newcomers in his own inimitable way, his cheery "How d'ye do," and warm handshake endearing him to all and sundry.

"E b'aint like 'is Pa," Roger Watts muttered to his neighbour Tom Tighe. "Sir Thomas were a good master, but allus so serious. Still, you could trust 'im to be fair."

"This one be all smiles," Tom's father, Josh, said across the table, "more like old Sir Frederick, eh? 'E were a jolly 'un." Josh and his son were not strictly tenants for they kept the Red Lion at Snargate but numerous relations were employed at Hollanders, and they had always been invited.

Will Apps, who was one of them, took a long pull at his ale, belched and wiped his hand across his mouth. He had been "looker" for Hollanders for nearly forty years and was past sixty, small and wizened. His son Abel helped him now with the sheep and it was Abel who lived in the old looker's hut at lambing time and turned out for a ewe in difficult labour, but Will refused to give up his work entirely. "Well, I 'ope Sir Frederick won't turn me off for bein' too old," he added gloomily. "'E may be all friendly-like now but 'e looks too fly to me. And what's a sodger know about sheep?"

"You're stupid, you are," Josh said. "'E's just Master Freddy growed up, and we all liked 'im, didn't we? Mr William'll show 'im 'ow to go on. Anyway, sheep's your business, not 'is."

"Maybe. Sir Thomas were a sailor when 'e come, but 'e learned, only 'e were a different kettle o' fish, weren't 'e?" Will was never happy unless he had something to grumble about.

However, they all raised a cheer for their new master when he made a short speech, telling them he was glad to be home and that he meant everything to go on as smoothly as in his father's day, which caused a knowing grin and a wink from the older ones who, even under Sir Thomas's firm rule, had not been averse to a spot of moonlighting. Cups and tankards were filled and the refrain was roared out:

Here's a health unto our master, the founder of this feast,
and all his works may prosper that ere he takes in hand.
For we are all his servants and all at his command –
So drink, boys, drink, and see you do not spill,
For if you do, you shall drink too, for 'tis our master's will'.

"Aye, so it is," Freddy called out. "Eat and drink as much as you wish, my friends – all of you." which raised another cheer.

Later on trestles were cleared, a fiddler struck up a tune and dancing began, the farmers wives and daughters and the staff from the two houses leaping about, laughing and sweating and enjoying it all, for this was, to them, the best night of the year when they feasted at the master's expense.

At last, after midnight, those who could still walk went home while those who had drunk too deep slept on the floor till morning.

Going along the corridor at Hollanders, Freddy saw a light under his mother's door, knocked and went in. She was propped up on pillows, reading by the light of a candle on the table by her bed. "Well?" she asked, smiling. "Was it a good supper?"

He sat down on the edge of the bed. "It went very well, I think. They all seemed to enjoy themselves and consume an extraordinary amount of food and ale. But do you know, Mama," sudden tears glistened in his eyes, "they cheered me, they said I'd be as good a man as my father and they sang 'Here's to the master', which I've heard them singing to Papa, and they threw their hats in the air and cheered me." He paused, searching for words. "But – the thing is, I'm finding it all so hard, sitting in Papa's chair at table, taking his place tonight, and down on the Marsh the other day, all the women bobbing to me and the men touching their hats. I can't ever be to them what he was."

"You will be yourself," she said, "and his son as well."

Indeed, she could not help being proud of him with his fine looks, his easy manner, his genuine pleasure in the people he met, his willingness to please. "Your Papa would be so glad that you are here filling his place. He always believed a man who owned land had a responsibility for it, though I could have carried on for many a day, my dearest, if you'd wanted to stay in the Army – you know that."

"Yes, I do know it," he said, "but once I had Angela to care for it made up my mind for me. You will be patient with her, won't you? She is finding it all so strange."

"Of course," she answered at once. "Now run along, she'll be waiting for you." And after he had kissed her and gone, she lay for a long time, the book on her knee, but not attempting to read. This morning Angela had walked round the house inspecting everything, looking into all the rooms; there was no reason why she should not, but there was that in her movements and her curiosity which reminded Isabel of a cat they had once had. Something about the girl put her hackles up and she castigated herself for being unjust. Angela was Freddy's choice and she must learn to accept her, hoping warmer feelings would follow.

Freddy meanwhile had gone along to the west wing, for his mother still naturally occupied the main suite and nothing had been said about a change. There he found candles guttering low and his wife asleep. He stood looking down at her, a little colour in her cheeks from the warmth of sleep, but as he began to undress she stirred and opened her eyes.

"You're very late. What time is it?"

"Half-past midnight. I'm sorry I woke you, my love. I do want to tell you all about the evening – it was such a success, all our tenants and William's, many of them married with families since I went away. I discovered Hinton's courting one of Obadiah's girls. They all gave me such a welcome."

"Oh, farmers and such, I suppose," she said with a big yawn.

"Of course, they're my people."

"I hope you don't mean to spend all your time fussing over them. Or expect me to go visiting them. I should think their cottages are very low and dirty."

Her tone was pettish and he felt a moment's twinge of annoyance. "That's hardly fair. Some keep their homes better than others, but it will be part of our duty to help anyone who's sick or in any sort of need. I mean to be a good master to them."

She looked up, her eyes fixed on him. "You said we were going to do so much together, go to London, see some society."

"Of course we will, but a little later on. As for society, you'll find there's plenty going on here. My darling, you'll see. It's just that tonight was a special night for my people. They gave me such a welcome and you should have heard . . ."

"Tell me tomorrow. And do get ready for bed, it's so late."

Rather dashed, he left her and went to his dressing room. Hinton had come back from the feast and was waiting to assist him – a good deal more efficiently than his old batman. While he prepared for bed and chatted to his valet about the feast, half his mind was on Angela.

It was natural, he told himself, that she could not understand how things were done at Hollanders, not yet anyway. And holding up his arms while Hinton threw his nightshirt over his head, he determined to be patient and understanding. He just wanted to hold her in his arms and assure her of his love and care for her, that she came first in everything, and that he would take her to London as soon as he could.

He went back to the bedroom, however, expecting to find her asleep again, but she was not. She was stretching her legs under the covers, freeing her arms, an expression on her face that sent him to her with every sense leaping. As long as she continued to look at him like that, to respond to his lovemaking as she was at this moment, it was all he desired.

In the morning he took her to Moon's End where they were introduced to his godson and namesake, Roddy Rokeby having been the other godfather while William stood proxy for him. Fred sat on his uncle's knee, wriggling with excitement and gazing ecstatically at the wooden elephant with gaily painted howdah on its back that was his present. Mary held out the baby to Angela, but she shook her head and said she knew nothing about children – indeed, it seemed to Mary who opened her arms to anything little, that this strange girl actually shied away from holding baby Isabel. After a while she rang for the nurse to take them away while she herself sent the men out, saying laughingly that she wanted to show Angela the house and have a nice long talk in her sitting room upstairs.

WIlliam took his brother's arm and they walked over to the stables. "Well," he said, "you certainly faced us with a great surprise."

"It wasn't meant to be like that. My letter was sent to prepare you all. Even if it had come, I knew Mama might not like it. Our coming like that must have been a great shock for her."

"And already married! She would have liked it better if she could have seen you wed in St Mary-on-the-Hill."

"I know," Freddy said patiently," but I've explained all that to her. Angela was so alone. I'd already fallen in love with her last Christmas – we met at a Mess party – but she hadn't said yes to me when the cholera outbreak took both her parents, poor darling. And then I heard about Papa – well, it seemed to be a bond between us. I told her about Hollanders and that I'd inherited it, and she was convinced I should come back. That was when she said she would come with me as my wife. As you can imagine, I was over the moon."

"Angela is a fine-looking girl," William said in his usual slow manner. "And I can see you're happy, dear old fellow."

"I should say I am. The chaps out there thought I was the luckiest man on the station. There was a scramble to buy my place when I sent in my papers, I can tell you, especially since I got my majority. And it only seemed sensible to marry at once so that we could travel together – there would have been so many difficulties otherwise." They had entered the stables and for a few moments looked over William's horses, Freddy saying how please he was with the mare his mother had bought him.

"And the saddle from Maeve," he added, but the smile faded then. "William, I am concerned about her. When I left she was a bright, happy girl but now, she seems very withdrawn, a bit sharp with me yesterday, which is not like her. And at dinner she was almost too – well, I thought her wit was on the acid side, as if it was all put on. Is anything wrong?"

"Well, as you can see – "

But Freddy was going on impulsively, "And why hasn't she married? I expected to hear of it anytime these last years. She's attractive enough to have had any number of suitors.

William leaned against a stall and slapped a chestnut's rump. "Don't be dense, Freddy."

His brother looked blank for a moment, staring at him. Then he exclaimed, "Oh, good God! You can't mean – all this time – because of *me*?"

"Of course I do." William felt a twinge of guilt. His wife had told him of Maeve's fierce instruction that Freddy was to be told nothing, but not only did he not see how it could be avoided, he was of the opinion that if Freddy didn't realise the position he might blunder in his good-hearted way, into awkward remarks.

Freddy was aghast. With his cheerful outgoing nature he was not a man of deep insight. He might even be insensitive at times, totally absorbed as he had been with his own affairs, with army life in India, and of late with his love for Angela. Hollanders had seemed far away; reality had been the heat, a stifling bedroom where his Indian servant fanned him, cleaned his boots, fetched and carried for him, billiards in the Mess in the evenings, drinking with his friends, dancing at Government house. He had thought of Maeve when letters came, but they impinged only briefly on his days and the whispered injunction to her when he left became in his memory nothing more than what it had been: the impetuous affectionate goodbye of a lad of barely eighteen who was going far from home. He had thought of her longingly for a time, it was true, imagining they might one day be man and wife, but those feelings had long gone. He had, like other officers, from time to time found girls in the bazars to amuse himself with; one, Anya, he had fancied himself in love with for quite a time. She had had no inhibitions, removing her clothes when they were alone with slow sensuous movements calculated to inflame desire – which they did. Her brown-skinned body, small breasts, rounded hips and slender legs had bewitched him, but of course it hadn't lasted, and when he met Angela every other girl was forgotten.

He quite believed Maeve would have her suitors and that he would hear in due course of her marriage. That he hadn't hardly seemed relevant, far away under the considerable influence of India. To be told, now, that she had thought only of him, rejected others, waited for him, was something of a shock to be compared with the one he had inflicted.

"I'll talk to her," he said, "explain – tell her – " Tell her what? He didn't know.

"I shouldn't," William advised. "Mary says she doesn't want anyone to speak of it."

"Then it has been talked of in the family? You all expected it?"

William shrugged expressively. "I can see now that we were mistaken in doing so."

"Good God!" Freddy said again. He and William regarded each other. William had been a schoolboy when he left, and he had come back to find him very much a man, for all he was still only twenty-three, with a wife and children, settled in the way of life he had always wanted. In their boyhood William had been his shadow, but the greater bond had been between him and Lionel and he wished that Li were here now. "I'm glad you've got Mary and Moon's End," he said at last. "Papa built you a fine house here, and you've done wonders with the place. I remember how ramshackle it was in Donavon Dacre's day. It's going to be so good to have you nearby."

William accepted the change of subject. "You mean to

settle at Hollanders, live there and take charge as Papa did?"

"Oh, yes. Angela likes the idea of being mistress of such a place."

"What about Mama?" William asked in his laconic manner.

"I hope she'll be happy to have a new daughter to teach about Hollander ways, and Angela will take some of the burden off her shoulders, "Freddy said blandly.

William was not given to showing much emotion, but his eyebrows shot up at this. "Can you imagine Mama standing down for anyone? She would have accepted – " He stopped abruptly, aware he was about to be tactless, but then felt he had to go on. "She was so sure Maeve would be mistress of Hollanders one day, and now she has to change, adapt to the new situation. Give her time, Freddy."

"Of course," his brother said impatiently, "Mama will grow to love Angela, you all will. I'm not stupid, you know. I understand my marriage has taken you all by surprise and it will take time for Angela to settle into the family."

"I expect so," William said rather formally, and Freddy laughed. "You never were given to accepting new things, were you, William? I remember the fuss you made about going to Eton and how you hated the first half."

"Every half!" his brother said with feeling.

"Well, maybe, but you'll see, you old slow-coach, everything will work out very well."

To make up for his obvious doubts, William tucked his hand through Freddy's arm and added, "We shall all do our best, you know."

"I know you will. By Jove, it's so good to be back. I just wish Li was here too." He stood for a moment in silence and then, seeming to make up his mind, said firmly, "You won't object if I borrow this beast for half an hour?"

Somewhat bewildered, William shook his head and beckoned to a groom to saddle the mare. When it was done and Freddy walking with it into the yard, he asked where he was going, adding, "Mary thinks you are both staying for luncheon."

"So we are, I'll not be above half an hour." Freddy set his

foot in the stirrup and swung himself up. "But I must see Maeve." And he clattered out of the stable yard.

William looked after him in pardonable exasperation.

Maeve was in the kitchen when Barlow came down to say that Sir Frederick was in the parlour. "Is the Vicar with him, or my mother?"

"No, Miss Maeve, they've gone over to the church to see the warden. They said they wouldn't be long."

She had been making bread, an occupation she loved, for it seemed to her both creative and pleasantly down to earth. She liked to pummel the dough, to see the loaves set to rise, and later to sniff the rich warm smell that wafted up from the kitchen as they baked in the bread oven. Mrs Jones, the cook, appreciated her help, "But I'm afraid you'll have to finish the kneading today," Maeve said and took off her apron, washing her hands and straightening her dress. Then she went slowly up the stairs, across the hall and in to the parlour. It would be the first time she had spoken to him alone and she was annoyed to feel warm colour rising in her cheeks, hoping he would think it was from her work in the kitchen.

He was standing with his back to the hearth where a fire burned brightly, for the autumnal days were getting chilly. Hands outstretched he came at once to her, seized hers and kissed her cheek. Without the faintest idea how to bring up the subject, he said, "Your man said you were bread-making. That must be a splendid occupation."

"I like it," she disengaged her hands.

"I can't tell you how good it is to be home again and visit everyone. I've just come from Moon's End."

"Were they all well?" Maeve asked coolly.

"Yes. I must say I'm enchanted by my little nephew, such a lively mischievous boy. William will have his hands full later on."

"Aunt Isabel says Fred is very like you were at that age."

Freddy laughed. "I suppose there is a likeness. She says I was an imp of Satan. It will be fun to watch him and the baby growing up. I hope to see Li's boys before too long."

"Do you mean to go down there?" Had he come just to make general conversation?

"Perhaps next spring. It's a long journey for Angela now the weather's getting colder. She didn't fancy the idea." Maeve had sat down by the fire, indicating a chair, but Freddy came to stand in front of her. "Maeve, I had expected – hoped – that is, I thought you'd be married by now."

He paused and she was even more aware of those two burning spots in her cheeks. "I could have been had I wished it."

"But you didn't. Why? Do tell me, I must know." And then he blurted out, "Was it – was it because of me?" She said nothing and he exclaimed, "Oh heavens, it was! William said – "

"What he should not have done!"

"Don't blame him. He thought I should know lest I caused you pain, which I can see I have, haven't I? Darling Maeve, I'm so sorry. You're the last person in the world I would hurt, and I can see I've been thoughtless." His remorse was genuine and in his desire to lighten the situation he added, "That's me all over, isn't it? I wouldn't have you turn into an old maid on my account, not for all the world."

His words could have been better chosen for, stung, she sprang to her feet, facing him. "You need not waste your pity on me. I am going to marry Sir Ralph Digby."

The moment the words were out she would have given anything to retrieve the furious statement. Aghast at herself, hardly seeing him, she stood where she was, her fingers curling into tight balls.

Freddy's jaw had dropped. "No one told me. Oh, this is splendid. I'm so glad. I couldn't bear to hurt you of all people. I see William was wrong and I was a conceited fellow to think – I wish I'd known – I wouldn't have – " He became entangled, aware that the door had opened. "Aunt Nell, Uncle Martin, isn't this wonderful news? I'm so happy for Maeve. From what you've all told me, Sir Ralph seems a good sort of man – and Welford Park! What more could we wish for her?"

The Vicar and his wife were standing transfixed by the door for they had opened it in time to hear their daughter's stark declaration. There was amazement on their faces, but Martin recovered himself quickly. "Yes, it is an excellent match for her. We are of course very pleased." He had pressed his wife's hand to convey to her what she must do and Nell gathered her scattered forces.

"Yes, indeed, it is quite delightful, but you must understand, Freddy, nothing is quite settled yet. He hasn't come for his answer, though we expect him any day now."

"Is that so? Well, I shall tell him how lucky he is to win our Maeve." He came to her and kissed her cheek, seizing her hands again and squeezing them. "Be happy, darling Maeve. I hope he and I will be the best of friends." He chattered on for a few moments about the pleasure of having Maeve as mistress of Welford Park before he recollected he must get back to Moon's End and luncheon.

"The whole family will know now," Nell said, on the verge of tears. "Oh, my dearest, why did you do it? You can't mean to accept Sir Ralph. You don't care for him, you know you don't."

Maeve had heard the front door close behind Freddy, the sound of hooves receding, and now moved over to stand looking out at the empty drive. She felt as if he had ridden out of her life, all hope gone. Even if she saw him every day, he was no longer to be cherished in her heart and mind. But she was quite resolute. Turning to glance at her stepfather she said, "You think well of Sir Ralph, don't you, Papa? You said you thought that if Freddy hadn't had my love for so long that Sir Ralph and I would suit quite well."

"I did," he agreed. "Come and sit down, both of you."

They obeyed and Maeve said, "Don't look so shocked, Mama. I've lost Freddy and it's no good saying it doesn't hurt, because it does. I didn't know I could be so hurt, but I must make something of my life despite that. Mustn't I, Papa?"

"Quite right." he agreed, "though I think you should take time to consider. You've done this in a moment of reaction and must try to reflect a little."

"You've said more than once that you don't like Sir Ralph." Nell was at the moment the most upset of the three. "Such a marriage couldn't make for any sort of content, let along happiness."

"I said that in a moment of irritation when he'd been

particularly tiresome – which he is sometimes, but then so am I, I suppose." She gave her mother a wavering smile. "Some marriages with even less propitious beginnings seem to turn out well. Don't you remember how we all thought Georgiana Rokeby was making a dreadful mistake? She cried all through her wedding as far as I remember, but look at her now? She quite dotes on Guy. And you know, Mama, that Sir Ralph and I have a great deal in common."

"There are plenty of other young men about," Nell said shakily. "You could have had Damian Havers, only it's too late for him now, but Lord Uttley said to me not long ago that Roger still hankers after you. Oh, my love, don't fix your mind on Sir Ralph yet just because of what's happened. You know you'd never have taken him otherwise."

"I wonder." Maeve leaned her head wearily on one hand. "I'm very fond of his mother, which is a good thing. I shall be Lady Dibgy, Mama, and mistress of Welford, and more than well provided for. You should be glad."

"Glad!" her mother echoed. "Of course I'd be glad to see you well settled if you cared a jot for him, but I'm sure you don't."

Maeve gazed beyond her, out of the window, looking over the low stone wall into the churchyard with its grey tombstones, here and there a more elaborate monument, among them an old yew tree. A beech near the gate was shedding its leaves as the soft breeze dislodged them and sent them fluttering down. She had a sudden sense of fatality. From the moment Ralph Digby had charged down that path between the graves he had made his presence felt. She had known, oh for a long time now, that his feeling for her was growing stronger but she had brushed it aside, an irrelevance when Freddy was coming home to her. She gave a deep sigh and said, "I may as well marry him as anyone else now."

Nell gave a gasp and her husband shook his head. "He deserves better than that, don't you think?"

Maeve caught her underlip between her teeth. "Oh, that sounded horrid, didn't it? But I must marry. I don't want to be a spinster living here all my life – as Freddy said."

"Did he? How singularly insensitive of him." Martin

frowned and Nell added. "As if we wouldn't treasure you being here with us."

"I'm sorry, Mama, that was horrid too. But I don't want to end up like Miss Mufferton. I've quite made up my mind. I hadn't until this morning, but I have now. I will marry Sir Ralph, and living at Welford I shall be near you all."

"It would be a very advantageous match in many ways," her stepfather agreed, but his wife looked at him in astonishment.

"I don't know how you can accept it like that. I can't see Sir Ralph making her a good husband at all."

"I can," he said. "I've come to know him better than you have, my dear. Oh, he may be outspoken and very much a man of the world, far beyond our experience in our quiet corner here, but I must admit to liking him very well. I told Maeve so after he offered for her."

"Yes, you did," Maeve said forcefully. "And I won't allow anyone, especially Freddy, to think that I'm going into a decline because of him. I'm not going to be such a poor creature."

Nell wiped her eyes. "I can't think what your aunt will say."

Her husband gave her a faint smile. "I'm quite positive she at least will understand."

"And Mary and William – it's going to be so difficult."

"You will manage very well," he said and got to his feet. "I must go. Robert Wiggins is coming to see me about that broken window in the vestry. If I find the young ruffian with the catapult . . ." Rising, Maeve came to him and laid her cheek for a moment against his black-clad shoulder. "Papa, you don't think I'm doing wrong in taking Sir Ralph, without loving him?"

"No, I don't quite think that," he told her gravely. He paused for a moment, wondering if he should tell her that Ralph suspected the truth, but he decided it would put too much strain on the new relationship. "But I do think you must try to put Freddy out of your mind. He belongs to someone else now and seems much in love with her. Give Digby at least your respect and trust him. Can you do that? Yes, I'm sure you can, and in time I'm sure too that it will turn out better than you think."

"I hope so." She gave a long deep sigh. The die was cast, the decision made. She had to live with it and for a moment the prospect filled her with a kind of weary dismay, but she revived to add determinedly, "But I shall tell him when he comes back that I'm not in the least in love with him. It's only fair. And then if he wants me despite that, it's his choice."

"I've a feeling he will," Martin said. "He seems to me to be sufficiently determined not to mind the terms."

"Oh?" Maeve looked a little blank. "I didn't realise – I thought perhaps it was just convenience."

"Oh, no," he said. "Something much more than that."

He went out and Maeve sat down beside her mother. "Dearest Mama, don't look so unhappy. Even if all our old plans are come to nothing, we can make the best of it. We shall have a wedding to plan. Don't you remember how lovely Mary's was?"

She managed to cheer her mother up as they talked, but all the while she felt inescapably wretched. Despite her rash proclamation to Freddy, her brave words just now, she knew she had set something in motion that could not be stopped. But she would not go back, nor let Freddy see he had shattered her dreams. She would marry Sir Ralph and that was that. Only thinking of her stepfather's words she became aware that she had been less than honest when she had said she thought it might be merely a marriage of convenience for him. Did he really care for her? And did she want him to? Would he not then ask too much of her?

There were the inevitable repercussions from the family. At first consternation on Isabel's part, and on Mary's, but William said, despite his wife's protest, that he liked Sir Ralph pretty well and would welcome him as a brother-in-law, while Isabel said, "My dear, my dear, are you sure? Can you hide what you feel?" And when Maeve said she thought she could, Isabel surprisingly added, "It is not so hard a thing to do if one is determined. We can find courage from somewhere to face all sorts of things." It seemed to Maeve she spoke out of experience and she wondered – her aunt and uncle had seemed utterly devoted, but perhaps it had not always been so. She had to live with all these conflicting reactions and felt herself a prey to emotions that wrecked her sleep. Freddy's whole-hearted pleasure was added pain, and Angela's remark, "I hope you will be as happy as my dear Freddy and I are," hardly added any comfort. She was far too wrought up by the thought of Sir Ralph's return.

A letter came from him a few days later, saying that he was back at Welford and announcing he would call on the morrow. He did not have to say why. Martin received him alone in his study, having instructed Maeve to wait in the parlour. She was nervous. Because there was no joy in it for her, which would have so coloured her response, she was not sure how to meet the moment and walked up and down the room, trying to calm herself. If only the door would open to admit – someone else. But it would not.

When it did open it took her a few seconds to bring herself to turn and look at him. He was wearing a dark green frock coat with gold buttons and the narrow trousers fastened under the instep that were becoming fashionable. He looked very well and green suited him with his thick sandy hair brushed up. His expression was hard to read. So engrossed in Freddy, she had forgotten what a big man Sir Ralph was, his presence filling the room. She felt, suddenly, suffocatingly afraid.

Closing the door he came to her and took her hand, putting it to his lips. "I am honoured that you have accepted my suit," he said formally, and then, in his normal bantering tone he added, "I wonder why?"

He could not have used a better approach. Thankful for that lightness, the teasing words, she answered in a similar manner. "I thought we might sharpen our wits very pleasantly on each other."

"Yes," he said drily, but his lips twitched. "I didn't delude myself that you had evinced undying love for me while I've been away."

She looked straightly at him. "I can't dissemble, you know."

"Nor would I want you to. Whatever reasons you may have, you must at least like me a little to consent to spending the rest of your life with me."

"I do," she answered swiftly. "These last months – " she

broke off. How should she speak of them? The contact with him, his mother, Welford, all tangled up with the waiting for a ship from India. Guilt swept over her. She had said she could not dissemble, yet here she was doing that very thing and she hated herself for it.

He saw the tension flitting across her face and at once took her hand in a strong grasp. "Tell me nothing you don't wish to – that is not like lying. Nor have I lived nearly thirty-five years without having a few secrets. Perhaps we can share ours later on, but for now shall we agree to take it all on trust, in the belief that we shall make each other tolerably happy?"

"Willingly," she agreed. "But you are crushing my poor fingers, as you did once before."

He released her at once. "When? How could I have been so careless?"

"Don't you remember? At your ball, when Mr Creevey told me about your marriage."

"Oh, then. Yes, I was annoyed, wasn't I? But I didn't want Creevey to be the one to tell you. Nor do I think today is the time."

It was her turn to say, "You need not speak of it at all, if you don't wish it."

"But I do, when the right moment comes. Only today I don't want to think of anything but that you have consented to marry me. Whatever your reasons I shall always be grateful and do my best to care for you. Maeve, look at me."

She raised her head and met his clear gaze. Something she saw there made her catch her breath. He bent to kiss her – he was wise enough to let the first kiss be gentle – his mouth warm on hers, his arms closing round her. Freddy had never kissed her like this, never kissed her at all apart from a cousinly peck on the cheek – but, oh, if only he had!

Now it was Ralph who was going to take possession of her, her life, her days and nights, and she feared he would not be satisfied with what she had to give. He had raised his head and was smiling down at her with a confidence that somehow warmed her. I will be a good wife to him, she told herself. Or at least I will try.

Chapter 8

Ralph saw no reason to wait. They were neither of them in the first flush of youth and he did not want to waste time on a long engagement. She agreed with him. If she was to do it, the sooner the better, then at least she would not be living in such close proximity to her lost love nor have to see him almost daily, with or without Angela.

Lady Digby was of course delighted. She swept Maeve into a fond embrace, saying, "This is what I hoped for, my dear, dear child. I'm so glad for you both. Ralph is a different man, I promise you, since you accepted him."

The warmth of this welcome touched Maeve and she thought to herself that one of the brightest spots in the whole affair was Lady Digby's affection. She also added, "What a pleasure it will be to hand everything over to you as the mistress of this house, and the one in London. I must admit I had been finding playing hostess at Ralph's numerous dinner-parties somewhat tiring. How I shall look forward to seeing you at the opposite end of the table to him."

Such generosity and acceptance could not but be pleasing and even Mufti's peck on the cheek and murmur of, "So nice, so very nice," was genuinely welcoming. She thought of her aunt's relationship with Angela, and considered herself fortunate.

A large party was given at Hollanders to announce the engagement which Martin, at Isabel's request, hosted, and when Maeve said hesitantly to her aunt that the year of mourning was not quite up, Isabel answered firmly, "This is what your uncle would want for you."

It was all a little overwhelming, as if she was on a tide that could not be stopped. In desperation one afternoon she rode over to Moon's End and said to her sister, "All this fuss! I shall be glad when it's over. Will I like being married?"

Mary laughed. "What a question! It's what a woman is made for – you'll see. And you must have observed what it is like for William and me."

Maeve was restless, walking about Mary's parlour, moving one ornament on the mantleshelf a fraction of an inch, straightening a chair. Over the hearth was a charming portrait of their mother in a rose-pink evening gown. "You and Mama," she said, "both so happy and content. But I don't feel as I would have done if –"

"Well, we were both lucky enough to love before we married," Mary pointed out, "but it wasn't easy for Mama when she was married to our father. You must remember the bad days after the fire?" Maeve nodded and she went on, "I am not so blind as not to know that all marriages are not as happy as mine, but even if you are not in love with Ralph as I was, and am, with my darling William, you must try to give him the best you can and wait for time to do the rest."

It was good advice, Maeve knew, but she sat and looked at Mary without saying anything, her thoughts transparent to her twin. "You must stop thinking about Freddy," Mary said firmly. "That is all over now and you must have observed how he adores Angela. Yes, I can see how that hurts you, but it is the truth and you must turn away from what has filled your head these last years. You must!"

"I'll try," Maeve said. "Sometimes I think it will be better when I'm married to Ralph and we're away together."

"I'm sure it will. Now I have some good news. I'm going to have another baby."

This had the affect which Mary hoped it would, of driving other things out of her sister's mind. Maeve hugged her and they sat talking of little Fred and one year old Isabel and Mary said William wanted another boy, but that she didn't mind in the least, so that when Maeve went home she felt more cheerful, determined to take Mary's advice.

There was one awful moment for her when Freddy said, "Of course Uncle Martin will be conducting the service, so I claim the right and the pleasure of giving you away."

Panic swept over her. Walk with him down the aisle of Saint Mary-on-the-Hill, where she had so often dreamed of coming out on his arm as his wife? She could not. But before she could find her voice, her stepfather came to her rescue. "I'm afraid that is my prerogative, Freddy. I've already arranged with the Vicar of Wittersham to perform the marriage."

Relief put the colour back into her face as Freddy laughingly yeilded, and later, back at the Vicarage, she threw her arms about Martin's neck and whispered, "Oh, thank you, Papa, thank you for that."

The marriage was set for the middle of December. There was a great deal of sewing done by the dressmakers of Rye, and Nell herself embroidered Maeve's new initials on sets of underwear. Isabel wanted to take her to London on a shopping expedition but there had been so much autumnal rain that the roads had become quagmires in the last few weeks, mists lying most mornings over the countryside and quite blotting out the Marsh.

"There is no point, Mama," William said reasonably, "in leaving Hollanders to be stuck in the mud halfway to London." Even Freddy, always more adventurous, agreed, and the women of the family pored over catalogues and hoped the carters would succeed in coming through on time. It was becoming fashionable to be married in white and when the charming gown was finished Maeve chose a deep bonnet of straw, the inside of the brim lined with the same material and trimmed with little white flowers and green leaves. Nell was ecstatic when her daughter tried on the whole ensemble for the first time.

Maeve moved through it all as if it could not really be happening to her. Ralph had given her a magnificent betrothal ring, a large emerald surrounded by diamonds, and she sat in odd quiet moments looking at it, as if in the whirl of happenings it was the one thing that kept reality before her. It was there, on her finger, his claim on her. He came nearly every day, calmly taking possession of her life until even her mother said, "Oh dear, here's Ralph again. We shall never get the fitting of your pelisse right and you must try the ball gown on again."

When the weather improved they rode together. Now that the hunting season was here, they followed the local pack across the wintry fields, revelling in the exercise, Centaur the black stallion and her Blanche making them a striking pair. Maeve found relief from tiresome thoughts when galloping at his side.

"By God," he said once in genuine admiration, "I've never seen a better horsewoman than you, my love."

"You should have seen my aunt in her hey-day," she answered, laughing, "I thought that of her." She had long since amended her early judgement that he was a bruising rider – hard, yes, and determined to be in control, but once master, careful of his animals.

Ralph proposed that they should live mainly at Welford for his mother's sake, but with occasional visits to London where the house in Bruton Street was being refurbished for them. There would also be visits to Brighton and to various country houses. Maeve was pleased with the prospect. A great deal of occupation would be better than a quiet life – and that she could not see Ralph leading. She was discovering that he had a seemingly inexhaustible fund of energy and she was well prepared to match it. He was arranging a long wedding trip – Paris, Switzerland, Italy, perhaps even Greece.

"How wonderful," was Mary's reaction, though without the slightest envy. "I can't imagine what it would be like to see all those places." And Ellen said that there was no doubt about it, she too would have to marry a rich man who would show her the world! She was in a state of high excitement over being a bridesmaid for the first time, an honour she was to share with Elizabeth Rokeby, and they gazed with awed admiration at the beautiful dressing case of shagreen, fitted with silver brushes and bottles and jars, that was Ralph's wedding gift to his bride. Maeve was somewhat overwhelmed and hoped her thanks were warm enough.

"I like to buy you gifts," was his answer, "I'm afraid you will have to get used to it!"

He had had, though she did not know it, a long talk with his future father-in-law and had arrived at a very fair assessment of Maeve's state of mind. Martin advised patience and affection in as quiet a manner as possible, and Ralph, for whom patience was not a virtue of which he had much knowledge, agreed that the Vicar was wise enough to see to the heart of the matter. Having met Freddy, he was well aware what he was up against.

Freddy pronounced Ralph a capital fellow who knew what he was talking about and that Maeve was bound to be happy with him; Ralph on the other hand summed Freddy up to his mother as good-natured, extremely amiable, and with plenty to talk about on the subjects of the Army and India, but without a great deal of perception.

"He had been away too long to grasp the politics of today," he said, "and the sum of his ambition seems to be to meet the Duke of Wellington. Perhaps I can contrive that."

Lady Digby gave him a swift glance. "That was rather sharp, my dear."

"Well," he shrugged his big shoulders, "it's how I see him. But I trust we shall get on well enough. Only I mean to keep Maeve away from Hollanders for a while."

"You think there was some attraction there?"

"I know it. Her stepfather admitted it when I asked him, straight out, on the day I offered for her, though she herself has said nothing, nor shall I ask her. Perhaps in time she will tell me, or perhaps –" he broke off.

His mother sat looking at him where he stood before the hearth, his back to a roaring fire. "Were you going to say that perhaps her life with you will succeed in putting that old affair into the past?"

"It was hardly ever that," he said. "She, all of them, put too much into too little, as far as I can understand it. His coming home like that, without warning, shattered her hopes. Now I have to set out to pick up the pieces and, if I can, win her love. At least she likes me enough to marry me."

"And you love her very much." Lady Digby let out a little sigh. "It's maybe a difficult road you're setting out on, but I wish you joy, my dearest boy. You have been a long time in choosing another wife and many marriages have begun with less." But at dinner a few nights before the wedding she found herself looking at the head of Hollanders House, and then at Ralph, contrasting them, and she went home certain that her son was the better man for Maeve. Her part would be to love the girl, as she did already, and make Welford a happy place for her. Yet there was a certain sadness beside the hope. If he meant to keep Maeve away from Sussex for a time it meant that she herself would be without either of them. She wished Selena could be at home for the wedding, though she and her daughter had never really got on – but Lord Hillingdon had gone to Russia on diplomatic business and they would not return for many months, certainly not during a Russian winter. So it meant a long lonely time for her too. But that, she told herself firmly, was the lot of old ladies who had outlived their usefulness.

Freddy, who had given the matter some thought, had decided in his mercurial mind that Maeve had quite got over any tacit understanding between them and must be happy with such a fellow as Ralph. He was still determined that she and Angela should be friends. Seeing quite plainly that adjusting to a new country and such a place as Hollanders was difficult for his wife he brought her often to the Vicarage, leaving her there while he went off, saying he had business to settle in Rye, or carrying away his uncle for an hour or two's pigeon shooting.

Maeve sat opposite the girl who had taken her place in Freddy's heart and wondered what to talk about. They seemed to come from different worlds. Once she said, "Tell me about your parents. Did you always live in Calcutta?"

"As my Papa worked for the Company, we had to," Angela said languidly.

"Is it a beautiful city? I imagine it must be."

"Oh, there are beautiful temples and palaces and such, and the Government buildings are thought very fine. Only there is much sickness and poverty and the streets are disgusting when it's very hot, which it usually is – beggars and all sorts are a nuisance." Angela wrinkled her nose. "I hate horrid smells and India is a place of smells."

"I never thought of that."

"I suppose you wouldn't. Our house was a little way out of the town and we had a pretty garden and servants to see to everything. My Papa was a quiet man and we didn't entertain much." Her eyes were shadowed. "Some English people hate marriages between an English gentleman and an Indian lady, however high caste she may be. There were places Papa was never asked."

"Did you get on well with your mother?" Maeve asked on impulse. "You seem so English yourself."

Angela twisted her head. They were sitting in the parlour at the Vicarage by a warm fire, the November day outside dull and misty. "I am – I mean to be. I hated my Indian relatives, there were so many of them. My mother always wore Indian dress and I couldn't see why Papa's wife shouldn't dress like a European. She and her mother tried to make me wear a sari but I wouldn't. I screamed and tore it."

Maeve sat in silence. This was something quite beyond the realm of her experience. Today Angela was wearing a gown of soft blue material which suited the gleaming fair hair, but one was always aware of that unusual colouring. She began to see what a difficult upbringing Angela had had, neither English nor Indian. "Your parents must have loved each other very much to have defied convention as they did," she said at last.

"I suppose so." Angela's voice was listless. "But as I grew up things changed. Everything got horrid, at least until Papa was promoted. One of the Governor's attachés brought him forward and we began to go to functions at Government House – at least Papa and I did, because I was turned seventeen. Mama never came. Oh, it was different then!" Her eyes lit up. "I love dancing, don't you?"

Maeve nodded. It was the first sign of animation she had seen in her. But it died almost at once. Angela said, "Then the cholera came and I was alone. I ran away from the house and went to a lady, a widow, who'd been kind to me."

"Had you met Freddy by then?"

"Oh, yes. He came to a ball at Government House and I'd gone to a Mess party with Papa, and then there was the garden party, and he came to our house with some other officers. He asked me to marry him before – before the cholera, but I hadn't accepted him. Only afterwards, he was so kind. He told me we would do so much when we came home, see London, go to parties. And now – now he is busy all the time, and there's nothing to do apart from driving out with my mother-in-law. And it's always so cold. I don't like being cold."

Maeve was slightly stunned by this burst of confidence but before she could say anything Angela went on, her eyes full of resentment, "He said I would be mistress of a large house and we'd entertain, but I have nothing to do with it. Lady Hollander does everything."

Unable to help feeling somewhat sorry for her, Maeve explained that it was still not a year since Sir Thomas had died, and though changes would come it might take time. As for Freddy, he was simply getting to know his people, making sure everything was being done as his father would have liked.

"As for my aunt," she added, "you must try to understand her. She lost her mother when she was very young and has been mistress of Hollanders for more then thirty years. She probably wants you to get used to how things are done here before you take on too much. Everything is new to you, isn't it – even our climate?"

Angela pulled at the fringe of her shawl. "She doesn't let me do *anything*."

Maeve had heard about a particular incident when Angela had sent for the cook to ask for Indian dishes to be prepared that she and Freddy liked. Cook objected and spoke to Lady Hollander when she came in and there was unpleasantness all round. "Foolish girl," was Isabel's comment. "She had much better wait before giving orders like that."

"And Freddy ought to have the master's bedroom." Now that Angela had begun she could not stem her resentment. "His mother says she will move back to the rooms she had as a girl but she hasn't done it yet. Freddy is the head of the house now and he and I should have it, but when I said so all he did was laugh and say we were very comfortable for the moment. It's not fair."

In the face of this catalogue of complaints Maeve hardly knew what to say. Though she adored her aunt she had the perception to see that Isabel Hollander might not be the easiest of mothers-in-law. Certainly she was not likely to retire yet in favour of an inexperienced girl who had never set foot in the country, let alone Hollanders, until a few weeks ago.

She said the first thing that came into her head. "When

Ralph and I are wed you and Freddy must come and stay with us in London. Ralph moves a great deal in society."

The unhappy look vanished from Angela's face. "I should like that very much. To see London and go into society there – perhaps even dance at court! How very kind of you, Maeve."

But after she had gone Maeve regretted her rashness. Having Freddy staying under the roof she would be sharing with Ralph was the last thing she wanted.

As the wedding day approached so Maeve's doubts and nervousness increased. Nothing Mary could say alleviated her confused feelings, and the very fact that her sister was happily pregnant again did nothing to ease her frame of mind. Once or twice she was snappish with Ralph and then apologised. He smiled and said, "I imagine all brides find it a trying time. You may snap at me as much as you wish as long as you walk down the aisle to me on the fifteenth," which she thought was very handsome of him. He kept their relationship on a light, friendly footing, rather than that of lovers, for which she was very grateful.

Her mother, always finding intimate talk with her daughters difficult, had given her a book called *The Female Instructor*, and turning over the pages the first sentence she came upon ran:

> If a young woman suffers an attachment to steal upon her until she is sure of a return, her misery is sealed. Although a superior degree of happiness may be attained in marriage, if she gives way to this thought she is in a dreadful situation.

She shut the book with an angry movement. It was finicking, depressing rubbish, but it disturbed her because she had done the very thing it warned against. She would do better to look at her mother and sister and her Aunt Isabel than to read a nonsensical book.

On the afternoon before the wedding she escaped the chaos of packing in the Vicarage to have one more solitary ride. The Marsh drew her as always, the pale sun of the December day putting a gentler aspect on the winter landscape. She went down the track past Beckett's Farm, past lonely Fairfield

Church dedicated to St Thomas à Becket, letting Blanche pick her way at an easy trot. She breathed deeply, drawing in the familiar scents of marshland, gazing at the wide acres of flat land under the great bowl of sky, loving it all. At Brenzett she saw the youngest of the Watts brothers emerging from the Fleur de Lys inn. He looked a little sheepish when he saw her and wiped his mouth with the back of his hand, well aware he should not have been in there at this time of day. But he was a personable young man and grinned up at her, saying he and his brothers wished her well, before he hurried off in the direction of Beckett's.

She rode on, turning towards Snargate, past the farm there and the lonely looker's hut out among the grazing sheep. Snargate had once been a favourite haunt of smugglers, who were not above hiding their contraband in the church itself, and it was here that her own father had died, shot in the head in a quarrel brought on by himself – he too involved in smuggling. She turned her head away, nodding to Tom Tighe who stood at the door of the Red Lion, and eventually came to the Military Road and the lane back to Hollanders. Perhaps she would come here with Ralph, but never again as her own mistress. She ached with love for the places where she and Freddy had ridden their ponies together, so long ago. The Marsh was the same, heedless of the comings and goings and the joys and heartbreak of ordinary people, only she would not be as she was today, still less as she had been then. Her throat was sore with the effort to swallow, not to weep.

Suddenly it became imperative that she should see her aunt, sit once more alone with her, for Aunt Isabel always understood everything.

There was even greater activity at Hollanders than at the Vicarage, for the reception was being held here, her own home not large enough for all the guests who were coming. As the weather had turned mild it seemed as if most would be able to come, and apparently Welford Park was going to be bursting at the seams with all the Digby friends and relations. In the hall boughs of greenery and pot plants were being set in place, servants hurrying about arranging chairs, setting glasses out on a long table, while the tall tiered wedding cake stood in all its splendour on a huge silver salver. Maeve stood in the middle of it all until Hinton came to her and said in his kindly way, "It's all very bewildering just now, Miss Maeve, but I promise you everything will be in order by tomorrow."

"I'm sure it will," she said and looked up at him as at an old friend. "Isn't it sad that my uncle isn't here? He was always such a good host."

"Yes, miss. We all miss him a great deal." Hinton was a tall man and strong and had been with Sir Thomas since his marriage to Isabel Hollander in 1798. Now at forty three, so Maeve had heard, he was contemplating marriage with Obadiah's twenty-year-old daughter Lily.

She asked, "Shall we be celebrating your wedding soon?"

"I think not, miss," he said gravely. "I have thought the matter over, but now that Master Freddy – I mean Sir Frederick – is back and wants me to serve him as I did Sir Thomas, his needs come first. I doubt if I can be a good husband to Lily at the same time. It's not easy for personal servants to marry, you know." He spoke with the ease of one who had and always would devote his life to the family.

"I suppose not," she said. "I hadn't realised –"

"Lily will find someone else," he added without a trace of self-pity. "She's that pretty. And I was too old for her anyway. It sort of came about when I used to have my dinner with Obadiah and Millie on my afternoon off. That was one of Sir Thomas's kindnesses, seeing that all of the staff in the servants hall had a free afternoon once a month. Most masters don't bother with that."

"I'm glad you mentioned it," Maeve said. "I will talk to Sir Ralph and make sure our servants get the same." She paused, thinking of Angela's complaint that she was allowed to order nothing, and how different was Lady Digby's request that her new daughter-in-law should take over all domestic arrangements. "What does Lily say?" she asked at last, suddenly sorry for both of them.

"I've talked to her, miss, and she understands. She's got a good place as housemaid at Lord Rokeby's, and it's better for her to stay there. Obadiah thinks so too – at least for the moment."

"I'm sorry, Hinton. In some ways it must be very lonely for you."

He allowed himself a smile. "Hardly that, miss. Not in this house! And now Sir Frederick is back, I have a great deal to do. Mr Ward, the new butler, only came yesterday and needs my help. If you want her Ladyship, she is in the upstairs parlour."

Maeve went slowly up. Hinton was still a personable man and she thought that Lily could hardly be happy to have had to give him up. She herself would soon have charge of a large house and be entertaining on a grand scale; she would have to deal with servants both in London and at Welford, and thinking of what Hinton had said she understood that in the running of a mansion servants who lived in could not cope with families of their own. People like Obadiah were more fortunate for they could be given cottages. He still lived in one called Mrs Gates' cottage, though his wife's grandmother had been dead for many years, and he came in to Hollanders every day, often from six in the morning until late at night, even sleeping in the tackroom with the under groom and stable boy if a mare was foaling. But women in service had to leave if they married and had children. She herself was taking Obadiah's second daughter Gracie on her wedding trip as her personal maid, and the first thing her aunt said to her this afternoon was, "I'm so glad you have chosen Grace Smith as your maid. Such a nice, quiet, well-behaved girl. But then Obadiah and Millie have brought up their brood to know how to behave. They are so glad for her."

"I'm afraid she will miss her family," Maeve said, thinking of the cheerful noise that seemed to emanate from Mrs Gates' cottage, six children crammed in there with their parents.

"My dear, for her to have a good place is the best thing for her. I have had Lucy since I was seventeen. Well now, are you packed and ready?"

Maeve sat down by the fire opposite her aunt. "I suppose so, though Mama is sure she's forgotten something. She made Gracie take everything out of my trunk because she could not remember whether my white evening pumps were put in, and of course there they were at the bottom. I was glad to escape for a while."

Isabel laid down her writing desk on the table beside her. "You have been riding on the Marsh, I expect?"

Maeve nodded and Isabel went on, "Just what I did the afternoon before I married your Uncle Tom. And are you content, my dearest, no last minute doubts? I have worried so much about you ever since Freddy brought Angela home."

Maeve did not answer directly. Instead, thinking of her talk with Angela, she said, "Is she settling in here? It must all be very strange for her."

"Oh, yes, poor little thing. She has not had an easy time from what Freddy says, and then that long journey home. I must say I worry about that marriage. To wed a girl who is half of another race does not make it easy. And I admit to finding it hard to talk to her."

"I think she's very much in awe of you." Maeve smiled at her masterful aunt. "Will she make a good mistress for Hollanders?"

"I really can't say, and certainly not yet. I expect you heard about that business with Cook, and she rings for a servant on and off all day with the most ridiculous requests. That may have been all right for Indian servants, but here they have their work to do and it must be kept within bounds. I try to explain. Well, we will see in time. Can you imagine her being able to deal with the day-to-day things that go on here? No, I'm not handing over yet. I've told Freddy so and he agrees with me."

"She doesn't seem happy about the rooms in the west wing," Maeve said cautiously.

"Oh, has she been talking about that? I suppose I must have my old rooms re-decorated. There's no dower house for me to go to, only the Stone House in the village and that has tenants." Isabel gave a rather sharp laugh. "Does she want me to go and live in the old tower, I wonder?"

"No, no," Maeve said hastily. "There's so much she doesn't understand, Aunt Isabel. I feel a little sorry for her."

"That's generous of you, my love. For Freddy's sake we all have to do the best we can to make her like it here. But we were talking of you. Do you think you can be happy with Sir Ralph?"

"I don't know," Maeve said, glad to abandon the subject of Angela. "We do like the same occupations. I'm always discovering new things about him – he really likes music for one. He didn't fall asleep the other evening when I was playing, as Freddy did."

"Shocking," Isabel said, laughing. "Freddy never was one for the accomplishments, was he?"

"No," Mauve said in a low voice, "but none of that would have mattered if – " she broke off.

Isabel seemed to brace herself. "There is something I feel I must say to you, my dear. Of course I wanted you to marry Freddy and when that could not be, I did fear you had hurried too quickly into accepting Sir Ralph, though I understood your doing it. I still think that may be so, but your Papa has persuaded me, all of us, perhaps, that he thinks it will all turn out all right. Only I wanted to tell you this – a sound and happy marriage need not begin with romantic love. In fact, it very seldom does."

"You told me once before that yours with Uncle Tom was arranged, but you always seemed so wonderfully happy together."

"So we were, but it wasn't always so." Isabel saw the surprise on the girl's face and went on, "At first we were not very compatible. Your dear uncle was so very reserved, so disciplined, which I wasn't. I made so many mistakes. And my father, you know, had brought me up like a boy, as his companion. I'm afraid my language was not always ladylike."

Maeve laughed. "One sometimes gets tired of being ladylike."

"True, but I had to mend my ways when the boys came along, and they made up for a lot. Only an estrangement grew up between us – oh, for reasons I won't go in to – and then we no longer shared a bedroom. It was more my fault than his."

Maeve was astonished, not only at the confession of something never guessed at, but that her aunt should tell her anything so intimate, and wondered why she was doing so.

Isabel was looking at her, so pretty and intelligent and lively, and she sighed for what might have been. She privately thought her son would have been far better off with such a girl as a wife, but there was no doubt he was deeply in love with Angela. With an effort she went on, answering the unspoken question, "I am telling you this because there is a point to the story and no one knows of it except your mother and your stepfather. While your uncle and I were estranged, Major Irvine came here to build the canal. Do you remember him?"

"I think so – very dark and fine-looking, in a scarlet coat."

A sigh escaped Isabel. "Oh, he was indeed handsome. Anyway, I fell very much in love with him and he with me." She stared into the fire, not looking at her niece now, but sensing her rivetted attention. "We could only meet very occasionally so that there was more pain than joy. I deserved that, I suppose, for it was very wicked of me, but we couldn't help ourselves." She paused, remembering – remembering an afternoon when she and Adam Irvine had sheltered from the rain in an empty looker's hut down on the Marsh, and the passionate and total love-making that took place there. But of that she could not speak. "Then he went away with Sir John Moore to the Peninsula War and was killed there at Corunna, almost at the same moment as Sir John."

Maeve reached out and took her aunt's hand. "You must have been so unhappy."

"I was – for a long time. Your uncle found out the day we got the news and that drove us even further apart. But gradually the wound began to heal, as all wounds do. Your uncle was unfailingly kind to me, far more than I deserved, and I began to realise how much I'd hurt him. I began to understand what sort of man he was, so good – I mean really good, as his brother is – so upright and fair in his dealings. I suppose I began to appreciate him for the first time. And then came that dreadful night when your father lured him into an ambush and tried to shoot him, only he shot me instead – in the arm so it was nothing. I tried to run between them. Foolish, wasn't it?"

"I didn't know that part of it," Maeve said, "but it sounds to me as if you were extraordinarily brave."

"Oh no, there just wasn't time to think. Anyway, you know the rest of it. Obadiah was forced to shoot your father to stop him killing Tom. I was soon recovered and your uncle took such care of me. That's when I realised how much I'd changed and how I'd grown to love him." The telling of the old story had been hard and Isabel wiped away two tears with her handkerchief. "After that – after that we found ourselves so much in love we were like a pair of romantic newly-weds – at our age!" She managed a shaky laugh. "It was a miracle really, far more than I deserved."

Maeve was so profoundly moved that her aunt had seen fit to tell her all this that she plumped down on her knees by her chair. "Dearest Auntie, I think I know why you have told me."

Yes, I'm sure you do. You see, the love I had for Adam Irvine – and oh, I did love him so much at the time – was wrong, impossible, and it was only out of all that heartache I discovered where my true happiness lay."

Maeve leaned her head against Lady Hollander's shoulder and let out a deep sigh. "I do try not to think of Freddy all the time, not to love him, but it's so hard. I've loved him for so long and now he's not mine to love."

"I know, darling, and no one understands that better than me. That's why I told you. Of course I want his happiness and I thought it lay with you, but he's found it elsewhere so I must support him and try to love Angela – while all the time I'm wishing you were my new daughter. So you see, we both have to begin afresh, to learn to see things differently. Perhaps an old story has helped you?"

"Oh, yes, indeed. Thank you for telling me."

"And you do feel something for Sir Ralph, don't you? Even if it's only liking, a companionship? Yes, I know you do. And out of it love may come as it did for me all those years ago. Oh dear, I do miss your uncle so much." But Isabel refused more tears, got up and drew Maeve to her feet.

"Think about what I have told you, dearest. But now we must go and do some of the hundred and one things that still have to be done!"

Half an hour later Maeve left and walked across to the stables, her mind turning over and over all that her aunt had said. It was an aspect of Isabel's life that she had never guessed at. It warmed her, the knowledge that her aunt had gone through a similar heartbreak and had in the end found such happiness. Could she find that with Ralph?

For a moment her heart sank. She didn't want to – she wanted to find it with Freddy, but all chance of that had gone. Yet somehow Aunt Isabel's tale of an old and lost love remained with her.

She turned into the stableyard and at once Obadiah ran Blanche out. As he touched his hat to her she said "I'll take good care of your Gracie, Obadiah."

He grinned. "I'm 'opin' as she'll take good care o' you, Miss Maeve. Will you go up?"

"No." She took the reins from him. "I went a long way today so Blanche can walk home."

She left, going round by the road as the short cut through the copse was not suitable for a horse, and as she passed the church gate she heard hooves on the road. For a moment, with a sudden twist of the memory, she thought it was Ralph. But this was not last January, nor was it Ralph. It was the groom, Jacob Hatch. He reined in and he too touched his hat.

"Art'noon, miss. Looks like it'll be a fine day fur your weddin' tomorrow."

"What are you doing here, Jacob? Have you brought a letter from Sir Ralph?" She had told her bridegroom he would be better out of the way today and wondered if he had written to her. Somehow she did not think him a letter writer.

Jacob shook his head. "Been to Rye, miss, for some tackle." He indicated the bundle tied to his saddle.

"You're out of your way for Welford then," she said rather sharply.

He grinned down at her. "I were quick about it and you can't blame a man for goin' to see his sister. It ain't far to Appledore."

"Well, don't be too long – I don't imagine Sir Ralph wants you careering about the countryside when you should be at Welford."

"No, miss. Ain't it odd as you and me'll be livin' in the same place – leastways you in the great 'ouse and me in one o' the rooms above the stables."

She gave him a steely look. "I should advise you not to say such things in front of Sir Ralph."

"Ah, you ain't told 'im about me then?"

"Certainly not."

"I wondered like. But I thought not, or 'e might 'ave turned me off, eh?"

"That's why. If you behave yourself and don't get drunk or

do something stupid, I'll not have you dismissed. But I advise you not to be familiar or Sir Ralph will send you packing, you can be sure of that."

"Yes, miss." He gave her a knowing look. He was very dark with thick black hair and black stubble on his chin. "I know me place. 'Tis a pity more folk don't." And with that cryptic remark he touched his hat again and rode off.

Irritated, Maeve turned down the drive to the Vicarage and handed Blanche over to Joe Smith. She wished Ralph had not taken on Jacob Hatch. She supposed she should enlighten him – it had hardly been necessary when Ralph employed him, but now the situation was changed. Perhaps if Jacob behaved it would not be necessary. She felt a little uneasy about it, but in the meantime there were far more important things to think about and the moment she entered her mother bore her away to decide between kid or lace gloves for tomorrow.

Through dinner and the quiet evening that followed she sat looking at every familiar object, thinking of the life she led here, the involvement in parish affairs, the happy drives with her stepfather, the companionship of her mother in household duties, Sunday mornings in the old church, the rides on the Marsh, the almost daily contact with Hollanders, her sister close by. From tomorrow she would no longer be the Vicarage daughter, but move into a world she did not know and in the middle of it all would be Ralph.

A year ago she did not even know him, nor guess that any other man than Freddy could be her husband – happily living in what her stepfather had called a fool's paradise, as they all had. She straightened sharply, thrusting the thought from her, and caught her arm against the table by her side, sending a small china shepherdess to smash on the polished wood floor.

"Oh!" She knelt by it to pick up the pieces. "Oh, I'm so sorry. I gave you this when you were married."

"Never mind, dearest," her mother said consolingly. "Perhaps it can be mended."

"I don't think so." Maeve sat turning the pieces in her hand. "I was so proud when I bought it all by myself in Rye with my own money. And so happy that you two were being wed and we were coming to live here. I wanted to give you something special."

Martin sent her an affectionate smile over the paper he had been reading. "You have given us much more than that over the years," he said.

She felt the warmth of their love for her, but as she sat on the floor by her mother, for a moment it seemed oddly significant, the shepherdess broken on the eve of leaving home, her life too broken and changed forever.

Chapter 9

The fifteenth of December was another pleasantly mild day with blue sky and pale winter sunshine. Gracie Smith, learning her duties, came early to her new mistress's room and opened the curtains. Maeve was already awake. After a restless night her eyes felt heavy and she had a headache. She would have liked to rest a while, to lie and think, but almost immediately her mother came in wearing her undress robe, followed by the footman and the bootboy carrying a tin bath. Cans of hot water were fetched and the bride was bathed and dressed, her hair done by Nell's Rose while Gracie watched.

Glowing after the bath, Maeve submitted to it all, listened to the cheery chatter, her mother hovering solicitously over the whole procedure. Mary arrived and joined in it all and by eight o'clock she was ready. In what seemed an incredibly short time she was standing dressed in her bridal gown and bonnet, a white cashmere shawl wrapped round her shoulders for the short walk to church. There were kisses and whispered good wishes and then everyone disappeared over to St Mary's. Her bridesmaids hovered about her, arranging the shawl yet again as she took her stepfather's arm.

"Are you all right, my dearest?" he asked gently, for it seemed to him that she was very pale and her eyes were shadowed. "Did you sleep well?"

"No, Papa, not much."

He pressed her hand where it lay on his arm. "In my experience most brides are nervous – except perhaps your sister. Marrying William was the most natural thing in the world to her. It is such good news about the new baby."

Maeve gave him a faint smile. "I wish I was more like her."

"You are yourself," he said, "and I consider Ralph to be a fortunate man. He's of the same mind himself."

"You are sure this is right, aren't you, Papa?"

"I think so," he told her gravely. "We can't see into the future but I believe it will turn out for you better than you think. If I didn't, I wouldn't resign you so willingly into his care. And we are all in God's Hands, you know, and He will watch over you."

"Yes, dearest Papa." For a moment she leaned against him, and then straightening herself, walked out with him into the sunshine.

Outside, the path through the churchyard was lined with villagers and Hollander tenants, all eager to wish her well. Families from Moon's End who had known her all her life had walked over and she caught a glimpse of Obadiah and Millie Smith surrounded by their three sons and two other daughters, Joe grinning all over his face. The Watts brothers were there with their families and the servants from Hollanders, and on a wave of good wishes she entered the porch, a fine old entrance built to celebrate the marriage of the victor of Bosworth field, Henry VII, to Elizabeth of York. On the far churchyard wall Solomon the peacock sat sleepily, feathers folded, unaware that it was he who had started the train of events leading to this day.

Her knees seemed to be shaking a little as Martin paused, gave her his own private blessing and then led her into the crowded church. Somehow the familiar surroundings steadied her, the old hatchments for long gone Hollanders along the walls, the memorial to the previous Sir Frederick and the more recent marble plaque to Sir Thomas reminding her of the day of his funeral. Underneath this was written, "The best of men, much loved husband and father, respected by all". Dear Uncle Tom, if only he were here today – but it was Freddy who turned in the Squire's pew to beam at her. It still hurt – oh, how it hurt – but she mustn't think of him, and she made herself smile at Angela. Freddy's wife was looking breathtakingly beautiful in a blue gown over which she wore a jacket of velvet trimmed with fur and a matching hat set on her gleaming fair hair. No wonder he had fallen in love with her! Maeve caught herself up on this train of thought and became aware of other faces, dear Aunt Isabel, Lady Digby, the Rokebys and the Derings, strangers who must be Digby relations, her mother, smiling and a little anxious.

They were nearly at the chancel steps now and she glanced for the first time at the tall broad-shouldered figure of her bridegroom. He looked very well in a mulberry cut-away coat with a buff striped waistcoat and buff trousers, the points of his shirt standing out, the white cravat high about his neck and held in place by a black stock. By his side his groomsman, George FitzClarence, was resplendent in the scarlet and gold of a Colonel of the Coldstreamers and it was he who turned and bestowed an encouraging smile on her.

Martin gave her hand into Ralph's and thought fleetingly that any woman should be proud to marry such a man. Why then did her heart sink, a terrible fear seize her? She tried to banish it by giving him one brief glance, glimpsing a strange expression on his face, as if he was deliberately revealing nothing. He had in fact seen that quick look towards one particular pew and his brows had drawn briefly together, his thoughts far from what they should have been, but he took her hand firmly in his as the Vicar of Wittersham began the service. He made his vows in a strong clear voice but only a few close by, after an imperceptible pause heard Maeve say: "I, Maeve Eleanor, take thee, Ralph Edward Lysander, to my wedded husband, to have and to hold . . ."

And then she was walking back down the aisle, the bells ringing out a triumphant peal as she came out of the church on the arm of her husband. It was done, his wedding ring was on her finger, and she must not look back, only up at Ralph to give him a little smile.

For answer he laid his other hand over hers as the villagers cheered them down the path to the waiting carriage, Ellen and Elizabeth Rokeby there to help her in so that her dress was not crushed.

It was like every other wedding she had been to. The breakfast was lavish, toasts were drunk, congratulations offered, a few arch jokes, and Ralph was clapped on the shoulder many times and told how lucky he was. He seemed to have a great many friends and relations. And Mr Creevey whom Ralph admitted to having invited, for one could hardly think of a celebration without him, came up to her and shook her hand heartily.

"Well, well," he said, "we never guessed, did we, when we went on that picnic to Bodiam last summer that you would be the next Lady Digby? I do wish you joy, my dear. No doubt we shall see quite a lot of each other in society." He gave her a beaming smile. "You and Ralph look very well together. That other marriage – so disastrous for him when he was so young. Ah, well, you will make him happy, I'm sure." She was called away to speak to someone else, but she knew a moment's curiosity. Ralph had not yet spoken of his first wife.

There was a great deal of cheerful talk and Colonel FitzClarence laughingly claimed the privilege of flirting with the bride. He kissed her cheek and took advantage of the moment to whisper, "I shall expect to stand godfather to your first, you know."

Lord Digby, the head of the family, had come all the way from Devonshire for the wedding, and he drew her down to sit beside him. "I'm afraid my days of standing about talking to people are over," he said, smiling. "Well, my dear child, you're very pretty and I think Ralph is to be congratulated. You must allow an old man to pay you a compliment. I hope he will bring you to Devonshire one day." He was Lady Digby's cousin and standing by him she added, "I'm sure he will. Dearest Maeve, come and give your second mother a kiss."

Their kindness, their welcoming her into their family, cheered her, and she stayed a little while talking with them. Ralph had gone to get a glass of wine for his mother, and for one moment he stood alone by the dining-room door, watching his bride as she gracefully accepted the good wishes. Was she happy? He didn't know, but he was thinking of that quick look towards the Squire's pew in the church when a soft voice at his elbow said, "So serious, Sir Ralph? I'm sure you've no cause to be anxious."

He turned at once to see his new sister-in-law smiling up at him. He said lightly, "I suppose every bridegroom must be aware of new responsibilities."

"That's not quite what I meant," Mary said, her eyes on her twin.

"No," he agreed, the smile gone. "I know very well what you meant. I've taken her on her terms, but I mean to make her happy, to open up a new life for her."

"And I'm sure you will." Mary laid her hand briefly on his arm. "William and I are so glad to welcome you as part of our family, and I hope so much it will be for your happiness too."

He looked down into her face, so like Maeve's, only softer in colouring, all warmth and concern and real affection. "You are very kind," he said. "I count your husband among my close friends now."

"I'm so glad. At one time I thought we must all seem very tame and countrified compared to London society."

"Not at all," he said. "Of course London has been my home for quite a long time and I hope Maeve and I will use the house in Bruton Street during the season, but the truth is I like Welford and living in Sussex far better than I expected. My mother likes it too and I know she will look forward to us spending much of our time there. As for being dull –" he glanced round the hall with its mass of gaily dressed wedding guests "– meeting you all could hardly be called that."

"I'm so pleased you find it to your taste. We wouldn't like it at all if you took Maeve quite away from us."

She was smiling at him, but he said gravely, "Oh, I don't intend to do that, only to introduce her to London and Brighton and other places."

"I don't know London at all, and I've never travelled," Mary admitted. "I've always been perfectly content here, but Maeve is different. I think she will enjoy it all exceedingly. You will judge what is best for her."

"You trust me to do that?"

"Yes, indeed."

"I hope I may – and thank you."

"What for?" she asked in surprise.

He took her hand and kissed it. "For talking to me like a sister!"

"How nice that sounds. I'm so sorry your own couldn't be here. Now I must go on being a sister and take Maeve upstairs to change. She can't travel at this time of year in that dress."

"What a pity." He glanced across at his bride. "She looks so well in it, but I expect you are right." He had arranged that they take their coach to Dover, spend the night at an hotel there and cross to France in the morning, and the weather was hardly likely to stay as mild for long.

Mary left him and exchanged a word with her mother. Nell was busy with so many guests and suggested the sisters should go and enjoy a few private moments together before bride and groom left. Maeve excused herself to Sir Edward Dering who was about to launch into one of his long tales that usually lacked a point, and turned to accompany Mary, but on the bottom step, answering one more guest, she stumbled momentarily. At once a hand was under her elbow, steadying her, and Freddy's voice was saying, "Careful now, dear Maeve. You don't want a fall on your wedding day."

His hand was firmly on her arm, a smile on his face, his brown eyes bright with affection.

"Don't," she said, "don't!" And catching at her skirts she hurried upstairs, leaving Freddy wondering what he was not to do. The incident, momentary though it was, had not escaped Ralph on the other side of the hall, for he had been watching her, but he calmly continued his conversation with an elderly man who had introduced himself as a cousin of Sir Thomas.

Upstairs, in the room set aside for Maeve to change her clothes, she was struggling out of her wedding dress as if she couldn't get it off quickly enough.

"Careful," Mary said, "you'll tear the silk. And it will be so useful as a ball gown." She took it and was sitting on the edge of the bed smoothing the creases when suddenly Maeve flung herself at her feet.

"What have I done? Oh, what have I done? How could I –" She broke into wild dry sobbing.

"Oh, my dear, my dear," Mary gathered her twin into her arms. "Darling, hush. It's only nerves. Everything will be all right."

"Will it? Will it ever?"

"Of course it will. Ralph loves you so much."

"He – he's never said so – and I don't know – I don't know if I want him to – I only wanted – " She was shuddering, the shattering sobs shaking her, and clinging to her sister as if to a life-line, while poor Mary, equally shaken by this breakdown, could only smooth her hair and hold her, murmuring soothing words. It was all so unlike her own wedding.

There was a knock on the door then and Gracie came in, sent up by Nell to help her new mistress. Maeve sprang up, dashed away the tears and began to talk, a little unsteadily, of the ceremony and how lucky they had been with the weather. "And only fancy old cousin Hector coming, and Mr Creevey, and didn't Colonel FitzClarence look handsome?"

Mary held up her travelling dress and Grace fastened it, tidying her hair and putting on her bonnet. When she was ready Mary handed her a muff and her gloves and set a little grey furred pelisse about her shoulders, whispering, "Darling, I can't bear it if you are so unhappy."

Maeve turned a brilliant smile on her, so unlike her usual one that Mary was hardly comforted. "I'm not, really I'm not. I was just silly. Forget all about it." She gave her a swift hug and was out of the door, Mary following with deep misgiving.

Ralph was waiting at the bottom of the stairs surrounded by guests, all crowding round as she came down.

"Are you ready?" he asked and crooked his arm. She put hers through it and answered, "Quite ready, thank you, Ralph."

In the carriage as it bowled away driven by Willis, Ralph's groom, she was surprised to see Jacob Hatch on the box. "Is Hatch coming with us?" she asked rather sharply. "I thought we were only taking Willis?"

"So we are. Hatch is coming to return our own horses home to Welford, while we take the carriage and hire horses at Calais. You do dislike him, don't you? Shall I dismiss him?"

She shrugged her shoulders, but was immensely relieved in her mind. "Not on my account. I just find him tiresome at times." And to change the subject she said lightly, "However did you come by the name Lysander?"

He gave her a boyish grin. "Isn't it dreadful? My father was obsessed with everything Greek: history, culture, art, military matters. Apparently my mother protested in vain, but at least it's not my first name. Selena fared a little better with Cassandra as her second name – it could have been Andromache!"

"I hope Lady Hillingdon will approve of me." From what Maeve had heard Ralph's sister seemed to be a rather forbidding woman. "She's older than you, isn't she?"

"By five years. But don't let her intimidate you – it's just her manner. She and mother can be very prickly with each other and sometimes have sparring arguments, but at heart Selena is a good sort of person. If she likes you, and I'm sure she will, she will be your friend for life."

"I hope so," Maeve murmured, but was rather glad Lady Hillingdon was safely in Russia.

"One should be very careful choosing names," Ralph remarked "I never owned to it at Harrow or I'd have been ragged to death."

"Children can sometimes be very unkind to each other," she agreed. She was conscious of the warmth of him close to her, the intimacy of the carriage increasing her nervousness.

"Boys can certainly behave like fiends to each other." he was saying with a laugh, "yet I shall want our son to go to Harrow. A good school can be the making of a man."

It was the first time he had ever mentioned children, but of course he wanted them, every man did, and so should she. Why couldn't she be like Mary? She would have, if only – I have to stop this, she told herself, or I will spoil Ralph's happiness and any chance of it I might have.

She had not answered him and he took her hand, holding it in silence. When he next spoke it was to say that they would stop at Hythe for some refreshment, and be at Dover by nightfall. His major-domo, Mr Flint, had already arranged their rooms at a superior inn and gone ahead to France to see that they had the best accommodation in Paris. Ralph's valet, Bridges, and Gracie, who was in a state between nerves at travelling so far from home and excitement at the prospect of going on the sea, were seated by Willis on the box while at the rear of the carriage where their considerable amount of luggage was fastened, Hatch stood on a step. It was certainly travelling in style.

Romney Marsh and the bare open acres slipped past. She would not see them again for months and she shared Gracie Smith's feelings. But there was more to it than that. It was blatantly before her – the truth that she, who would have yeilded herself so joyously to Freddy, must tonight accept complete intimacy with a man she did not love. Liked yes, at least most of the time, but did not love. It was the lot of many, perhaps most women, she knew that, but she had had the chance of something more and Freddy had killed that. No, not Freddy but Angela. She hated Angela, almost hating Freddy too, for between them they had wrecked what should have been hers.

Looking out of the window she saw that they were passing the Ship at Dymchurch, a few men hanging about the entrance, a smugglers' haunt, a fisherman's inn, today just an ordinary day. But it was not ordinary, for tonight Ralph would come to her, become her husband, take the virginity she had kept for one man. The coach lurched and she wished she did not feel so sick.

Chapter 10

Christmas in Paris, snow in the Tuileries Gardens and the Place de la Concorde, morning service in the Embassy chapel. When the snow melted, to the warmer Mediterranean shores, the busy port of Marseille, the blue sea sparkling in the sunshine, ships docking and sailing in ceaseless activity. Then Italy, and a wonderful few weeks in Florence seeing the churches, the galleries, the wealth of art. It all passed in a fascinating diorama, leading to Easter in Rome, the great bell of St Peters announcing the glorious day of the Resurrection, the sun warm and spring in the air.

Over breakfast a few days later Ralph suggested they should hire horses and ride out into the Roman hills. Maeve was delighted with a chance to get into the saddle after so much coach travel and ran up to their room to change while Ralph went out to find the livery stable recommended by their hotel proprietor. Gracie brought out the blue habit and soon had her mistress ready. She was still bemused by her good fortune, that she, a plain Marsh girl, should be seeing so much of the world.

Dressed, Maeve suggested that if Bridges was willing and as neither of them would be needed for a few hours, they might go out together to see the sights of Rome, Bridges being middle-aged and eminently respectable.

Gracie clasped her hands together. "Oh, ma'am, I'd like that for sure. I never know'd, living on the Marsh, there were such places, so much to see. They won't believe it at home when we go back. The furthest I'd even been were Rye, and Lydd on market days."

Maeve smiled. "Run along then and get your cloak and bonnet, and I'll speak to Bridges."

With that satisfactorily settled, she went down to the hotel parlour to wait for Ralph, standing by the window to watch the busy crowds outside. Their hotel was near the Ponte Milvio and there was a constant stream of carriages, riders, men with handcarts, others hurrying about on business, while those at leisure strolled in the sunshine. She thought it a fascinating city and had bought a set of little drawings of the various churches as a present for her stepfather, while presents for her aunt, for Mary and Ellen had been purchased in Paris, silks and perfume and gloves and handkerchiefs. However, she thought Ralph was beginning to get a little tired of a diet of churches and museums and was sure a ride this morning would please him as much as herself.

It was four months since her wedding and she seemed to herself to be a different person, separated by travel, by a perspective of the wider world, by wifehood, from the girl she had been. Like Gracie she had known only her small corner of Kent and Sussex, and no people except her own countrymen. She was glad to have a fair knowledge of French, taught to her by her stepfather, discovering that Ralph spoke not only French but Italian and a smattering of German, as well as some Spanish picked up during the Pensinsula War. His father had evidently been a much travelled man, and finding in his son a flair for languages had added to the Latin and Greek of school, teaching the boy himself during his holidays – being of the opinion that spare time only induced the young to get into mischief. Poor Ralph, Maeve thought, it did not sound as though he had much fun during his boyhood, none of the wild games she and Mary and the three Hollander boys had got up to, she and Freddy always together.

Apparently, after his father's death, and the débâcle of the "Elegant Extracts", followed so soon by his wife's death, Ralph had travelled extensively and knew what he was doing in foreign cities. In Paris he had spent one morning at a fencing school, using the foils being one of his pleasures, and Maeve planned to walk in the Champs Elysée accompanied by Gracie, to browse in the shops. Knowing Paris better than she did, Ralph said at once that Bridges would accompany them, and when she demurred, seeing it as unnecessary, he had simply said, "I insist." So Bridges had walked discreetly behind them. While in Paris they had been invited to dine with the British Ambassador, who had been acquainted with Ralph's father, and had met a pleasant company of people.

Yesterday Ralph had received a letter from an old Harrovian friend, Harry Blake, who had married an Italian girl and now lived in a house on the estate of her father who owned several vineyards in the south. They were pressed to spend a week or two there and tomorrow would leave to accept the invitation. It would be a refreshing change from hotels and inns, Maeve thought, though everything had always been arranged for her complete comfort. She had discovered that if one were as wealthy as Ralph it was easy to travel in the utmost luxury. He was always solicitous, at his best, she thought with some amusement, though occasionally there were flashes of the old Ralph who could swear with great fluency at a clumsy groom or a careless porter, but for the most part Mr Flint had arranged everything so well there was little need for it.

Using their own carriage, slung aboard the packet boat in a manner that amazed her, they hired post horses the other side of the channel. Mr Flint had engaged the best rooms at every stop, evidently quite accustomed to doing this.

"I didn't know you'd been abroad so often," she said once and Ralph replied, "As often as I could – after Alice died." It was the first time he had mentioned her by name and Maeve waited expectantly but he said nothing further, other than that before Napoleon was defeated it had of necessity been to such places as Hanover, where he polished up his German. He had also been to Spain once Wellington had cleared that country of the French, and had seen the grave of Sir John Moore, carefully tended by the people of Corunna. After Waterloo, of course, Europe had been open once again to English travellers and he had taken full advantage of that, travelling sometimes with one of his friends, once or twice with his mother, before she found the process too much of an effort. No wonder, Maeve thought, he had planned their journey with such authority.

In Paris he had taken her shopping, bought her day and

evening dresses, elegant hats, gloves and shoes, until he was forced to invest in an extra trunk to accommodate them. She protested that he was pandering to her woman's vanity, whereat he laughed and said it pleasured him. She knew he liked to see her well dressed when they went to the opera or to dine at the best restaurants – it was a side of him she hadn't expected.

Really the days had been delightful, with so much to see and do. Ralph's manner towards her was light and teasing, seldom lover-like, never intense, and under this treatment she was able to recover her poise, put aside the dreadful emotions of her wedding day. Both here and in Paris it could not help but be gratifying when they met other English travellers that he was so obviously pleased to have her on his arm, and it was more enjoyable than she had expected being Lady Digby and squired by such a striking man. If only there were not the nights!

She watched as a man with a barrow of cabbages tried to avoid a rider and had his cart upset, the cabbages rolling all over the street. He was jumping up and down in a fury, shouting and gesticulating, while the man on horseback rode on, taking no notice whatsoever. A dog started barking and a woman with a pail of milk tripped over a cabbage to sprawl in the dust, her milk making a white stream down the gutter. In a moment the whole street seemed to be involved in the turmoil and one young urchin gathered up a couple of cabbages, tucked them under his coat and fled. Maeve gave a momentary laugh but she was too deep in her own thoughts for much diversion.

Oh, the nights! She knew she had failed him there. In the day she could be bright and cheerful, entertained by everything without any falsity for she *was* enjoying it all. There was not a great deal of time for repining and Ralph kept her too busy to think much of Hollanders and home. But when the dark hours came, the moments of intimacy, when he got into bed beside her, his hands touching her, caressing her breasts, his mouth on hers, it was then that she could only think of Freddy – Freddy who should have been the one possessing her. She grew stiff, rigid, not quite afraid but resistant, her body tense, not yielding. When he came to her, took her – and nothing in her life had quite prepared her for the reality of this – with his weight on her, she wanted to cry out, to push him away, to weep for Freddy to whom she would have yielded her body with such joy, and the dark hours became her dread, a sort of purgatory.

If she thought Ralph unaware of this, she was mistaken. He was only too aware that he shared his marital bed with a third person, shadowy and far away, but there as surely as if he was present in the flesh. Determined to be patient as long as necessary, Ralph tried to dispel the tension, to bring forth a response, but as the weeks went by and nothing changed he became first desperately disappointed and then resigned. So, the union of the flesh was disagreeable to her – well, he would accept the delightful companion of the daylight hours and hope that before too long she would become pregnant. Perhaps motherhood would soften her; loving their child, she might come to love the father as he wanted to be loved. He told himself it was early days yet, but he began to fear for the future, that nothing would be as he had hoped.

One night, lying beside her after he had blown out their candle, he put his arm about her and felt the inevitable stiffening.

Quietly he said, "Maeve, it would be so much better if you didn't resist me, if you could accept –"

In a stifled voice she murmured, "I can't."

"Try, I beg you, my dear. You must know by now how much I want you, need you."

"You have me," she whispered. "I am your wife."

"I have the right, yes, but don't you understand? There is a world of difference between enduring what you clearly don't like, and giving on your part. My dear, try to understand." He was caressing her, his hands moving over her. "I want all of you, not just certain rights. I want us to be one in every way."

She gave a little sob. "If I could be – what you want, I would, but I can't. It's only this – in the daytime –"

"Oh, I grant you we do very well then, but do you think I'm satisfied that my wife finds it hard to bear with my presence at night? Good God, am I asking so much?"

"No – no – it's just that –" But his mouth had come down on

hers as if he didn't want to hear the rest of the incoherent sentence. He made love to her then, with passion enflamed by frustration, and when he rolled away to fall instantly asleep, she allowed a few tears to trickle down her cheeks. Did he, she wondered, compare her to his first wife? What was the long dead Alice like? Had she loved Ralph in a manner that she herself could not? It was clear that her death had devastated him, that even now he could not speak of it.

Leaning her head against the jamb of the window on this bright May morning she felt a curious oppression. Her stepfather had been so sure this was the right marriage for her and yet now here she was knowing she had failed Ralph. The fault was hers. She could not conquer or suppress her feelings, nor generate those she thought she should have, but she had once said to Ralph that she could not dissemble and she had discovered this extended to the physical things as well. She could not pretend to want him when she wanted another man. Did that make her marriage vows a lie? Oh, I am wicked, wicked, she told herself, and wished she could run away, go home, hide anywhere. And she could never speak of it, nor had Ralph mentioned the subject since that one moment in the dark when he tried to make her understand. She could never ask advice, for one didn't talk of such intimacies. She had chosen to accept Ralph and must now make the very best of it that she could. But oh, Freddy, Freddy, she murmured to the busy street outside, how could you have driven me to this? And she still loved him, would always love him.

However, Martin's teaching and example had not been in vain. She straightened herself. Given that one area in which she could not please him, in every other she would try to be all her husband wanted, and that at least would be no lie, for she liked his companionship, shared his tastes. It had to be enough.

When he came in a few minutes later she turned to him with a smile and said, "How I'm looking forward to a ride. Did you find suitable horses?"

"Fair enough," he said. "Not perhaps up to Blanche and Centaur, but they should give us a good outing. Shall we go?" She took his proferred arm and they went out together into the sunlit courtyard where Willis was holding a roan and a chestnut ready for them, the roan with a side saddle. It was going to be a perfect day, she thought.

They rode out of the city and into the blue hills. The whole panorama of Italian scenery unfolded before them: pine trees, groves of shady oaks, lush valleys, hillsides covered with olive trees and vines, small white farms, peasants working in the fields. One or two men touched their hats as they passed, women with washing baskets or gathering vegetables turned to stare at them, children stood gaping. Here and there was a little Romanesque church, sometimes a wayside Calvary.

"How I wish Papa could see all this." she said. "He would love Italy, all the art and the buildings and these beautiful old churches."

Ralph was watching her. "You are enjoying it, aren't you?"

"Oh, yes, indeed," she smiled across at him in genuine pleasure. "So much, Ralph. You've given me a tour I shall never forget."

"I'm glad," he said, "but I wonder now if even you have had enough of picture galleries and museums."

"Oh dear," she laughed, "have I been so tiresome, wanting to see everything?"

"Insatiable," he teased her, "but I must admit that twice round the one yesterday began to pall a little. Never mind, we go to the Blakes tomorrow and I shall have some respite. It will be good to see my friend Harry again."

He seemed to have a gift for friendship, she thought, for he had innumerable friends. "It will be nice to stay in their villa," she agreed. "It's very hot. I wonder if there is anywhere we could get some refreshment?"

He pointed to a small white-washed farmhouse. "Shall we try there?" They rode up to it, hens and ducks scuttling away, and he spoke to the woman sitting on a stool at a table out of doors and cutting up onions, a baby in a cradle beside her.

The table was in the shade of a big leafy oak and they sat down there to a luncheon of bread and an unusual cheese, with olives and a rich dark wine.

"This is delicious," Maeve said, sipping it. "I shall have a lot to tell them in my next letter home. What a darling baby."

He looked at the cradle and then at Maeve, but all he said

was, "You will have written a book, I shouldn't wonder, by the time we get back. I'm sure your letters have gone all round your family."

There was a little edge to his tone, but she was not aware of it, watching a two-year-old boy playing with a long-suffering dog of indefinable breed. "I'm grateful that you've done the same for my mother," he went on. "She will have enjoyed hearing from you. I'm afraid I've not been much of a letter-writer over the years. One of those things one is always going to do tomorrow, but now I've got you to do it for me."

"I like writing to them all. What a view." It lay stretched out before them – green hillsides, a river winding away below, cultivated fields, all tranquil in the early summer warmth. They sat in quiet content, finishing their wine. The woman did not want to accept any money, but Ralph insisted, leaving some coins on the table. "For the *bambini*," he said. He collected the horses and, cupping his hands, threw his wife up into the saddle. She was in so many ways the perfect companion, and impulsively he reached out his hand. "I shall remember this place."

"So will I," she answered at once, but her eyes were on the distant blue hills and she did not see the proferred hand. He withdrew it and put the reins into hers. And there their perfect day ended.

They had not gone a mile when they came upon an ugly scene. Two men were trying to get a horse to pull a loaded cart up the hill. The wretched animal was emaciated, its head drooping, legs scarcely able to bear even its paltry weight, its rib cage standing out like a skeleton's. One of the men was tugging mercilessly at the rough rope bridle while the other, sitting on the cart, was raining blows on it with a whip.

"Oh!" Maeve said in horror. "How can they? The poor beast can't pull that cart, it's half dead."

"Bastards!" Ralph said under his breath. "Damned bastards." He swung himself out of the saddle, threw his reins to Maeve, and with a sharp command of, "Stay here. Leave this to me," strode over to the cart. The men had turned in surprise at seeing him dismount, the one in front pausing in his efforts to force the trembling animal up the hill.

"*Fernati*," he commanded, "*Fernati, dannato!*" They took

no notice and he raised his voice. "*Lascie stare la povera bestia, miserabile codardo!*"

They stared at him. They were both very dark, unshaven and wearing breeches and torn dirty shirts, so alike it was clear they must be brothers. The one at the head gave a derisive laugh at this interfering stranger and, ignoring Ralph's order to stop, went back to his efforts. The horse's mouth was torn and bleeding. With a smothered curse Ralph caught him by the shoulders, swung him round and dealt him a swift left to the jaw. The fellow went down without a sound while the horse, released, collapsed in the shafts, its pathetic legs giving way so that it was half-suspended by the leathers. Ralph bent over it, looking at the rolling eyes. The animal was in obvious agony and he drew the pistol he always carried out of his pocket to make an end.

The other man had given a screech and now he leapt down from the cart, lashing out with his whip at Ralph. Seizing it, Ralph wrenched it away with his left hand, his attention on the dying beast, the pistol levelled. The man, pulled over by the force of Ralph's action, fell against the shaft and steadied himself. It was then that Maeve saw his hand go to his belt and the gleam of the knife. Abandoning Ralph's horse, which promptly took to its heels, she spurred forward, raising her crop and striking his assailant across the side of the face. He swore and launched himself at her, scrabbling at her skirts to pull her down. Nearly losing her balance, she had some trouble controlling her frightened horse. Ralph thrust the pistol away and in two strides was beside her, seizing the Italian from behind. He forced the threatening hand across the man's back until the knife fell from limp fingers.

Then Ralph flung him away with such force that he was thrown against one of the wheels. His brother was recovering now, rubbing his jaw and eyeing Ralph with some caution. Maeve calmed her horse and with one not too pleasant glance at her to assure himself she was unhurt, Ralph went back to the cart horse.

It was not quite dead and without hesitation he cocked his pistol and finished the business, the shot echoing over the hillside. He then turned on the men and in a flow of Italian told them what he thought of them, their cruelty and stupidity, and their general unfitness to be part of the human race.

The one who had fallen against the wheel staggered up and screamed abuse at him, gesticulating and pointing at the dead beast. Ralph put his hand in his pocket and pulled out a few coins which he threw on the ground. "Buy a new animal," he said sternly. "Treat it properly and it will serve you better."

The men shuffled their feet in the dusty road, standing together muttering and staring at him, aware of the pistol still in his hand. He was coolly re-loading it. Then they looked at the dead horse, a crop of flies already at its nose. Shrugging, they bent down and gathered up the money before running off, presumably to find another animal to pull their cart.

The angry red light was still in Ralph's eyes. "Where the devil's my horse?" he demanded in the voice she had first heard in the churchyard nearly a year ago.

"I'm afraid I let her go when I –"

"When you interfered, quite unnecessarily. Do you expect me to walk back to Rome?"

"No, I – I see it was careless of me."

"Careless?" He put a wealth of scorn into that one word.

"I'm so sorry. Perhaps I can find her." She glanced all round but there was no sign of the livery horse. Then she felt the reins wrenched out of her hand.

"Thanks to you, I shall have to ride pillion back to Rome. Very dignified, I must say." Suddenly he turned on her. "How dared you? How dared you disobey me? I told you to stay where you were."

Shaken by his vehemence, she retorted. "I saw the knife – you had your back to him."

"I was quite aware of him. Great God, do you think I can't deal with a pair of scum like that?"

"I'm sure you can." she said sharply, "but I was not going to sit there and see you knifed in the back."

"That would not have happened," he said crushingly, "but coming into it as you did, you could have been badly hurt. He nearly had you off. And learn this, Maeve, I will be obeyed."

She was now almost as angry as he was. "Don't be so absurd, Ralph. Do you think I'm such a ninny that I'd sit there without coming to your aid? I brought up a weal on that man's face that he won't lose for a while."

"Oh, no doubt you think very well of yourself, but it is beside the point. If I give you an order like that, you are to obey me – do you understand?"

She was struggling with indignation, surprise and resentment. "I see! You are going to turn into an unreasonable tyrannical husband. Do you imagine I have no will of my own?"

"No, I don't think that for a moment," he retorted, "but, by God, my girl, I am going to master you as I once told you I would master the black stallion. Do you remember that? You would do well to do so."

She looked at him in disgust. "Now you are being coarse. Or do you think you are a mediaeval baron? I believe they beat their wives and chained them up if they'd a mind. No doubt you would like that."

"Now it is you who are being ridiculous."

She hardly heard him. "I suppose you want to turn me into a 'yes, Ralph, no, Ralph' prissy sort of wife. Well, I'll not."

"Of course I don't want that," he said roughly, "and you know it. Your spirit is what I've always liked about you. But when I give you a direct order, you will obey me. Is that quite clear?"

She flushed. "You make me almost wish I'd let you be knifed in the back."

They faced each other in the hot dusty road.

"Oh," She put a hand to her mouth. "I didn't mean to say that, really I didn't."

"I wonder," he said slowly. "The truth comes out when we are in a heat. Would you have minded too much?"

"Ralph! You are being unjust, hateful. After these months together, how can you say such a thing to me?"

"No, I suppose that was unfair." But he added, "Anyway it wouldn't have availed you anything, would it?"

She stared at him. "What can you mean by that?"

"Nothing – nothing." He turned his head away, looking at the city of Rome lying below them. "For God's sake, let's forget the whole damned, ridiculous business."

"Willingly," she agreed coldly. With one swift movement,

surprisingly easy for so big a man, he vaulted up behind her, put his arms on either side of her to hold the reins, while she sat, conscious of her uselessness. It was a silent, ignominious ride back to Rome where they found Ralph's horse returned to its stable to the consternation of the livery man.

Dinner was a chilly affair and he did not make love to her that night. Their first quarrel, she thought, lying in the dark, barely able to hear his quiet breathing and wondering if he was asleep. If he was, he didn't deserve to be while she lay here, too annoyed and irritated for any rest.

It was her duty to obey her husband, of course it was, but she had a will of her own – a spirit that he said he liked – and she was glad he knew it. At the same time she could not deny a certain admiration at the way he had dealt with the situation. Many men, foreigners in a strange land, would simply have ridden past and conversed on the cruelty of the wretched peasants, but Ralph had not done that. He had reacted as she would have had him do, and she wished he had not been so angry with her for what were after all the best of intentions.

Her own motives she didn't subject to scrutiny, other than thinking she would have done the same whoever had been her companion. He was unjust and heavy-handed and she finally fell asleep, still very much put out.

In the morning she woke to find him lying looking at her. Half asleep, she said impulsively, "Ralph – are you still very angry with me?"

He leaned up on one elbow and with the other hand touched her cheek. "It was only my care for you, you know. And it was your fault we had to come back in that stupid fashion."

"Oh, yes, and I am sorry. Sometimes I think I don't deserve the care you give me." She felt a sudden desire to weep.

Quietly he said, "Why should you not? Is there any reason for that remark?"

"No." She thrust the question away. "This tour, the lovely places we've seen – you've been so good to me."

"You have been a companion such as I never hoped to find." he said. "Yesterday's incident was, shall we say, unfortunate. Or perhaps not. Perhaps it has taught us something about each other."

She gave him a little smile. "Maybe. It might have been better if you had wed me when I was seventeen, before I formed such bad habits of independence."

He looked down at her, a grave expression on his face, not taking the remark lightly. "If you had been seventeen I doubt if I would have seen the qualities that come with a little experience of life, the qualities that made me ask for you."

She gazed back at him, unable to read his expression. "Then I must assume you knew what you were doing and so should take me as I am."

"On my own head be it, eh?"

"Well," she said honestly, "I think if you had been a youth I might not have taken you. I'm sure at that stage, before you mastered it as you want to master so much else, you must have been subject to abominable fits of temper!" She was half laughing up at him, but to her astonishment his face changed utterly.

He had been reaching for her, to put his arms about her and his mouth to hers, but he withdrew at once, and turning his back got out of bed.

"It is time we dressed for breakfast," he said in his hardest tone, but before he got as far as the adjoining dressing room she sat up, exclaiming, "Ralph, what is it? What did I say that was so dreadful? I only meant it in fun."

"It's nothing." He threw the words over his shoulder. "I'll ring for Gracie."

The door shut, she lay back in bewilderment. What could have upset him so much? Something to do with his temper? Had he done something in the past because of it? Perhaps during his first marriage, intuition suggested. And what had he meant by his innuendo that she might not have cared if he had been knifed? Did he know, could be suspect anything, guess that her feelings for Freddy had been warmer than those of a cousin? For the first time she faced the fact that he must know at least something – it would account for a lot.

When Gracie appeared she dressed for the journey south to the Blakes' house and then went slowly down the stairs. He was waiting for her in the hall and in silence gave her his arm into the dining room.

By great good fortune a letter which had finally caught up

with them was brought in to engage their attention.

"It's from George," he said in his usual tones as he scanned the neatly written sheets. "He says Prinny, I mean His Majesty, is going to be at Brighton by August and plans to stay several months. A good company will be there and he suggests we might like to take a house in the town for a while. What do you think? We were planning to return to England after visiting the Blakes, weren't we?"

"I should like it very much," Maeve said, following his lead and ignoring both yesterday's quarrel and this morning's words. "But ought we not to spend a little while with your mother first?"

"I thought of that. We could be home some time in July and stay at Welford for two or three weeks, seeing your family as well. You will want to visit your sister. She must be near her time."

"If the baby had not arrived by then," Maeve said gaily. "It will be so good to see them all again."

He said he would set the matter in hand. They conversed, if a little stiltedly, over their coffee and rolls and afterwards Ralph disappeared. Maeve wondered where he had gone but went upstairs and was busy for a while, supervising her packing, though by now Gracie had become very good at this.

In the carriage as they left the city Ralph silently held out a small package. When she opened it, she saw it contained one of the most beautiful brooches she had ever seen, a sparkling sapphire in the centre surrounded by intricate gold filigree work. She hardly knew what to say and felt her eyes fill. "Oh, Ralph!"

"A peace-offering," he said, and his mouth curled. "Am I forgiven for what you rightly called my abominable ill-temper?"

"I should not have said what I did," she answered. "I don't know what is worse, a lovers' quarrel when one is seventeen or the arguments of two people who are set in their ways."

He looked out of the window at a grove of cedar trees. "I suppose we must learn to bear with each other's foibles."

"Yes," she said. "If we don't, it mustn't be for the want of trying, must it?"

"No," he agreed. "And I think we must allow each other to bury our separate pasts."

A little silence fell. Maeve remembered what he had said when he had proposed to her; "I have not reached thirty-five without having a few secrets." Which, he implied now, she had too.

She sat turning the brooch in her hand, and then with a little smile said, "Perhaps it should have been in the shape of an olive branch."

He laughed in response, but it seemed to her that an indefinable barrier had risen between them, its limits clearly set.

Chapter 11

William Hollander, coming in with a gun under his arm and a springer spaniel, Lasher, at his heels, had enjoyed the morning's shooting. No one recalled quite how Lasher had got his name but he was an offspring of Sir Thomas's dog Rigger and a bitch of Obadiah's, and has proved himself an obedient and diligent animal. The library door was open and Lasher pricked up his ears and barked. A visitor, William thought, and raised an eyebrow as his footman appeared and said, "Sir Ralph Digby, sir, and Lady Digby has gone up to see Madam."

William nodded and handed over his gun. "Put that in the gunroom, Parker. I'll clean it later."

He went in, Lasher trotting after him. The next minute he was wringing his brother-in-law's hand, while the dog leapt up and down in great excitement. "Down," William said sternly. "Ralph, my dear fellow. Down, Lasher. This dog can't distinguish friend from foe. In fact, he thinks all the world his friend, which is good news for troublesome poachers. When did you get home?"

"Last night," Ralph said, "and nothing would do for Maeve but to come straight over this morning and see her sister. My mother tells me that you are to be congratulated."

"Yes, a fine boy, thank God, born three weeks ago. But sit down and take a glass of sherry. I gather Maeve is upstairs."

Ralph accepted the glass and they sat by the open window, the summer garden full of colour. "She went straight up. I hope all went well?"

"No trouble at all." William stretched his booted legs in

front of him in a satisfied manner, Lasher settling at his side, his eyes fixed on the newcomer. "I'm glad you are home. We postponed the christening in the hope you'd soon be here. We thought of calling him William Ralph, and hoped you'd stand godfather."

Ralph could not help but be gratified and accepted with pleasure.

"The other godfather is to be my brother Lionel whom you've yet to meet. It will be some time before he is in home waters again, perhaps next summer. That's what comes of being a sailor. I would like you to see him – he's the walking image of our father. Tell me about your trip. Maeve's letters have been quite graphic!"

Upstairs Maeve was sitting on the window seat in her sister's bedroom. Mary was up and dressed and determined to go down on the morrow, but now she settled for the luxury of a few moments alone with her sister. "I want to know all about your travels."

Maeve laughed. "Oh, we had a wonderful trip but I am sure my letter told you most of it."

"Not quite perhaps?"

"It was a journey I shall remember all my life. Such wonderful places, so much more than what one gets from books. Ralph assures me we shall go abroad again, but in the meantime we are going to Brighton. Ralph has taken a house there as the King will be at the Royal Pavilion, and Colonel FitzClarence and quite a company, I gather."

"You will meet the King? How exciting."

"I never guessed when we first knew Ralph that his closest friend was the King's nephew, nor that he moved in such circles, though I do remember Miss Mufferton saying something about it. But she is such a gossip I didn't set too much store on it. It is very good of you to give the baby Ralph's name and ask him to stand godfather. My mother-in-law will be so pleased."

"I hope you will soon have a baby of your own – that will give her the greatest pleasure. Are you – ?"

"Not yet," Maeve said swiftly. "No doubt it will happen sometime." She changed the subject. There were some things she did not want to confide, even to Mary. "But I must tell you about Paris."

"Yes, but later." Mary was not so easily to be put off. "Angela shows no sign of anything yet either. I'm sure Freddy must be very disappointed. He does so want an heir." She looked closely at her sister. "You look very well. You are happy, aren't you, dearest?"

"Of course. All that sunshine and warmth was so delightful. Ralph had arranged everything so well."

"That brooch, did he give you that?"

"Yes, in Rome. He really is ridiculously extravagant, but it was after we'd had a – a stupid quarrel."

"Oh, dear." Mary tried to think if she had ever had a quarrel with William. "What was it about?"

"Nothing – at least, nothing much." Maeve hastily diverted the talk from herself and asked when she was going to see her new nephew.

Mary rang the bell and when her maid came, sent her to tell the nurse to bring the children. Annie came with the baby in her arms, Isabel just two holding her hand, little Fred running ahead. Annie had been nurse to Freddy and his brothers, and to Ellen. She was in her forties now and plumper than she used to be, and Mary had said there was no one else to whom she could so happily entrust her children.

Fred hurled himself at his newly returned aunt.

"There, old fellow," she laughed, extricating herself, "Don't strangle me. Goodness, how you've grown. Annie, let me hold the baby."

He was to be called Will, his mother said, so that there shouldn't be any confusion in the house, and Maeve, looking down at the sprinkle of fair hair, said, "I wonder if he'll be like Uncle Tom. He has his colouring." She kissed the top of his head and handed him back to Annie so that she could take the shy Isabel on her knee. After her six months away, Isabel did not seem too sure who her aunt was.

There was a knock on the door and the two men came in. Ralph was shown his godson, while Fred jumped up and down and helpfully acquainted him with the baby's names.

"Ralph is after you, Uncle," he said. "It was a good idea of Papa's, wasn't it?"

"Very good," Ralph said gravely. "It quite makes me one of the family, doesn't it?"

"Oh, yes," Fred agreed and took his hand. "A proper uncle, not one of those we call uncle just because it is polite."

This drew a laugh and then, as Master Will seemed disposed to cry, Annie took the children away and Ralph said, "You have a splendid family there, worthy of the Monarchs!"

Maeve felt a sudden ache of the heart – she knew only too well what Ralph wanted and she avoided her sister's eye, saying after a few moments that they should ride over to the Vicarage.

This brought another happy reunion, Nell delighted at her daughter's bright looks, and in a brief private moment Martin said "I can see matrimony is suiting you both. Is all well, dearest?"

She gave him a quick kiss and said, "Oh yes, indeed, Papa. Ralph is the most thoughtful of men." But she hadn't said what he wanted to know. Not yet, he told himself, and prayed that it would come.

Nell had no such doubts. "You were right," she said to him that night. "They both look so – so content. I am so glad she has realised that her feeling for Freddy was just a youthful fancy." Leaving Martin wishing he could agree more wholeheartedly with her, though he kept this to himself. Three days later, when it was considered that Mary could make the short journey, there was a family dinner party at Hollanders House. Isabel was out of full mourning now and wearing a grey silk gown though her cap was still of black lace. She was back in the saddle most days and after no more than a few minutes Maeve could see that all her old vigour was present, that she still presided over the household, and that there was a sulky look on Angela's face.

Freddy was his usual self, cheerful and extrovert, in his element playing host to the assembled family. The only person absent was Lady Digby who had a head cold, and though disposed to come had for once listed to Mufti's earnest entreaty that she should stay indoors – or perhaps it was that she rather enjoyed acceding to the advice of her new daughter-in-law. Outside the family the only others present were the Rokebys who were considered almost as relatives.

The talk was at first of the wedding trip, both Ralph and

Maeve describing the places they had visited, ending with the very agreeable visit to the Blakes.

"Their house is quite delightful," Maeve said, "all white and looking out to sea, with pine trees on the hillside and so many flowers in the garden. I wish I was an artist. Do you remember, Mama, how Mr Hebden from Rye tried so hard to teach me to draw and I was such a dunce?"

Nell laughed. "I'm afraid you were. The artistic talent in this family all went to William."

"That picture you brought us is quite beautiful," he said. "We've hung it in the parlour. You must come and see it, Mama."

"And now we are going to the sea again," Maeve said. "Ralph's man of business, Mr Harding, wrote this morning to say he had leased a house for us in Brighton for three months, and Mr Flint is going down to set all in order."

Ralph added, "His Majesty is to be there soon and we are to be invited to the Royal Pavilion. Colonel FitzClarence and his wife have already gone down and I understand the Russian Ambassador and his wife Princess Dorothea are coming, Lord Sefton too, Mr Creevey of course, and the Duke of Wellington is expected."

Freddy leapt on the words. "The Beau will be there? By Jove, how I would like to meet him. He's every soldier's model of what one should be." He barely paused before being struck with an idea. "Ralph, old fellow, do you think Angela and I might join you for a while? If there is room in your house, of course?"

"I believe there are half a dozen bedrooms," Ralph said in a voice devoid of expression.

"Well then, what could be nicer? Angela, my love, would you like it? If the King is to be in residence at the Pavilion I'm sure Ralph could procure us an invitation. What do you think?"

There was no doubt about Angela's response for her face lit up when he mentioned the King. "I should like it above all things. There will be so much society there, won't there?"

Freddy turned, smiling, to Ralph. "Well, what do you say? Maeve?"

There was nothing they could do but agree. Ralph's face revealed only polite acceptance but Maeve, giving him a quick glance, wondered how much the idea pleased him. It was the last thing she wanted. The thought of Freddy under her roof was dreadfully disturbing, and accompanied by Angela, even worse. But she would have to play hostess and in the face of Angela's obvious wish to join them – or even more, Maeve suspected, to get away from Hollanders for a while – she would have to endure it.

When the ladies had withdrawn to the parlour Angela contrived to sit beside her while Lady Hollander was busy with the tea tray.

"I am so glad," she began confidentially, "I'm sure we shall enjoy it a great deal. It's quite the best thing since I came to England."

"Aren't you happy here? I thought you might be more settled by this time?" But settled might have meant pregnant and Maeve was guiltily aware that she did not want to see Angela big with Freddy's child, the next moment despising herself for the thought.

Angela was shrugging her shoulders "Oh, it is so much more boring that I expected. Your mother is kind to me and sometimes takes me with her when she goes parish visiting but it is hardly entertaining. Everyone seems to have something to do except me. I do sometimes write letters to one or two friends in India but that doesn't take up much of my time."

Maeve pitied her. For herself she had never been bored. There was seldom enough time in the day to do all the things she wanted to do, and as for parish visiting, she had always liked to see the village families, knowing all their joys and troubles and helping where she could. And there was always riding on the Marsh, something Angela didn't appear to want to do. She asked her if she liked reading, suggesting Miss Austen's works, several of which were on the shelves in the study. "And my mother-in-law has just given me a copy of Sir Walter Scott's latest novel, *Woodstock*. I'm sure you would like that."

Angela yawned. "I tire of reading after about a quarter of an hour. We went to London in the spring and that was very pleasant. There were parties and balls and drives in the park. Freddy went to his grandfather's gentleman's club and made some acquaintances as well as meeting one or two fellow officers, and that led to other things so we went about a lot. But after only a few weeks he insisted that we come back for something or other he had to do. He's a councillor now in Rye, only they call them something else."

"Jurats."

"Yes, that's the word. He seems to like it, and Rye too, though I think it is a steep pokey little town without any interesting shops."

"I'm sorry you don't find it pleasant," Maeve was beginning, but hardly pausing Angela went on, "Still, I'm sure I shall like Brighton and going to the King's court. Have you seen him? What is he like?"

"Very fat and elderly now, "Maeve told her, "but he likes music, Ralph says, and lively conversation in the evenings." Her misgivings about the visit of Freddy and Angela to their house increased and she wondered how Ralph was taking the assumption that he would procure them an invitation to the Pavilion.

"It's very good of you," Isabel Hollander said later when she and Maeve were briefly alone on one side of the room. "Really, I don't know what to do with the girl. I can't find occupations she likes, nor can I play cards or Chinese Checkers, which she seems to have a passion for, during the day. I have far too much to do. It is a great pity she doesn't like riding. There's no sign of a child yet, more's the pity." Her eyes flickered over Maeve's neat figure and when she shook her head Isabel added, "Well, there's plenty of time." She smiled at her niece. "How very elegant you look. That is a charming gown. French, I'll wager?"

In the carriage going home to Welford, Maeve said tentatively, "Did you mind Freddy inviting himself and Angela to stay with us in Brighton?"

"I? Why should I?" Ralph's tone told her nothing and she could not read his face in the dark. "Did you mind?"

"Oh, no." She turned her own face away towards the window. "Though I hope it won't be for a little while."

"Freddy told me after you ladies had gone upstairs that he couldn't get away for a week or two."

"I'm glad of that – I mean, we shall have time to get settled in," she added hastily. "I don't find Angela the easiest person in the world."

"Whereas you've known Freddy all your life," he said drily. "I wonder quite why he married her."

Shaken momentarily by his words she could think of nothing to say, and it was he who went on, "I can see the attraction of course – she's amazingly beautiful – but the mixed blood shows and I cannot see that they have the least thing in common to make for a comfortable union."

"The same thing crossed my mind," she agreed, able to talk of it a little more collectedly, "and I know Aunt Isabel feels the same. I think she will be quite glad to have Angela off her hands for a while."

"It has hardly been easy for anyone," he said – another of his remarks that made her feel uneasy. He added, "Your aunt is a splendid person and I admire her very much but I can't help feeling it might be better for that girl if Lady Hollander would step down a little, or even retire to a small house in the village. Though I can't see her doing that!"

"Neither can I," Maeve agreed with some amusement, but the thought of the forthcoming visit was disturbing.

Ralph said as much to his mother later when Maeve had gone to bed and he lingered in Lady Digby's room.

"Don't you think, after your long wedding tour, that she has got him out of her head?" she asked.

He stared broodingly as if he was not really seeing her. "I wish I knew. Even if she has, I know I've not yet filled his place."

"Oh, my dear." Lady Digby was very much concerned. "Are you sure? You seem so content together."

"I think we are," he agreed, "but there are certain bounds – I very much hope – am I being conceited if I say that I hope that a few weeks of Hollander and his wife in the same house will convince Maeve that I am the better husband for her?"

"Not conceited, honest," his mother said. "Did I tell you that Selena expects to be home shortly. Her husband has been recalled. I very much hope she and Maeve will get along together."

"Selena coming? I shall be glad for them to meet. But I do beg you, my dear mother, to say nothing of all this to her."

"As if," his mother retorted, "I should do anything so stupid!"

160

The house on Marine Parade, facing out to sea, was among the handsome new buildings which had sprung up when Brighthelmstone, a simple fishing village, became Brighton and a fashionable seaside resort.

"All due to Prinny and Mrs Fitzherbert, of course," Ralph said. "We only caught a glimpse of it as we came in but I thought tomorrow we would take a walk about the town."

"The Pavilion seems an extraordinary place."

"It is, I promise you that! Now I'll leave you to talk to Mrs Gibson while I see Flint."

The housekeeper from the Bruton Street house had come down three days ago to see that everything was in readiness and had engaged further staff above those she had brought with her. Maeve, inspecting the house from top to bottom, found her a stiff woman, obviously inclined to be suspicious of a new young mistress. However, by the time that they had looked into the bedrooms, Maeve acceding to the suggestion that she should have the largest facing the sea, the dining room which could seat at least sixteen, and a spacious parlour, she had shown herself interested in every aspect of running the house while at the same time making it clear that she trusted Mrs Gibson to know her business.

She did not go down to the kitchen which, like many, was below stairs, but merely said, "I'm sure I can leave all that side of things to you, Mrs Gibson. You will know all Sir Ralph's likes and dislikes."

The housekeeper unbent so far as to say, "And pray let me know yours, your ladyship."

"None in particular," Maeve said, "though I'm not fond of a large breakfast. I like good fresh bread, for I often made the bread at home and was considered a very passable baker."

Mrs Gibson looked pleased and confided later to Mr Flint that she liked a lady who was not above understanding good housewifery. "Of course," she added, "you will understand, ma'am, that the house in London is far superior to this in its facilities, but if you and Sir Ralph entertain, as I'm sure you will, we'll do our best."

Maeve gave her a warm smile. "I'm sure you will. You and Mr Flint know how Sir Ralph likes things done."

"Yes, your ladyship," Mrs Gibson agreed. She would have no trouble with young Lady Digby.

Over what turned out to be a very good dinner, Ralph said that Mr Flint had informed him that the King was believed to be arriving the day after tomorrow.

"I think I shall be a little nervous meeting him," she said.

"Oh, Prinny is very amiable and he likes a pretty woman," he smiled across at her," though I must say not all his mistresses have been remarkable for their beauty. Lady Jersey was, and still is, an attractive creature – but more because of her vitality than her looks. Lady Hertford I never cared for. The odd thing about Prinny is that he has always seemed to be genuinely fond of them all, even when long discarded. It is hard to understand the appeal of the present occupant of that position."

"Oh? Who is that?"

"Lady Conyngham. Not a brain in her head, only a hand held out for the next diamond necklace, and two mountains to put it on."

"Ralph!"

He grinned at her. "That was not original. I forget who said it but it's very apt. So was old Sheridan's remark that he was too much a ladies' man to be a man for one lady – certainly not for Queen Caroline. She never washed, you know, and was very coarse. She could behave like a fishwife, and frequently did! After meeting her for the first time, he hastily retired to his own room and demanded a brandy."

"I didn't know she was like that."

"It was the shortest cohabitation in history," he said drily, "and fortunate for him that she produced from it the Princess Charlotte, a delightful girl. We were all so saddened when she died. I'm afraid Prinny will have no heir but his brother York."

"Will we see some of the Royal dukes?"

"I doubt if York will come down, he's been in poor health for some time. Cumberland, who is quite abominable, is, thank God, in Hanover. Sussex may be here, a pleasant enough little fellow, and as George is coming, it's possible his father may come down. Clarence was a sailor and is something of a buffoon with quarter-deck language at times, but good enough at heart. You will like his duchess."

"Lady FitzClarence told me how kind she is to all the Duke's children by –"

"Mrs Jordan, the actress? Yes, she is. No beauty but a thoroughly nice woman. It's a pity George and his father don't get on better!"

"Oh?" Maeve was fascinated by all this. "Why don't they?"

"Well, the Duke has ten of them to support – no, nine, since poor Henry died in India – and George does like to live up to what he considers his birth entitles him to, even if it was on the wrong side of the blanket. He's always inclined to extravagance and his being in debt most of the time is a bone of contention between them. He borrows a little too freely, poor old George."

"Does he owe you money?" Maeve asked, and instantly wished she hadn't for at once he answered, "That's a matter between gentlemen, my dear, and need not concern you."

"No," she said at once. "You are quite right, Ralph."

At that moment the bell rang. "Talk of the devil," he exclaimed. "It can only be George. No one else knows when we were arriving."

It was indeed Colonel FitzClarence, not in uniform but in evening clothes, and he brought with him a gold-embossed invitation from his uncle the King that they should dine and attend a concert at the Pavilion on Friday evening. "He'll be here on Thursday," he said, and added to Maeve, "I'm sure you will never have seen anything like my uncle's taste in building. It is bizarre, to say the least, not at all like Carlton House before the fire ruined it, or any of the other London buildings he has had a hand in. Are you satisfied with this house? Your man was lucky to find it. I believe Lambton offered for it and then cried off because of his gout. At any rate, he's not here."

"It seems very suitable," she said. "I'm so glad you and Lady Mary are here, Colonel. It will be nice to see one or two familiar faces when we go to the Pavilion."

"Oh, you will see more, I'm sure. Lord and Lady Sefton, whom you met at Welford, are here, the Millbankes, and of course Mr Creevey."

She laughed. "I love the way everyone always says 'and of course Mr Creevey'."

"Well, he is somewhat ubiquitous. One certainly expects to trip over him somewhere or other."

Ralph leaned over to pour wine into a glass for his guest. "Well, George, what's the news in town? We are very much out of touch."

"Let me think." The Colonel sipped his wine with a connoisseur's air. "Now I wonder where Flint found this? I could do with a dozen or so in my cellar. Let me think – Charles FitzRoy is to marry Miss Cavendish. Well, they're welcome to each other, no humour either of them, but she must be worth forty thousand. My sister Elizabeth seems to be very happy with Errol, they married in the spring, you know. My father's new house near St James's is all but finished, to be known as Clarence House of course, but he still likes the unpretentious place at Bushey best. He's here with my step-mother. The Conyngham has come, another 'of course', but whether her husband came with her I don't know. Poor fellow, no one notices him. The Broughams are not here, he's tied up with some legal business. Just as well, he's been in bad odour ever since he defended Queen Caroline in that absurd divorce case. Count Lieven is here with Princess Dorothea; she's a deuced pretty woman. York's too unwell to make the journey, his doctors don't expect him to last many months."

"That will change your father's prospects," Ralph remarked drily.

"Won't it just?" George's face lit for a moment. "Liverpool's ill too. It's thought Canning might head the next Government, but the King don't like him above half." He rose. "Mary told me to ask you if you would dine with us tomorrow? You will? Good. By the way, Dig, there will be several of your friends gathering at the Old Ship tonight. Do you remember Captain MacDonald? Yes, I thought you would. He's stationed at the cavalry barracks on the Lewes Road. It's his birthday and I'm sure he'd be glad to see you – unless you'd rather not come out after your journey?"

"Oh, I'll come," Ralph said, "and drink his health with the rest of you."

When George had gone, Maeve said, "I'm so glad he and Lady Mary are here."

Ralph emptied his glass. "You must be prepared to see the company at the Pavilion somewhat more easy-going than you are used to. I know the country has its wild sparks and its scandals, but I think you will find the court more outspoken."

"I've never had my eyes shut to what goes on," she retorted, a little defensively. "My own father hardly lived an unblemished life. In fact, he caused a great deal of scandal, and his reputation in his last years hardly bore looking into." She paused and saw Ralph looking at her as if he expected her to say more, but she decided this was not the moment. He was going to be angry enough when, or hopefully 'if', he found out about Jacob Hatch. She wished she had cleared that matter up a lot earlier, but it was not something she was proud of.

"Well," Ralph said, as she did not elaborate, "you will have to get used to the complicated business of relationships. The Duke of Devonshire has children by his wife, and by Lady Elizabeth Forster, plus one the Duchess had by Lord Grey, all growing up together in Devonshire House but with different surnames. As someone once said, 'The vices are wonderfully prolific among the Whigs!'"

She was lightly shocked by this, it was rather more blatant than she had expected. "Well," she said at last, "One can't help but think such licence is hardly exemplary."

"Don't be parochial, my love. It won't do at court."

She was annoyed. "I never thought myself parochial, as you call it, but maybe I am. I wonder you did not remark it before. After all, you found me in a vicarage, didn't you?"

"I was using the word in its broader sense," he said coolly.

"But I thought you were accusing me of being narrow?"

He paused, his hand on the back of his chair. "Are you trying to quarrel with me, Maeve?"

"No," she said swiftly, "it was you who called me parochial."

"Which clearly you didn't like. I apologise. Now I think I'll stroll down to the Ship and see who is there to toast MacDonald. I hope you won't mind a solitary evening?"

"Not in the least. I am not so simple that I would expect you to stay at home every evening that we are not going out together. And I have plenty to do."

But when he had gone she began to wonder if it was to be the pattern of things to come. They were no longer on their wedding trip.

He came in very late. She was almost asleep but she heard him moving about in his dressing room, knocking something over, and once his voice, rather slurred, saying, "Damn you, Bridges, leave that till morning." She heard his valet depart, the door shutting, and then there was silence. He did not come through the intervening door to share her bed. Why, he's drunk, she thought. And then commonsense told her that men were in the habit of drinking deep among their own friends. Ralph had obviously met some at the Old Ship.

Chapter 12

In the morning she dressed in her prettiest cotton print dress and went downstairs to breakfast. Ralph was not there and as she drank her coffee and ate her rolls – freshly baked and up to her standard – she wondered if he had forgotten they were to go out together and found something else to do. But a quarter of an hour later he came in, everything neat about his clothes as usual, and sat down opposite her, looking none the worse for last night's carousing.

"It's a fine morning," was his opening remark. "Are you ready for a walk about the town?"

"Yes, indeed." She glanced across at him. "Did you have pleasant evening with your friends?"

"Very convivial. I'm afraid I was late home. I hope I didn't disturb you?"

"I heard you come into your dressing room."

"I'm sorry. One tends to get clumsy in one's cups. But it was good to see so many old friends. "He saw no necessity for any further comment on the matter and went on to talk of the acquaintances he had met, and as soon as he had finished suggested she fetched her bonnet.

Their house was at the beginning of Marine Parade so they were quickly down the slope and Ralph pointed out the Chain Pier.

"It was finished three years ago," he told her, "when Prinny came down occasionally to walk on it, but it's beyond him now, and so is sea-bathing, though he used to bathe whenever he was here."

She watched, fascinated, as two ladies in enveloping

costumes with frilly caps on their heads emerged from the door of one of the peculiar huts on wheels, drawn by horses to the water's edge. They stepped into the softly lapping waves with little shrieks at the coldness of it, splashing each other and apparently enjoying themselves hugely.

"It must be very refreshing on such a warm day," she said enviously. "I've never seen it done before."

"I'll arrange it for you," Ralph said. "But I must warn you that some of the young blades in the houses on the sea front keep telescopes in their rooms to watch the ladies disporting themselves."

"Should you mind if they did?"

He laughed. "If they find pleasure in seeing my beautiful wife in the waves, why should I? I've been young myself. I shall buy you the appropriate dress, and Gracie shall watch over you, as you must have a companion."

Hog boats were drawn up on to the shingle and nets laid out to dry while men unloaded the morning's catch, and she watched the scene for a few moments. A great many people were promenading by the pier and on it and Ralph suggested they should take a walk on it themselves. It seemed so strange to stand there with only the sea beneath and she said impulsively, "I've seen the sea often enough at home but I never thought of it becoming a pleasure for people to enjoy like this."

He laughed at the wonder on her face and presently led her off and on to the glazed pavement of the Steine. There were more people walking there and in the gardens.

"It's so pretty,' she exclaimed, her hand in the crook of Ralph's arm, "so well laid out. And, oh, how the Pavilion gleams! I've never seen anything so extraordinary."

In the bright sunshine the domes and minarets shone, the pale walls gleaming, and the whole giving the appearance of an eastern palace.

"A monument to the King's idiosyncrasies," Ralph said, "but magnificent in its way. He got the idea from some Chinese wallpaper that was sent to him, and now it's a mixture of Chinese, Moorish, Indian and heaven knows how many other influences as they happened to strike him, but at least it's built of English Bath stone."

"How Freddy will enjoy seeing this," she said impulsively, and added hastily, "and Angela, of course."

She felt rather than saw his quick glace at her, but he went on smoothly, "It was begun by Mr Henry Holland and finished by John Nash. Did ever architects have such fantastic instructions!"

"I do want to see the inside, if it is anything like this."

"Oh, it is. You will see it on Friday. Poor Prinny has been reviled for creating such a monster, but personally I am of the opinion that he will be remembered for it as much as for Buckingham House and his other noble buildings in London. He pays such attention to detail, and I've been there when he's been interviewing decorators and plasterers and upholsterers himself, not considering he could leave that to underlings."

"He sounds very approachable."

"He is, but I'm afraid he's not what he was, though something of the old Prinny is still there. I didn't, of course, know him in his best days but my father did and talked much of him, tales that he kept for after dinner when the ladies had retired!"

As they walked along Ralph was constantly being hailed. "Hallo, Dig old fellow. Where have you sprung from?" This from two young men, while a few yards further on an army officer called out to him and slapped him on the shoulder. Several ladies and gentlemen greeted him and Maeve was introduced to so many people she could not retain all their names.

"That's Donaldson's library." Ralph pointed to an elegant building on their right and led her inside where she gasped at the size of the place and the vast number of books on the shelves. It made Rye library seem a pokey little place. Papers and magazines were spread out on tables and there were plenty of chairs for customers.

"Card parties are held here," Ralph said, "and often concerts. I saw the great Rossini conduct one of his own pieces here two years ago."

The library was full of people coming and going, for it was a great place to meet one's friends, and sure enough they were hailed and turned to see Mr Creevey.

"I am so glad to see you," he said, shaking them both by the hand. "Lady FitzClarence told me you were coming to

Brighton, and I might have guessed, Lady Digby, you being such a great reader, that I would find you here. Where are you staying?"

"We have a house on Marine Parade," Ralph said. "I hope you will do us the honour of calling on us."

"Of course," Creevey said warmly. "That will be a pleasure I'll promise myself. So Sir Ralph is showing you the town, Lady Digby?"

"Yes," she answered, "though we only arrived last night and haven't see much yet."

"I trust you will be going to the Pavilion. I understand his Majesty arrives soon."

"Yes, we expect to be there on Friday evening," Ralph said "Shall we see you then?"

Mr Creevey beamed. "Indeed you will. I am going with Lord Sefton. Poor fellow, he lost his daughter, you know, Lady Georgina, a few months ago. He positively doted on her, and she leaves five young children behind. Poor Grenfell is utterly cast down and Lady Sefton is gone to see the children, poor little mites. But his Majesty so begged Sefton to come for a day or two that he is here. I am spending most of my time with him to try to raise his spirits, but it is a great loss."

"I imagine it must be," Ralph said.

"Well, I mustn't detain you," Mr Creevey added, and then launched into another tale. "You will be delighted with the Pavilion, Lady Digby. I first saw it – oh, twenty years ago, the autumn of the victory at Trafalgar and the loss of poor Nelson. I was out walking with my dear wife, still with me then, and my step daughters here on the Steine when Prinny saw us. He was sitting over there on a bench and talking to old Lady Craven – she's gone now, poor soul – and he beckoned us over. I presented my family and he was most affable, inviting us to the Pavilion, and I think there was scarce a day during our stay when we were not there."

He paused, sighing. "Ah, we were all a lot younger then and he was a positive Prince Charming. You will hear all sorts of bad tales about him, Lady Digby, some of them true, no doubt, and some people call him selfish and he can be heartless, but I can only speak as I find, and I am proud to be one of his friends, for I think I may call myself so. Now I must leave you for I'm sure you are waiting to choose a book and I am going riding with Lady Augusta. I will see you on Friday."

He hurried off and Maeve laughed. "He really is a most amusing man."

"An amiable gossip," Ralph agreed, and added, "I'm sure at least half the tales about the town are spread by Creevey himself but there's no malice in him. It's just that he must be at the heart of everything." They came out of the library and he went on, "The latest that I heard last night concerns him for a change. They are saying that he is in fact Sefton's half brother."

"Oh? How can that be?"

"Well, as you know, the Sefton estate is in Lancashire and Creevey himself comes from Liverpool. Rumour has it that the old Lord Sefton comforted Creevey's mother too well during one of his father's absences. He was a sea captain, so was away a lot. It is a rum tale, but the more one thinks of it, the more likely it seems."

"I'm astonished," she said. "Does he know?"

"I should think so, but one can't tell. Certainly he and Sefton are devoted to each other, or perhaps I should say Creevey is devoted to him and Sefton takes pleasure in bringing him forward. However, there'll be another piece of tattle to eclipse that next week."

They walked on round the Steine to the west side and there Ralph pointed out the stables with its gleaming glass dome topped with a green cupola, and after that a house, white-painted with verandahs, long windows open to the morning air.

"That is Mrs Fitzherbert's home." he said. "It was built for her by Prinny in their happier days so that they could be close together, and she has lived there most of the time since. She is very well liked and respected in Brighton.'

"Poor lady." Maeve surveyed the small and tasteful house. "I have always been sorry for her, though I didn't know much about how it all happened."

"Prinny has always said, despite everything that has happened since their estrangement, that she was the wife of his heart and I believe him. Of course he behaved abominably to her, in his own inimitable manner, while she is a lady without a stain on her character. As she is a Catholic, that wedding conducted in her drawing room was illegal for the heir to the throne – and under age at that. They may have considered themselves married in the sight of God but," he added drily," unluckily for them the law of the land carried more weight."

"He must have truly loved her to have risked so much for her."

"According to his own lights, yes. I must say the Royal family always treated her kindly but it had to be pronounced no marriage, brutally so by Fox in Parliament, for all he was supposed to be one of Prinny's closest friends. And one or two people, including old Lady Sefton, Sefton's mother, chose to cut her. Then they married him off to Caroline of Brunswick and nothing could have been more disastrous."

"Does she still live there?" Maeve gazed but there was no one in sight.

"Yes. I'll take you to call on her sometime for I've known her for many years. She must be seventy now and it's too early for a call, but you won't be able to help liking her when you meet. Never a breath of scandal in all the time since their parting. I don't know that Prinny deserved such devotion."

They walked on into North Street, Maeve pondering with something like awe on the character of the woman who had sacrificed so much for the First Gentleman in the land. North Street was the busiest place in Brighton. From here coaches set off may times during the day for London, Lewes, Hastings and Portsmouth, and were continually arriving and departing, causing riders to pull out of the way. There were shops all the way up and a constant stream of ladies and gentlemen meandering past. At a milliner's Maeve fell in love with a large shady straw hat decorated with pale yellow ribbons which Ralph insisted on buying for her to protect her from the sun. He then took her to a draper's and they chose a bathing dress, Ralph over-riding her hesitancy. Would she really wear this odd garment and plunge into the sea, she wondered, but the adventure of it appealed to her.

A little further up, while Ralph was inspecting a hatter's window, she became aware of a man staring at them from the opposite side of the street. He was of medium height, strongly built, in his thirties she guessed, and though his hair was light brown, his face was burned an even darker brown by more than English sun.

"Ralph." She turned to catch his arm. "There's a man on the other side of the road staring at us as if he knows us. It can't be me – do you recognise him?"

Ralph swung round. "Where? I can't see anyone looking at us that I know."

She scanned the people on the other pavement. "Oh, he's gone."

"Well, no doubt he will catch up with us if he wants to make himself known. What was he like?"

She described the stranger but Ralph shook his head. "I've no idea who that could be. I think I like that brown beaver hat. Shall we go in?"

Soon after, both with purchases to be delivered to number twelve Marine Parade, they walked home for luncheon and Maeve pronounced Brighton to be the most charming and delightful place.

They ate dinner with the FitzClarences, the only other guests being two of his sisters, Sophia and Elizabeth, who was not long married to Lord Errol and seemed very happy with her father's choice of husband for her. She was a very handsome woman and Maeve liked her. Lady FitzClarence had given birth to a second son last February, William George being two years old, and afterwards in the parlour upstairs children were the general topic of conversation which left Maeve with a longing which she seemed unable to fulfil. Nothing had changed between her and Ralph, she liked the nights in their shared bed no better, but if she could only give him a child it would surely make up to him for so much.

On their short walk back to their own house, listening to the waves lapping on the shore below, a moon hanging low over the dark water she said she thought the Colonel made an excellent host and that Lady Mary seemed so content.

"I'm sure she is," Ralph said, and added, "surprisingly for one of his family, George has never been involved in scandals of a delicate nature – only in extravagance, and Mary seems unable to curb that."

On Friday evening they set off for the Pavilion in their carriage, and remembering the sharp words they had had on their first night here, Maeve determined to do or say nothing that would make people dub Ralph's wife "parochial". Joining a queue of carriages they were eventually set down by the octagonal and pillared entrance hall. She felt more than a little nervous as she took Ralph's arm and went in. Flunkeys in powered wigs stood each side of the door as they passed through to join the throng of elegantly dressed ladies and gentlemen. Ralph spoke to several acquaintances, some of whom she had already met, and Mr Creevey joined them for a while before trotting off to speak to Lady Augusta Millbanke. Mark Millbanke was with his wife, a neat compact man with a predilection for horse-racing and who was a fair jockey himself. They were devoted to each other but over the years he had learned to leave the conversation to her.

Maeve was too fascinated by the extraordinary decorations to be conscious of much else. Passing through the entrance hall they came into a larger reception area, well lit and spacious, with a row of painted glass windows. She gazed at the chinoiserie on the walls before moving into a long corridor which Ralph told her was called the Chinese gallery. Here groups of people were standing talking and they moved to join the FitzClarences.

Lady Mary tucked her hand into the crook of Maeve's arm. "It is rather overwhelming on a first visit, isn't it?"

"There is so much to see. Oh, the delicate porcelain, and the wallpaper – and that beautiful cabinet!" Maeve hardly knew what to comment on next.

"There is more to come," Mary told her. There was a sudden burst of laughter and she added, "I see – no, I hear – Lady Augusta is in a cheerful mood. Gusty, here is Lady Digby come to the Pavilion and quite amazed by it."

Lady Augusta Millbanke, outstanding in a jade gown decorated with pearls, said at once. "Oh, I remember Lady Digby, only of course you were Miss Dacre then, from that delightful picnic at the castle."

"Bodiam," Maeve said. "How do you do, Lady Augusta?"

"Gusty, please. Everyone calls me that. And I shall call you Maeve – we have known Ralph long enough, if you will permit the intimacy. What a crush. Ralph, you look very well – you like matrimony, eh?" She dug him in the ribs, forgetting if she had known that he had been married before. "I wish our sovereign would hurry up, I'm starving. I know a lady shouldn't say that, but I always look forward to a good dinner here. His Majesty has, naturally, the best French chef in the kingdom."

A passing lady heard and stopped. "A great deal too rich for us, Lady Augusta. How nice you look, my dear."

"Ma'am." Lady Augusta dropped a curtsey to a rather plain lady in a simple but well made gown of pink silk. "Sir Ralph of course you know, but I think you have not yet met his wife." She turned to Maeve. "The Duchess of Clarence, my dear."

Maeve too curtseyed. "Your grace."

The Duchess was smiling and Maeve remembered what Ralph had told her of this kindly woman.

"How very pleasant to see you, Lady Digby, and you, Sir Ralph, We heard you were travelling round Europe. William, here is Sir Ralph back with us, and with his bride."

The Duke of Clarence, the King's next brother after the Duke of York, paused to shake them both by the hand. "Well, I hope you enjoy the evening," he said to Maeve. "Always to much food and too rich for me. It gave me the gout and a queasy stomach the last time I was here. We live much simpler at Bushey, don't we, my love?" The Duchess nodded, and he patted Maeve on the shoulder. "You must get Sir Ralph to bring you down to us one day. I'm just a plain sailor, you know, so we don't do things the grand style but our hospitality is none the less warm for that." He beamed and moved on, a corpulent man in a plain blue coat with gold buttons and white breeches, for he still liked to look like a naval officer.

There was a sudden stir and a bustle of people moving back as the King came down the stairs, a lady on his arm whom Maeve guessed correctly to be Lady Conyngham. In contrast to his brother he wore a rich purple velvet coat decorated with orders, the garter star standing out among them. He was enormously fat, his stomach held partly in check by a corset which, half way through the evening, he was likely to disappear to remove. Legs and thighs so thick that he was inclined to waddle, he was very conscious that he had lost all the old Prince Florizel looks, and his face was painted to hide its florid look, the little red tell-tales marks of an extreme over-indulgence of wine. But he was smiling at the company, calling out greetings, and Lady Augusta whispered in Maeve's ear, "When you are presented, don't let him kiss you. It is a most unpleasant experience."

As Lady Augusta's whispers tended to carry round the room, Maeve was acutely embarrassed, but though one or two ladies tittered the King had not come close enough to hear. When he did, however, he observed Ralph and shook him firmly by the hand. "So you're back, dear boy. George said you would be able to make use of our invitation. You know you are always welcome here."

Released, Ralph bowed. "May I present my wife, sir?"

"Ah, your bride. Welcome to my country cottage, my dear." His eyes ran over her appreciatively with the critical look of one much experienced, and he leaned towards her. She hurriedly made a deep curtsey so he contended himself with pinching her cheek. "Ralph, you can bring this charming bride of yours at any time. My dear," to Maeve, "you must meet our dear Lady Conyngham." Maeve wondered if she should curtsey again and how much deference was to be paid to the King's mistress, but that lady was merely nodding to her. Flamboyantly dressed, her enormous bosom barely covered by rich crimson satin, her jewelled fingers on the King's arm, she passed on down the room with him.

"Well done, my dear Maeve. His breath is quite odorous, and heaven knows where Lady C. buys her perfume but it's not to my taste – though come to think of it, she never buys anything out of her own purse, nor do her considerable family." Gusty exchanged an amused glance with Maeve as they followed their sovereign into the banqueting room.

It was dazzling. The ceiling was a forty-five foot dome of blue filled with green foliage, huge copper leaves, a winged dragon in the centre; a fountain of crystal formed the central chandelier, festooned with jewels and surrounded again by dragons of which the King seemed to be inordinately fond, enormous lotus flowers of tinted glass spouting from their mouths. Four other similar lamps on tall stands stood in each corner of the room with lotus leaf bowls. All were a blaze of light.

"How are they lit?" she whispered to Ralph. "I don't see the candles?"

"You won't," he told her. "This is the wonder of the day – gas! It is piped in – makes a better light, don't you think?"

"It's amazing. And all those dragons! The wall paintings are all Chinese, aren't they? And what huge mirrors."

An elaborate Axminster carpet of dragons and oriental figures covered the floor and set against the walls huge sideboards were decorated with yet more dragons, holding golden candelabra and silver and gold vessels of all sorts. Taking her place she found herself separated from Ralph with Lord Sefton on one side and a Mr Manners on the other. He was a relative of the Duke of Rutland and hastened to tell her so, making her think the relationship must be somewhat distant if he needed to mention it so swiftly. He engaged her at once in conversation, claiming Ralph as an old friend – which Ralph told her later was an exaggeration, their acquaintance confined to a few meetings. He was, Mr Manners informed her, secretary to his noble relative who was at present away on the continent, and his wife was a cousin of the Seymours.

"You will know the Marquess of Hertford and his lady, of course," Mr Manners was saying, and though she murmured that she had not yet had that pleasure, he went on as if he had not heard, dropping noble names with all of whom he professed if not close friendship, at least a nodding acquaintance. He was a small man, rather plump, fortyish, and had once been passably handsome though his face was now rather puffy. Once he laid a pudgy hand on her arm to emphasise something and she withdrew it hastily, turning to Lord Sefton who was asking her how she had enjoyed the Eternal City. For a while they talked of Rome but she thought he looked very melancholy compared to the man she had met last summer at Welford.

She asked if his wife was with him, and at once his eyes filled with tears. "Not just now, Lady Digby. She is gone to see our poor little motherless grandchildren."

"Oh," she murmured, "I am so sorry. Mr Creevey told us – "

"It is hard to lose a beloved daughter," he said quietly. "She was everything to me, and I have no heart for banquets or the court or anything else these days, but his Majesty sent me so kind a letter that I decided to come, at least for a few days. And my friend Creevey is the greatest support."

She was very sorry for him and began to talk of Brighton and how much she liked it, giving him a chance to recover himself.

Mr Manners then engaged her again while Lord Sefton answered a question from the lady on his far side, merely toying with the food on his plate. Ten courses were served, each with at least half a dozen or more side dishes, all brought on magnificent gold plate by footmen in colourful livery. Once she heard Clarence belch and murmur that he'd rather be eating plain boiled mutton.

"You ought to serve some, my dear brother." He leaned across the table towards the King. "You'll be the ruin of my stomach."

His Majesty laughed. "As long it's not of anything else, I'm content," he retorted. "You and I at least won't fall out. York's worse, did you know? Taken to his bed and not likely to get up again, poor dear fellow." He and his brother Frederick had been brought up to do everything together and there was a strong bond between them. After the turmoil in royal circles at his marriage to Mrs Fitzherbert, he had been heard to say he would never marry a princess to get an heir but leave all that to Frederick. York however had no children and his death would change things for the Clarences. However the Duke was genuinely disturbed. "Poor fellow. Always fond of York. For God's sake take those things away," as a dish of escallops stuffed with truffles was offered to him. However when the patisseries were brought round he weakened enough to eat an elaborate confection of meringues stuffed with whipped cream and doused in liqueur.

"Which I shall regret," he muttered gloomily while spooning in mouthfuls. His Duchess smiled and when he had half finished signed to the footman to remove his plate.

"Hey! Oh, well, I suppose you're right, m'dear."

Maeve watched all this in some amusement. She ate sparingly of the courses for Ralph had warned her that there would be many, but the food was delicious, cooked to perfection and served in ingenious ways. Mr Manners told her the chef was the best in the world and she believed him. He continued to entertain her, often witty at the expense of absent politicians or public figures, sometimes she thought rather coarsely, and he pointed out various people to her, among them the Russian Ambassador Count Lieven and his very pretty wife Dorothea who had dark curling hair, a delicate pointed face and brilliant brown eyes. She was always in the forefront of the talk and her corner of the table resounded with laughter Beside her sat a man whom Mr Manners named as Count Balakov, an attaché at the embassy and one of the handsomest men Maeve had ever seen. The Duke of Wellington had not yet come, but the Duke of Sussex, the King's youngest brother, was there, small and lively, rather like his Majesty in feature and obviously popular, with two of his sisters, the Princesses Sophia and Augusta.

Maeve listened and looked. Mr Manners was rambling on with a story of a mishap to the King's horse at the recent races and she only half attended. it was very hot from all the lamps and candelabra and she began to wish the interminable meal would end, at the same time wondering if it would be ill-mannered to use her fan. No other lady was doing so however and she made up her mind to endure the heat. At least she was thinly clad and she pitied Ralph who, she could see across the table, had beads of sweat on his forehead. He didn't seem to mind for he was talking animatedly to a lady in red silk whom she learned afterwards was one of the Devonshire daughters. The King was totally taken up with Lady Conyngham and when plates of dainty biscuits were set out she playfully placed one on each capacious bosom and told the King he might purchase them with a kiss, which he did, scooping them off her skin with his lips. There was a good deal of laughter at this. Maeve managed a smile but she thought it a tasteless exercise. Am I really a prude? she wondered. The Pavilion and its royal host were totally outside her small experience.

In the music room, to her astonishment, the King suddenly beckoned her to set beside him on the green satin settee he favoured, and when he asked her how she liked his 'little retreat', she said honestly she had no words to described her amazement.

"It does catch the eye, doesn't it? he agreed. "I have spent a little money on it," an understatement for an expenditure well in excess of a hundred and fifty thousand pounds.

"I've never seen anything so – so captivating," she said, "so much beauty in every room. My cousin, Sir Frederick Hollander, is just back from India and coming to stay with us soon. He would so much enjoy seeing this, and his wife is part Indian."

He looked pleased for he never tired of hearing praise of his achievement. "It was just a little farmhouse when I first saw it," he told her, and added, "You must bring your cousins one evening. Sir Frederick and Lady Hollander, you said?"

She was to learn he never forgot a name or a face. He asked if her cousin was an Army man and nodded in a pleased manner when she said he had been a dragoon.

"My own regiment were Hussars, you know – the Prince of Wales' own. Yes, of course you know. Sir Ralph was with them once. I designed their uniform too. Ah," he sighed in happy reminiscence, "It's a good life for a fellow," forgetting he had never been a serving officer in any sense of the word. After a little more talk he pinched her cheek again and said, "Now you go off and find some young company. I'm sure you know several of my guests." She assured him she did and this time he succeeded in kissing her. She curtseyed and left him, hoping it would not be repeated too often. But despite his unhealthy appearance and his tainted breath, there was something about him still that made her enjoy talking to him.

Presently there was music, a small orchestra playing works by Rossini and Mozart, and a Haydn string quartet which she knew well, it being a favourite of the little orchestra in Rye. But the heat, the brilliance of the scene, coupled with the rich food and wine, made her feel oppressively tired, and when the music finished Mr Manners who was behind her chair said softly, "I think, Lady Digby, you would be glad of a quick turn on the lawn."

"I would," she answered gratefully, and taking his arm went out through the long open doors into the summer night where she stood drawing deep breaths of the cool refreshing breeze off the sea.

"There – isn't that better?" He pressed her arm, walking very close to her, and began to talk of the entertainments planned in Brighton over the next few weeks. "I hope I shall have the pleasure of meeting you at many of them," he finished. "You are an adornment to our society, Lady Digby."

She decided he was becoming a little too friendly and was about to say she wished to return to the music room when Ralph came up behind them. He did not look affable.

"My dear," he said, "the King has retired and the guests are leaving. Our carriage will be here any minute. Your servant, Manners." He took her hand firmly through his arm and swept her inside, nor did he speak again until they were being driven back to Marine Parade. Then he said, his voice grating a little, "That was not wise of you, Maeve."

"What was not wise?"

"Going into the garden with Manners, alone and in the dark. Such things cause gossip and his reputation is not all it might be where your sex is concerned."

"I didn't know. I was so hot, and I didn't realise – I must sometimes seem very simple to you, Ralph."

"Not simple," he said at once, "refreshingly innocent."

"That sounds worse!"

"No, indeed." He laughed and took her hand in his. "I wouldn't change you, my love, but moving in the King's circle you must be a little wary. There are women, plenty of them, who play the game with few rules and whose husbands, poor cuckolds, look the other way, but I would not like you to be thought one of them. Nor indeed would I tolerate it."

"Ralph! You know that I wouldn't – I couldn't –" she broke off, unable to convey what she meant.

He interpreted her words in a different way. "I know you couldn't" he said. "At least these last months have led me to think that – but perhaps it is only so far as *I* am concerned."

Tired, hot, and a little overwrought, she burst into tears. "You think I'm cold, that I can't love you as – as I should. I've not given you a child – and you must wish you'd never married me!"

"Good God, what's all this?" he exclaimed. They had reached the house and their footman was already opening the door. Ralph sprang out, handed her down and took her straight into the parlour. There he shut the door.

She was struggling to control herself, to find a handkerchief to mop up her stormy tears, and coming to her he produced his own large one and performed the operation for her. "Dear me," he said, "we do get across each other sometimes, don't we? That was an unkind thing I said, Maeve. Please forget it. It isn't your fault and on the whole we do better than many married couples, don't we?"

"Yes." The word came out on a gasp. It seemed almost an

admission of defeat and turning away from him she sat down by the empty hearth. "I do like so much that we do together, Ralph. It's only that – I know how much you want a child."

"So do most men," he said lightly. "We are conceited enough to want to project something of ourselves into the next generation and provide heirs for our property, such as it is. But, my dear, there's plenty of time. My friend Hastings, whom you've not yet met, waited five years for his wife to produce an heir and now he has three. I do however wish, sometimes – " he stopped the damaging words. "But I'm glad we spoke of this. We have all the time in the world, you know."

She leaned her head on her hand. "You are very kind – and understanding."

"Am I? Not always, I fear. I have had no one but myself to consider for far too long, and one doesn't change easily."

"No," she answered in a low voice, "one doesn't."

He gave her a swift glance and then said, "My dear, it is far too late for discussions and you look very weary. Shall we go up?"

She rose and laid her hand on his arm. " I will watch my step at court, Ralph. I promise you I won't be so stupid again, it's just that it is all so new to me."

"Of course it is," he said bracingly, "as sea-bathing is. Would you like to try that tomorrow? By the way, I thought you conducted yourself very well with his Majesty."

She was grateful. The remark did much to restore her confidence, and she went to bed determined not to do anything to annoy him when they next went to the Pavilion. As she was drifting into sleep she murmured, "I did think Mr Manners very tiresome."

She heard him laugh in the dark. "So do many of us! He has an eye for the ladies – and more if he gets a chance."

"Well, he won't with me." she assured him, and heard him laugh again. But she was to remember the little exchange some time later.

Chapter 13

A good night's sleep quite restored Maeve's vitality and she found her first bathe in the sea invigorating, surprised at how delightful it could be, splashing around in the cold clear water. There were several 'dippers' there, women employed to help the ladies into the sea, including the daughter of the famous Martha Gunn who had been the first to hire out her services in such a manner. Afterwards Gracie rubbed her dry with a thick towel so that her skin glowed, and over lunch she enthused to Ralph over the experience.

"I thought you would like it." he said. "At one time Prinny bathed most days when he was here, but he's not gone into the water for some time now. Too fat, poor old fellow."

"I wondered if we might go riding on the Downs this afternoon," she suggested. "Now that our horses have arrived."

"I'm sorry, my dear, not today, though Willis can take you out, if you wish There's a new boxing parlour opened and I've engaged to take a look at it with Mark Millbanke and MacDonald, and perhaps try a bout or two."

"Oh – isn't that for younger men?"

"Good God, I'm not as old as all that! Tom Cribb who was one of the finest and has a parlour in London still occasionaly puts up his fists and he's well into middle age. I've had many a bout with him, and with Gentleman Jackson too in his time at his sparring place in Old Bond Street."

"Well, I'm sure I hope you'll enjoy it and not come home with a bloodied nose."

He laughed and left her to her own devices. Having no

mind to explore the Downs without his company, she went to call on Mary FitzClarence and found her entertaining the elderly Marchioness of Salisbury.

"I do hope I'm not intruding,' Maeve said. "Your butler didn't say you were entertaining."

He has orders to open the door to callers this afternoon." Mary beckoned her in. "I'm so glad you came. Lady Salisbury, may I present our friend and near neighbour, Lady Digby?"

The Marchioness was seventy-six years old, dressed in lavender silk, a lavender bonnet on her thin grey curls. She had been at the centre of society for many years and caused a stir or two in her time. Even now, despite her advanced years, she still had the beautiful complexion of her youth.

Maeve looked at her with considerable respect and remembered that though she was ten years older than Prinny, Ralph had mentioned that she had once been his mistress – along with the others who had filled his days after Mrs Fitzherbert had lost her hold on him.

She nodded to Maeve and said, "You are Ralph Digby's bride, are you not? I've known your mother-in-law these forty years."

Maeve sat beside her and for a while they talked of the Digby family before the Marchioness asked her about her own, whereupon the old lady said she was sure the Marquess had known old Sir Frederick Hollander. She asked Maeve how she liked Brighton.

"I've only been here a few days, ma'am, but I like what I've seen very much. I love riding and I was hoping to explore the Downs with my husband, but he has gone off to a boxing parlour with some friends.'

"How long have you been married, my dear?"

"Since last December. We only came back from our wedding trip a few weeks ago."

"Then let me give you a piece of advice. One's wedding tour is a very small part of married life and not one to set a pattern by. Don't try to tie your husband to your apron strings. Gentlemen must have their own occupations and amusements, you know."

"Yes, ma'am," Maeve said meekly. "I suppose I have much to learn."

"Sensible child. Come to my card party next Wednesday." and as Maeve hesitated she added, "Now don't say you will see if your husband has plans. Tell him you are engaged with me."

"Yes, ma'am," Maeve said again, and could not keep back a smile. "Perhaps you will give me your direction? I'm afraid I don't know Brighton very well yet."

"Lady FitzClarence is promised to me so you can come together. I am in Sussex Square, a little out of the town but a great deal quieter."

When she had gone Maeve glanced at her hostess. "Do you think she is right? About husbands, I mean?"

Mary laughed. "I'm sure she is. You have had Sir Ralph to yourself for these last six months, a very long time for a honeymoon, but you are back in the world now and must let go a little. One must not make one's husband a laughing stock."

"No, indeed," Maeve agreed. "But I never thought myself possessive." She was silent for a moment. The last thing she wanted was to appear in that guise to their friends and acquaintances but she saw that all the delightful things they had done together touring Europe had made her expect his company and it surprised her that she should mind if now he began to go his own way. She was rather glad that a curricle drew up with more callers and she was able to take her leave, so that she could walk slowly home and think about the eminently sensible advice given her. Why indeed should it worry her?

Ralph came in later with no evidence of any mishap and informed her that a prize fight between a fellow called Johnny Longshanks and a famous fighter nicknamed the Croucher was to be set up somewhere off the Lewes Road, and gave the opinion that most of the gentlemen in the town would be off to attend it.

"Including myself," he added.

"It seems horrid to me," she said, "grown men battering each other half to death for no good reason."

"It makes men of boys," he said. "Shall we ride in the morning? I engaged with Millbanke that they would join us."

As the days went by she saw a pattern emerging, as Lady

Salisbury and Mary FitzClarence too, had said it would. Ralph was among his friends again, the society he knew, and was often out. Apparently he expected her largely to make her own amusements, generally in company with others.

He was often out and she might have been lonely had not it been for Mary FitzClarence who took her under her wing. They made calls together, went shopping and to card parties, and one morning paid a visit to Steine House.

The King had built this for Mrs. Fitzherbert at the height of their relationship, and the wife of the young Prinny's heart sat this morning in the charming drawing room surrounded by friends. Lady Augusta was there and Mary's sister-in-law Lady Errol, another of Lord Egremont's illegitimate brood; the Duke of Sussex was leaning against the mantelshelf, his shoulders barely reaching it, while the Russian attaché, Count Balakov, displayed himself in a gilt chair, his long legs stretched out, well aware of how his bizarre and colourful uniform set off his superb figure. The talk was lively, on a variety of subjects, and for the most part Maeve listened. She thought Sussex entertaining and without the disregard for others that his brother Clarence could show on occasions, or the downright rudeness of Cumberland, but it was their hostess who most intrigued her, though she restrained herself from staring.

The woman whom the young Prince of Wales had loved to distraction had grown fat but she had lost none of her sweetness of expression and spoke in a warm tone to Maeve, welcoming her to Brighton. "London by the sea," she added, smiling, "for that is what it has become."

"They say you are the Queen of it, ma'am," Maeve said impulsively, and then went scarlet. "Oh, I beg your pardon, I only meant – "

Maria Fitzherbert's face wore a look of ineffable sadness, but she reached out and took one of Maeve's hands in hers. "My dear child, you meant it for a compliment, I know that. Now tell me about yourself." She smoothed the matter over and the morning passed pleasantly. Count Balakov chatted lazily to Maeve while the Duke of Sussex told her that he liked the county of his title and talked of the charm of Rye and the strangeness of Romney Marsh and its people.

"My carriage once lost a wheel when I was coming back from Dover to Brighton," he remarked, "in the middle of a storm, it was, and the nearest shelter while it was being repaired was a Martello Tower! Well, did you ever? A strange edifice, but vastly interesting. A good vantage point for the coastguards, I should think. Is there still a deal of smuggling thereabouts?"

Maeve told him not so much now that the taxes had been reduced and he laughed and said, "Well, that's one good thing this government has done."

Other people arrived, among them Mr Manners, and when coffee was served, he drew up a chair to sit beside her. She disliked his marked attention and was glad when Mary FitzClarence said that it was time they left.

Walking back, she was still shaken by her faux-pas. "How could I have said such a stupid thing?" she said unhappily. "I am so ashamed."

"You need not be," Mary took her arm, "because it is true in a sense. The people here do love Mrs Fitzherbert and you can see why. Many remember when she and the King, he was Prinny then, were seldom seen apart, and she received as low a bow as anyone except him. She was a much ill-used lady and we all love her. If the marriage had been allowed, what a difference it would have made. Oh, the King would have had his little conquests no doubt, but they would not have amounted to anything if she had been given her rightful place at his side, and she would have known it. George is devoted to her."

"I wish I had not said such a foolish thing."

Mary smiled. "Who hasn't said something amazingly stupid some time or other? I remember more than once wishing the floor would swallow me up. Do you go to the ball at the Old Ship tomorrow?"

It was the largest gathering Maeve had ever been to, the room of the hotel crowded with people, the ballroom lavishly decorated with flowers, an excellent orchestra at the far end. Ralph danced with his wife and then surrendered her to George. After that he hardly saw her again for she was on the floor for practically every dance. As a bride of not yet a year she was introduced about by the Duchess of Devonshire Lady Errol and Lady Ellenborough, who had been a Miss

Digby before her marriage and was a distant connection of Ralph's. At one point Lady Augusta bore down on her and made her known to William Lamb who had been married to the tempestuous Caroline Lamb. Maeve thought him a very good-looking and charming man and she remembered that Ralph had said that Caroline's death had shattered him despite the misery of their broken marriage.

About halfway through the evening there was a stir at the entrance and a gentleman came in with two or three others, pausing to survey the scene. Maeve had no difficulty in recognising him at once from portraits she had seen, even if her partner, a Captain Hemmings, had not said, "By Jove, it's the Beau!"

Wellington was a fair height with a high forehead and the famous nose that had earned him the sobriquet of 'Old Nosey' or 'Old Hookey' among his soldiers. He was plainly dressed in a dark green evening suit on which were several of his dozens of medals and orders, among them the magnificent Garter Star.

He moved to speak to Lady Augusta and presently took the floor with her. Maeve gazed at him with awe. The victor of Waterloo had been her greatest hero since she was a child, and the thought that Freddy had been part of his triumphant army when hardly more than a boy lent him an added glamour. She hoped he would stay in Brighton until Freddy's visit, on the chance that they might meet. Not expecting to be introduced herself, she was standing beside Ralph in the pause for refreshments when George FitzClarence came in their direction, talking with the Duke.

He stopped at once and said, "Your Grace, do you recall my friend, Sir Ralph Digby?"

Wellington subjected Ralph to one of his penetrating stares. "Digby? Yes, I do remember. One of the Elegant Extracts, eh?"

Ralph bowed. "I am surprised you recall that, sir. It's a long time ago. May I present my wife?"

Wellington turned to Maeve and shook her hand. "Good evening, Lady Digby. I hope your husband has grown into a more sensible fellow – it was a thoroughly bad thing, that, and they were a bad lot, you know, a very insubordinate lot."

But he was smiling, and returning that rather shy smile she said, "So I've heard, your Grace, but wiser now perhaps? Certainly Colonel FitzClarence and he are reformed characters."

He gave his high neighing laugh. "I hope so. It was a thousand pities, Sir Ralph, that you threw up the army. Did you ever regret it?"

"Very much, sir, "Ralph said, "but circumstances partly dictated my behaviour. I would have given anything to have been at Waterloo."

"Would you, by God? The best of you Peninsula fellows had been sent off to America and I was left with an army of the worst scum imaginable – drunk half the time, most of them. They frightened me to death, but I needn't have worried – they did worse to the enemy. Splendid fellows, every one of them," he finished in complete contradiction. "Do you dance, Lady Digby?"

A waltz had begun and he held out his arm, ignoring a young lieutenant from the cavalry camp coming to claim her, and Maeve took to the floor with perhaps the most exalted man in Europe, a staunch Tory, a man covered with honours and offices, among them the Lord-Lieutenancy of Hampshire, and Constable of the Tower, as well as Master of the Ordnance. He loathed the Foreign Minister, George Canning, and was deeply involved in the machinations of Canning's enemies – a pity, Ralph had told her, for he was a better soldier than politician.

He danced well and made easy conversation, interested at once when she spoke of Freddy as being one of his youngest officers at Waterloo, begging leave to present him if the opportunity arose.

Wellington said at once, "Of course, of course. Never forget my officers, though I didn't know 'em all by name. I am staying here at the Old Ship so bring him to see me."

"I would like to do that, sir. He has been serving in India for the last nine years, but he is out of the Army now and recently come home."

"Ah, I had some good campaigns there," he said, "many years ago now. A strange country, too hot for my liking. What did your cousin think of it?"

"He used to write wonderful letters describing it all," she said, "but he is settling down to be a country gentleman now that his father had died. He was Sir Thomas Hollander – you may recall him from when you were our member of Parliament?"

"Some twenty years ago," he said in surprise. "Yes, I do remember, and Sir Thomas was an excellent fellow. I dined with him several times. But you cannot be old enough to remember that."

"No, sir, I was a little girl then. He died last year."

"I'm sorry to hear it. I recollect he was much concerned in the building of the Military Canal. I hope that it is of use and justifies all the public money spent on it?"

"It serves local people, sir, and in the summer there are always pleasure craft out on it."

"Now what was it dug for, eh? Well, never mind, we did everything we could for the safety of our country at that time."

She smiled up at him and said, "You, sir, surely more than anyone."

"Ah, those days are long gone. I was at my best on a battlefield. But the morning after – no, I wouldn't wish that again. The weight of so many deaths on one's shoulders is a terrible burden. Please God I'll fight no such battle as Waterloo ever again. Now I'm a crusty old politician."

He left her at the end of the dance and later she confided to Sir Ralph that she liked him very well.

"He's a great man," was Ralph's comment. "I'm glad I served under him, if only for a while."

At that moment, with a rustle of skirts and a sudden little shriek, a lady whom Maeve had not seen before swept down on them. She was not pretty but rather striking, with a mass of red hair confined in a jewelled fillet, and she had sharp green eyes that flew at once to Maeve and then back to Ralph. Thrusting her hand through his arm she said, "My dear, dear Ralph, I hoped so much to see you here. We came yesterday but have only just got ourselves settled in – a poky little place in St James Street but it was all we could get."

"Caroline." He disengaged himself, putting her fingers briefly to his lips. "This is my wife. Maeve, Mrs Trenchard."

They shook hands and the newcomer said, "Ah, yes, I heard that you had married, but you know what rumours are in London. I was not sure if it was actually true. Ralph, you naughty fellow, sneaking off to wed like that without us knowing. Emulating Prinny, eh?"

Active dislike rising in her, Maeve said, "I assure you, ma'am, our wedding was not at all private. In fact a great many of Ralph's friends were there."

She gave a laugh that was slightly insincere. "Oh, my dear, don't take offence. I promise you, I meant nothing. I daresay we were away at the time. But dear Ralph, you understand, is one of my oldest and very dearest friends."

Maeve returned the look. "I am discovering that as my husband has been in court circles for many years, he has a large number of friends."

Mrs Trenchard laughed again, her hand once more on Ralph's arm. "I think I can claim to be one of the nearest, You come from this part of the world, I believe?" And when Maeve mentioned Rye she said, "I am afraid I don't know Sussex at all – except Brighton, of course. We prefer London life, so much more going on, but when our dear Prinny chooses the sea coast what can one do but come? I suppose you are very quiet in the country?"

"Not entirely." Maeve heard her own voice sharpen.

"Well, I'm sure Ralph must find it so – don't you, my dear?"

"Hardly," he said, "seeing I have just bought an estate and brought my mother to live there."

She glanced up at him, smiling into his eyes. "What times we've had in the past, eh?"

"In the past," he agreed. "But times change, Caroline. We are all a little older."

"Oh, you are ungallant, sir," she laughed and tapped his arm. "None of us ladies would admit to being older. Do you recall that visit to Oxford in – when was it – the spring of '19?"

"I recall it," he said, "rather as I recall follies which should be left where they belong – in our youth."

"Well, let us enjoy the present then. You must bring your wife to London, my dear."

"I mean to," he said. "Is your husband here?"

"Somewhere about." She waved a vague hand. "Oh, they are playing a waltz. Lady Digby, may I capture your husband for it?"

Maeve inclined her head and said coolly, "As I am promised to Mr Creevey, Ralph may do as he pleases, unless he is engaged elsewhere."

"I shall claim priority," she said gaily, and Maeve was thankful that Mr Creevey came up at that moment to claim her.

After two turns and some desultory conversations she asked if he could see Mr Trenchard. After a moment's glance round he said, "Yes, there he is over there, the short fellow in that appallingly cut brown coat."

"I've not met Mrs Trenchard before, nor have I heard my husband mention the name," she said casually. "Do you know them, Mr Creevey?"

"Dear me, yes. She's a fascinating creature, as you must have observed. Lord knows why she married Trenchard, but I suppose it was because, although he's an insignificant man, he has significant relations!"

"Oh? Who?"

"No less than the Conynghams. I'm sure Sir Ralph will have told you how Lady C. persuades our sovereign to find places for all her relations. Mathew Trenchard is assistant to Sir William Knighton – he's dancing with Lady Augusta at the moment, the King's physician and secretary, and his Majesty goes nowhere without him, but he's not well liked and as for his assistant, nobody notices him. Mrs Trenchard, however, is another matter altogether." As usual Mr Creevey was full of information. "She was a nobody from somewhere in Essex, I believe, and I suppose she saw Trenchard as a way up the ladder. A long way up to the Pavilion, eh?"

Maeve glanced across the floor. Mrs Trenchard was turning in Ralph's arms, laughing and evidently teasing him, for she had her head on one side and was drawing a reluctant smile from him. There was something altogether too possessive about her attitude.

"A word of advice, Lady D.?" Mr Creevey said softly, and when she nodded went on, "If you are planning any entertainment, you would not find the Trenchards very congenial guests."

"Oh?" she looked up at him. "I wonder what you mean by that?"

"Nothing of any moment," he said lightly, "but I doubt whether on further acquaintance you would care for her, and he has no conversation at all."

"I don't think I like her now, "Maeve said, and then added hastily, "Oh dear, what an unkind thing to say. One shouldn't make such quick judgements, should one? She says she is an old friend of Ralph's, so I suppose . . ."

"He may not wish to renew that acquaintance. And I think in this case your judgement was instinctive and very apposite."

"Maybe, but I shouldn't have – "

"I like people to speak their minds, Lady D, even though it can be dangerous, but not among friends – for we are friends, aren't we?"

"I hope so." She gave him a warm smile as the dance ended. And she had a feeling that if ever she needed a friend, he would prove to be a loyal one.

She danced next with Captain MacDonald whom she found to be an affable man. Promotion had passed him by, he was nearly forty now and unmarried, and in the circle he was by reason of his friends. She found him a little over-solicitous, insisting on fetching her a glass of lemonade after their dance and obviously considering himself a gallant where the ladies were concerned. She danced next with Mark Millbanke and they talked horseflesh which was much more to her liking.

The dancing finally ended at one o'clock and she said regretfully to Ralph that she could have gone on till dawn.

He laughed. "You are insatiable. Did you like our Beau?"

"I've never enjoyed meeting anyone so much. Perhaps it's because one knows so much of his tremendous achievements over so many years."

"Including his time in India?" Ralph's tone was devoid of expression.

"Of course," she said, nettled. "At home we all had a natural interest in that country."

"Of course," he echoed and left it at that.

The next morning at breakfast he suggested it was time that they gave a dinner and she said at once that the same thing had been on her mind. Over the next few days this occupied much of her time. She had long talks with Mrs Gibson, planning the menu and deciding that the dining-room table could be made to accommodate eighteen to twenty people. Mr Flint organised what needed to be hired in the way of extra chairs and staff, as well as asking her for her preference for flowers to decorate the house. She and Ralph sat over the list of guests deciding to whom cards should be sent – the FitzClarences, of course, the Millbankes, Count Lieven and Princess Dorothea, Mr Creevey, Captain MacDonald, Lady Hertford, the Errols and the Ellenboroughs, the Devonshires.

"Do you think," Maeve said tentively," the Duke would come? To see him at our table – "

"We'll send him a card," Ralph said. "I'm sure if he's free he'll come. He's long forgiven me for being an Elegant Extract!"

The list was fairly full when, prompted by she hardly knew what, she said, "And your friends the Trenchards? Do you wish to ask them?"

He looked surprised. "But you hardly know them and I've not seen them for some years."

"I was thinking of what Mrs Trenchard said, about being one of your oldest and closest friends."

"She exaggerated. I don't believe we should include them." Which remark only made her wonder the more why Mr Creevey had been of the same opinion.

The cards were sent and only two of the Devonshire tribe refused on the grounds of prior commitments. The Duke of Wellington accepted, to Maeve's delight, and her first reaction was to say, "How I wish Freddy was going to be here," to which Ralph replied, "I'm sure you do," whereupon she rather wished she hadn't.

But she was looking forward to her first big entertainment as mistress of Ralph's house, beginning to feel very much part of the Brighton scene, and in the intervening week before the big day her time was filled. She rode on the Downs, sometimes with Ralph, often with the Millbankes, sometimes with

George and Mr Creevey who had stayed on when his friend Lord Sefton, unable to stomach any more gaiety, departed to rejoin his wife. There were evenings at the Pavilion, a dinner at the Millbankes, and the weekly ball at the Old Ship. One evening as they came in from cards at the Pavilion, the King's favourite Ecarté, Ralph said suddenly, "I hear nothing but compliments on every side. You are doing very well, my dear." Which in itself was a compliment, and Maeve could not help but go to bed in a happy frame of mind.

On Sunday they went to the Chapel Royal. The King was there with his brothers, Clarence and Suffolk, and the Conynghams, as well as most habitués of the court scene. The long sermon was about the seed that fell among rocks or on stony ground where it could not produce anything and the thought led Maeve to wonder miserably if she was to be that ground. She could see Mary FitzClarence with the swelling under her gown beginning to show while she herself had no sign of a child. Was she to be that biblical reproach, a barren wife? Tears pricked her eyes but she would not shed them. She wondered what her dear stepfather would say to her – surely that she was foolish to worry so soon, that she should trust in the One who ruled all their lives.

She prayed then for the child that would surely change her life, end once and for all the longing that would not die, make up for what she had not been able to give Ralph. Even in the midst of this new, busy and highly entertaining life, Freddy was still in his place in the core of her heart and it did not occur to Maeve that it was for her to find a way to clear that space for someone else, that as long as she kept him there no other could enter. Actually in this busy life they led there was sometimes a whole day when she did not think of him at all – but how would it be when he was here with them? If only she were with child, could tell him so, evict him from that secret place so that he was in fact just a cousin. I won't think of it, she told herself, and then perhaps it will happen. A child surely was the answer for her and for Ralph? She stole a glance at him. He was sitting with his arms folded, looking extremely bored with the parable of the sower which had had more than justice done to it.

It was the Duke of Clarence, yawning loudly and saying,

"Is this fellow never going to stop?" who brought the unhappy preacher to a swift and confused conclusion.

They dined with the Devonshires the next evening. The Duchess had been a great society hostess for many years and it was she who had given the famous ball in Brussels on the night before Waterloo from which all the officers were summoned back to their regiments. Freddy had not been there, being far too young and junior to be included, but he would, thought Maeve, enjoy meeting the Duchess when he came to Brighton. She herself was fortunate to be seated next to Wellington, who had Lady Augusta on his other side, and the table resounded with a great deal of laughter.

After dinner they went on to an evening's music at the Pavilion and found the South Drawing Room crowded as usual. Ralph was captured by Lord Errol and asked if he was to be at the races next week, in which Mark Millbanke was riding, while Maeve walked further into the room, looking for Gusty to see if she meant to go, when a strident and oddly familiar voice said, obviously in answer to a remark, "What? Where?"

Maeve turned, saw Mr Creevey beckoning to her from beside a lady seated on a small settee. She walked over, thinking it was a new arrival that he wished her to meet, but then as she came closer a suspicion entered her head.

The lady was not fat but of large proportions, obviously tall and magnificently dressed in deep blue satin with diamonds about her neck. She had sandy hair tinged with grey which spilled from under her lace headgear, and clear, very direct blue eyes.

She looked up at Maeve and said in a rather strident voice, "So you're the little girl from the vicarage!"

Chapter 14

There had by mischance been a momentary lull in the talk around and a sudden ripple of laughter filled it. Maeve felt her colour rise but she lifted her head and said coolly, "Yes, ma'am, I am – and you, if I am not mistaken, are my husband's older sister."

Several people were looking at them, amused by the exchange. The lady on the sofa stared for a moment and then burst out laughing, a very familiar sound to Maeve. "Touché! Yes, my dear, I am Ralph's sister – and older at that! Come and sit beside me. Give her your place, Creevey, there's a good fellow. I want to meet my new sister-in-law."

He rose at once and stood back, smiling, as the people around returned to their conversations, making way for Ralph who, hearing the brief exchange, broke off his talk with Millbanke and came over to them.

"Well, Selena," he said pleasantly and bent to kiss her cheek. Then without changing his tone added, "I should have thought years in the diplomatic world would have taught you to mind your damned tongue."

"Ralph, "Maeve protested, "I'm sure Lady Hillingdon didn't mean anything."

Ralph's sister pressed her hand. "Selena, if you please. We are sisters now, you know, and I shall certainly call you Maeve. Such a pretty name. Irish, I suppose? Of course I meant nothing unkind. Ralph, take that chair beside us and don't be disagreeable."

He obeyed but said, "Your remark was ill-judged to say the least. Where's Hillingdon?"

"Reporting to our Foreign Secretary. When Mr Canning releases him he'll join me. I wrote to Mama from London and she gave me your direction so I've had the impertinence to have my bags set down at your door, but you may throw me out if you wish. Only the Ship and the Royal Oak are full and I have no desire to tour Brighton looking for a tolerable apartment, if indeed any are available."

"Doubtful at this time of year and with Prinny here, "Ralph said. "Of course you must stay with us. I trust you're not inflicting my nauseating nephews on us? How are they? As bad as ever?"

"Not quite. Harrow has improved their behaviour somewhat. At least they've progressed past the frogs in the bed stage. Their jokes are more sophisticated now. They are in Cornwall at the moment, no doubt causing mayhem there." Lady Hillingdon glanced at Maeve. "I'm afraid my sons are always up to some devilry. Do you have brothers?"

"No, ma'am, but I have three cousins who were very mischievous in their school days. The eldest is married and he and his wife are coming to stay with us shortly."

"Then I hope Hillingdon and I will not be inconviencing you?"

Maeve shook her head. She felt somewhat at a loss with this forthright lady, so like Ralph in looks and, it seemed, in manner too. "No indeed," she said formally, "you are very welcome." But nevertheless wished Ralph's sister had deposited her bags elsewhere.

The King came in then and the music began, but for once Maeve was unable to settle to enjoy it. She was still very much discomposed by her sister-in-law's remark, laugh it off though she might, and later that night, after seeing Lady Hillingdon to one of the guest rooms, she waited in her own room for Ralph, sure he would have some comment to make.

He did. Stalking in from his dressing room, he said, "I believe I must apologise for my sister. My mother no doubt told you she is the most tactless woman alive."

"I'm sure there was no malice meant," Maeve assured him. "I do hope to get along very well with her, Ralph. I mean to try anyway."

"Oh, Selena is good enough at heart, but I do not like my wife to be the butt of the latest society on-dit."

"I expect it will soon be forgotten," she retorted." In any case it's true and I'm not in the least ashamed of it. Nor should you be – or is it because I am 'parochial' that you are so annoyed?"

He was even more irritated. "You can't forget that, can you? But I am not ashamed either, as you put it – what a ridiculous word to use. Selena really is incorrigibly deficient in tact."

She wanted to say it was not a virtue he himself possessed in any degree, but she realised his pride was pricked. She thought it rather foolish of him but he knew society better than she did and was well aware that the unfortunate epithet would be repeated with much amusement and some superiority in the drawing rooms of Brighton.

The first days of his sister's visit were so busy, with old friends calling or visits being made, that they gave Maeve time to study her new relative. Selena was almost of a height with her brother, but her features were more classical and she was really a very good-looking woman. Her hair, a little darker than his, was the colour of ripe corn and her French maid dressed it to perfection. It was soon obvious that for all her reputed lack of tact she had a great many friends and, like Ralph, was welcome anywhere. She made herself immediately at home, clearly delighted to see her brother again, and their verbal sparring amused Maeve, for she could see that underneath it there was a great deal of affection. Neither liked to admit to any sort of indulgent sentiment, but she was sure it was there, enhanced perhaps by the age difference.

On the third morning after Selena's arrival Ralph announced that it was the day of the prizefight and he was off to see it with George, Captain MacDonald, Millbanke and a few others.

"Good," was Selena's response. "We have hardly paused since I have been here and perhaps Maeve and I can have a leisurely day together. I hope you enjoy what I consider to be a low sort of pastime, though if Hillingdon were here no doubt he would join you."

"I'm sure we shall, "Ralph retorted in brotherly fashion. "It will be a change from escorting you on a tour of most of the shops and all of the society in town!"

"For my part," Maeve added, "I shall be glad to have you out of the house today. I hope you haven't forgotten it is our dinner party tonight?"

"Of course not. I shall be home by three or four o'clock. You and Selena will have a fine time fussing over the last details."

When he had gone his sister settled comfortably in a chair by the window. "There, now we can see the world go by. What a fright that woman looks. People with that colouring should never wear crimson. She looks like an overblown paeony. I think it's going to rain, that confection on her head will get very wet."

In short while the street was almost deserted and when Maeve said she ought to see Mrs Gibson and ensure that everything was in order for tonight, Selena caught her hand.

"One moment, my dear. I want to talk to you. I'm sure the estimable Mrs Gibson and Flint between them have everything in hand. How many do you expect?"

"Eighteen." Maeve sat down on the window seat beside her. "Nineteen with you."

"Oh dear, now I've thrown your numbers out as I did dear Prinny's last night, but he would have me dine with him. Shall I go out and bring in a spare man from the highway?"

Maeve laughed. "That won't be necessary. I'll send a card to Count Balakov. Ralph won't mind. We nearly put him on the list anyway. The Count is very beautiful and knows it, but he's quite amusing. I'm sure Flint will be able to rearrange the seating."

Lady Hillingdon waited while Maeve sat down at the small escritoire and wrote out a card for the Russian attaché, and when this had been despatched she said, "Now we can talk. My dear, I must tell you how different I find my brother. Mama told me you had made a new man of him."

"Your mother is so kind," Maeve said warmly, "I really am very fond of her."

"As I can see she is of you. But Ralph *is* changed. Oh, not on the surface – there he's much the same sharp fellow he always was – but I think you have laid his unhappy past to rest."

"I don't really understand . . ., but then I had only known

him a short while, less than a year before we married." Maeve found herself thinking of the man who had ridden into the churchyard, cursing his runaway horse and the raucous cry of the peacock, all disrupting her Uncle Tom's interment. He had been different then and she remembered how at first she had disliked him intensely.

"Well," Selena said honestly, "my mother told me how you had met – that was Ralph all over, blundering in where he shouldn't have been. He always had a temper and his manner is not always what it might be. We all thought marriage to Alice would improve his wild ways, and so it did for a time, until her tragic death. Then it was worse, for he grew so bitter." She looked keenly at her sister-in-law. "You know about Alice?"

"Only that she died in childbed, but I have often wondered, from things people said – Miss Mufferton, Mr Creevey . . . whether there was more to it. But Ralph never told me there was. In fact, he has never talked of it."

"Well, it was all so long ago, and both Mufti and Creevey talk too much."

"Is there something I should know?"

"If Ralph has said nothing to you, then that's how he wants the matter left. There is no reason for him to talk to you about his first wife. In fact, in my opinion it would not be at all the thing, and serve no purpose either."

Maeve gave her a direct look. "Then there was more to it? I thought there might be. His joining the army, going away, not living in the house and then selling it, made me wonder."

Selena shrugged. "It had a profound effect on him. Mind you, I was away in Cornwall with my in-laws at the time and when Hillingdon and I eventually came up to Durham he had gone to the Peninsula, but even some years later I could see how the tragedy had changed him." She shut her mouth suddenly and when she spoke again it was of her own husband. "Hillingdon's estate is in Cornwall. His family, you know, made a great deal of money from the tin mines there. Then he became a Member of Parliament and later a diplomat, so we were and are often abroad – Germany, Italy after Waterloo, and lately Russia. I shall be able to make conversation with your attaché." She had moved the conversation neatly away from her brother's first marriage, but after a few moments Maeve reverted to it.

"Is there nothing more you can tell me about – about my predecessor? I would like to understand."

Selena gave her a forthright stare, so like her brother's. "You are curious, aren't you? And it is rather pointless to drag it all up." Maeve made a deprecatory gesture. "Oh, well, if you must have it. Alice had a fall, from the top to the bottom of the stairs – it was a tall house and they were steep – and the baby was born that night, two weeks or so early. Alice died a few hours later and the baby the next day. As you can imagine, Ralph was out of his mind with grief. He was only twenty, poor lad, and very much in love. He began to hate the house, could hardly bear to walk up and down those stairs."

"Oh, I see. Poor Ralph." So concerned was she with sympathy for the young Ralph and the even younger Alice, imagining the onslaught of grief he must have suffered, that it did not occur to Maeve to wonder how his wife had come to fall.

The rain had ceased, a breeze dispersing the dark clouds, and Selena suggested that they should fetch their bonnets and take the air as far as North Street, as she wanted some ribbons for the gown she would wear tonight. "My Célie can sew them on this afternoon," she added. "French maids are so clever in the way of fashion."

She found the colour she wanted, after having every ribbon in the shop laid on the counter, and as they came out Maeve suggested they should go a little further as she had a fancy to wear sandals tonight.

"Very dashing," Selena said. "Oh, how tiresome! I must have left one glove in the draper's. Wait for me here, I won't be above a minute or two."

As they were by one of the coaching offices, Maeve stood watching as a great lumbering vehicle prepared to leave, passengers boarding, luggage being loaded, the horses held by an ostler, her mind more than half on her first big entertainment, feeling both nervous and excited. The passengers were nearly all aboard now and the post boy had picked up his horn, the coachman gathering the reins, when suddenly the last gentleman, his foot already on the top step, withdrew it to hurry across Maeve. It was the man she had seen staring at her and Ralph on their first day in Brighton.

He lifted his hat. "Pardon me, ma'am, for speaking to you. I am aware I am unknown to you, but I wonder if you would tell me if that was Ralph Digby with you the other day?"

"Yes," she answered in surprise. "I thought you must know him. He is my husband, Sir Ralph Digby."

He looked down at her, the oddest expression on his face. The post boy blew his horn and the driver called out for him to hurry or miss the coach. He bowed. "Then you have my commiserations, ma'am," he said and leapt on board before the astounded Maeve could say another word.

The coach drew out into the busy street and a voice in Maeve's ear said, "Good God!"

She turned to see her sister-in-law staring at the receeding coach, looking almost as amazed as she was. "Do you know that gentleman?" she asked. "He stared at us the other day near here, but by the time I'd called Ralph's attention to him, he'd gone."

"Oh, yes," Lady Hillingdon answered slowly. "I know that gentleman well enough, though I never saw him above half a dozen times."

"Then who – ?"

Selena took her arm and walked her away from the crowded yard. "That," she said, "is Ralph's brother-in-law, Alice's brother, Gervase Oglethorpe."

Maeve was even more surprised. "Then why on earth didn't he come over to us?"

"He wouldn't, "Selena said shortly, "unless it was to cause trouble. Nor would he expect a very warm welcome."

"Oh? Didn't he and Ralph like each other?"

"Like! I wouldn't be exaggerating if I said the mutual feeling was more like loathing. But he's been abroad since Alice died, so I suppose he may have changed with the years. It's very odd that he should be back here in Brighton just when we are – and that you and I should have been talking of him. The sort of coincidence one doesn't want."

They had reached the Steine, both having forgotten about

the sandals, and Maeve's curiosity grew. "Why did they hate each other?"

"My dear," Selena said, "it is an old story and best forgotten. I'm sorry he's back."

"I wonder what Ralph will think?"

Selena paused. The clouds were scudding up, the sunny interval over. "I would advise you most strongly to say nothing about seeing Mr Oglethorpe. At least, thank God, he appears to have left Brighton, one hopes for good. What was he saying to you?"

"Such an odd thing – he gave me his commiserations! If they hated each other as you say perhaps that would explain it in part, but why should he pity me? And why –"

"Good heavens, it's going to pour." Selena took her arm. "We must hurry home if we don't want a soaking."

"But surely Ralph should know?"

"No," Selena said as they started up Marine Parade. "Take my advice, my dear. One doesn't have to tell one's husband everything – heaven forbid – and let us trust we don't see the wretched man again. Here comes the rain." And they hurried indoors as the first drops fell.

Maeve was a trifle uneasy about keeping the occurrence from Ralph but the afternoon was too busy for her to worry any more about it. There were the decorations to oversee, the setting of the table with their own glass and silver, brought down by the reliable Flint, the rearranging of the drawing chairs and a panic over the non-arrival of the champagne. However Flint dealt with that and the bottles were soon stored in the cellar to keep chilled.

When Ralph came in he was full of the prize fight, describing the skill with which the Croucher floored Johny Longshanks, after a good many rounds, complete with broken nose, black eye and cut lip.

"Disgusting," his sister said. "Gentlemen's sports are sometimes quite beyond me. But I should like to go to the races on Friday. Will you take us, Ralph?"

"Certainly," he said. "Prinny has a horse running and Millbanke is to ride his own."

They were on the point of going up to dress when they heard a carriage rumble to a halt outside the window.

"It can't be guests yet," Maeve said in horror. "It's far too early."

Ralph was glancing out. "It is guests," he said rather shortly, "but not those we are expecting. Hollander and his wife are here."

"Oh!" For a moment her face lit up, and then consternation followed. "Oh no, not today! How could they not tell us they were coming?"

"Very inconvenient." Ralph said drily and Selena added, "That will put Flint in a fuss."

A moment or two later their footman was announcing, "Sir Frederick and Lady Hollander."

They came in a flurry of eagerness, Freddy impeccably turned out in mulberry coat and grey trousers caught under the heel, Angela in a pretty muslin dress with a light cashmere shawl over her shoulders. He held out his hands to Maeve and kissed her on both cheeks. "Well, here we are, and so glad to be here. Ralph, old fellow, how do you do?"

Maeve kissed Angela, Ralph introduced his sister, and when they were all seated Maeve said tentatively, "We didn't realise you were coming today."

"Didn't you?" Freddy queried vaguely. "I thought I wrote in my last letter . . ."

"You only said towards the end of August, but never mind. You couldn't be more welcome."

"I hope we haven't inconvenienced you," Angela said stiffly, aware of the critical eye of Ralph's sister on her.

"Not in the least," Ralph said smoothly. "We have a number of guests for dinner tonight so it will serve as an introduction for you into Brighton society."

"Unless it would be tiring for you after travelling?" Maeve turned to Angela. "You could have a tray in your room if you wish."

"What, and miss all the fun?" Freddy exclaimed. "I've never known Angela too tired for a party, eh, my love?"

She shook her head, looking round the room at the flowers, the preparations for the evening, and Maeve added, "I must tell you that the Duke of Wellington is among our guests."

"Really?" Freddy almost bounced out of his chair. "That's

splendid. I hope – but I hardly thought I'd find myself at the same table as the Beau on our first night."

"I will ask Flint to rearrange the seating," she said. "He can put Angela next to his Grace and you opposite, Freddy. Now I must see to your rooms."

He could not resist giving her a quick hug as she went to the door. "We're so glad to be here. What a good time we shall all have together. I've brought letters, by the way, from Mama and Aunt Nell. Now, Ralph, about stabling . . ."

She left them, aware of a warmth in her cheeks, this sudden arrival having momentarily shaken her. To see him in her drawing room, laughing and full of eager talk, ready to enjoy everything – in other words, his usual self – was disturbing, and for a moment she paused, her hand on the bell rope, gathering herself for what must be done.

The major-domo was admirably restrained. Quite used to dealing with sudden comings and goings and changes of plans, he merely said, "Leave it to me, madam. I will see that the seating is re-arranged. Mrs Gibson, I'm sure, will not worry about two extra covers."

"I'm afraid it will be a tight squeeze at the table. Now as to rooms . . ."

"Dolly is already upstairs preparing the large guestroom and I have had their trunks taken up. Will that suit, madam?"

Maeve gave him a quick smile. "What would we do without you, Mr Flint?"

"I trust you will not have to," he said gravely, but with a hint of a smile. He liked young Lady Digby. He had been with the family for many years and had thought Sir Ralph's first wife inclined to be a little hysterical which, in his opinion, had led to her sad demise. This new mistress, so calm and sensible, was far easier to oblige.

She went back into the drawing room where Selena was trying to draw Angela out, while Freddy was admiring the prints of famous race-horses which Ralph had bought only yesterday, to have framed and hung at Welford.

Upstairs Maeve showed Angela her apartment with its attached dressing room. Hinton was in the process of setting down his master's large amount of luggage, while Jamala was disposing of Angela's dresses.

"I'm very glad to see you, Hinton, "Maeve said, "and you, Jamala. While you are here we must contrive on a quiet afternoon for you to have an hour off to look about the town."

"Thank you, my lady," Hinton said while the Indian woman, when Angela had translated, raised her hands to her forehead and bowed. Hinton disappeared into the dressing room and closed the door and Angela added, "You are very familiar with the servants. It is not how we conducted things in India. They are there to do as you tell them, aren't they?"

Disliking her tone, Maeve said, "I've known Hinton all my life. At home and at Hollanders we always found servants did their work better for a kindly word now and then. Of course sometimes a man turns out to be a thief or drinks too much, or a girl gets into trouble, and then they have to go. But the principle is right. My Aunt Isabel has always found it so."

"Oh, my mother-in-law!" Angela wandered restlessly about the room. "You all think her perfection, I know."

Maeve sat down on the edge of the bed, not answering but merely asking if she had everything she wanted. How did Freddy deal with this beautiful but tiresome creature?

She went away soon to dress and took a long time over her toilette, wanting to look her best. Gracie had learned a great deal during her nine months as a lady's maid; she had become adept at dressing Maeve's dark hair in the most becoming way and had developed a flair for making a gown sit perfectly; a twitch here and a stitch there, and something extra was added. Maeve had chosen a gown of palest primrose with ruching at the low-cut bodice and a wide row of frills about the hem. A dark green sash surrounded her waist, falling behind to the length of the hem, with knots of the same coloured velvet decorating the bodice. The combination of colours was striking and when she had finished putting the last touch to the fall of the sash, Gracie sat back on her heels and said, "Oh, ma'am, I never did see anything so – so beautiful!"

And when Maeve went downstairs, Ralph, waiting in the hall, turned to see her and on his face was a look that made her catch her breath. But almost instantly it was gone and he merely took her hand and put it to his lips.

"My dear, you would grace any man's table. I'm proud that

it should be mine. I think I shall get Sir Thomas Lawrence to paint you in that dress."

"Oh, Ralph." Suddenly she didn't know what to say, glad to have pleased him. She remembered it later as a moment of promise that was so soon lost.

Angela came down then on Freddy's arm, looking ravishing in white with hyacinth blue trimmings, the full skirt emphasising her slender waist. Freddy glanced proudly at Maeve, who said at once, "Angela, my dear, you look lovely. You will break some hearts tonight." A remark which afterwards she wished she hadn't made.

The guests began to arrive, champagne was served, and Ralph and Maeve moved among them, making sure they were acquainted, which most of them were. Freddy and George FitzClarence struck up a conversation about army service in India, George confiding to Freddy details of the book he was writing on his experiences there, while Lady Augusta endeavoured to make something of Angela. Wellington was a little late. Maeve at once captured Freddy and presented him to the Duke as: 'My cousin, Sir Frederick, whom I mentioned to you."

Wellington was affable, listening to Freddy's enthusiasm about Waterloo and turning off the effusions by saying, "There is only one thing worse than winning a battle and that is losing it. I do not consider war a glorious thing, Sir Frederick, only a thing that has to be done in extreme circumstances."

Freddy was slightly dampened by this, but flattered by the attention the Beau gave to Angela during the meal, talking to her of his great interest in the country she had only lately left. The conversation at the richly laid table had all the brilliance Maeve had hoped for. Princess Dorothea was sparkling, her pretty face always alert, and some of her remarks on the politicians of the day were merciless at the same time wickedly funny. Gusty's laugh rang out and Mr Creevey topped some of the anecdotes with even racier ones.

Someone mentioned a lady recently come to Brighton who had come up in the world by marrying a wealthy gentleman much involved in the racing world. She was embarrassingly eager to join the Pavilion set but had no idea how to dress, covering her hair with feathers and tulle in a manner at least twenty years out of date. George said earnestly, "She is, I believe, somewhat overwhelmed by the company she finds herself in, but I'm sure at bottom she is a very good sort of woman. You rode with them yesterday, Creevey – what do you think?"

Mr Creevey turned his wine glass, a smile twitching his lips. "As to that, sir, I'm not acquainted with the lady's bottom, but I find her deuced comical at top."

There was an explosion of laughter and Gusty, who was next to him, playfully slapped his hand. "Lord, Mr Creevey, only you could say such a thing."

Unrepentant, he said, "But aren't I right?"

More laughter and a few nodding heads. Maeve, from her place at the end of the table, had become used to such free talk and she had to smile, but she couldn't bring herself to like it, particularly at her own entertainment, and she was thankful that Ralph turned the conversation by speaking of the forthcoming races while his sister was leading some lively talk about the new production of one of Mr Sheridan's plays. The mention of the Brighton theatre brought George back into the discussion. He never forgot that his mother had been an actress and took a keen interest in that profession.

Count Gregor Balakov, sitting on Angela's other side, engaged her attention for a great deal of the lengthy meal; he made her laugh, and she listened while he talked of St Petersburg and the Winter Palace, of the River Neva frozen in the winter and the Hermitage with its wealth of art treasures, describing the golden onion domes of that city until she clapped her hands together and said, "Oh how I would like to see it all."

Maeve was occupied by the Duke who was on her right, their conversation more sober, talking of horses and hunting, and he told her of his old favourite, Copenhagen, who had carried him through the day on the field of Waterloo.

"Buried at my place at Stratfield Saye," he finished. "Good old fellow, he deserved a decent burial. Do you know my part of the world, Lady Digby?" When she shook her head, to her astonishment he said, "Then you and Sir Ralph must visit me some time – if you would care to? Not very exciting. Can't offer much entertainment, I'm afraid, but the riding is good."

From what Ralph had said, she knew such invitations were not often issued and she accepted, saying quietly, "I am country-bred, you know, sir, and would enjoy such a visit very much."

He nodded, understanding her, and her liking for him grew.

After dinner they all assembled in the drawing room. Ralph asked Princess Dorothea to play for them on the pianoforte that the room boasted and she complied willingly.

"Our Snipe plays well," Mr Creevey murmured in Maeve's ear during the applause at the end, and she turned and asked why he called her that.

"Oh, my dear, that pointed nose. Pretty and well-shaped, I grant you, but into everything. Haven't you noticed she has something to say on every single matter?"

She could not help smiling, but added, "That is what makes her so delightful a dinner guest."

George, who had a fine baritone voice, sang a duet then with his wife, and Count Lieven's deep bass came over well in a Russian folk song.

There was a little lull after that and Freddy said tentatively to Maeve that if she would like it, Angela would dance for them, accompanied by her maid on an Indian instrument.

Surprised, Maeve said, "I didn't know she danced as an entertainment. Aunt Isabel never mentioned it."

"No," he answered in a low voice. "You know Hollanders, it was not likely to be suitable so I never suggested it, but here – only, not if you wouldn't think it acceptable."

"I'm sure it would be delightful," Maeve said, and went over to Angela to make the suggestion, Without hesitation she slipped out of the room.

She came back some time later, entering at an appropriate break in the conversation – Maeve was sure she had listened for it – and all heads turned. She had changed into an Indian dress of scarlet and gold, her hair loose, her sari embroidered with dragons and exotic flowers, her feet bare with jewelled anklets above. The whole effect was breathtaking. Jamala followed her carrying a sittar, and when Maeve said Lady Hollander would dance for them, a space was cleared in the centre of the room.

Slowly, as Jamala plucked the strings, Angela began to move, her bare slender feet bearing her swaying body, turning and twisting in a sensuous manner, the anklets tinkling, her hands and fingers all part of the dance, lifting and gesticulating.

The gentlemen were captivated. Count Balakov couldn't take his eyes from her, Mark Millbanke was openly staring, George recalling his days in India when he had seen such dances performed and whispering something in Mary's ear. Mr Creevey's eyes grew wider, a little smile on his lips as if he was relishing the gossip this would provide tomorrow, and even the Beau looked on in approval. Freddy was a little flushed, delighted at the effect of his wife's performance, but Maeve felt hot and somewhat embarrassed. There was no denying the appeal of such a display on the men present, for it had an overt sensuousness of which they were more than aware. She glanced at Ralph, but he too was rivetted. She caught Selena's eye and saw one eyebrow raised but more in amusement than anything else. Only one or two of the ladies were not smiling, Lady Hertford with a sour look on her face and Lady Ellenborough apparently occupied in studying her fan.

The music ceased. Angela lowered her arms and sank to the floor. There was an outburst of applause. Ralph came to her and gallantly raised her while Mark Millbanke called out, "Splendid performance, Lady Hollander," and George said, "I've never seen it better done, don't you agree, my Lord?"

"Heartily," Wellington nodded. "We who've visited India know how well you danced, my dear."

Freddy was glowing and Maeve was afraid someone should suggest that she danced again, but fortunately at that moment the tea-tray came in and Angela slipped away with Jamala. When she returned fifteen minutes later, changed back into her evening gown, she was immediately surrounded by gentlemen, laughed with them and talked easily, clearly relishing the adulation.

"Well," Maeve said to Freddy, "she has certainly contributed to the success of my party."

"Wasn't she wonderful? The first time I saw her do it, I was quite bowled over, I can tell you." Which, Maeve thought, explained a few things.

But much later, after all the guests had gone and Freddy and Angela retired, when Maeve made the same remark to Ralph, concerning the success of the evening, he said drily, "Oh, she was quite a hit, I agree. But if I were Hollander I would not want my wife exhibiting herself in such a manner. It was fascinating, but provocative to say the least. Better suited to the theatre, I should say."

Maeve sat down, suddenly tired, in the now empty drawing room, only Ralph's sister with them. "What did you think, Selena?"

Lady Hillingdon shrugged. "Entertaining enough, but Ralph is right. It was suggestive, which is doubtless why all the gentlemen liked it."

"Including her husband," Ralph said. "But I must admit to being surprised at his proposing it in the first place."

Maeve found herself flushing and rose in instant defence. "I suppose he is proud of her talent, which one can't deny."

"Never having seen Indian dancers, I can have no opinion on that, though George and the Duke seemed to agree," Ralph said. "Only one wonders at his naivety. Shall we go up?"

Chapter 15

If Maeve wanted something to make people forget 'the little girl from the Vicarage' remark she certainly had her way. Angela's dancing became the subject of a great deal of talk and no doubt the motive behind many invitations – to dine, to picnic on the Downs, to attend card parties and balls. She performed at the Millbankes, though Lady Augusta said to Maeve that she thought it positively indelicate. "Only Mark will have it that it's art," she explained. But in reality she was not at all put out at seeing it in her own drawing room: "At least before Mark's aunt Lady Melbourne arrives," she added with a smile.

Mr Creevey could talk of nothing else. When Angela, who never rode, joined a picnic party in flowing pink muslin, her carriage was surrounded by young men eager to hand her out, several officers having heard the tale from Captain MacDonald, and she became within a week the toast of Brighton. The Duke of Sussex who had been at the Millbankes told his brother of it in glowing terms, the upshot of which was an invitation from his Majesty for Sir Frederick and Lady Hollander to attend an evening reception, with the added request that Lady Hollander should dance for them.

The King was delighted, clapping his hands and asking for more. He had always admired artistic talent, the more exotic the better, and it was hardly surprising that young Lady Hollander should intrigue him. Afterwards he called her to sit beside him, showed her his Indian treasures, and escorted her through each room, puffing and ungainly, to exhibit his considerable collection of Oriental art.

At every entertainment the Russian attaché contrived to be among those most often at her side, and when they danced together at a ball at the Old Ship all eyes were on them, both of them so physically beautiful that together they were an astonishing combination.

During the evening Angela danced three times with Count Balakov and Maeve, waltzing with Freddy, said, "It is not very discreet of her, you know. A married lady should not dance more than once with a single gentleman."

"Oh, stuff!" was his laughing answer. "As if I should be worried. She is always sought after wherever we go. I'm proud of her. Don't you think I should be?"

"Of course," Maeve said. "But she doesn't know English society, and for all the easy talk there are some things one must be wary of – I've had to learn that."

"Darling Maeve." He squeezed her hand. "I'm glad to see you so happy with Ralph, who's a splendid fellow. We went to Lamprell's bathing establishment today and he's a dashed good swimmer. He says he learnt by being thrown in the river at Cambridge!"

"Oh," she said in surprise, "I didn't know that. I know he likes to bathe in the sea, but the ladies and men are kept separate on the beach so I've not seen him in the water. Anyway it's too cold now."

"What a long way all this seems from Hollanders," he said. "I don't know how I shall get Angela home again. I'm afraid she's not as happy there as I could wish. Not riding or hunting or liking any country occupations, she and Mama just can't seem to get on, try as Mama will. She seems fond of Ellen who thinks her Indian background fascinating, but then Ellen is more often than not out riding herself. This," he indicated the ballroom, "is what Angela likes." He brightened and added, "And so do I, by Jove! After Christmas I've promised that we'll go to London for a long stay."

So much, Maeve thought, for his leaving the army to come home to be master of Hollanders. He seemed not only to have lost his heart but also his commonsense over Angela, and with his innate good nature tended to see only the best in her. Maeve's sympathies went out to her aunt.

During all the socialising that went on through the autumn,

while Angela was fêted and scarcely missed a single entertainment, the attachment of Count Balakov set tongues wagging. Maeve even heard it was being obliquely suggested that there was more to it than met the eye. But she said nothing to Freddy. There didn't seem to be much point, for she was sure he would have laughed it off. Ralph had not referred to the subject since the night of their first dinner party, for reasons she could guess at.

In the game of flirtations Mr Manners continued to be a nuisance, striving to bring his horse alongside Maeve's, his chair next to hers, to be one of her set whenever they were at cards. Once when he slipped his hand on to her knee under a table at Donaldson's, she slapped it hard and said in a low voice, "Mr Manners, permit me to tell you that you are most inaptly named for it is obvious to me that you have none at all."

Far from being set down he chuckled and said, "How I like a woman with wit – but not, I hope, a Miss Prunes and Prisms?"

If she had hoped to shame him, she had quite failed. It was clear he would like the flirtation to go on, to what end she could imagine, and it began to worry her. Once when he had been among a party walking on the Chain Pier he elbowed another gentleman aside to be her companion, and later when they were returning to Marine Parade she said to Ralph, "Why didn't you come to my rescue? Surely you could see Mr Manners was being tiresome?"

He raised an eyebrow. "What did you expect me to do? Call him out? I would make myself ridiculous if I behaved like a watchdog."

"If you had walked with me instead of squiring Mrs Trenchard, I would have preferred it."

"I should have thought you could have dealt with an ape like Manners. Anyway I don't wish to become a laughing stock – as your cousin is."

"Oh!" She was highly indignant. "I don't believe it. I've never heard –"

"Probably you wouldn't. But he does rather make himself a cake over his wife."

"I don't know which attitude is worse," she retorted, and

then remembered old Lady Salisbury's words of warning.

Instinctively she turned to Freddy for support, thinking perhaps he needed it too, but he appeared for a while to be blissfully unaware of any such thing. Over the next week or so, however, she sensed an unease creeping into his manner when they were occasionally alone. He called Balakov a pertinaceous fellow and added, "I have told Angela not to encourage him, but she laughs it off."

As you did once, Maeve thought. But they were caught in a whirl of rather hectic pleasuring and there appeared to be nothing to be done about it while the King stayed in Brighton.

Lord Hillingdon arrived, a long, lugubrious man who regarded life as a serious matter but on occasion could have a twinkle in his eye. Maeve liked him at once and was enjoying her house full of people. She and Ralph seemed to have little time together, sometimes only meeting in their bedroom, and often then if he was late she pretended to be asleep when he came to bed. Their bedtime conversations so often ended in sharp words.

Ralph and his brother-in-law seemed to get on extremely well, sharing a large circle of male friends quite separate from the younger group around Freddy and Angela, and while she was holding her court, Maeve and Freddy were left more and more to each other. They shared old jokes, old memories, talking often of Hollanders, of Freddy's father, of childhood days and games on the Marsh, Riding on the Downs with a party of friends, their horses generally came together. Freddy had bought a magnificent bay which he had called The Beau in honour of the Duke of Wellington, and there was nothing he liked better than cantering him alongside Maeve's Blanche. Mr Manners became aware he had competition. Not one to be worried by a husband – indignant, annoyed, or complacent – a rival was another matter and once or twice he twitted her on preferring the company of Sir Frederick.

"He is my cousin," was her retort, but nothing daunted him.

"I know his sort," Freddy said, "I'll fend him off for you." Which, Maeve thought, was more than Ralph was doing.

It was for her a time of happiness and heartache. To be close to Freddy, sharing so much with him, brought all the old longing back; seeing his smile brought such a response that she felt for a while back in the old days. But it was not the old days. This was dangerous, and she knew it. And if she thought Ralph unaware of what was happening, she was wrong.

One evening at the Pavilion Angela was sitting beside the King, somewhat to Lady Conyngham's annoyance, and Freddy came towards Maeve, to the empty seat beside her. Ralph also was set in the same direction and Caroline Trenchard, taking his arm, said, "I see Sir Frederick is about to keep Lady Digby company, so do, Ralph, come and take a place by me. There are two chairs."

He hesitated, his face expressionless. Looking towards his wife, he saw her smiling up at her cousin and without further ado offered Mrs Trenchard his arm.

A voice on Maeve's other side said, "A chair here, if you please, Hillingdon," and as Selena sat down she added in Maeve's ear, "Insufferable woman! We can't avoid her in society but if she calls on you, don't receive her."

"She has already," Maeve whispered back, "but I was out. Only how can I refuse her if she comes again? I'm sure Ralph would not like me to."

"One need not," Selena said in a crushing tone aimed at Mrs Trenchard's back, "be forced to receive one's husband's mistress – or rather ex-mistress, which at least is the situation in Ralph's case."

Maeve felt her face flame and then turned cold as the colour ebbed. Her throat felt dry and no words would come. She managed to say, "I didn't know."

"Well, he was hardly likely to tell you," Selena said casually, before she realised the effect her remark was having on her sister-in-law. "Oh, my dear, I didn't mean to upset you. Believe me it was some time ago. And surely you didn't think there had been no one between Alice and you?"

"I never thought about it at all." Maeve began to recover herself a little. "But I see – naturally one could not expect – "

"It's the way of men. Dear girl, don't let it bother you."

"I wish she wasn't here. She – she makes such a point of seeking him out and I don't know whether he likes it or not." She wondered if she sounded like a querulous complaining wife.

"I doubt it," Selena said. "She really is beyond anything. Men do like a little flattery, but Ralph is not likely to be drawn into that web again." She regarded her sister-in-law. "He thinks far too much of you, you know." She saw another wave of colour come. "It is only the way of society that we all mix around, for the most part quite harmlessly. I had a whole summer, years ago, of being pursued by Lord Grey, after the Duchess of Devonshire had thrown him over. Mind you, it went too far with her and one of her brood is his. I never went that way! But I can have a word with Ralph, if you like?"

Maeve sat stiffly in her chair. Freddy, thankfully, was engaged in conversation with Lady Augusta and not aware of Maeve's low-voiced talk with her sister-in-law. "No, thank you, Selena. I'm sure he would resent that. And, anyway I must fight my own battles."

"Very well, my dear," Lady Hillingdon said complacently, "I won't say a word. But I shall certainly not receive Mrs Trenchard when we are back in London, nor talk with her here except for the scantest politeness. I can make myself felt, you know, and a little flank attack never did any harm."

Maeve was quite sure her sister-in-law could be a formidable opponent – and a staunch ally. She pressed her hand. "Thank you. Dear Selena, I'm so glad you came to Brighton."

Lady Hillingdon laughed. "The feeling is mutual. My mother said that if once you and I got over a little initial fencing, we would get on very well."

"Ralph told me that once you were someone's friend, it was for life."

"Did he now? That was handsome of him, and true, I hope, in our case. And don't let Mrs Trenchard bother you. She is just an incorrigible, rather ill-bred flirt who once trapped an unhappy young man. Oh, it is to be Handel tonight. How delightful."

But the music that Maeve usually so enjoyed was lost on her this evening. She could not take her eyes off Ralph, sitting beside Mrs Trenchard, and was beset by thoughts she would rather not have had. Ralph had cuckolded – horrid word – Mr Trenchard. He had been the lover of this woman with the amazing red hair and greenish eyes who was looking up at him in a manner that spoke of old intimacy; or even, Maeve thought in revulsion, of hopes of renewing it. She might be all the things that Selena called her but of her physical charm there could be no doubt. It was all hateful, but such affairs were part of the world she now lived in, and anyway how could she blame Ralph for anything he had done before he met her? And if it were to start again, would she have driven him to it? Unpleasant thoughts came into her head. If she was not the sort of wife he wanted, if she had failed to live up to his expectations, would he turn to Mrs Trenchard again? She would not be able to laugh it off as some women did, or take a lover herself. She could never, never do that – she was too much the Vicarage daughter – nor could she ever do violence to the principles her stepfather had inculcated into her.

She thought of Selena's remark, that Ralph did care for her – so much, Selena had said. Was it true? A longing rose in her, a different longing, for things to change, to be right as they might once have been. She braced herself. One had to deal with the situation as it was, and she was fast learning that to bemoan the past was a quite fruitless occupation. She was not going to give up, look the other way. She was going to fight, as she told Selena, but just at this moment she didn't know what weapons were to hand – and the reason for this determination to vanquish Mrs Trenchard quite eluded her.

The round of parties and outings continued as autumn drew on, but the King returned to Windsor and gradually people drifted away. Count Lieven and the Princess Dorothea went to Windsor with his Majesty, Wellington had gone to London when Parliament reassembled to deal with the crumbling government of Lord Liverpool, Mr Creevey departed to be the guest of his friend Lord Sefton at Croxteth. Angela began to look dejected but one morning when George FitzClarence had returned to London about his duties, his wife's eldest brother, another George, called on Ralph and Maeve to say that he was taking his sister to Petworth to see their father, and his Lordship had said in his usual hospitable way that they might bring any guests they liked. The Millbankes had already been invited and he proposed that the whole party from the Digbys' house should join them.

"The hunting is excellent," he said, smiling at Maeve, "and the park well stocked. I do hope you will all come?"

Ralph looked pleased and Angela was obviously delighted. Freddy murmured something about it being time to go home, but she said at once, "Oh, pray, let us go to Petworth. I can't think of anything more pleasant than continuing the delightful time we have had here."

Freddy conceded. He seemed to be incapable of refusing her anything, but later he said to Maeve that he would have to write a conciliatory letter to his mother, informing her that they would be another two weeks returning home.

"You've not been there a great deal since you came back," she pointed out. "Aunt Isabel must be looking forward to your settling at Hollanders."

"I know." He sighed. "But you must see how happy Angela is to be in such lively company. I wish I knew what to do."

It was not like him to sound so depressed and she was sorry for him, but she hardly knew what to advise. That night Ralph came out of his dressing room to say, "You will like Petworth, once you accept the Wyndham eccentricities. For some reason Lord Egremont failed to marry Elizabeth Ayliffe, the mother of his six children, until after they were grown up, so they are all illegitimate. She died four years ago. The title, I believe, must go to a cousin, but George Wyndham will get Petworth and the old man will certainly look after Mary and FitzClarence. I shall enjoy taking you there."

Two days before they left they attended the theatre to see a new production of one of Mr Sheridan's plays and Maeve found herself walking in beside Mrs Trenchard.

"Such a crush," that lady said. "There always is here, isn't there, despite so many people going away. Do you go to London this winter, Lady Digby? It's the only place to find any entertainment at this time of year."

"No," Maeve said, "at least not as far as I know. We are to visit Petworth before going back to our house, Welford Park, for Christmas."

"Oh!" Mrs Trenchard gave a tinkling laugh. "Such an odd old man, Lord Egremont."

"Have you been there?" Maeve asked, and when Mrs Trenchard shook her head, adding that everyone knew how peculiar he was, Maeve added, "Personally I find it very ill-judged to remark upon people I haven't met."

Mrs Trenchard looked sharply at her. "Dear me, it's easy to see you have not long mixed in high society, my dear. Listening to talk is as good as meeting someone sometimes."

Maeve was about to make a swift retort, but perhaps fortunately they came to their box and Ralph handed her in. As they sat down he said, "Was it necessary to be quite so rude to Mrs Trenchard?"

"I don't like her," Maeve said shortly.

"That is obvious. Why?"

"One is hardly obliged to like everyone," Maeve retorted, "and nothing suits her better than to say something to me to remind me of the 'girl from the vicarage' remark."

"You are reading too much into that," was Ralph's only comment as the curtain went up.

It was with very mixed feelings that Maeve prepared to leave Marine Parade. It had been home for three months which on the whole, apart from a few rubs, had been enjoyable. She was thankful that the Trenchards were scarcely known to the Wyndhams and had not been invited to Petworth. Mr Flint was organizing the giving up of the house and the return of staff and goods to Welford, and all the other details. Bridges, Ralph's valet, and Gracie were of course accompanying them to Petworth, and the whole party would travel together.

On the last day, after seeing to the careful packing of her jewellery and personal things, Maeve slipped out to make a final call on Mrs Fitzherbert. Ralph had gone to bid farewell to Captain MacDonald and other friends, the Hillingdons too, while Freddy and Angela had driven ahead to spend a night on the way with an old friend of his from the East India Company.

Maeve wrapped a warm cloak about herself for there was a chill wind off the sea, and she remembered how calm and blue it had been on the hot day when they had first arrived here. Mrs Fitzherbert was alone, and Maeve was glad. She had come to like the elderly lady so much and to be the only caller was a rare privilege.

"Brighton is emptying fast," Mrs Fitzherbert said while her footman served coffee, "but a circle of friends now live here, as I have done for so many years, and there is still the theatre and the Assembly Rooms to give us entertainment, as well as out winter addiction – almost daily card parties! When do you go, my dear?"

Maeve accepted her cup and took a sweet biscuit. "Tomorrow, ma'am, but we are not returning home just yet. We are to stay at Petworth for two weeks."

"I'm sure you will enjoy that. I've not been there myself but I met Lord Egremont in the old days and found him charming, if a little eccentric. But I sometimes think eccentricities are what makes people interesting, don't you? He did so much to bring Mr Turner forward, and dear Mary FitzClarence gave me that delightful painting he did of a woodland scene at Petworth."

Maeve glanced up at the picture over the mantelshelf that she had admired each time she came. The long windows were closed today and a cheerful fire burned in the hearth. "I shall ask Ralph to try to buy one of Mr Turner's works to hang at Welford. It would be an addition to our drawing room, I think."

"And you are looking forward to being there, I can see. Has your stay here been a pleasant one?" Maeve met the direct and very kindly look. Mrs Fitzherbert was someone she felt she could confide in. "Mostly," she said. "Oh, that sounds ungrateful. So much of it has been quite delightful – going to the Pavilion and the balls and picnics – but sometimes I have felt . . ." she searched for words ". . . a little overwhelmed."

"A very different scene for the girl from the Vicarage?" Mrs Fitzherbert queried softly. "Yes, my dear, that *bon mot* reached me. I'm very fond of Lady Hillingdon but she does speak her mind. Or rather, I should say, the first thing that comes into it – sometimes rather unfortunately!"

"Yes. I admit I didn't like it, nor did my husband. It – it seemed like a slur on the home I came from, that it should be the cause for such amusement."

"The clergy and the Church are often a butt for wit," her hostess said, "and indeed some parsons deserve little else, for all they seem to think of is hunting and socialising and the table and putting their duties on the shoulders of a poor curate, but I'm sure your papa is not like that."

"Oh, no, not in the least. He is so good and our people love him, though he isn't soft," Maeve added, smiling. "I've seen him deal very firmly with shiftless fellows and lazy good-for-nothing girls in the village. When he married my mother – he had loved her for a long time, while my real father was alive – and we went to live in the vicarage, we were so happy."

"Then you must be proud to be the girl from the vicarage," Mrs Fitzherbert told her. "I can see, dear child, that the society gathered round his Majesty cannot have been totally congenial to you."

"Well," Maeve twisted her hands together, "Most people have been very kind to me, and Ralph has so many friends whom I've enjoyed entertaining. I can hold my own in most situations and sometimes find the right words to cap a remark –"

"As Lady Hillingdon found – oh, yes, I heard that too."

Maeve could not keep back a smile. "I'm afraid it was very rude of me. But when it comes to the licence that goes on – oh dear, I don't mean to be a prude, but I can't help but feel . . ."

"I know only too well what you mean, no one better." Mrs Fitzherbert's smile was a little sad. "When my dearest Prinny first fell in love with me and I realised how deep it went and what he wanted, I fled, you know. I travelled in Europe – I was a widow then – but Prinny's friends persuaded me to come back, telling me he was threatening suicide. So I came. But I would not be his mistress. I had a tussle with my conscience and my Catholic beliefs which meant, and still do, so much to me. And then that marriage . . . it satisfied him for a while but there were others out to destroy him. I could never forgive Mr Fox for his treachery. Nor could I hold my husband – that is how I think and will think of him to the day of my death. But he was heir to the throne and our marriage was against the law of the land, so it all came to an end, oh, twenty years ago now. There has been no one else for me and I watched in great sorrow the wretched misery he had with the woman they chose for him. Poor Prinny, it was no wonder he turned to others."

"I wish he had turned back to you," Maeve said impulsively.

Mrs Fitzherbert stared out of the window at the grey scudding clouds. "It was not possible. But I think I could have kept him from the ruinous life of drink and women and wildness of all sorts. Ah, well, it is no good repining the past. But you see, my dear, why I can understand your feelings. I was not a frivolous person, nor are you, that is obvious. Take your Ralph home and be happy there, where you can live the sort of life you really like."

"Oh, yes," Maeve said on a long drawn-out breath. She had a sudden rush of pictures into her head: Welford with its lovely garden taking shape, Hollanders on its ridge commanding such panoramic views, the Marsh stretching away below, the dear old vicarage and its homely rooms. "Oh, yes," she said again. "Thank you for understanding, ma'am."

"Write to me sometimes," Mrs Fitzherbert said. "I should like to know how you go on. I hope to hear of you with a family coming along soon."

"So do I – I long to please my husband in that way." There was a knock on the outer door and she got up suddenly. She would have liked to pour out all her hopes and disappointments to this wise lady who had had no children herself, but it was too late and as another visitor was shown in, Maeve said with some regret that she must go.

To her surprise Mrs Fitzherbert kissed her on both cheeks. "God bless you, child. Sir Ralph is a lucky man. I hope he knows it."

Maeve walked across the Steine, aware of a warmth, a kindness, that she was sorry to leave behind, combined with a sense of guilt. What would Mrs Fitzherbert have thought if she had confessed to being in love with another man? She would surely think less of her, and remembering that lady's last words to her, Maeve was aware of a certain wistfulness. If she had known the truth would Mrs Fitzherbert have thought Ralph so lucky?

She recalled that first walk here, on his arm, and how excited she had been at the prospects before her. To be a constant visitor to the Pavilion and to come to know the Prinny of so much fame and gossip, meeting the real man and discovering, apart from all the dissipation people accused him of, how cultured he was, how he loved music and art. She had made so many new friends, found so much that was exhilarating, but there was another side to the coin. She was having to accept things about Ralph that she had not known – apart from his one-time liaison with Mrs Trenchard there was his preoccupation with various sports, his seeking of male company, his brusque way of dealing with their not infrequent arguments. Yet Selena said he cared very much for her. Did he? Or was their marriage becoming like so many others, a mere surface convention? It seemed to her he had withdrawn a little from her. Having Freddy and Angela in the house had no doubt contributed to that. They were a part of the family scene now and Welford was very near to Hollanders. They could not avoid meeting each other nor could she help treating Freddy as she had always treated him.

She wished she knew how Ralph felt about that. He was polite always, but she sensed he only tolerated Freddy and actively disliked Angela. She would have liked to talk to Selena about it but could she do that without betraying herself? No, it was out of the question.

What a coil it was, and mostly of her own making. Glad to reach Donaldson's, she returned her last loaned book and came out to turn up St James Street, meaning to cut through Charles Street to Marine Parade. It was then that she saw the door of a house opposite open, and to her astonishment Ralph came out.

Having no idea who lodged in the narrow building she paused, seeing him look up to a window on the first floor where a woman stood by the curtain. Ralph lifted his hat and Caroline Trenchard blew him a kiss.

Then he ran down the steps and Maeve fled back into the sanctuary of Donaldson's, her heart thumping in a most unpleasant way. He had lied to her, had gone not to Captain MacDonald but to that woman! She felt sick, shaken, and stood by a shelf, staring blindly at a row of books. A slight acquaintance spoke to her but she barely answered, and as soon as she was sure he would be out of sight, she followed Ralph home.

They dined alone on this last evening and at once he asked her what the matter was. "Are you ill? You look very pale."

"I am perfectly well," she said, and knew her voice sounded snappish as she crumbled her roll.

"I expect you are tired, what with preparing to leave and all the farewell visits. Are you sorry to be going?"

"In some ways, though I shall be glad to be home again." And then, because the opening was there, she was unable to resist it. "How did you spend your day?"

"As I told you, saying my own goodbyes to various people whom we shall not see at Petworth."

"Including Mrs Trenchard?" She hated herself for saying it, knowing it was a stupid thing to do, but the words would come out.

He put down his glass and regarded her. "Now who saw fit to inform you of that?"

"I saw you," she said, not meeting his gaze. "I went to Donaldson's to return that book I finished last night."

"I see." He flicked his fingers for the expressionless footman to leave them, and then said, "And what are you making of it?"

"I don't know – nothing. At least – " she floundered.

"It was a courtesy call on an old friend," he said shortly. "Courtesy such as you blatantly refused to show her."

"An old friend?" Not a wise remark either, emphasising the word 'friend'. She could see the tell-tale signs of his rising annoyance, but she wanted it out in the open.

"I gather someone has been gossiping. Do I detect Selena's hand in this? Yes, I thought so. Her lack of tact is really phenomenal."

Maeve stiffened. "She merely told me she would not be receiving Mrs Trenchard and suggested I should not either."

He continued to keep his pale eyes fixed on her. "And why is that?"

"Well, Selena said she was once – " Aware she should never have got into this conversation, Maeve felt the colour flooding her face.

"Yes, once what?" And as she did not answer he added, "Do you want me to be more explicit?"

"Oh!" she clasped her hands together. "You have no – no –"

"Delicacy?" he queried in a mocking tone. "But then you have always known that, haven't you? My dear girl, you are being singularly stupid. Whatever Caroline Trenchard was to me in the past, I can assure you it is very much in the past. Did you imagine that before I met you I had lived the life of a cloistered monk?"

"No," she said jerkily. "No, of course not."

"Then be sensible. I am sorry Selena should have informed you of it. It would have been better left decently buried."

"I – I would not have thought anything – but Mrs Trenchard made such a set at you, even at the Pavilion –"

"Good God!" he said irritably. "You are making far too much of this. I'm sorry for Caroline and I would be a pretty poor sort of fellow if I turned my back on her. She and her husband don't get on and she's not popular – too many of the aristocratic old cats shun her. She could do with a little friendship. And if we are to cast stones, you have spent more time with Hollander than might be considered seemly."

"But he's my cousin," she retorted, as she had to Mr Manners.

"Ah, but not as close by blood as I once thought. Your mother is only distantly connected with the Hollanders, I believe."

"Yes, but you know perfectly well we were all brought up together and Sir Thomas and Lady Hollander always as uncle and aunt to Mary and me. You are being quite ridiculous to compare that with your relationship with Mrs Trenchard."

"I have no relationship, as you put it, with her," he said crushingly. "I merely went to say goodbye – I could do no less. But why I should explain myself to you, I don't know."

"I am your wife."

"But not my keeper." Throwing down his napkin, he got to his feet. At the door he paused, and in a very different tone he added, "At least if you are jealous, there's some hope for me." After which extraordinary remark he went out, leaving her staring after him, a prey to confused emotions. That night he slept in his dressing room and so ended their last day in Brighton.

Chapter 16

Petworth House was a magnificent place, set in sweeping parkland designed by 'Capability' Brown, and as their carriage was driven through the little town to the entrance, Maeve was quite unprepared for the vista that stretched out on the far side.

Servants in blue livery with silver-crested buttons leapt to open doors and carry in baggage, and in an entrance hall smaller than might have been expected a sedate butler met them and conducted them past the great staircase into a marble reception room. Maeve had a brief impression of walls adorned with paintings, sculptures on stands, and then she was being presented to her host, the Earl himself.

Lord Egremont was seventy-five years old, genial, eccentric and generous, a big man with a jutting hooked nose. He seldom left Petworth now. It had been his purpose in life to make the great art collection housed here; his stud had been famous and in the past he had had winners of both the Derby and the Oaks. He had created a house, once the home of the Percies of Northumberland, a pleasure garden, and a park of amazing beauty and loved to fill it with people.

"A great inn," Mr Creevey had told Maeve before he left Brighton, obviously sorry not to be with the party bound for Petworth, "but with rather poor service, despite having more servants than any other house in the kingdom, I should think." As always he had an anecdote to tell. "Do you know once I couldn't get a glass of wine at ten o'clock at night. And why? The butler had gone to bed! Did you ever?"

The Earl greeted Ralph with great affection and gave

Maeve a gentle welcoming smile. "Well, my dear, I'm glad to see Ralph with a pretty wife at last. I hope you enjoy your stay here, and if there's anything you want there are plenty of servants to look after you. Do you like pictures?"

"Very much, sir."

"Then you'll enjoy my little collection. I received the Allied sovereigns here in this room when they were visiting England, the year before Waterloo it was, and the Tsar of Russia took a great fancy to that bust there of the Roman Emperor, Septimus Severus. I think he hoped I'd present him with it, but I don't part with my treasures. They're here for everyone to enjoy. Ah, Lady Hillingdon, and you, my Lord, how pleasant to see you again."

Maeve moved on and Mary FitzClarence hurried over to greet her. "Let me show you round, my love. Ralph, you will find George somewhere, probably in the stables."

She swept Maeve on from one elegant room to another of the house where she had grown up, pointing out favourite paintings. "I love that one of the Thames at Windsor. Mr Turner has a studio upstairs, you know – my father was his patron and brought him forward – but he hasn't used it for many years. He's so famous now and his work is much in demand. Isn't that a fine portrait?" She pointed out a large picture of a Tudor gentleman sitting by a table and leaning his head on one had. "That's Henry Percy, the ninth Earl of Northumberland. He was known as the Wizard Earl because of his interest in scientific things. Oh, and there is my special favourite, by Angelica Kaufman – fancy a lady being a famous painter. But you will see more tomorrow. I expect now you would like to see your room?"

Unable to take it all in, Maeve said she would and Mary, after introducing a sister and another brother, rang the bell. Maeve followed the summoned footman who led her majestically up the grand staircase to the long corridors above. The door of a large apartment at a corner of the massive house was flung open and there she found Gracie unpacking her clothes. There was a door slightly open to a dressing room beyond and she caught a glimpse of Bridges bent over his master's valise.

"Oh, ma'am," Gracie sat back on her heels, "Isn't it a big

place, and so grand?" The maxim that servants did not speak unless spoken to had escaped her.

"It is indeed." Maeve gazed round the room. It was decorated in blue and gold, the hangings rich brocade, a thick blue carpet woven with yellow and bronze flowers, while the furniture was all of the most expensive and in selective taste. A little Boule writing desk, furnished with pens, ink and paper for her use, was set against one wall and a huge gilt pier glass hung between the windows. The chinoiserie style of it reminded her of the Pavilion. There was a marble-topped table by the sumptuous bed with its mahogany head and foot boards, and on a washstand were basin, ewer, and small dishes.

Maeve went to one of the windows and looked out at the fine trees of the park, the garden area ending in a ha-ha to keep the deer from straying into it, and she anticipated the pleasure of riding there. "You are right, Gracie, it's quite magnificent," she said, and turned as Ralph came in.

"Well?" he queried, "what do you think of it?"

"I thought Hollanders was large, and Welford too, but this! Shall we ride tomorrow?"

"Indeed we will, if the weather is suitable. We shall find horses at our disposal, which is why I sent ours home. His Lordship has a vast stable – I believe something approaching three hundred."

"Good gracious, does he mount half the county?"

Ralph grinned, "Certainly all his guests. He likes his dinner unfashionably early, at six o'clock, so I suppose we had better change."

Everyday matters had set the tone of their conversation on the journey here, neither she nor Ralph mentioning Mrs Trenchard again. This morning in the bustle of leaving he had appeared his usual self and she had followed his lead. It had been stupid to tax him with the affair, over it seemed before she knew him, and she certainly didn't believe he had taken it up again. But his remark last night remained with her. Was she jealous? Could she be, knowing she didn't love him? But undeniably her feelings towards him were changing. Perhaps I'm just getting used to being a married lady, she told herself, and went down to dinner on his arm, thankful to put that unhappy end to the Brighton stay behind her.

The house-party consisted mostly of people she already knew, except the Wyndham brother and sister, some cousins and a nephew of Mr Fox whom she found very foppish. George FitzClarence had gone back to his duties at the Horse Guards, but Mary stayed with her children, the elder two adored by their grandfather, and Maeve was touched, as she had been at Moon's End, by Ralph's popularity with the little boys, considering he never fussed over them and treated them as small adults, without any concessions to their age. She thought he would make a good father, if he was not too severe with his own. But that prospect had no foundation for hope.

The dinner was good, even if it had lost a little of its heat on its long journey from the kitchens, and the evening passed pleasantly. Their host was well-read, an intelligent man able to lead a great deal of brilliant talk. Mr Manners was there, his 'noble patron' being a friend of the Earl's, and as they left the table he contrived to walk with Maeve into the drawing room.

"Brighton was very pleasant," he remarked, "but I must say I dislike the thought of winter. There was a very heavy mist this morning and it does not suit my constitution."

"I am country-bred," she answered, "and quite used to this sort of weather. Romney Marsh is often covered by mist in the winter and I ride in all weathers."

"Myself, I prefer London," he said. "I have information that my relative Rutland will be home from the Continent shortly, so I have to go back there certainly by the end of the week. I shall miss your company."

"No doubt Sir Ralph and I will be in London some time," she answered.

"Ah, yes, in Bruton street."

"You are very knowledgeable, sir."

"I have been in society for a long time," he said archly, "and I think I may say my acquaintance is numerous. When you are there I shall give myself the pleasure of calling upon you."

"Sir Ralph will no doubt be pleased to receive you," she said formally, and he squeezed her arm.

"Silly child, I mean to call in the hope of seeing *you*."

She removed her arm from his clutch. "I am not a child, Mr Manners, but a happily married woman."

"I meant no harm," he assured her, "only that I find you most engaging, and as a widower a little congenial company is very pleasant. You wouldn't deny me that?"

"I didn't know you had been married," she said in surprise. "You never mentioned it before."

"It was some time ago. My poor wife caught a fever and never recovered. We had no children, to our great sorrow, and so I am very much alone. In fact my employment with my noble patron and his kindness in bringing me forward is what has kept me going."

She felt a swift sympathy for him, seeing in him a little man striving to combat loneliness by trying to make a niche for himself. "I am sorry," she said, "it must have been very sad for you."

He captured her hand again. "It was, but it's all in the past now. I contrive to enjoy myself, as a gentleman should."

Not quite sure how much he meant by this, she was glad they had reached the beautiful white and gold room where tables were set out for cards.

It was the first time she had stayed as a guest at such a large country house and that night in their bedroom she said to Ralph, "The hospitality amazes me. Everything is so lavish, and Mary says the Earl does not like to sit down with less than twenty guests and would rather have more!"

"He is the most generous man. Every year he opens the grounds to the villagers for a cricket match and probably feeds above a thousand people. I was here two years ago and playing myself."

"Oh? I am always learning things about you, Ralph. I didn't know you played cricket."

"I began at Harrow, and I've always liked it. What should you think if I set up a Welford team? I've seen some promising players on the village green."

She smiled at him where he lay, leaning on one elbow, looking at her as she prepared to come to bed. "You are full of ideas for Welford, aren't you?"

Rather more seriously, he said, "Now that the place has a mistress, it puts a new complexion on all my plans." He held out his hand to her and she came to him, blowing out the candle. At least she could share all his interest in Welford.

Breakfast, Maeve discovered, was served at any time between nine o'clock and mid-day in the small dining room as guests tended to appear in twos and threes. She and Ralph found only the Millbankes at table. The rolls were warm and crisp, the coffee excellent, and feeling restored after a night's sleep she watched Ralph tuck into great slices of ham topped with fried eggs, sauteed potatoes and devilled kidneys.

"You won't get luncheon before two," he told her, "so make a good meal now."

She smiled and accepted some scrambled eggs, but breakfast was not her favourite meal of the day. Lady Augusta suggested that they should ride together this morning and Maeve wondered whether Angela and Freddy should soon come down so that Freddy could join them. But Gusty swept her away to change into their habits, saying the morning was the only time for riding on these winter days.

Experienced grooms saddled horses for them, expertly choosing mounts to suit them. Gusty said crisply, "We want a good gallop, so no gentle hacks for us, Simmons, if you please."

The groom, who knew her of old, gave her an appreciative grin and answered, "Certainly not, your Ladyship. There's a fine gelding here to suit you."

"And for Lady Digby? What about that mare?"

"She's skittish, ma'am!"

"Just what I like, "Maeve said. "Let me have her, if you please."

Ralph was mounted on a big stallion of seventeen hands, well up to his weight, and the four of them roamed the park for most of the morning. At one point Mark challenged Ralph to a race and, watching them, Maeve said, "Mark really is a brilliant horseman. Has he ever ridden that roan before?"

"Never," his wife answered. "He has a natural affinity with any horse. Two years ago at Doncaster he was racing and I was watching, standing in a phaeton to see better. There was a dreadful mêlée, several horses fell and I saw Mark go down. My dear, I fell too, to the floor in a dead faint! I thought I'd lost him. Mr Creevey raised me and there was Mark, a great bruise coming up on his forehead, but as well as could be. I fear he won't stop racing until the years catch up with him." She gave a great sigh. "I am so very unfashionable as to be deep in love with my own husband."

"You are fortunate, Gusty." Somehow the story had filled Maeve with a strange sort of envy.

Without turning her head from the riders, Lady Augusta said, "I'm sure you care very much for Ralph. If you saw him fallen to the ground –"

After a moment's pause Maeve said in a low voice, "I fell once, at a hedge that was too high for me. I suppose I wanted to show off my horsemanship. Ralph was so cross, but he said afterwards that was when he knew he wanted to marry me."

"How romantic."

"Not really, when I was lying flat on my back, very muddy and bruised, and knowing I had been stupid and careless of my poor Blanche."

"Things like that bring out our real feelings," Lady Augusta said and Maeve, remembering the incident, thought that anger and shame and irritation with him for being right were her main sentiments at the time.

Mark had won the race, a head in front of Ralph, and they were both laughing, Mark saying he wished he had wagered fifty guineas on it.

Maeve gathered up her reins. "I won't wager as much as that but will you race with me, Mark? Round that tree and back?"

"Race with a lady? Can't do that," he said.

"Of course you can, and you are not to let me win either. Fair and square? Ten guineas?"

Ralph glanced at her. "You don't know your mount, my dear."

When he called her 'my dear' in that rather superior manner, it annoyed her. She patted her mare's neck and said firmly, "I know her well enough to realise she has speed. Well, Mark?"

He grinned at her. "If you insist, but I'll not take money from my friend's wife."

"You have to win it first, sir," she retorted.

The mare served her well, capable of speed and a swift

turn; the wind caught the plumes in her hat, her face was flushed and her eyes sparkling as they sped over the rough grass. He did win, of course, but by no more than to make her feel she had put up a creditable performance. She felt exhilarated, loving every minute, and as she caught him up at the finish he said, "Oh, splendid! By God, Ralph, you have a fine horsewoman here."

"I know it," he said, "reckless too if she gets a chance." And there was a certain pride he could not keep out of his voice. He had watched her throughout the race and thought, as she sat easily in the saddle, alive with the fun of it, that she had never looked more beautiful. He lowered his gaze and lapsed into silence. Oh God, would she never care for him as Augusta cared for his friend? He wanted to beat his fist against the pommel of his saddle for he was not a patient man. He thought of last night, of love-making in the opulent bed; she had been submissive, patient, enduring perhaps . . . but giving, responding? No!

Gusty was saying that not many women would have given Mark such a run, and they rode back together, Maeve flushed and happier than she had felt for a long time, so that it was something of a disappointment when Mark said, "By the way, Ralph, there's a horse sale in Winchester in a day or two. Have you a mind to come? George Wyndham told me about it. He's going and suggests we sleep at the King's Arms there. I believe they keep a good table."

Ralph said at once that he would join them. "I'd like to look for a pony for our nephew, Fred. What do you think, Maeve? I'd like to give the boy a present."

"I'm sure he would be quite transported," she said at once. "He has been wanting to learn to ride, as soon, his father says, as he can get his fat little legs across a saddle. The Monarchs will think it very kind of you."

"The Monarchs?" queried Lady Augusta," Now who can they be?"

"My sister and my cousin who are married to each other. Their names happen to be William and Mary, hence the nickname."

Augusta, who knew her history, thought this highly amusing, and as the ride ended and Ralph lifted her down,

Maeve was conscious that she would miss him when he was away. When they went indoors, however, Freddy was in the Marble Hall and Maeve's previous thought was swept away as something in her leapt to meet him. Deliberately she took Ralph's arm, knowing it for an empty gesture and hating herself for it.

As the November days darkened there were cards in the afternoon, music after dinner, and enjoyable times for Maeve just walking about and looking at the pictures and sculptures. The Earl would wander in among his guests' occupations, often with his hat on his head, beaming at them all and expressing his hope that their stay was proving pleasurable.

Freddy and Mark were frequently engaged at the billiard table while Count Balakov hovered about Angela. On the second night he begged her to dance for them, glancing towards their host, and when George Wyndham seconded his request, the old Earl nodded amiably. She conceded at once.

"And how she loves the applause," Lady Augusta murmured in Maeve's ear. "Conceited puss!"

On the morning of his departure for the horse sale, Freddy having joined the other three engaged on it, Maeve was barely awake when Ralph came in from his dressing room, fully dressed.

"Goodbye, my love. I'll see you the day after tomorrow, I expect. You will all be singularly short of dancing partners tonight. Too many ladies, eh? But no doubt Manners will capture you."

She sat up, half laughing. "You can joke about it, but he is so tiresome. Do you know, he has already asked me to go in to dinner with him tonight as you won't be here?"

"Damn his impudence," Ralph said cheerfully, "but I think I need hardly consider him a serious threat?"

"I should think not," she retorted, and turned up her face for his kiss. "I hope the trip will be worthwhile."

It was raining so Maeve spent the morning studying the wonderful collection of pictures yet again, and in the Carved Room a Sir Joshua Reynolds painting of a naval officer attracted her, reminding her of her cousin Lionel still away on his voyage to the South Seas. She thought how hard it must be for Madeleine, and all Naval wives, to be without their husbands for so long, and surprised herself by realising how much she was disliking Ralph being away.

She was looking at the magnificent Van Dyck of Charles I on horseback when Lord Egremont came trotting towards her. "I see you are enjoying my collection," he said. "Now, I'm particularly fond on this Reynolds – the lady is Kitty Fisher who was no better than she ought to be, but was, shall we say, very popular. Come into my library and I'll show you some more of my treasures."

She spent a delightful morning with the old man whom she thought particularly kind, and he took her by surprise, in the middle of a conversation about Dutch Masters, by suddenly ringing the bell. When a footman appeared he sent the man off to a storeroom to bring down a certain picture. This turned out to be a small Dutch landscape by Aelbert Cuyp, executed during the last century.

She admired it and he astonished her by saying, "It's yours, my dear. Have it hung in your house to remind you and Ralph of your stay here – I hope the first of many."

She was quite overwhelmed, particularly in view of his earlier remark about not giving his treasures away, and hardly knew how to thank him.

He patted her hand and said, "Well, it's no great matter, and my pleasure. Take it as a wedding gift."

The picture was duly removed to be packed ready for their departure and she felt honoured and touched by his generosity and looking forward to showing it to Ralph.

The party seemed somewhat depleted that evening, as Lord Hillingdon too had departed, for business in London, though Selena stayed on, intending to go with Maeve and her brother to Welford for a stay with her mother.

Playing whist, Maeve felt she owed it to Freddy to keep half an eye on his wife who was sitting on a settee plying the Russian Count with questions about his country. Angela had apparently spent the morning being introduced to the game of shovelboard by the Count who had recently discovered this occupation himself and played with the delight of a child. Mr Manners, who had got himself placed at Maeve's table, said in a low teasing voice, "I think your mind is not on the game, Lady Digby. I hope you are not missing Sir

Ralph too much. And all the other gentlemen," he added archly.

"Yes, no – it is only for two days," she answered, not liking his innuendos, and later when the game was over and they moved away, he added, as if there had not been half an hour since his last remark, "Well, perhaps I can make up for his absence. Will you ride with me tomorrow?"

"Very well," she said, only half attending, as Angela and Balakov had also left their table. They were drifting away, her hand on his arm, towards the North Gallery where Lord Egremont kept a great many of his favourite paintings, and there was something intrinsically intimate in their manner.

"And tonight?" Mr Manners was murmuring, "May I help to make the time pass? A little favour, eh? Perhaps even the final one?"

Not even listening to the tiresome man, nor getting his drift at all, Maeve nodded absentmindedly and then said, "Excuse me," and thinking she owed it to Freddy, walked off after Angela. She thought at first that the gallery was empty and wondered where they had gone. Then she saw them deep in and alcove at the far end that housed a Roman head on a pedestal. Angela was in the Count's arms and he was kissing her, seemingly with her full consent for she was making no protest at all.

Maeve stood rooted to the spot, unable to take her eyes off them. The Russian lifted his head, there was some soft talk between them, which she could not hear, and then he bent his head again over the woman in his arms. Apparently unseen and unheard, Maeve slipped away and fled upstairs.

Not ringing for Gracie, though it was nearly time to dress for dinner, she sat down by the bright fire burning in the grate. A soft November dusk was following a glorious sunset now that the rain was over, but still she sat on. What should she do? If Ralph were here she might on impulse have confided in him, but sober thought warned her to keep the matter to herself. She had not believed Angela would let it go this far, for it was no light kiss she had seen. Flirtations had been the order of the day in Brighton, which no one paid serious attention to, and of these Angela had her share, but this was different, and done when Freddy was not here. Always believing that the strange girl was deep in love with Freddy, it was a shock to see her actively betraying him with the undeniably attractive Russian. Obviously Brighton and the high society there, coupled with her own success in it, had completely turned Angela's head.

She felt suddenly angry, incensed that Angela could be so irresponsible, so uncaring. Didn't the wretched girl know how she would hurt Freddy if she persisted in this? But would she let it go on? In a week they would all be going home and surely that must be the end of it? She wondered if she should speak privately to Angela, or even to Freddy when he came back, but having no answers to these questions, her main desire at the moment was to box Angela's ears. However, she decided that discretion was the better part. Even if the Count had turned the silly girl's head with his attentions, once back at Hollanders it would all have to be forgotten – because it was unthinkable that it should go any further. Yet, a niggling thought persisted, Angela was not happy at Hollanders, and who knew what she might do?

Maeve leaned her head on her hand, desperately anxious for Freddy yet angry with him that he had seemed so blinded by Angela's popularity in Brighton that he had not seen what was under his nose, and it was in a heavy and abstracted mood that she submitted to Gracie's ministrations.

A table somewhat denuded of men assembled for dinner that night, but Count Balakov was there to hand Angela in and Mr Manners held out his arm to Maeve, while Lord Egremont insisting on having Lady Augusta on one arm and Lady Hillingdon on the other. During the meal Mr Manners chatted away about this and that but Maeve only gave him monosyllabic answers, too disturbed to pay him much attention. She was finding it hard not to keep glancing at Angela who was smiling as she sat next to the Count, and blushing a little at something he said.

Afterwards, under cover of listening to Mary Wyndham playing the piano, Selena said in a low voice, "What is the matter with that girl? She was behaving like a coquette at dinner."

No need to ask which girl she meant. Maeve whispered back, "Not being brought up in English society perhaps she doesn't realise how silly she is being. I shall be glad when we all go home."

"Should you not speak to her? At least before it comes to Sir Frederick's ears? You know what prattlers people are."

"I had rather not. It is only for a few days more." The thought of tackling Angela or marring Freddy's apparent happiness was not appealing and she was glad that Selena did not pursue the subject. The rest of the evening passed pleasantly enough with the Count singing one of his Russian folk songs and Angela gazing at him with rapt attention, but when he had finished Maeve made sure she herself took the seat beside Angela.

Mr Manners came to stand behind her and said, "Won't you play for us, Lady D?" To which she replied, "Not tonight, sir. I'm rather tired."

He touched her shoulder lightly. "Not too tired to be comforted a little, I hope?"

Having no idea what he meant, Maeve ignored the remark and turned away to ask Selena where she would spend Christmas.

"In Cornwall, if Hillingdon can get away," she said. "The boys will be home for the holidays and they love being there. London is a bore for children."

"Well, if you don't go there – it must be a very long journey in the middle of winter – do consider coming to Welford. We should all like that so much."

Selena pressed her hand. "So would I – if Ralph could bear with what he is pleased to call his 'nauseating nephews', though indeed they are really much more tolerable these days."

Maeve went up feeling unusually weary, her excuse to Mr Manners being genuine enough, and yet when she was in bed there were too many thoughts chasing round her head for sleep to come. She had told Gracie to leave the candle burning by her bed and took up her old favourite *Emma*, always finding Miss Austen soothing, despite her own slight headache. She had read a chapter and was contemplating seeing if sleep would come, when after a slight tap, the door opened. She glanced up, thinking it was either Selena or Gracie having forgotten something. Instead it was Mr Manners, resplendent in a crimson dressing gown embroidered with flowers.

Maeve sat bolt upright in bed. "Sir! Mr Manners, what are you doing here?" Hastily she pulled the covers up about her shoulders.

He gave her an arch look. "Such an opportunity, eh? You can't be going to scold me for taking advantage of it." And coming to the bed he scrambled on to it, seizing one hand and kissing it fervently before she could pull it away.

"How dare you?" she searched for words to express her outrage. "Are you out of your mind? Go away at once."

"Oh, come," he laughed, "a little modesty is all very well but you can't deny you have encouraged me today to hope a little." Untying his dressing gown he let it fall to the floor, his nightshirt flapping about bare legs as he tried to take her in his arms.

Shocked, she pushed at his shoulders. "Oh, let me go – let me go at once, you foolish man! How *dared* you think I want you to – to –"

He was still trying to hold her, to put his mouth to hers, murmuring that she was coming it too strong. She twisted her head away, wrenched one hand free and tried to smack his face, but he caught it, laughing.

"Dear girl, we shall have a famous night of it, you'll see. I love a woman with spirit. And I am considered quite a man of parts myself. I shall tickle you into pleasure, you'll see." And this time he succeeded in kissing her, the other hand fumbling for one breast. He was stronger than she would have thought, refusing to believe her behaviour was anything but a coquettish lure to draw him on, while she was only aware of such fury rising in her that it gave her added strength. There was an undignified struggle and she cried out, "Stop! Stop! I'll ring for my maid, I'll shout, rouse somebody, if you don't go away this instant. I mean it!"

At that moment, to her overwhelming relief, the door opened and Lady Hillingdon stood there, tall and immensely dignified in a long dressing robe.

Maeve had never seen so welcome a sight and gasped out, "Oh, Selena, thank heaven!"

Selena was holding the door open and in a voice that sounded exactly like her brother's at his very worst, said, "Mr

Manners, I believe you should be in your own room. Had you not better remove yourself there before the whole household is roused?"

He had jumped off the bed, but was not a whit abashed. "My dear lady – I had thought – well, you can't blame a fellow for hoping."

"No, but you can blame him for trying, "Selena retorted. "Go, sir, and take that ridiculous dressing gown with you. I should advise a dose of honeysuckle juice to cool down your ardour, or better still, castor oil."

He was trying to put his plump feet into a pair of equally ridiculous and ornate slippers. "Well, that sounds somewhat drastic – and I never took you for a spoil-sport, Lady Hillingdon."

"I can be far worse than that," she retorted, "when it comes to my own. And if I may proffer a further piece of advice, you would be wise to find a reason for leaving tomorrow – before my brother returns."

He did look a little set down at that. "Oh come, ma'am, it was only a little fun, part of the game we all play. You wouldn't apprise Sir Ralph . . ."

"We do not all 'play the game', as you put it," she said coolly, "and it is for my sister-in-law to decide whether or not Sir Ralph should know of this. If he does hear of it, I think you may expect his challenge before many days."

"Surely not? I mean – no harm done, eh?" He looked appealingly at Maeve. "I meant none, I assure you."

She had seized her wrap and put it about her shoulders. "Just go away, Mr Manners, at once if you please."

He gave a shrug and then bowed, well aware that his 'noble patron' would not like him to cause a scandal in Lord Egremont's house. "I beg your pardon, Lady D. It seems I misunderstood. I bid you both goodnight." He marched out, giving Selena an impish look as he passed, and the door closed behind him.

"Well!" Maeve exclaimed. "Of all the effrontery! I'm sure I never said – I never encouraged him – in fact, I've been rude to him. It was only when he told me about his wife that I was nice to him."

"Foolish man, he's used that loss to great advantage for a

good number of years." Selena sat down on the bed beside her. "I think you'll find him gone in the morning. He's too small a fry to want to risk us bringing down a husband's wrath on his head. Unless you want to tell Ralph the whole silly business?"

"No," Maeve said shakily. "As you say it was a silly business, but Ralph would be so very angry, and rightly so. Selena, how did you know?"

"I didn't. I just happened to come past your door. Mary FitzClarence wanted to borrow my copy of the *Ladies Magazine* and I took it to her. I heard your voice and it told me enough. I thought you might need assistance to put a stop to whatever was going on, before everyone else was aware of it."

"Thank God you did! I'm sure I could have eventually got rid of him, but it was horrid."

"Did he hurt you? Did he –"

"Certainly not," Maeve retorted with spirit. "I made my feelings quite plain to him, wretched little man. To take advantage of Ralph's absence like that!"

"Well, thank God you are not going to have the vapours. That I couldn't be doing with," Selena said in some relief. "But would you like me to sleep here with you?"

"I would," Maeve said. "I'm sure he wouldn't dare to come back, only I'd feel more comfortable." But she had been shaken, first by the realisation that Mr Manners had thought her ready to be seduced, and then by her own foolishness that she had not seen during the day where all his talk was leading. She was glad that by the time she went down with Selena to a late breakfast the next morning he had found that his 'noble relative' had sudden need of his services and taken himself off, with profound excuses to his host.

"Come and go as you please," Lord Egremont had said. "I never mind as long as people enjoy themselves." Which was hardly the feeling uppermost in Mr Manners' mind as he rode regretfully away. Such a pretty little thing, Lady D., what a pity she was so strait-laced.

The day was not very enjoyable for Maeve either. It was tedious waiting for Ralph and the others to come back – a ride with Gusty lacking the zest of the racing a few days ago. The whole ludicrous business of last night would not leave her and she wished Ralph had never gone to the horse sale. Consequently when he did arrive, as she was changing for dinner, she was betrayed into exclaiming, "Oh, Ralph, I was never more glad to see anyone in my life."

His hands went out to her, but almost at once, suddenly embarrassed by what she had said, she turned aside to pick up a bracelet and added, "It was very dull without you gentlemen."

His hands fell to his sides. "I'm glad we were missed," he said drily.

"When do you plan we should leave here?"

"The party seems to be breaking up on Saturday," he answered in some surprise, "but I thought you were enjoying it all?"

"Oh, yes, I am. Lord Egremont has been so kind." She told him about the Earl's gift, and in some gratification he said they would have to find it a place of honour at Welford.

Maeve gave a deep sigh. "It will be so nice to be home again, to see everyone."

He nodded and went away to his dressing room, wondering whether in fact by 'home', Welford, Hollanders or the vicarage was uppermost in her mind.

Chapter 17

Ralph had bought a pair of peacocks to grace the lawns below the south terrace of his house. The male was a fine bird with a great fan of tail feathers when he chose to spread them, which was never when visitors wished to see them. The smaller female followed him about in total subservience and Ralph hoped they would mate. They seemed to like the terrace and when not strutting on the grass, pecking at the soil, they sat there in comfortable harmony.

"Do you like them?" he asked Maeve, and she answered, "Oh, yes, I've always thought them beautiful birds. They remind me of Hollanders and Old Solomon." Which was hardly the answer he wanted.

The fifteenth of December was the anniversary of their wedding, and in the morning when she was dressed and about to go downstairs he came to her room with a package. "You see I've not forgotten the day," he said.

She opened it and found a gold fillet for evening wear in the hair. It was made of fine filigree work and embellished with diamonds, each one set in the heart of a wrought flower.

"Ralph!" She looked up at him. "It is quite lovely. Thank you so very much."

"I'm glad you like it. I thought we should mark the day." And then he swept her into his arms and kissed her with sudden intensity.

She was surprised, for he was seldom demonstrative during the day, and stood passively. Then, as abruptly, he let her go, saying, "I hope it has not been such a bad bargain."

She moved out of his embrace to lay the fillet on the

dressing table, half laughing. "What a thing to say – when you have just given me such a gift. I wish I had something to give you." And was aware of a moment's guilt that it had not occurred to her to have found a present for him.

"You have," he broke in. "But whether you will ever give it, I don't know. Are you ready to come down to breakfast?"

Bewildered at the sudden change of tone, but aware instinctively of what he meant, she took her cue from him, made a remark about the weather and went down. Somewhere inside her there was a dull ache.

That night when he drew her into his arms she thought about their wedding night in the inn at Dover and her own shock and revulsion. She had never got over it, never been able to conceal it, always in her mind believing she could only ever have given herself wholly to one man. But now shame and guilt ate at her. Thinking of the past year, of his generosity and consideration she wished she could make him some return, knowing full well what he wanted from her – his remark this morning had made that clear. Could she not pretend, put her arms about him, try to respond? But it would be a lie and he would know it. For a man who did not deal in polite conventions, who was no hand at drawing-room conversation, he was surprisingly perceptive, adept at seeing through any sham. And that was what it would be. But, oh, she wished she could. All she managed to do was not to draw away, and even that seemed a sort of betrayal of something she had kept sacred for so long. Afterwards he said in a low voice, "No regrets, my love?"

Why was it so hard to lie, to try to make him happy? All she could say was, "You have been so good to me, Ralph, and I am grateful – really."

He withdrew himself, settling for sleep. Gratitude! As if that was what he wanted.

They had hung the Cuyp in the small parlour where they generally breakfasted and it looked very well there. Lady Digby approved of it and Mufti, always inclined to over enthusiasm, made some banal remark about the cleverness of painters to which no one paid any attention.

There were celebrations of Christmas all round the county and on Christmas day the whole party from Hollanders and the vicarage came to Welford for a splendid dinner. To sit at her own table and see all her family and numerous friends, including the Rokebys, was to Maeve a new and delightful pleasure. Ralph had struck up a friendship with Lord Rokeby and rode with him often, and they were soon deep in talk about breeding which Maeve thought better suited to the port afterwards when the ladies had withdrawn, but that was Ralph!

After the meal there was dancing and later Ellen and Elizabeth Rokeby entertained them with a scene from *Twelfth Night*, carefully rehearsed. Elizabeth had grown into an attractive girl and though quiet by nature she was intelligent and put a great deal into the part, making a stately and charming Olivia, but it was Ellen, in a borrowed suit of Elizabeth's brother's clothes, who held the audience. Acting the part of Viola she looked a lively and appealing boy and put so much into 'Make me a willow cabin at your gate', that at the end Freddy cried out, "Bravo!" and led the applause. Elizabeth blushed as she curtseyed, giving Freddy a quick glance and then lowering her eyes.

Oh no, my dear, Maeve thought, that is no way for you to go. But perhaps it was no more than a little hero-worship, and as she herself glanced in his direction, seeing how handsome he looked in his black evening suit and silk stockings, she could only think how she had dashed herself on the same rock. Only too aware of the effect Freddy had on people, more especially the female sex, she turned away and said to Ellen, "That was splendid. How well you remembered the words."

At fifteen, and out of the schoolroom, Ellen had become the darling of the family, and she was glowing with pleasure at the reception of her performance. "I love Shakespeare so much, it is easy for me. Isn't it a shame a lady can't be an actress? I would so much like to perform on a real stage."

Maeve laughed. "Well, that's one thing you can't do. Aunt Isabel would have a fit – and as for your brothers! But I think you would have been very good at it."

"So do I." Ellen perched on a table and dangled her silk-clad legs. "Just think of it, a large theatre – I can imagine it though I've only been inside the little one at Rye when there were some ballet dancers there last year. All the people listening and applauding afterwards, a dressing room full of flowers – from gentlemen admirers, of course."

Maeve was smiling at the excited girl. "What an imagination you have. And come off that table. You look such a hoyden sitting there in those breeches."

"I like my breeches. Don't you think I have a good turn of leg?"

"Very, but your mama is trying to make you into a lady."

Ellen giggled, "She says it is uphill work. Anyway, you told me that Colonel FitzClarence's mother was an actress."

"That," Maeve said, "was a very different matter. Off you go and change into more respectable clothes. Your dress for tonight's party is very pretty."

Ellen jumped down and ran off obediently while Maeve turned to speak to a slightly shocked matron.

At the end of the evening mulled wine and little sandwiches were served and Freddy, munching one, came over to Maeve and said, "This has been the best Christmas I've had for years. It was never the same in India, you know, not in the heat. And we could never teach our Indian cook how to make a real Christmas pudding. He couldn't seem to understand about boiling it in a cloth."

Laughing, Maeve said, "Mrs Gibson has excelled herself. What does Angela think of an English Christmas, I wonder?"

"She enjoys any celebration." He glanced across at his wife, but it seemed to him that despite the dancing and the general fun, she was in low spirits. But if he suspected why he kept it to himself and went on, "Last year, of course, we were still in mourning for Papa and you and Ralph were in Paris, if I remember rightly, so this year is as it should be."

"I'm so glad Welford is near Hollanders so that we can all be together," she said. "Are you happy to be back there, Freddy?"

His smile faded. In a low voice so that only she could hear, he said, "I am, yes, and so is Mama to have me back. It's where I should be, what I came home for. But – for Angela – I wish she liked it better."

Maeve hardly knew what to say. She was hoping that away from Count Balakov Angela might learn to be a contented wife, but it was easy to see she was not. Would anything ever make her like Hollanders? Her attitude towards it had always filled Maeve with incredulity.

When the carriages were called for, hung with lanterns for the journey home, William asked his brother if he meant to join the hunt tomorrow.

"Rather," was Freddy's answer. "I wouldn't miss it for anything. Maeve?"

She said she and Ralph intended to be there and Mary added that perhaps now they were settled back at home, Angela might learn to ride.

"She's afraid of horses," Freddy said as Ralph handed his wife and mother into their carriage. "I have tried, but it's really no good."

William went on to speak of young Fred's delight in the new pony his Uncle Ralph had given him and the aptitude he was already showing. "He's no fear," Freddy added, "and that's the age to learn."

There was a slight edge to his voice, something unusual for him, and Maeve suspected that the first rapture of his marriage to Angela might be passing. How the two of them would survive years together she did not know. Nor did his mother, and said as much privately to Maeve a week later when she was at the vicarage.

Nell Hollander had taken a feverish chill and as Mary was anxious about little Isabel, who had a cold, Maeve elected to be the one to spend a few days at their old home and care for their mother.

Ralph had offered to come with her, but Maeve said firmly that she could be more useful on her own and he did not argue. She settled in to her old bedroom, relished the quiet times sitting beside her mother, with a book if Nell was asleep or chatting comfortably as if in the old days. Dinners with her stepfather were equally pleasant and he did not press her to any confidences for which she was grateful. Only once, after she had been talking about Brighton, did he take her hand and say, "I am more at ease about you now, dearest. I can see Ralph has turned out to be a very good husband."

"Oh, he is," she had answered. "Don't worry about me, Papa." She gave him a quick smile and turned the conversation to something else, which left him with just the reverse of the ease he had professed. She began to speak of Petworth and confided to him, as she had to no one else, what she had seen in the gallery there. He said she had done right to keep it to herself. It was probably no more than a silly flirtation and he expressed the hope she shared that Angela might now try to become part of Hollanders, but he sounded equally doubtful.

Freddy came over to enquire after his aunt and he and Maeve sat companionably over the fire for a while, moments that both relished but which left Maeve more disturbed than she liked.

He was followed a while later by his mother, and in answer to Maeve's conventional enquiry after Angela, who had not accompanied her mother-in-law, Isabel said, "I am singularly worried by the whole situation. I wonder if I should move out? After all, we have several properties with tenants in and I could make use of them, I'm sure. But then, what would happen to Hollanders? Angela hasn't the remotest notion how to go on and no wish to learn." Maeve murmured something about Freddy teaching her, but his mother shook her head. "I doubt if it would serve – heaven knows I've tried – and if he does what he wishes to do, follows in his Papa's footsteps and becomes involved in the affairs of Rye and the county in general, which I would like so much – can you imagine Angela dealing with the house and all the entertaining, to say nothing of making herself known in the villages and among the tenants and so on?"

"No," Maeve said flatly, "I can't. But perhaps in time –"

"I think time will have very little to do with it. A child perhaps?" Isabel sighed. "They have been married for nearly two years now and no sign. She doesn't like me, you know. We have no common ground except Freddy himself. And I'm no longer sure he's happy. For the last two days he has been moody, which is not like him. It is very bad of me, I suppose, but I do sometimes long for what might have been. Still," she braced herself in her familiar manner," we have to make the best of things. At least I am beginning to like your Ralph very much. I didn't at first – well, that was hardly surprising – but he's a man of such energy, and though he may be lacking in charm he makes up for it in forthrightness which is a virtue I have always liked." She touched Maeve's cheek and added, "It is like old times to have you here again."

But it was not old times. When her mother was well enough to come downstairs Maeve said that perhaps she ought to return to Welford and sent a message to Ralph to say she would be coming home soon, but still she lingered, finding it hard to tear herself away.

Ralph, however, when the end of the week came without either Maeve herself or a message, decided to take matters into his own hands, and if her mother was really on the mend, to fetch her home himself. He had been doing a great deal of thinking over the time of her absence and on an impulse drove the curricle first to Moon's End.

Mary Hollander was still breakfasting when Sir Ralph Digby was announced and as he came in, she looked up, smiling, to say, "I'm afraid you have found me very behindhand today. The baby was so fretful with her cold last night that I was late to bed."

"I'm sorry," he said, rather formally. "I hope she's better this morning?"

"She seems so, thank you. But you look cold, Ralph. Pray sit down and let me pour you a cup of coffee."

"Thank you." He sat next to her and accepted the cup, stirring it more than was necessary. "Have you heard how your mother is? Maeve said several days ago that she was better and that she would soon be home, but I've heard nothing since."

"Oh, yes, William was there last night and she's apparently quite herself again. I shall go over as soon as Isabel allows me to leave her."

Ralph was silent again and Mary eventually said, "I'm sorry William is already gone out, to Rye on some business. Did you wish to see him?"

"No – no, it was you I wanted to speak to. I'm glad I've found you alone."

"Oh?" In sudden anxiety she added, "I hope there's no bad news?"

"None in the least. In fact I'm on my way to the vicarage to see if I can bring Maeve home."

"But something is wrong." She waited while he stirred his half empty cup again, and then in her quietly sympathetic manner added, "Can you not tell me? I have a feeling you must have come for that purpose."

"I did," he said, and got up to stand by the hearth, his shoulders against the mantelshelf.

"There is something amiss between you and Maeve? You seemed to be going along so capitally."

"Oh, we are," he said with a bitter note in his voice and suddenly found the ability to say the words he needed. "We are, on the surface, very well suited. I am congratulated by all my friends! At table we talk of horseflesh and our plans for Welford, and of Brighton and our friends. Maeve is an excellent keeper of my house and she and my mother get on capitally. I have nothing to complain of. But we seem to be endlessly quarreling, over trifles mostly, and in our private moments – " He saw Mary's cheeks colour a little, but he went on determinedly, "There's nothing for me. Oh, she's dutiful, which is as much, I suppose, as many men get. But she doesn't love me, you see."

"Oh, Ralph!" Instinctively her sympathy went out to him.

"I understand," he went on, unable to stop now that he had started, "that many people want no more than we've got – compatability, shared interests, our growing concern for everything to do with Welford – but I know there could be more. You and William are proof of that. I wouldn't mind waiting if I thought . . ." he stopped abruptly, but only for a moment. "If I thought she would come to care for me, I wouldn't mind how long I waited, but there's no sign. Perhaps it's my fault. I don't know."

"I'm sure she does care," Mary said at once, though she was far from being unaware of what he meant.

"Oh, maybe, as a companion, but not otherwise. You see I know, I've known for a long time, that when you were all young together it was always you and William, and Maeve and Freddy. I was soon aware when he came home that she had wanted to marry him." He saw her start of surprise and went on, "It was not too difficult to understand. To be still single at twenty-four and talk of him as she did – and then after he brought Angela back she lost all her brightness, for a while anyway. She married me as second best. I sometimes think it was an act of defiance, bravado, if you like."

"Oh, surely not?" Mary said, but she was remembering the day of their wedding and her sister weeping on the floor. "Ralph," she went on earnestly, "believe me when I say that I think you are far more suited to her than ever Freddy would have been, much as we all love him." His eyes were fixed on her, and she persevered, "Only give her time and I believe she will see – oh, many things. Just be kind to her, and patient too."

"I don't know how," he said bleakly. "I've tried. God knows I've tried to be patient. I give her everything I can, and I try sometimes to prick her, tease her into response, but it always ends in a quarrel – we can quarrel mightily, you know!"

She said nothing for a moment, thinking how different their relationship was compared to hers with William.

"What can I do?" He had come back to the table and, sitting down, grasped her hand without realising it. "She thinks only of him."

Very gently Mary said, "I don't think that's true any longer, but you must understand that she thought of him in that way for many years and the hurt when he came back was correspondingly deep. It is taking a while for her to adjust, that's all. I realised at the time that she should not have married you so soon, but she would not listen to any of us."

"What can I do?" he asked again, his voice harsher than ever. "What am I doing wrong?"

Mary covered his hand with her other one, despite her smarting fingers. "Nothing, I'm sure, that can't be mended. Make the most of all the things you do enjoy together, keep everything as – as everyday as possible." She gave him a quick smile. "I know that is not perhaps quite in your nature, but it is the way to be kind to her. Don't ask her for love yet. I know it's hard but I'm convinced it is the way with her."

He pressed her hand and then released her poor bruised fingers. "You are a wise woman."

"I'm a happy one, and I want you both to know what William and I have. What's more," she added with conviction, "I truly believe you will for you are already more to her than she knows. Being twins, you know, makes us very close, and I think I understand her."

"That is why I came to you." He got to his feet." I wish I could believe what you say. At any rate, I'll try to take your advice."

"That's what sisters are for," she said affectionately, and for the first time he smiled back.

"I'm afraid mine would have told me to go out for a long gallop and not to talk nonsense."

Mary laughed. "Perhaps that's not such bad advice either."

In the hall they found Fred bouncing down the stairs. He was four now and had graduated from petticoats to a little brown jacket with a white shirt and white pantaloons.

"Uncle Ralph!" He jumped the last three steps. "I am glad you're here. I was just going out to see Maisie. Annie said I could," he explained to his mother, and when she smiled approval he went on, "Maisie is just the best pony in the world. It was very kind of you to buy her for me. Will you come out to the stables and see her?"

Ralph ruffled the boy's head. "I'm on my way to my curricle so I'm sure I can spare a few minutes. How are your riding lessons progressing?"

"Papa says I'm doing very well. He takes me out nearly every day now and I like it so much."

Ralph kissed his sister-in-law and departed with the happy little boy, a great longing growing in him as Fred tucked a small hand confidingly into his.

At the same time Maeve had been riding on the Marsh. It was a bright January morning, crisp and clear, the pale sky arching over the wintry marshes, few birds about, fewer people, only the sheep grazing everywhere. At breakfast Martin had suggested the ride. It was the best day they had had for some time and she had been cooped up in the house for long enough. He was only sorry parish business prevented him going with her.

Nell, when consulted, said at once, "Yes, go, darling. I really am quite better and I shall be downstairs soon. It's time I answered a few letters so I shall be well occupied." She still looked a little frail, but satisfied she was really recovered Maeve went out, refusing young Joe's offer to accompany her. Glad of the solitude, she took her mother's gentle horse, though Nell seldom rode these days, and patting the mare's neck, said aloud, "I doubt if you're much in the business of galloping any more." And passing down the lane beside Hollanders she saw Solomon sitting on the wall by the gate that led into the paddock. "You old villain," she said to him, "You don't know what havoc you once caused."

The peacock stared at her with a small sharp eye, unmoved, and she went on towards the Marsh, aware of how good it was to be here again, surrounded by the familiar. Drawing deep breaths of the invigorating air she trotted by Beckett's Farm, her gaze wandering over the loved scene, realising how much she had missed it.

Today it was clear, friendly, not menacing as it could be when overhung with mist, losing travellers, hiding villains, keeping sensible folk indoors. But the high days of smuggling were gone, though it still went on in a small way, and today everything lay open and visible, no evil lurking. There was something about the expanse that always drew a response from her, relaxing, peaceful, putting all her anxieties into perspective and she rode slowly, letting the mare pick her own way.

The peace, however, was short-lived. She had left Fairfield behind and gone nearly as far as the Romney road when round a bend where a few trees grew by a barn she saw a man leaning on a closed gate. It was Freddy, the reins of The Beau hanging idly over his arm.

As she came up he heard hooves and turned. The black look that was on his face disappeared at once into a smile. "Maeve! It must mean that Aunt Nell is much better for you to be riding down here."

"She is, and Papa said I should go out of doors."

"What good luck for me that you came this way. Will you come down?"

She nodded, unhooking her leg. He lifted her down from the saddle, setting her on her feet to hold her for a moment longer than necessary. "Darling Maeve, it's so good to see you. In fact, you don't know how good."

They looked at each other and then he released her. Maeve said, as her sister was saying at that moment at Moon's End,

"What's the matter? Something is – I can see it, Freddy."

"Yes," he answered, and leaned on his gate again.

"Can you tell me?"

"You, if anyone." He scuffed at the rough ground at his feet, and The Beau, tired of standing still, shook his head in protest and then snuffed at the mare. "Quiet," Freddy said, and Maeve fondled the horse's soft neck.

"I expect he wants a gallop," she said, "which is more than I can get out of dear old Flossie."

"We came down at a good speed. I had to get away for a while."

"Oh, Freddy, what is it? Do tell me."

He drew a deep breath. "Have you not thought that Angela and I have been married for two years and have no child yet?"

"Aunt Isabel is always telling me there is plenty of time." As if he hadn't heard, he went on, "God knows I would never have reproached her for something that wouldn't have been her fault – if that had been the case – but it is not. The other night I did say – something."

She had never seen him so grave, so wretched, so unusually reluctant to reveal what was on his mind. "But you can't have given up hope yet? I know how much you want an heir and I'm sure that in time –".

"Time will do nothing for me." He stared out across the Marsh while Maeve waited for him to speak. At last he said, "Angela told me, the night before last, something she should have told me a long while ago. She can't have children."

"Oh! But how can she know?" Maeve was shocked into swift pity for Angela, facing barrenness – a dread she knew herself.

Freddy turned back to face her. "Apparently when she was about fifteen she had some dreadful Oriental disease and the doctors told her it would be almost impossible for her to bear a child. Well, that wasn't her fault, poor girl." He drew a deep breath. "But she didn't *tell* me, Maeve, before we were married or after. When I talked about wanting an heir she agreed – she said of course I would, with a place like Hollanders. I don't know what then she imagined it was like. But she lied to me, she kept the truth from me. and the worst of it is, she doesn't seem to mind that we shall have no children – or how much it has upset me."

Maeve hardly knew what to say. She could only murmur his name helplessly.

"And it has made me see so much else." He switched savagely at a clump of grass with his riding whip. "When I was courting her – with half a dozen others, I might say, wives being in short supply out there – it was not until after I had told her about Papa's death and my being the new 'Bart' and owning Hollanders, that she accepted me. It excited her, the prospect of all that, and going to England. And – don't you see? – she thought that if she told me I would never have an heir, I might not have married her. I would – of course I would, at least as I felt then – but she didn't trust me enough to tell me first. To let me think – to marry me with a lie between us – I don't know how to bear it!"

Maeve understood the depth of his bitter disappointment. Freddy was the most honest, the most open, man she had ever known, and the deceit was a blow from which he would not easily recover. It was a betrayal, a using of his love. She had no doubt Angela found him immensely attractive, had perhaps loved him in her own shallow way, but not enough to trust him with the truth before the knot was tied.

"I am so sorry," she said. "What are you going to do?"

"What can I do? She's my wife and I must try to make her happy, but she's wayward, Maeve. I never know from one day to the next what mood she's going to be in. You know how she feels about Hollanders. She thinks I want to bury her in the country when she expected life to be like Brighton all the time – which, thank God, it isn't."

"Amen to that," she echoed.

"And she treats the servants badly," he went on, "That's something we've never done at Hollanders, and she causes Mama endless trouble in a dozen ways. Mama is very good about it, but she was never the most patient of women and you know how she can speak her mind." He gave Maeve the glimmer of an unhappy smile.

"It must be hard for you," she said, thinking that for a man of his easy, even temperament, a wayward wife was not going to make for an equable life.

"And another thing," he added. "I'm sure you all thought I was blind at Brighton. Oh, at first I liked all the adulation

Angela got. It made me proud – after all she is my wife – but then that damned fellow Balakov behaved as if he was courting her, as if she was free to receive his advances. He meant to cuckold me, I'm certain of that. Or try anyway, curse him!"

Maeve said slowly, "You never gave any sign. I wasn't sure if you suspected."

"How could I? A pretty fool I'd have looked, playing the jealous husband. But I imagine you and everyone else was well aware of what was going on?"

"Well, perhaps, but then there was so much harmless flirting, I don't suppose it meant anything. One had only to have a few moments' conversation to one side for everyone to remark it."

He glanced at her. "Quite. But I can't think that anything untoward happened in Brighton. I never let her far from my sight, and in any case I believed – I still believe – that she loves me. It was just that so much admiration turned her head." He gave a heavy sigh. "I'm in a cleft stick, you see. She's not happy here, and to be too much in the top society as we were then would be dangerous. When I was away, when I went horse-buying with Ralph, I suppose that tiresome Russian was even more obnoxious, damn him?"

Maeve thought of the North Gallery at Petworth. No, she couldn't tell him that. Instead she said, "Well, now you're home again she's not likely to see any more of him."

He gave another long, deep sigh. "If only it were as simple as that. One can't see ahead, but nothing has turned out as either of us hoped."

She said nothing for a moment. What was there to say?

He seemed to rouse himself. "I have promised to take her to London in the spring and I can't break my word. She wants me to buy a house there so that we can spend more time in town."

"Will you?" she asked. "Would it be wise? You would be back in society again, no doubt meeting the Count who always seemed to be in every drawing room in Brighton."

"I shall be on my guard now, and if a house in town is what she wants, then I must see if it makes her more content."

Privately she thought it was only likely to make Angela

want to spend even more time away from Hollanders. It was one thing to make occasional visits to a London home, as no doubt she and Ralph would do, but quite another to make it the reason to turn her back on Hollanders. And she thought of all the wasted years when she had dreamed of being mistress of the house that Angela seemed to hate. Gazing longingly out over the Marsh, she thought how eagerly she would have shared Freddy's love for it all. Yet she could have borne her own personal tragedy if Angela had been the sort of wife he wanted, sharing his love for his home. At last she asked, "What does Aunt Isabel think?"

"She says I must do as I think best. God knows it isn't what I want to do. But I'll have to take Angela up in the spring and see how she likes London. Only I'm very much afraid it will be just what she does want and I'll have to become a London society man, riding in the Park instead of here." He swept out a hand to encompass the wide pastures. "I'll have to join clubs, be a gentleman of leisure and waste my life." His voice took on a rare cynical note. "And I'm not so stupid as not to know she will always attract men. If it's not Balakov there will be others, though perhaps in time – " He broke off. "And how much will I see of Hollanders, which is my responsibility and my pleasure? It doesn't bear thinking about! And how Papa would hate to see me abandon it all. But if I don't – my God, what a mess! I never thought – but that's been my trouble all along, hasn't it?"

Slowly she said, "It isn't fair on you."

"Is life ever fair? Perhaps once I thought it was. I had so much: the Army life that I loved, with the prospect of being master of Hollanders in the distant future. I never thought dear Papa would die so suddenly."

"No one did. We all loved him so much. But he knew Hollanders would be safe with you, he told me so, when he hoped – " Abruptly she stopped that train of thought.

He turned towards her, his brown eyes dark with anxiety and bitter disappointment. "At least you are happy, aren't you? Ralph seems such a splendid fellow." Which was generous of him, considering Ralph had never set out to make any sort of friend of him. "Why, Maeve, you're crying. What's wrong?"

"It's for you," she whispered, and wiped away the few tears with a gloved finger." And – and for what might have been."

There was a long silence. Then he said slowly, "When I came back I think I was very dense – William told me I was – not to see that you had waited for me. You did, didn't you?"

"Yes." She could not keep the word back.

"Oh, Maeve, darling Maeve! I think, I know now, I made the most dreadful mistake. I hope you didn't as well? His forehead wrinkled as he grappled with the situation. "I had thought you were happy with your marriage but you only took Ralph because I came home with Angela, didn't you?"

"Yes," she murmured again.

"What can I say? Oh God, what can I say? I've ruined everything. When I realise – if we'd married, how happy we would have been here. Mama loves you, everyone at Hollanders loves you, and it would have been your rightful place. But I fell so desperately in love, at least I thought it was love, and now everything's gone wrong. Oh, don't cry."

She could no longer keep back the tears. He put his arms round her and she wept into his coat. After a few moments he found a handkerchief, wiped away the tears and she straightened.

"How stupid of me. I'm sorry."

"Are you so unhappy?" He held her, looking down into her face.

"No – no, really I'm not. Ralph is so good to me, and I do like Welford, and I love his mother. I have nothing, nothing to complain about." The only thing that's wrong, she thought, is me, myself.

"I see that you didn't love Ralph when you married him, but do you love him now?"

"I'm fond of him, of course I am, and we share so much, but – I can't – it was always you."

His hands fell to his sides. "I've wrecked both our lives, haven't I?"

"No!" Sturdily she shook her head. "No, we can't let that happen. I'm sure, somehow, Angela will settle down, even if it means a few years in London. She can't intend to let Count Balakov, or anyone else, really ruin her marriage. Perhaps even in time she'll learn to like Hollanders. I do believe

London would be very tiresome if one was always there."

"Well, perhaps when she's older, more mature." He hesitated." Or if Mama should decide to live elsewhere. I think Papa bought the Stone House in the village with a view to it being a Dower House for Hollanders, and there are only tenants in it. Much as I love darling Mama, it might be better – not yet perhaps, but later on."

"There. You see, there are always possibilities for the future. Lionel will come and bring his boys, and little Tom will be your heir."

"Yes," he said slowly, "only it won't be quite the same as if it were my own son. Still, when dear old Li knows the truth, I'm sure he'll let Tom spend time here and learn to love the place as we do."

"Of course." She managed a smile. "And as for me, I enjoy my life with Ralph, really."

Slowly he said, "You are right. We mustn't bewail the past or the 'what might have been'. It's pretty pointless, isn't it?"

"Yes," she agreed firmly. "What's done is done."

He stood for a moment looking at her before glancing round. There was no one in sight. "Will you let me kiss you, just once – and not as the brother I've always been?"

She couldn't speak, only look up at him, her longing in her face. He bent his head and put his mouth to hers, for longer and more deeply than he had intended, feeling her respond, her lips clinging to his, parting under his, both of them savouring one short moment of sheer joy. Then they drew apart.

"No more," she said. "Not again, Freddy. I couldn't bear it. Will you help me up?"

They rode back together, the horses moving slowly, past the lonely old church and Beckett's Farm, up the lane to Hollanders and round to the vicarage. They hardly spoke, for everything seemed to have been said. At the entrance to the stables he reached out his hand, she put hers into it, and he lifted her fingers to his lips. Then he turned his horse's head and rode back to the big house.

Suddenly weary from all the emotion of the last hour, she let the reins lie slack as the mare picked her way across the yard. And there, his curricle waiting, the horse being walked up and down by Joe, was Ralph, his hand already on the latch of the door into the vicarage. It was obvious he had seen them.

He waited until Joe had lifted her down. "Very touching," he said, and there was a sneer in his voice. "Are you by any chance ready to come home?"

Chapter 18

The journey back to Welford passed in silence. Maeve refused to change, and Ralph drove the curricle with Gracie squeezed in beside her mistress. No one spoke, for conversation was not easy under the circumstances. In their own yard it was Jacob Hatch who ran to hand her down, while Ralph threw the reins to Willis. Maeve went into the stable, wanting to have a look at Blanche and assure her that she was not forgotten, while Willis was dealing with the curricle, unhitching the driving horse. Ralph followed his wife in, in the grip of a deep corrosive anger that he was incapable of throttling.

All pretence gone, he said, "I suppose you managed to see Hollander every day you were there? Is it too much to hope you will ever get him out of your head?"

"Oh!" She gave a gasp. "What can you mean?"

"Don't prevaricate," he snapped. "He's at the heart of everything for you, isn't he – married or not?"

She stood very still. From the first she had dreaded this moment, while hoping it would never come – certainly not on top of the emotion of the last hour. She tried to speak, but her mouth was dry.

"Do you think me totally lacking in perception?" he enquired crushingly. "Of course, I've always known. Your ride, I suppose, was an assignation?"

"No!" She was stirred into a swift denial. "I went out alone."

But he hardly heard her. "And now that his wife is playing fast and loose, he and you feel free to – "

"You had better stop," she threw the words at him, "before

you say something you will regret. I tell you, today's meeting was not planned."

"No? Well, even if it wasn't, no doubt you took advantage of it." He became suddenly aware of the transfixed stable boy. "You – out!" The boy fled, and Ralph went on, shaking with the culmination of months of repressed emotion, "How could you expect me to be so simple as not to know you imagined yourself, and no doubt still do, in love with your cousin? It was obvious to me from the beginning. I know you took me because you couldn't have him."

"Oh?" she cried out again. "I never said – but, Ralph, I didn't lie to you. I never pretended love where I didn't feel it."

"No, indeed, and no doubt that salved your conscience." His voice was biting. "You certainly never let me think you loved me, but I wanted you enough to believe – one day – but I see now I was deluded. What a poor fool I've been."

"Don't, don't! I can't bear it." Repeating the words she had said to Freddy. "After all you've done for me –"

"For God's sake, stop harping on that tack. Obviously it was not enough to win the one part of you I want. You are hard, Maeve – I should say obdurate – clinging to your love for a man who spurned it and who, I might say, hasn't half the intelligence that you have."

"You've no right to say any of that," she flared. "He couldn't help falling in love with Angela, but he knows now – he's been deceived. He told me –"

"My God!" Ralph's anger flared still further. "You *have* been having a revealing talk on the Marsh! No doubt declaring undying love for each other, regardless of those useless impediments, a husband and a wife. Commiserating with each other over your mistaken choices, eh?"

"She hesitated for one tell-tale moment, and he shouted, "Don't lie, I won't have it."

She was trembling but managed to retort, "I won't then. How can I kill what I feel – what I felt for him so long before I met you? But that's the end of it. As you so rightly say, he has a wife and I have a husband."

"And one, by God, who won't put up with secret meetings. We can't get away from Hollanders, more's the pity, but I forbid you –"

"Ralph! I won't – I wouldn't – whatever we feel I wouldn't sink so low as to – to betray you. Oh, you must know that?"

"Must I? I saw enough today to make me wonder." For a moment he stared at her, her cheeks flushed, her eyes flashing. "Yes, I've always known there was passion in you, if I could rouse it, but you've kept it for him, you – "

His hand came up, still holding the whip, and she screamed. Jacob Hatch, thinking a horse must have kicked her, pelted in, saw the raised whip and, without a moment's pause, sprang at Ralph from behind and seized his hand, taking his master so much by surprise that he was able to wrench it away.

Flinging it on the floor, he shouted: "Don't you touch 'er! Leave 'er alone!"

To Maeve's astonishment, Ralph was white-faced and shaking, staring down at the whip. Then he recovered himself and swung round on the groom. "What the devil –"

Hatch planted himself in front of Maeve who was clinging to the upright post of the stall, while Blanche, sensing the charged atmosphere, pawed the ground and shook her head.

"Don't you 'it 'er," he screeched. "I won't let you, d'you 'ear?"

"Damn you to hell, how dare you?" Ralph swore at him. "I won't tolerate this, by God. You are dismissed! Go – get out of here."

"Not until you promise not to touch 'er."

Maeve caught his arm. "Jacob – it's all right. I made Sir Ralph angry. He won't hurt me."

"I ain't so sure. Go 'ome, missy. Don't you stay 'ere, not with 'im."

Ralph picked up his whip. "Do you want me to use this on you, Hatch? You won't catch me unaware a second time. What we do is not your affair."

"Oh, yes, it be," Hatch retorted. "Do you think I'd let you 'urt me sister?"

There was an instant's silence. Maeve, stricken, clung to her post. Ralph's face was suddenly suffused with blood. He drew a deep, throttling breath.

"Sister? *Sister*? What the devil do you mean?"

Hatch said nothing, but he stood his ground. Maeve didn't move.

Ralph looked from one to the other. Then he seized Jacob by the collar. "Get out, get out! You are not to set foot in this place again. Willis!" His coachman came running. "Take this man to Flint and get him paid off. He's to go at once." He half threw Jacob towards him.

Willis caught the luckless groom by the arm. "Come on, you." And as he seemed about to protest, added, "If Sir Ralph says you've got to go, you go."

Hatch gave up with a shrug. "Sorry, missy," he said to Maeve. "I shouldn't a' said. I 'opes you'll be all right."

"of course I will," she managed to say. "Go to your sister, Jacob. I never wanted it to end this way."

Willis propelled him out and Ralph gave her one look. "Inside," he said, and walked with his hand about her wrist across the yard and into the house. There, he drew her to the nearest place they could be alone, which happened to be the empty gunroom. "Well? You had better explain."

She had never seen such anger, even hatred, in his face. It was all over then, all pretence stripped away. "It's quite simple." She controlled her voice to sound equally cold. "My father, my real father, was a disreputable man – I'm sure I told you that. I'm not proud of him. There are, no doubt, quite a few of his bastards on the Marsh. Jacob just happens to be one of them."

"Now we're getting down to plain speaking," he said. "But why did you never tell me, why did you lie?"

"When you took him on, I hardly knew you," she retorted. "Certainly marriage to you was the last thing on my mind." She saw him wince, but she forced herself to go on, "It seemed a good place for Jacob, a chance for him to make something of himself. Apart from a liking for drink, I know him to be a good hand with horses."

"Perhaps that's the only thing that commended *me* to you," he retorted. "But you kept up the lie when you married me. To think that that fellow working in my stalls was your bastard brother! How could you cheat me like that, live a lie? And not the first, by God! I wonder how much more there is? I wonder what else I don't know about you?"

"Stop, stop! There's nothing. And you lied too – you and Mrs Trenchard –"

"I wondered when you'd throw that at me. I told you the truth, but you wouldn't believe me." He had let her go and was leaning against the gun rack, his arms folded.

"Any more than you believe me." She was half sobbing now. "I'm sorry about Jacob. I know I should have told you when we married, but he was doing well and wouldn't have risked his place by saying a word about it if you hadn't tried to strike me."

"If you hadn't driven me to it," was his bitter retort. "To see you and Hollander together like that –"

"I wish you hadn't," she burst out. "You're making a mountain out of it. I did love Freddy – I can't deny it – but he's married and so am I – nothing left but old vain affection."

"And nothing for me?"

"I always knew you cared for me and I did think we were growing together, fond anyway, but – out there in the stable, you would have hit me if Jacob hadn't stopped you. And you nearly called me something – something I didn't deserve." She broke into sudden weeping. "I suppose you would like to use one of these guns on me!"

He put his hand to his head. "Maeve –"

But, wrenching the door open, she fled along the passage and into the hall. There, Lady Digby was on her way to the library. "Maeve, my dear, you're home. I'm so glad. How is your mother?"

Maeve hurried to the stairs. "Excuse me, I must change."

Blindly she ran up. Ralph had followed her into the hall, and there, seeing his mother, he stopped.

Sharply she said, "I hope Mrs Hollander isn't worse? You said she was well enough for Maeve to come home."

"So she is," he answered, in such a tone that she paused and stared at him. "Then what have you been doing to upset dear Maeve?"

"Behaving like the brute I am," was his retort, and he went into his study, slamming the door.

Lady Digby paused for a moment, leaning on her stick. Wondering what on earth could have prompted such a quarrel, she sent up a brief prayer that her son's temper was not going to wreck this marriage as it had the first.

I'm too old for all this, she told herself, and went sadly into the drawing room where, finding Mufti at her eternal embroidery, she vented her desperate anxiety. "Not yellow, for heaven's sake, Mufti, not next to that crimson. They're supposed to be fuchsias, dear, fuchsias!"

The quarrel was patched up, if not mended, after a week of icy silence, of bare politeness at meals, which reduced Mufti to confused attempts at chatter and Lady Digby to remarks about the weather or her plans for the garden.

The servants could not help but be aware that something was very wrong. Their master was in one of his blackest moods, which since his marriage they hadn't seen, while their mistress looked pale and abstracted. She went riding as usual, but it was always alone, or with a young groom taken on in Jacob Hatch's place; in an indirect way they had heard that he had gone to Hythe and enlisted in the army. "And a good thing too," Willis said darkly. The tale of the scene in the stables had, however, reached the servant's hall, not through him, for he had learnt to be the soul of discretion, but through the stable boy who couldn't resist telling the kitchen maid.

One morning, Bridges found Gracie snuffling into her apron and enquired what was the matter, though he guessed well enough.

"It's my lady," she whimpered. "I ain't never seen her like this, so quiet, so unhappy, her what's always so bright and cheerful."

Bridges had paused at the door, a pile of his master's clean linen in his arms. "Well, I admit Sir Ralph is not at all his usual self," he said, "but it's not for us to be questioning what our betters do. It's their affair, Gracie Smith, mind that. Our work is to serve them as best we can. You look after your mistress as you always do, and keep a still tongue in your head. D'you understand?"

"Yes, Mr Bridges."

He nodded loftily and went to the dressing room, well aware that the bed there had been slept in every night since the mistress had come home.

The situation came to an end, at least for a while, when the

King's next brother obligingly died. Lady Digby, with Maeve and Mufti, was awaiting luncheon when Ralph came in with the latest copy of *The Times* in his hand. "Old York is dead," he said, "not unexpectedly. He was ill when we were in Brighton. A very decent man, by and large."

"I always liked him," Lady Digby said. "When my father first brought me to London, I danced with him at several balls. And I believe my father thought him quite smitten with me. But he didn't come up to scratch and I took your father, Ralph, who probably brought me far greater happiness. So the Duke's gone. Well, well."

"The funeral is next week. I think I shall go up for it – after all, apart from a short interval over that wretched business when his mistress was accused of selling commissions, he had been Commander-in-Chief of the Army for many years. All the military men will be there, including Wellington and George FitzClarence, of course, and no doubt a number of Peninsula veterans."

Maeve managed a smile. "The Elegant Extracts, I suppose? Even if it is a sad occasion, you will enjoy seeing them. How long do you plan to be away?"

"I don't know, a week or so I expect."

She nodded and said nothing more, but Lady Digby suddenly saw an opportunity, a chance to grasp at a change of scene that might resolve the present unhappy state of what she could only term 'armed truce' between her son and his wife.

"Why don't we all go up?" she suggested. "A change would be very pleasant and we shall be into February in a few days. Maeve, dearest, we meant to go in the spring, didn't we, so shall we go with Ralph now and have the shopping spree we promised ourselves? I need some grey silk to trim a bonnet to go with my new dress, and I can't find any in Rye or Hastings."

Mufti exclaimed, "Oh, how delightful. It will be so pleasant to be at Bruton Street again and at the hub of things."

Obliged to fall in with the suggestion, Maeve said that she would like to see the London house. She glanced at Ralph, but his face gave nothing away. He merely said, "Certainly, if you all care for it. But it's turned very cold and there was a hard frost this morning."

"We don't mind that," Lady Digby said cheerfully, "and we shall be very snug after the journey at Bruton Street."

"Then I'll send Flint up to get everything prepared for our coming."

To Maeve's secret distress, Freddy rode over the following morning to ask Ralph if he proposed to go to the funeral.

"I thought you would," he said, accepting a glass of mulled claret, his riding boots dropping mud on the carpet. "I plan to, of course. The dear old boy was our Chief."

"Is Angela going with you?" Maeve asked.

He nodded. "As you know, I'd planned to take her up anyway. I expect we shall look for a house."

Maeve wondered in dread whether Ralph would invite them to stay again. Surely he could not do that now, it would be more than she could bear at the moment, but Ralph merely mentioned the name of a house agent he had heard recommended.

Freddy thanked him and added, "We shall be at Pultney's Hotel, so I expect the four of us will meet now and again." Unaware of the quarrel and determined for his own part to do nothing to embarrass her, he smiled at Maeve, bowed to Lady Digby and took his leave.

Maeve was by turn grateful to him and then to Ralph.

Later, when Lady Digby was resting and they were alone in the parlour, Ralph reading the paper, she said, "Thank you, Ralph."

He looked up, laying down *The Times*. "For what?"

"For not asking them to stay with us."

"You didn't want me to?"

"Certainly not."

"You don't like Angela, do you?"

Maeve said, "I think I'm more sorry for her than anything else."

"Indeed? I thought she had everything you wanted." He rose, adding, "Excuse me, my dear – I must see Willis about leaving," and walked out of the room, leaving Maeve nonplussed, staring at his empty chair and abandoned paper.

Two days later they set off in the carriage for London. Not sorry to be leaving Welford, the scene of such recent unhappiness, Maeve began to hope the move might ease things between her and Ralph. She hated the estrangement. It hurt her more than she would have believed possible. Somehow, his act of ungovernable temper in nearly striking her hurt less than his words, and for those she knew herself at least partly to blame. It was stupid not to have told him of Jacob Hatch and their connection, but she had thought it would be hard to lose Jacob so good a place. So she had let a lie stay between them to add to the other and greater lie. And now it seemed he had known all along about Freddy, as in her heart of hearts she had guessed he did. Various remarks of his came back to her, making her think herself very foolish. Hoping against hope that her love for Freddy would die, she hardly realised that it was she herself who had kept it alive – for until that moment with him on the Marsh with its revelation, Freddy had been too wrapped up in Angela to see more than that his cousin was Ralph's wife and apparently happy to be so. He had received a shock of his own and the kiss between them was the fruit more of unhappiness than of love.

Ralph had not spoken to her other than the necessary communication of everyday affairs. He looked strained and tired; he did not come to her at night, nor had he said one word of apology. Perhaps he thought she didn't deserve it, and she lay at night alone in their large bed, miserably aware of the cold, empty space beside her. She was so used to it being filled by his large warm body and was amazed to find how much she was missing his presence. Was he lying in his dressing-room bed equally lonely? Was he as hurt as she was? It was all so wretched, the culmination of lies and small deceits. Was it only pride keeping them apart? Surely he must regret his behaviour in the stable, whatever had driven him to it? She had always known he had a temper and the strength of it had frightened her at the time, but now, oddly, she wanted only for him to know she didn't hate him for what he had done. Yet she felt restricted, unable to be the one to be the first to speak, afraid in her heart of rejection, afraid he would turn from her, refuse the proffured hand, and then everything would be even worse. She wept into her pillow and could tell no one of her misery.

When she rode over to say goodbye to her parents, her stepfather, seeing her pale cheeks and shadowed eyes, tried to have a few minutes alone with her but, for the first time in her life, she evaded this, leaving him so deeply worried that he went over to the old church and stayed there until dusk fell, praying for her and for Ralph. That something had gone very wrong, he could not doubt.

She was less successful when visiting her twin. Mary had the whole incident of meeting Freddy on the Marsh and finding Ralph at the vicarage out of her without too much difficulty.

"Really, Maeve," was her comment, "you do court disaster sometimes." Which Maeve had to admit was true enough, and was glad for once to be going away from her observant family.

The house at Bruton Street was like many others in London, tall, and tastefully, even elegantly, furnished. The drawing room had double doors that opened out to make a long area for dancing, the dining room with its mahogany table could seat a great number of guests, while upstairs was a charming parlour for everyday use. She and Ralph had adjoining rooms, Lady Digby a fine apartment. There were guest rooms above and servants' quarters at the top. The kitchens, Mrs Gibson said gloomily, were dark and plagued with cockroaches, but she managed to produce the usual excellent dinner.

On their first evening Maeve went upstairs fairly early and was about to get into bed when Ralph knocked and came in, wearing his dark green, frogged dressing gown.

"I wanted to speak to you," he said, and looked across the expanse of the bed. "I have been trying to do it for days."

She looked at him mutely and he went on, "Whatever causes we have – and God knows, we have them – for the disagreements between us, my behaviour in the stable was unpardonable. Can I ask you to believe I bitterly regret it? I assure you no such thing will *ever* happen again."

She was so overcome she could only murmur, "I'm sure it won't – oh, Ralph, I did provoke you."

"Yes," he said without any dissembling, "you did. And disappointed me. I know now that I've no hope of winning your affection, but I trust we can go on as before, at least tolerating each other?"

"Yes, yes –" she felt herself trembling, tears threatening. "I wish it too. But, oh, more than that if we could –"

He hardly seemed to hear the last words, having said what he had screwed himself up to say. "Good. We will both try to make life possible for each other. Goodnight, my dear." And he went back into his dressing room, where he shut the door and set his back to it.

God, what a fool he was! Couldn't he have swept her up into his arms, begged for her love? Perhaps, perhaps! He hated himself, hated his pride, dominated by his own fear of a rejection that would be the last humiliation, and he threw himself on to his bed in a moment of utter despair mingled with rage at a whole array of circumstances.

On the day of the funeral, Lady Digby went out to visit her old friend Lady Salisbury and Maeve took a hackney to Upper Belgrave Street. Mary FitzClarence was at home.

"Such a fuss this morning, and so early," she said. "George threw down three stocks before he was satisfied and he had his man nearly brushing the nap off his uniform."

"He always looks so well turned out," Maeve said, taking a glass of Madeira from the footman's tray.

"Yes, but you see our circumstances are so changed now." Mary saw her querying look and went on. "His father is now heir presumptive and will doubtless be King one day – and not so far distant, I should think. The Duke is far less given to excesses than his brother. And when the King goes, my father-in-law will be on the throne of England."

Maeve thought for a moment. She saw Mary's suppressed excitement at the thought of her husband becoming a King's son.

"I see what you are thinking," Mary said, and smiled across at her. "Of course, my dear, George can't be his father's heir or ever be King himself, but think of the position he will have! His father will have to give him an earldom at least. And he wants it so much."

"Do you?" Maeve asked.

"Oh, yes – for him. Most men are ambitious, aren't they? And you see, if one is illegitimate as George is, that has to be overcome first. It's – it's a sort of compensation, I think."

"I suppose so. I see that it can't be easy for him."

"He doesn't think of it much. He loves the Army and his

writings and scientific interests, but today's funeral – well, it does change things." Mary gave a deep sigh. "I do believe he would make a good King, it's such a shame, everyone likes him. But as things are – it will be little Victoria who inherits the crown. All those brothers, and among them only that child as the rightful heir."

"It is unfortunate," Maeve agreed, and driving home remembered Mr Creevey telling her that day at Bodiam that he considered George FitzClarence to be 'the best of the bunch'. She was rather glad suddenly that Ralph was not ambitious. Never putting himself forward he seemed content with his position, his more than sufficient wealth, his sports and his friends – and until recently with her. Which brought her back to their own present unhappy situation.

Ralph came home in a far from pleasant mood. Finding his wife and mother in the upstairs parlour, he came to the fire. Standing with his back to it his first words were, "What a shambles! Nothing was ready. Inside the chapel it was even colder than outside and we were kept waiting an hour and a half until the procession started. Wellington looked blue in the face, the Duke of Montrose sat huddled in his great coat, talking to Cumberland and blowing on his fingers. Sussex and I walked up and down and he said he wished he'd put on an extra shirt. George, of course, was in the guard of honour."

"The authorities who arranged the funeral should be thoroughly ashamed of themselves," Lady Digby said. "It is no way to go on, and very disrespectful to the dead."

"Was his Majesty there?" Maeve asked.

"Yes, though I wondered at it. But poor old Prinny was much attached to York, more than any other of his brothers. He looked cold and ill and very upset. The news is he is going at once to Brighton, or so Creevey says."

"One might have guessed he would be there," Maeve remarked with a slight smile.

"Nothing would keep him out, though I don't know who provided his invitation. Sefton, I suppose. Canning was looking positively furious at the delay. They say he will be the next man to form a government."

"Is Lord Liverpool worse?"

"I believe so, at any rate he wasn't there." Ralph paused while a footman brought in a tray of punch, which he had ordered to warm his cold limbs. "Myself, I think Wellington is the more likely contender, and the best. The talk was all of the Corn Laws and Free Trade and the plight of the Catholics, which Wellington is very keen to ease – he had some very good Catholic officers under him in the army."

"But what a place to be talking politics!" Lady Digby shook her head.

"We had to do something to take our minds off the cold." Ralph refilled his glass. "And politics certainly warm one up. When at last it did begin, Billy Clarence said to Sussex in a loud voice: 'We shall be treated very differently now, Brother Augustus, from what we have been.' I should think the entire congregation heard it."

"How tactless." Lady Digby shook her head. "Sometimes I think he really doesn't care whom he upsets. If one didn't know he was really a good person at heart, one would be annoyed with him most of the time. He takes his sailor's bluffness too far."

"Too far by half!"

Maeve wanted to ask if Ralph had seen Freddy there, but their last quarrel left her in no doubt that it would be unwise to do so. However, Ralph answered the question for her. "I saw your cousin there, by the way, in an aisle set aside for officers. And as he turned up in uniform, I presume he thought himself entitled, serving or not." Maeve said nothing at this little piece of spite and he went on, "A most odd thing happened afterwards. As I was leaving with Sussex, a man stepped out of the crowd – and had the confounded cheek to confront me. Nothing could have more added to the annoyance of the day than it should turn out to be Gervase Oglethorpe."

There was no very pleasant expression on his face, and his mother glanced swiftly at him and then at Maeve. "He was Ralph's brother-in-law, Alice's brother. Did you speak to him, my dear?"

"He spoke to me, some remark about my moving in such circles. He planted himself in front of me and indulged in some further unpleasantries." Ralph broke off with a swift glance at his wife. "Well, he was his usual obnoxious self. I didn't want a scene so stepped out of the way and one of the guards lining the path to the carriages ordered him to take himself off."

"I'm glad to hear it," Lady Digby said indignantly, "but I don't like the thought of his being back in England. I hope he won't importune you again."

Maeve said, "I imagine Ralph could soon send him off – he's half Ralph's size."

They both turned to her and Ralph said, "How the devil do you know that?"

The sudden question caught her short. "Oh – I saw him in Brighton. Do you remember that first day when we went shopping, I said a man was staring at us? It turned out to be Mr Oglethorpe."

"But you'd never seen him, how could you know who he was?" She was aware of his tone growing even harsher and that this was not the moment to add to his annoyance, but she was trapped. Even her mother-in-law was looking at her in some astonishment. "I – I did see him once again, just after Selena had come. I was waiting for her where the coaches leave for London, in North Street, and he came up and spoke to me. He asked if the gentleman with me the other day was you, so I said it was and that you were my husband." She came to an abrupt halt, feeling rather than seeing Ralph's gaze burning down on her.

"Well," he said, "what more? All of it, if you please."

"He – he gave me his commiserations." She tried to turn it off with a laugh, but Ralph was far from being amused.

"What damned, bloody impertinence! By God, I've a mind to find the little toad and call him out."

"You would be well advised to do no such thing," his mother said sharply, and Maeve added, "Oh, it was such a silly thing to say. I didn't give it any mind, I promise you. Then he had to board the coach, just as Selena came up. She told me who he was."

"And neither of you thought fit to tell me?"

"To be honest," she said, "I wanted to, but Selena explained to me that you and he were never on good terms, and that as he had left Brighton there was no point in teasing you with it."

"Selena really does ride roughshod," Lady Digby said, sometimes despairing of the ability of either of her offspring to use their common sense. "It would have been far better – "

"Of course it would," Ralph interrupted tersely. "I will not have such things kept from me, Maeve. Do you understand?"

"Ralph!" his mother protested. "None of this was Maeve's fault. How could she know how you would feel?"

"I will make it plain then. Good God, do you and Selena think I am a child to be protected from such a man as that?"

"I didn't think anything of the sort," Maeve retorted. "It merely seemed to me that Selena's advice was right – as I can see by your reaction it was!"

"I shall have words with my interfering sister when I see her," he snapped.

"I hope you won't." she begged. "I am very fond of Selena and I know she only acted out of thought for you."

"That's what I am complaining of," he retorted. "She can't forget she is five years older than I am and must presume upon it. Now if you will both excuse me, I am going to bed. It has been a damned irritating, tiresome day."

He left them and Lady Digby looked across at her daughter-in-law. "I apologise for him, my love. It is a great pity he saw Mr Oglethorpe at that particular moment. Let us hope he does not bother any of us again."

Chapter 19

The results of the long wait in the cold Chapel were widespread. The Dukes of Sussex and Wellington were struck down with feverish chills, the elderly Montrose retired to his bed, announcing that he was unlikely to leave it except in his coffin, and Mr Canning only dragged himself from his to attend a Cabinet meeting.

George FitzClarence and his father, however, seemed none the worse, and Ralph, apart from the inroads on his temper, showed no ill-effects. They had not seen Freddy and Angela since they came to London and Maeve waited for a chance to call on them and find out if Freddy had taken cold at the funeral. Two days later it came. She had spent the morning having a wildly extravagant and thoroughly enjoyable shopping expedition in Bond Street with her mother-in-law and Mufti. In the afternoon, not surprisingly, both elderly ladies retired to rest. Ralph had gone out, so Maeve ordered a hackney and had herself driven to Pultney's Hotel.

There, she was told that Sir Frederick was keeping to his room and, saying she was his cousin, had herself shown up. Freddy was indeed in bed, but Angela was not there.

"Oh." She hesitated. "I didn't realise Angela was out."

"Come in, come in," Freddy said thickly through a stuffed up nose. A newspaper and *The Gentleman* magazine lay on the coverlet and a nightcap was perched on his head, one of Angela's shawls about his shoulders. "Shut the door, Rogers, you're making a draught. Come to the fire, Maeve."

She couldn't help laughing. "You do look comical. Is your cold very bad?"

A momentary scowl turned into a grin. "Devilish. That wretched funeral! I wish I hadn't gone, but I felt I should. I suppose Ralph told you how they kept us waiting for hours?" He threw off his nightcap and ran his fingers through his hair, as thick and curling as when he was a boy.

"Yes, he gave us a graphic description. They say Lord Montrose is quite likely to die of the chill he caught. Where is Angela?"

"She has gone for a drive with Countess Lieven. She has been very bored here with me ill and nothing to do, so when Princess Dorothea sent a message inviting her to take a turn in the Park, I made her go."

Maeve had sat down, not by the fire but on the edge of the bed, and Freddy, without hesitation, took hold of her hand. "It is good of you to visit me. I trust that Ralph is not ill?"

"No, he's gone to a fencing place this afternoon and won't be back until dinner."

"And you came to see if I was at death's door? That was good of you, Maeve."

They smiled at each other and he put her hand briefly to his lips. "How are things with you?" he asked. "After I'd said goodbye to you that day at the stables, I caught sight of Ralph's curricle in the yard. I gathered afterwards he'd come to fetch you home."

"Yes," she said pensively. "I'm afraid he'd seen us together and thought – we had a dreadful quarrel."

"I'm sorry. I wouldn't for anything have been the cause."

"Well, it was not only that we'd been riding together and you kissed my hand, as you've just done. It was other things as well."

"I hope it's mended now?" he asked anxiously.

"Not really."

"Darling Maeve, if I hadn't got this beastly cold, I'd take you in my arms. You're made for loving."

She released her hand. "Oh, Freddy, don't talk like that. It doesn't help."

"I don't know how he can't see it," he went on, and she answered "He does, he does – it's me. I don't want to talk about it."

"Can't you tell me?"

"No." She shook her head a little wildly. "Not even you, Freddy." And was thankful that, just then, Angela came into the room. Her cheeks were glowing, her eyes alight. Maeve sprang off the bed and Freddy said, "Well, my love, was it pleasant in the Park?"

"Very." She gave Maeve a brief greeting and then, untying her bonnet and slipping the furred cloak from her shoulders, went on, "Would you believe it? Count Balakov was riding, and when he saw our carriage he insisted on dismounting and giving his reins to our coachman while he himself drove us around the lake. The sun was shining and it looked so beautiful, and he was a most amusing companion as always."

"I hope you haven't taken cold," was all Freddy said, to which Angela replied, "Oh no, I was well wrapped up and it was so enjoyable."

Soon after, Maeve took her leave and, in the hackney going home, it seemed to her that Angela was either shameless or naive. Somehow, she thought it was more likely to be the latter, but that one day the girl might take one step too far. Then her thoughts turned to her talk with Freddy and her own situation. While still believing herself irrevocably in love with him, she was aware of change – that last quarrel with Ralph and his present coldness were more distressing than she could have believed possible. She wanted to mend it, but how – how? That she could go to him, put her arms round him and tell him so, hardly seemed a possible situation.

Back in Bruton Street, there were no visitors and the four of them had a quiet dinner. Lady Dibgy remarked that in Maeve's absence they had had a call from Lady Salisbury, the upshot of which was an invitation to return to Hatfield with her for a week or two.

"I know the weather is inclement, but I should very much like to see Hatfield again," Lady Digby remarked. "I think we'll venture, eh, Mufti?" And to Maeve, "You wouldn't mind, would you, dear? I'm sure you will be occupied with friends, and your cousin and his wife will be on hand for a while, won't they? I'm sorry you found Sir Freddy unwell today."

Maeve assured her that, though in his bed, he seemed only to have a cold, and as for herself she would have plenty of occupation. But she was aware even as she spoke that Ralph had gone suddenly rather silent.

Half an hour later and almost ready for bed she had just dismissed Gracie when, without the usual tap on the communicating door, Ralph came in. He too was undressed, his green dressing gown over his nightshirt. Her heart gave a sudden turn. His expression frightened her.

Without any preamble, he said, "I understand you called on Hollander and his wife this afternoon? I presume as he was in bed you didn't see him?"

"Well, yes, I did for a few moments," she admitted truthfully.

"Then I suppose his wife was there?"

"No". Maeve grew even more reluctant. "She had gone for a drive with Princess Dorothea. Freddy wasn't ill enough to need – " she broke off. "But she came in later."

Ralph seemed to be fighting with himself. Then he said, dropping each word into the silence, "Am I to understand then that, in a public hotel, having arrived in a hired hackney, you visited Hollander, *alone*, in his bedroom? Or had you a modicum of propriety left and was someone else there?"

Stiffly, still sitting at her dressing table, she said, "No one was there. I never thought of it – Ralph, remember, we grew up like brother and sister."

He gave what could only be construed as a snort. "What a simpleton you must think me, if you believe I'd swallow that excuse! Neither you nor he are in the nursery now. Nor, if I'm not mistaken, have your feelings been as platonic as that for some time."

She turned away. "You are making something of nothing. It was a simple call on a sick relative."

"For God's sake," he broke in, "let us have an end to such ridiculous pretence. I'll not ask what passed between you, but I'll guarantee you did not sit on the opposite side of the room." He saw her face crimson. "Ha! I thought so."

"Oh, stop!" she cried out, and threw her hairbrush down. "You are wrong, Ralph, in thinking either Freddy or I want there to be anything between us. There was once – I can't deny it – I loved the boy who went away, but I soon learned that the man who came back was no longer mine. Only you can't expect me to suddenly treat him like a stranger."

"No, I see that is the last thing on your mind, or his! He is not finding marriage to that vain, wilful girl the sinecure he expected, is he?" Suddenly, all the pent up emotions of the last weeks blazed up into a deep anger, an unstoppable resentment. His face went leaden, his eyes slate-coloured. In two strides he crossed the space between them, seized her wrists and dragged her to her feet. "But I've had enough, by God, I have. Tonight, at least, I'll make sure there is no room for Hollander in your head or in our bed."

Still gripping her, despite her struggle to free herself, he sank his mouth on hers, so hard her lips felt pinched and bruised. When he raised his head he muttered, "You drive me mad. Don't you understand what jealousy can do? But tonight, I swear it, you won't think of him." One hand was at the back of her head, forcing her closer to him, his mouth searching. "I'll make you feel – I'll drive him out –"

Momentarily twisting her head away she cried out, "Ralph, stop! Oh, don't. Listen to me –"

But if he heard her, he gave no sign. Almost throwing her onto the bed, one hand pushing back the bed clothes, he came down on her. She felt her nightgown wrenched aside, his hands on her as he possessed her with a strange and overpowering passion that seemed to have more hate in it than love. He was thrusting mercilessly, hurting her. Her sense spinning, she felt as if her head would split, but oddly her only thought was: have I driven him to this? Is he so hurt, so jealous? She wanted to calm him, tell him not to be afraid – which was odd in this moment of violence. And then she felt suddenly, for the first time, that she wanted to put her arms about him, hold him, only they were pinioned. A yielding crept over her and the most delicious, utterly unknown, sensation flooded her body. At the same time, Ralph wrenched himself away. She had one swift, revealing glimpse, in the light of the flickering candle, of his face – a Grecian mask of anguish, grief and pain.

"Ralph!" she cried out. But he was gone into the adjoining room and the door shut between them, the key turned in the lock.

She collapsed against the pillows, uncertain whether to cry, laugh or have hysterics.

Lady Digby, to Maeve's surprise, came down to breakfast the next day. She was sitting alone, crumbling a roll which she was not eating, wondering where Ralph was, wishing he would come, when her mother-in-law entered with Miss Mufferton.

"We must get on with our preparations for Hatfield," Lady Digby said. "Mr Flint is sending up my small trunk and we shall spend the morning deciding what to take – at least, knowing my Rosalie, she will already have decided. Where is Ralph?"

"I haven't seen him this morning," Maeve said in what she hoped was a natural voice. She still felt bruised, shaken but curiously aware that nothing seemed relevant until Ralph came. When he did, she would tell him – oh, what would she not tell him? And then all would be well between them.

But he did not come. She asked Flint if he had seen his master this morning.

"Yes, my Lady," the major-domo said, "he went out early. Mr Bridges had packed a valise for him, but he did not accompany Sir Ralph."

"Oh," Maeve said, and then summoning a smile added, "Of course, I remember now. He won't be gone long."

But she did not know that. And feeling cold and a little sick with an unnameable fear, she went up to the parlour to occupy herself writing to her mother. It was three o'clock when a note was brought to her.

She opened it and found it was headed from White's club.

My dear Maeve,
It seems I am always apologising to you and now must do so again. I see we are quite unsuited as husband and wife and I will not force my attentions on you again. If you can forgive my quite unforgivable conduct, I shall be eternally in your debt. I thought it best for us to be apart for a while and am going to my friend Hastings at The Mill House, Dedham, for a week or two. If you need me, pray do not hesitate to write.
Always your humble servant,
R E L Digby

She laid the note down. I mustn't cry again, she told herself, I mustn't. But the tears were not far away. How could he go away and leave her after the trauma of last night – and when she wanted him so much?

For a moment she was tempted to call the footman and order the carriage to drive her to Dedham, wherever that was. But she couldn't do it. She couldn't turn up unexpectedly and maybe have another scene with him in front of his friend. Waiting would be almost unbearable, but she must do it, for both their sakes, so that, calmer and quieter, they could somehow put right their life together. But, oh, it would be different now. It must be. She must make him see that Freddy, her once beloved Freddy, was no longer a threat.

With a sudden rush of insight she knew it to be true. That was in the past. Something would always remain between them, the memory of one kiss by a gate on the Marsh, but that was all. It was true, at last it was true, and she sat there in a sort of daze. It was Ralph, tempestuous, dictatorial, with a shocking temper, strong and independent, a man in every way for all his faults and foibles, that she now knew she loved.

She longed for him to come back so that she could tell him so, yield herself to him with joy, as he had always wanted her to do. It would be bliss. Her cheeks suffused with colour, so that she was glad to be alone.

And then, into these blessed moments, came a knock on the door and a footman announced, "Mr Gervase Oglethorpe, my Lady."

Dragged from her reverie, she asked in bewilderment, "Did you not tell him Sir Ralph was away?"

"Yes, my Lady, but he said he wished to speak with you."

Not having the faintest idea what Alice's brother could have to say to her, she supposed she had better see him and inclined her head.

He came in briskly, his face pink from the cold outside. She did not offer her hand, he merely bowed.

"Well, Mr Oglethorpe, what can you possibly have to say to me? No doubt our footman told you my husband is not here."

"I only came because I knew that," he answered. "I was in the street this morning when he left with a valise. By an odd coincidence, I had been spending the last few days of my stay in England with a friend in Albermarle Street, so I was nearby."

"You are leaving?" She thought she was being rude and suggested he should sit down, but he merely said, "Thank you, no, ma'am. I shall not inconvenience you for long. Yes, I leave for Liverpool in the morning and sail in two days' time. I came to settle my son at Stowe School and see some of my family. That done, I must get back to my plantation in Virginia."

"Why then could you possibly wish to see me?" She decided she disliked his manner. "If you waited until my husband had gone out, I find that distinctly odd. I doubt very much if I should have received you."

"You may be glad that you did!" He took a turn about the room and then said, "I saw Ralph at the Duke's funeral. I thought the procession would be worth viewing, but I did not have the privilege of a place as he did. Did he tell you we met, if you could call it a meeting?"

"Yes, he did speak of it."

"As always, he was offensive," Oglethorpe said. "I wonder ma'am, how much did he tell you of my sister's death?"

"Very little," she answered in further surprise. "Only that she had a tragic fall downstairs."

"Fall?" Oglethorpe paused, and then looking as if it was the answer he wanted, went on, "That is as I expected. He would not dare tell a prospective bride the truth."

"What truth?" Maeve asked sharply. "What are you trying to say, sir?"

"That he was responsible for her death." He ignored her indrawn breath and went on, "He struck her, ma'am, stuck her with his whip, and she near her time." His face was scarlet now and his voice shook. "I thought he would not have told you – a nice piece of revenge for me, eh? Be careful, ma'am, be careful. Your life too may well be in danger. He killed her and he might –"

A voice broke in from the doorway. "Mr Oglethorpe, I think you had better leave at once." It was Lady Digby, drawn up to her full height, majestic in black, her eyes flashing in anger.

He looked startled, as if he had not expected her to be

there, and gave a sketch bow in her direction. "I've said what I came to say."

"Too much indeed." She moved further into the room, glancing at her daughter-in-law who was standing rigid in shocked amazement. "Now will you leave, or must I call the footman to throw you out?"

"Oh, I have done." He looked indeed well satisfied. "Ladies." And then he was gone and the front door banged behind him.

Maeve's legs seemed to be shaking and she sat down abruptly in the nearest chair. Lady Digby closed the door and seated herself opposite. "My dear child, I would not have had that happen for the world. Where is Ralph? It is a pity that he wasn't here to deal with the man."

"He – he's gone away for a few days, a week or so perhaps."

"Gone away?" Lady Digby looked blank. "Without so much as a goodbye? What possessed him?"

For perhaps the first time in her life, Maeve told a deliberate lie. "His friend Mr Hastings needed him, so he went at once. He – he sent me a note and asked me to make his apologies to you."

"Sent you a note?" his mother exclaimed, "What an odd thing to do. It is extremely discourteous of him and not at all like his usual behaviour."

Maeve forbore to mention the early morning departure with a packed valise before anyone was even up, and only said he didn't want to disturb anyone.

Lady Digby was displeased with her son, even more with their visitor, and began to say something about paying him no attention, when Maeve sat upright.

"Forgive me, dear ma'am, but I want to know the truth of all this now. Ralph has never told me what really happened. I spoke to Selena about it in Brighton when we saw Mr Oglethorpe briefly there, but she didn't say anything other than to mention the fall. Now Mr Oglethorpe has left a horrid suggestion in my mind. Was he – was he right?"

Lady Digby gave a deep sigh. "Oh, my dear – we none of us wished it raked up again. Least of all, Ralph. It is all so long ago now and when he wanted to marry you, I saw no reason that the details should be known – though I did say at the time that perhaps it was dangerous not to tell you the whole truth."

"Tell me now – please, ma'am."

"Lady Digby looked suddenly much older and rather weary. "Very well, you shall have it all." The door opened and she snapped "Not now, Mufti," and her companion whisked herself out again. She paused only momentarily and then braced herself to do something she had prayed she would never have to do.

"They were very young, you know, he and Alice, and very much in love – though I must say she could never have been to him, as the years went by, the companion you are."

Maeve said nothing. There was no colour in her face and she had both hands gripped together, dreading she hardly knew what. "Please go on."

"Yes, well, Alice was a pretty little thing and very sweet, but without a great deal of sense. Her brother was a year or two older, an unpleasant youth and totally without principle. He had got into bad company, gambling, and losing heavily. Ralph was always generous, but behind his back Gervase was borrowing every penny he could from Alice. The climax came one afternoon when Gervase was being dunned for his debts. Ralph was out hunting. Gervase went up to Alice's room where he persuaded her to let him pawn the beautiful necklace Ralph had given her for a wedding present – foolish, foolish girl, she paid for that folly with her life."

Maeve could only whisper, "And then?"

"Gervase came out on to the landing in the act of putting the pearls into his pocket just as Ralph came up the stairs, back from hunting. There was the most dreadful scene. They had never remotely liked each other and Ralph hated him for his behaviour to Alice. You know I fear what a temper my son has."

She paused again and Maeve whispered, "Yes, but – sometimes I think he does hate himself for it." She thought of last night and the misery on his face afterwards. "What happened next?"

"He struck out at Oglethorpe with his whip and they were struggling together when Alice, hearing the noise, came out of her room as I had come out of mine. I ordered them to stop, but they were past listening, venting all their antipathy on each other. Alice - silly, silly girl, in her condition - tried to run between them to prevent her brother, as she must have thought, taking a beating. As you so rightly said, Ralph is twice his size."

"And then?" Maeve could see what the telling of the story was costing her mother-in-law.

"Then – " Lady Digby paused, gathering herself for the end of the unhappy business " – Ralph raised his whip to strike Oglethorpe again, Alice was in the way and the blow fell on her. She screamed and tripped backwards to the top of the staircase, lost her footing and went down. The fall brought on early labour and she died that evening, and the poor little baby the next day."

"Oh! How awful. What happened afterwards?"

"It was very dreadful. Ralph was nearly out of his mind with grief. At one point I really thought he would try to take his own life. The Oglethorpes threatened him with the Sheriff, with prosecution, accusing him of murder, but they soon saw it would involve their own son equally, that in fact it was his misdeeds that were really responsible, and they calmed down. The Sheriff saw no cause for action and the whole affair was hushed up as far as was possible. But the burial was a miserable affair, Ralph in a terrible state, the Oglethorpes refusing to speak to us or come near us." She gave a mirthless laugh. "There were so few people at the house afterwards that we gave the funeral baked meats to our tenants and villagers."

"And when it was all over?"

"The Oglethorpes packed Gervase off to America to make his own way there – which apparently he has done if he can send his son to Stowe. As for Ralph, he had to get away too, he couldn't bear the house. And as for the stairs . . ." She shook her head. "He went away to join the army, we let the place and came to London. Ralph's father died shortly afterwards. He had no heart for anything any more. He doted on Alice and never really forgave Ralph. The rest you know."

"Yes," Maeve said huskily, "the rest I know." She left her chair and came to kneel beside her mother-in-law. "Dear, dear ma'am, I wish I hadn't asked. It has hurt you to tell it."

"No, my child, it was only right that you should know."

"It was an accident," Maeve said, "a most unhappy accident, but no more, surely? Mr Oglethorpe was wrong to say Ralph killed her. I see he was the cause, but unwittingly, and it was just as much Mr Oglethorpe's fault for treating his sister as he did – stealing from her, taking her wedding gift from Ralph."

She put her arms around her mother-in-law and, for a few moments, they clung together. Then Lady Digby resolutely wiped away the few rare tears. "You are generous, my love."

A little silence fell and then she murmured, "We should have told you, trusted you in the first place – but for years Ralph had refused to consider remarrying, he thought he could never trust himself again, and so became reconciled to it. Then he met you. He told me he fell in love with you when he saw you lying on the ground after that tumble, an nothing would satisfy him but to wed you. He believed he had learned to master himself over the years. And now – I do pray you won't judge him too harshly?"

"For what they did?" Maeve said shakily. Then she leaned back on her heels, a whole new concept of Ralph forming in her mind. "No, ma'am, I don't. If I blame anyone, it's Oglethorpe. And Ralph has had to live with this all the years since. Oh – " she took the wrinkled hand in hers, "I understand now, better than I ever did. I understand what has made him the man he is, the blame and the guilt he has lived with, some of the things he has said to me. It has been behind all our quarrels, it has formed him, driven him." She thought of the quarrel in the stables, the whip, then Ralph's ashen face as it was wrenched from him. She did not know it, but an odd look of relief came over her face. "Don't you see, it all makes sense now? Now that I understand, everything will be different, so much better between us."

Lady Digby looked at her with a mixture of surprise and then dawning respect. "You are indeed the girl I've always thought you were, my dear, and the very one for him. I've always believed, hoped, it might be so. For a moment I feared that, hearing the truth, you would turn from him, even leave him –"

"I might once," Maeve said honestly. "but not now – oh, not now, ma'am. I lied to you this morning. He has gone away because he thought – he thought he had hurt me – though he has indeed gone to Mr Hastings, but his reason was different from what I said. Only now, when he comes back, I will put everything right."

Lady Digby leaned back in her chair, exhausted. Too much emotion, she thought, not good at my age. "I think perhaps I should put off my visit to Hatfield and stay with you."

Maeve jumped up. "Oh, no, ma'am, pray don't. I shall be perfectly all right here. Of course you mustn't disappoint Lady Salisbury. I have so much reading to catch up on, and letters to write too, and Mr Flint will look after me. I'll have plenty to do."

Lady Digby nodded, considering wisely perhaps that it would be better if she and Mufti were not in the house when Ralph returned. The depth of their quarrel couldn't be guessed at, but that Ralph needed the balm of his wife's new understanding she was sure. When all the explanations were over, there would be, there must be, a new happiness for them. "I think I'll take a little rest before dinner," she said. "I must confess to have found this somewhat tiring."

"Of course," Maeve said, "and don't worry about me, dear ma'am. It isn't necessary."

And looking deeply into her face, Lady Digby believed her. Her son, if he would only grasp the chance, was going to be happy at last, and she went upstairs, rather thankful to be going to Hatfield where she and Sally Salisbury could recollect, in the tranquillity of old age, their own somewhat tempestuous youth.

Chapter 20

When the carriage emblazoned with the Salisbury arms had borne Lady Digby and Miss Mufferton away, Maeve wandered about the house, suddenly glad to be alone. The servants, however, took their charge of her very seriously. Mrs Gibson came to discuss dinner, Mr Flint said Willis wondered if she would like a drive or a ride in the park, and the bootboy made up all the fires to be sure she would not be cold.

She smiled a little, chose her dinner and said she might drive the curricle herself round the park this afternoon.

By the Serpentine, she saw Angela wrapped in furs in a phaeton driven by Count Balakov. Angela waved as they passed in the opposite direction. Stupid girl, Maeve thought, how can she do it when she has Freddy for a husband? And then realised she had not thought of him for quite a while. Poor Freddy, his impetuous marriage had not brought him happiness, whereas her calculated one to a man she almost disliked was about to achieve a depth she could as yet hardly dare to believe. She thought of Ralph coming back, wanting to make amends, afraid of his reception perhaps, and her cheeks warmed as she saw herself reaching out to him, driving away all fear and self-castigation, all the sense of failure. What was it he had said? "I know now I can never win your love . . ."

A little smile curved her lips and she could only thank God that after the way she had behaved to him, he still wanted her. Her blush deepened as she thought what their reunion could be – if only he would come soon! But he had said a week or two. She could write, of course, but putting what she felt on paper was quite impossible. She would have to wait.

Two days were occupied in paying calls and on the third morning, deciding she would take a stroll to the library, she was in the hall in a walking dress, pulling on her gloves with Gracie ready to accompany her, when there was a ring at the bell.

It was Freddy, without a greatcoat despite the chilling frost, his hat set askew, his face pale and strained. Without preamble, he said, "Can I speak to you, alone?" He threw the hat to a nearby footman who, with some skill, caught it.

Maeve led him into the drawing room where a freshly lit fire burned cheerfully. "Where's Ralph?" was his abrupt question.

"Away," she said. "Did you want him?"

"No." He looked totally unlike his usual self.

"What is it? Is something amiss?"

"Very much. Angela has run away with that damned, despicable, treacherous Russian!"

"What!" Silly and short on common sense she had thought Angela, but this! "Tell me."

Freddy was too distraught to stand still. "I haven't been out since I had my cold, but today I felt so much better, I thought we could take a drive together. I was almost dressed when I heard Jamala scream. I ran into Angela's room and there was the silly woman having hysterics. She jabbered at me that Angela's valise was gone, and some of her clothes." He ran his fingers wildly through his hair.

Aghast, Maeve said, "Gone? Gone where?"

"I questioned the hotel people, of course. They said she went out very early, and one porter told me he had seen her enter a carriage which was waiting outside and a gentleman helped her in. I asked what the man looked like and he was pretty vague, but it sounded like Balakov. So I went straight to the Russian Embassy – the Lievens have gone to Brighton with the King and they told me the Count left this morning without a word to anyone, they assumed for Brighton as well, but it's plain enough, isn't it?"

"Freddy, dear Freddy, I'm so sorry. How could she be so crazy? What are you going to do?"

"I'm going after them, of course. It was a hired carriage and the porter said the driver was ordered for the Dover Road."

"And if you catch them?"

"I'll call the damned fellow out, kill him if I have to. And bring her back."

"Suppose she won't come?"

He stopped abruptly in front of her. "None of you really understand Angela. She's a woman, as I of all people have come to know, but she's part child too. She knows little of our world. What will this fellow do with her? He can't marry her. He'll use her for a while and then abandon her – I know his sort. She may think he'll love her forever, but I doubt it. She needs me, Maeve, to protect her. It's all been a big failure – I don't need to tell you that – but I must do the best I can. After all, I did marry her and I won't abandon her. She – she can be intoxicating, you know."

"I could see that," Maeve murmured. "But, Freddy, do be careful. If you catch them, who knows what Count Balakov may do."

"I'll deal with him," Freddy said through closed teeth. "But the thing is, Maeve, will you come with me?"

"Come with you?" she echoed. "How can I?"

"Well, you say Ralph's away. What's to stop you? I need you, Maeve. If – when – I find them, I'll have to deal with him. I can't take Jamila, she's useless in a crisis, and Angela will need someone, a female, to be with her and come home with her. Don't you see? And who better than you? You've always been kind to her."

Maeve was trying to think, to grapple with the situation. There was nothing to stop her going, no one here to mind what she did, she would be back before anyone missed her. Ralph wouldn't return, probably for at least ten days. Yet some instinct told her that if he found out about it – and it might be hard to keep a secret – it would make him angrier than ever, just when she was going to make everything right between them. Oh, why did it have to happen, why did Angela have to be so mad, so utterly irresponsible? All these thoughts were chasing visibly across her face and Freddy came to her, taking her hands.

"I need you," he said urgently. "Maeve, darling Maeve, I'll explain to Ralph if necessary. We won't be gone long."

"You're so sure we'll catch them."

"Of course," he said. "I must. She doesn't know what she has let herself in for. I don't trust that fellow, not one inch. I must bring her back."

And what would he do with her then? Maeve wondered. Shut her up at Hollanders?

He had her hands in his. "Please Maeve. I do need you so much. I've got to get her back and you're the only one who can help me."

For one moment she resisted, but the appeal was stronger than her presentiment of danger. How could she desert him in this crisis?

"Very well," she said helplessly. "I'll come."

"Oh, God bless you for that. I knew you wouldn't fail me. By the way," he added, "you'd better bring your night things, we might have to stay in Dover. Unless we catch them soon, we can't be there and back in a day – and I think it's there we'll find them. Let's pray they have to wait for a packet for Calais."

Maeve gave a gasp. She had not thought of having to sleep away from home, but it made sense. "Very well," she said, "but I'll take Gracie with me."

He nodded. "Good idea. She can look after you and Angela. Only hurry, please."

Maeve fled upstairs, calling for Gracie to follow. In about a quarter of an hour her valise was packed, a few belongings in the startled Gracie's little canvas bag. Coming down again, Maeve told a new footman she would be away for a while but Mr Flint, coming up from the nether regions, heard and asked when they could expect her return.

"I don't quite know," she said cheerfully. "Don't worry about me, Mr Flint, Sir Frederick will look after me and I have Gracie with me."

"And what would you like me to say to Sir Ralph when he comes home, madam?"

"Oh, I shall be back long before Sir Ralph," she said, and took Freddy's proffered arm out to the waiting carriage, with the Hollander escutcheon painted on its door panels. But as they set off, crossed the river and turned south, gradually leaving the streets behind, she felt a sick dread, an uneasiness, that she was making a great mistake. Yet what could she do? How could she abandon Freddy, the long-beloved Freddy, in his time of need? She glanced at him, at the familiar profile, his usual ruddy cheeks paler today, his eyes almost black with the weight of anxiety – no, she could not have refused him. He sensed her gaze, turned to her and gave a little smile. "Thank you," was all he said, for Gracie was inside with them, Maeve thinking it far too cold for her to be on the box.

The trail was not hard to follow. The distinctive Balakov, the outstanding looks of Angela, were not easily forgotten. They had stopped at Maidstone and then at Ashford for refreshments and a change of horses, but when Dover was reached and enquiries made, it seemed they had caught the packet for France an hour since. There was nothing for it but to wait until morning. Freddy found the best inn, ordered dinner and rooms.

"We'll cross in the morning," he told her.

"But I can't leave the country," Maeve exclaimed in a shocked voice. "Whatever will Ralph think – or, even worse, do?"

"He won't know," Freddy said dismissively. "We'll be back before he is and, anyway, we can't stop now. I've got to find her. Surely you understand that?" He sounded impatient at such quibbling.

She did not understand. He was labouring under a dreadful strain but, though every instinct urged her to go back to London, she couldn't desert him here. He was, after all, Freddy and she had loved him, still did in an odd way, but differently.

She shared her bedroom with Gracie, who was thoroughly excited by the whole adventure – to be chasing after an eloping wife would be something to tell when they got home again. But long after the girl was asleep, Maeve lay awake, too worried to sleep, desperately sorry for Freddy but far from liking the mad pursuit herself. And then it occurred to her with a cold shock that she should have left a note for Ralph, explaining what had happened. In the rush she hadn't thought of it. Only that she'd be home in no more than a day or two, long before his return. How she wished herself back in

Bruton Street. Yet here she was, dashing off with a Freddy who wouldn't be stopped. At that moment, she could willingly have throttled Angela. She dozed fitfully and the morning saw them on the first packet for Calais. There was a fresh wind, it was bitterly cold and Gracie was sick. "I'm sorry, it's so bad a crossing," Freddy said, "but we'll soon be there."

In Calais they picked up the trail. Yes, the gentleman and lady had hired a carriage and set off for Paris. After some difficulty, Freddy managed to do the same but a broken wheel caused them so much delay that nightfall saw them still some way from the capital.

A poor sort of inn in a small village was the only place to stay. The landlord said he did not usually accommodate quality, but at Maeve's insistence eventually said that he had a very small room for her, and monsieur would have to share with a young English gentleman en route for Paris. The maid could share his kitchen girl's bed. This turned out to be in little more than a cupboard, but Gracie, in the spirit of the escapade, said cheerfully that she didn't mind. Maeve's room was indeed tiny and none too clean, but a fire was lit and it was tolerable.

Over a poor dinner shared with their young compatriot, he told them he was on his way to study art in Paris, sponsored by his uncle who thought he had talent, but that his papa would have nothing to do with it.

They sat for a while drinking indifferent coffee and then Maeve said she would go to bed, hoping to sleep after last night's restlessness. Gracie helped her prepare and then Maeve sent her off to her attic. Sitting on the edge of the bed, in her flowered dressing robe, rather doubting the sheets were clean enough to enter, she was thinking longingly of Ralph. Through this tiresome day, when Freddy had been irritable, impatient, and with his lack of French unable to provide better for them, she could imagine how Ralph would have commanded, bullied and cajoled to get a fresh carriage, better accommodation in a better place, and was imagining him at Mr Hastings' house in Suffolk, oblivious of what was happening to her. She had just decided to venture between the sheets when there was a tap on the door.

Thinking it Gracie having forgotten something, she called, "Come in."

It was Freddy who stood there, candle in hand, in shirt sleeves and stockinged feet.

He managed a laugh for the first time since yesterday morning. "I am a refugee from that youth in the other half of my bed. He tells me he always reads poetry aloud to himself in order to be able to get to sleep. Well! I thought that was the outside of enough and left him to it."

Maeve laughed at him. "Then you'd better sit down for a few minutes by my fire. Shall we ring for some punch – if this wretched inn can supply it? I can't imagine you listening to poetry into the small hours. Such torture!"

"You are an unfeeling woman," he said, and came to stand beside her.

Their eyes met and the laughter died suddenly. A wave of colour swept through her cheeks. Then he pulled her into his arms and, bending his head, kissed her again as he had on the Marsh, his arms tightening about her, his body pressed against hers.

For one moment desire swept them together and then he raised his head and said in a thickened voice, "We may never be alone again like this. Let me stay – for God's sake, let me stay."

But she was already pushing him away. If this had come sooner, before they had come to London, she might have yielded, but not now. For her, at least, the sudden emotion was over. "No – no, Freddy." She managed to release herself. "You don't really mean it. We've come far beyond that. It is only because you are so anxious and upset."

He shook his head, still swamped with the desire that had seized him. "Oh, Maeve, my darling – if only – "

"It's too late," she said. "You can't think that I'd be your mistress?" Her head was clearing. "I don't love you in that way. Oh, I did once, but not now. I didn't love Ralph then, but I do now."

He caught his breath. "Yes, it's Ralph, isn't it? I can see it in your face. You don't care for me any more." he sounded like a jealous boy.

"What would have been the good?" She slid away from him, though the smallness of the room prevented her going far. "It was because we were unhappy that we kissed on the

Marsh, thought we loved each other. I love Ralph. I've only just found out how much."

All the urgency seemed to go out of Freddy, leaving him pale and weary.

"And I only found out on the Marsh how much I love *you*. It's the very devil, isn't it? If I'd realised, had any sense – oh, long ago – but you're right, there's nothing to be done." He stared helplessly at her. "I have to try to get Angela back, look after her, for the rest of my life make something of our marriage. But now – my God, I just don't know how."

He put a hand to brush off the sudden tears.

"Oh, my dear," she whispered, "what can I say?" She went to him, put her arm about him. "I pray it will be better for you when you find Angela. Perhaps then she will know how much she has in you and Hollanders."

He had put his head for a moment on her shoulder, but now he raised it. "I don't believe that – but maybe. I've nothing else left, have I? Goodnight, dear Maeve. I'm sorry I tried – "

"Don't think of it," she said gently. "Time slipped for a moment so that we were – as we once thought we could be. But we shall always be friends – always – and friends don't turn their backs on each other in the bad times, do they? Now I think we should get some sleep."

He nodded, and taking her hand, pressed his lips into her palm. "Thank God you came with me. I couldn't have borne it alone."

In his shared room his bed fellow stirred, opened his eyes and said, "You're late to bed, sir. I hope she was pretty – and accommodating."

And Freddy, who would normally have made a laughing retort, told the youth to shut his bloody mouth. Then he sat down on the edge of the bed and buried his face in his hands.

They reached Paris in the afternoon of the next day and Maeve suggested Freddy should tell the hired driver to take them to the Hotel de l'Europe. It was the only one she knew as it was where Ralph had brought her on their honeymoon a little over a year ago. She was shown up to a large comfortable room on the first floor, where she found herself recollecting the repugnance she had felt for the intimacy of married life with the big man she had chosen to wed, and was thankful now that she had left that innocent, erratic girl behind.

Freddy said, "This is a splendid place. You see, I couldn't have managed without you," and added that he was going out at once to make enquiries.

Tired after the journey, the disturbed nights and uncomfortable upsets, Maeve took off her dress and lay down on the bed with her dressing gown over her petticoats.

The winter light faded and she slept until it was quite dark when Gracie returned with candles to help her put her dress in order. Having no idea she would end up in Paris, she had not brought an evening gown and had only her walking-out dress, not at all suitable for the dining room, but it couldn't be helped.

Freddy came back, looking wretched. "I've walked the streets," he said, "tried every damned hotel I could find. Shall we have something to eat and then I'll go out again? Perhaps it's worth going across the river to the south side of the city."

They ate an excellent dinner, Maeve conscious that she was improperly dressed in her gown of dark blue with pale blue check inset from the shoulders reaching to a point at her waist. It was one of her favourite dresses but hardly suitable for the dinner hour. Afterwards, Freddy growing impatient, they went up to her room where he had left his hat.

"Wait until morning," Maeve begged. "They won't be going anywhere now."

"I can't," he said. "They might leave at dawn. I'm sure they're here – they must be."

"Very well," she said helplessly. Another night away and, much as she pitied him, her unease grew and she wanted only to go home. "But wrap up well. I wish you had brought your greatcoat." For he had forgotten it in his rush to search for the runaways. "I'm sure it's bitter out."

He gave a deep sigh. "I think I'm half afraid – of what I shall find."

"I'm so sorry for you," she said again. "And I can do so little to help you."

"You will – when we find her." He gave a shaky smile and at that moment there was a knock on the door. "I told them to send up a mull," he added, but instead of the door opening to admit a waiter with the wine on a tray, it swung back to admit the last person they expected.

Chapter 21

"Ralph!" Maeve cried out, "Oh, Ralph!" in so a stunned a voice that he could be pardoned for his next remark.

"Well!" he said in a voice of ice. "May I enquire whose bedroom this is? Or is it relevant? You two seem to have a predilection for meeting in bedrooms."

They both spoke together. "Ralph, you can't think – " from Maeve, while Freddy broke in, "You've got it all wrong – but how on earth did you find us? I thought you were in Suffolk?"

"It was not too difficult," Ralph retorted, ignoring the last question. Closing the door, he set his back to it and said, "If you meant to cover your tracks, you made a poor job of it. You not only drove off in a Hollander carriage, but with both Gracie and a valise into the bargain. What was I to deduce from that but that you were running away with my wife?"

"The devil you did!" Freddy said in sudden irritation. "How could you think anything so stupid? It's *my* wife we're running after."

"Yes," Maeve said, "it's quite dreadful, Ralph. Angela has gone off with Count Balakov." By now she had had a few moments to recover, to take stock of Ralph's appearance. His face looked grey with fatigue and strain, a deep furrow between his brows. He was unshaven, though he had so light a beard it hardly showed, but it indicated his state of mind. His boots were muddied, his coat dirty, and his stock loosened. Her last words left him looking staggered.

"It's true," she said. "Ralph, you can't have believed anything so stupid as that I'd run away with Freddy? And if I had, I'd hardly have done it so blatantly, would I?"

He was getting a little tired of being called stupid. "It seemed an obvious deduction in the lack of anything so helpful as a note."

"Oh, I did think of that afterwards," she said penitently, "I did – do forgive me, Ralph. But I never thought you'd be back as soon. I was sure I'd be home before you knew I'd gone. It's true about Angela – really it is."

Ralph seemed to be struggling to grasp this after his long ride south, the nightmare of finding her gone and the chase across to Paris with his mind in an agonised turmoil. Drawing several deep breaths he said, "Then it's that foolish girl who's caused all this – this trouble?"

"If you want to blame someone," Freddy retorted bitterly, "blame that damned Russian. He started it all, turned her head. And blame me too – I shouldn't have brought her to London, maybe not even to England. Only it's no good going over all that."

Ralph turned to his wife. "But I don't understand why you are here."

Freddy answered for her. "She's here because I begged her to come, though we did think we'd catch them the English side of the Channel. We never meant to end up in France."

"Freddy thought Angela might need me, that I could be of use when he found her," Maeve put in, and Freddy added, "When I've put a sword or a bullet through the cursed fellow, Angela will need a woman, a friend, and Maeve was good enough to come."

Ralph passed his hand over his eyes. "I thought – but I see I was wrong."

"Yes, you were," Freddy said forcefully. "For God's sake, sit down before you fall down. You look dead beat."

Ralph ignored this. "And have you found Angela? And Balakov?"

"Not yet. I've been scouring Paris. I was about to go out again when you came."

In something of a daze Ralph said, "I'm beginning to understand. It was utterly foolish of you both to dash off together. What a choice piece of scandal if it became known! But I see I misjudged you."

"No, you didn't," Freddy answered unexpectedly. "I've

regretted the mistake I made – I wish to hell I'd married Maeve before you came along, but I didn't and that's an end of it. I've got to lie on the bed I've made."

"And you?" Ralph turned to Maeve. She was trembling and had sunk down suddenly in the nearest chair. It seemed as if Ralph would never believe her, that the harsh, cold voice would never soften. "Oh, Ralph, it's been so awful – there was a moment – but its over and now . . ."

"Yes?" he asked intently, "Now?"

Freddy snatched up his hat. "Don't you see yet? It's you she loves, not me. She told me so. And now I must go and look for my wife."

Ralph paused, summoning all his forces. "I beg your pardon, Freddy. I came here wanting to put a bullet into *you*, believing what I did – " He broke off that tack and held out his hand.

Freddy took it. "Thank you. Now I'll go."

"Wait a moment," Ralph said suddenly. "Do you know your way around Paris?"

"Not at all," Freddy admitted. "I've never been here before and I was never much good at learning their damned language."

"Then I'd better go with you. I know the city well and my French is passably fluent – that is, if you'd care for my company?"

They looked straightly at each other, and then Freddy said. "It's been hellish, trying to find hotels they might be in and getting lost into the bargain. I'd be damned grateful if you'd come." He glanced at Ralph and then at Maeve. "You'll want a few minutes – I'll wait downstairs."

The door closed behind him. Ralph was gazing at her, seemingly searching for words "Is it – can it be true – what he said?"

Maeve sat up. It seemed suddenly the moment that would set the pattern for the rest of their lives. Quite deliberately she came across to him and did what she had been longing to do since he went away. She put both arms about his neck, and looked up into his face. "Oh yes, yes, yes. Ralph, you must believe me."

Slowly he closed his arms about her. "I've – I've been to

hell and back these last few days. I thought you'd left me and I didn't know how to bear it, knowing it was all my fault."

"It wasn't – it wasn't. Thank heaven you came back so soon. But why did you?"

"Because I couldn't stand it, because I wanted to put things right, to grovel at your feet if I had to, but to beg you to forgive me. That night . . ."

"Oh, that night," she whispered, "It was then I knew I loved you."

He looked at her in amazement. "How could you, after what I did? I must have hurt you, I was a brute, but I was crazy with jealousy."

"I don't know." She gave a little half sob, half laugh. "I only know I saw for the first time how much I'd hurt *you*, how blind I'd been. I thought once I could never love anyone but Freddy, and then I saw it was nothing but a fantasy, from my girlhood really. I saw that it was you that I wanted – in every way." Colour came into her cheeks, but she kept her eyes on her face.

"Dear God!" he said. "My darling, darling girl. Why didn't you write, call me back?"

"Everything happened so fast. Mr Oglethorpe came – "

"God damn the man – am I never to be rid of that devil? What did he want?"

She told him, explained the interview and her long talk with his mother afterwards. "So you see" she said, "he's gone, he won't interfere in our lives again, but I'm glad he came. If he hadn't, perhaps I'd never have learned the truth about Alice – which would have been a pity for it's taught me to know you better, to understand everything, even that business in the stable."

For the first time since she had known him, she saw tears in the blue eyes that were no longer cold. "I should have told you," he said hoarsely "at the beginning, but I didn't want to lose you."

"Knowing has done just the opposite," She gave him a slow smile filled with new love. "You may bark and swear as much as you like, for I know you now. I understand."

"Never at you," he said. "Never again. Can I believe it – you really love me?"

"I love you," she answered, and lifted her mouth to his. They stood there clinging together, one as never before, but at last, reluctantly, he said, "I must go. Freddy will be waiting."

"It is good of you to go with him," she said gratefully.

"Well, he looked quite done up and obviously didn't know what he was about. I have my wife back – in every way – but he's lost his. Even if he gets her back, what will life be like for him – or her?" He was holding her as if he could hardly bear to leave her. "I'd give anything to stay, but I hope we'll be back soon. In fact, I rather hope we don't find the wretched girl"

"But that would be no solution," Maeve said sadly.

He let her go and then put her hands, one after the other, to his lips. "No," he agreed, "you're right. We may be hours, so go to bed, my darling, and try to sleep."

But there was too much on her mind for her to rest, alternating between thrilling joy and desperate anxiety and pity for Freddy; she twisted and turned until the small hours when, with no sign of the two men, she drifted into a doze, only to wake as the first grey slit of light showed where the curtains failed to meet.

She became conscious that someone was in the room, and, turning her head, saw Ralph standing the other side of the bed. "I'm sorry to wake you," he said, "but I have to tell you what has happened."

"Oh, what?" She sat up abruptly and he took up a shawl to put about her shoulders for the room was cold. "Did you find them?"

"Yes," he said abruptly, "we found them, and a devilish business it was."

"Where? Ralph, tell me."

He sat down on the bed and took her hands in his. "It was after midnight, I suppose, when I remembered a hotel off the Quai D'Orsay, the sort of a place Balakov might choose if he wanted to be secluded. We roused the porter and made him show us the register – well, a few francs in the palm helped there – and so we found them. The porter told us to go away till morning but Freddy pushed past him and rushed up the stairs, and I followed. He practically kicked the door in. I'd snatched up a candle and there they were, tucked up in bed together!"

"Oh!" Maeve clasped her hands. "Poor Freddy, how dreadful for him."

"Dreadful it was. Angela gave one shriek – we must have seemed like a pair of avenging angels – Freddy seized Balakov by the nightshirt and dragged him from the bed. Then he hit him so hard the wretched man was sent half across the room to crash over a stool to the floor."

"Freddy must have been so angry."

"I didn't know he had it in him. Anyway, Balakov got to his feet and I kept them apart. Only blood-letting could solve the business and Freddy challenged Balakov to meet him this morning. He wanted to pull Angela from the bed and make her come away with us, but Balakov got between her and Freddy, and short of a fist fight I thought there wasn't anything to be done but to persuade him to leave her there for the moment."

"But what did she do? Didn't she see – "

"She was having hysterics and screaming that they would kill each other. A pretty scene, it was, roused half the hotel guests I shouldn't wonder. Anyway, I got Freddy out, after Balakov had named a Russian at the Embassy to act for him. We went round there and made the poor fellow get up from his bed. He had no English, but he and I managed in French. They are to meet in – " Ralph took out his watch and glanced at it," – "an hour's time in the Bois."

"Oh, Ralph, wasn't there any other way to settle it?"

"None."

"Have you and Freddy had any sleep? You didn't come to bed."

"No," he said. "It was past two when we got back. I looked in, but you were asleep. In any case, Freddy needed some company. We sat with a bottle of brandy I'd prised out of the porter – more francs doing the trick, for he had to unlock the cellar – and Freddy talked about Angela, about how it had all happened in India, about how his eyes were opened first in Brighton and then in London. He was in too bad a state for me to leave him. And then nothing would do but that he should make a fresh Will – he'd made one when he came back to Hollanders, of course, but he said that would no longer do. So he wrote it out and I got the porter up – more francs, of course –

and he and I witnessed it." He took a paper out of his pocket and, going to the mantleshelf, laid it there under a candlestick. "I'll leave it in your charge."

It was then that the full realisation of what was about to happen hit her. "His Will! Oh – couldn't you have stopped it?"

"I'm afraid not. It's the only way they can settle it."

"It's wanton – hateful – one of them may be killed."

"I agree with you, but it's the only way between gentlemen."

She was twisting her hands together. "If Freddy is killed . . ."

His eyes were on her face. "It would mean so much to you?" And then, seeing her expression, he added hastily, "No, no, I didn't mean that. It was a cheap thing to say, but I haven't yet got used to knowing you are truly mine. I've been jealous of him for so long. These last hours, I've come to know him better. Poor boy, he has suffered a great deal."

Poor boy! Maeve blinked. Was it really Ralph calling Freddy 'poor boy.'

He came back and kissed her. "Freddy assures me he's a crack shot – it's to be pistols – and so he should be, being an Army man. But Balakov's an unknown quantity."

"Have you had anything to eat?" she asked. "It'll be so cold."

"We got the porter to fetch us up some coffee. I'll be back as soon as I can, or send you a note. Try not to worry too much."

"Ralph, be careful."

He smiled at her from the door. "It's not I who am to fight this morning." Which was a comforting thought, but hardly eased her anxiety. Men were stupid, stupid, to think the only way to settle a quarrel was by trying to kill each other. She rang for Gracie, dressed, and then went down to breakfast, but found she couldn't swallow anything, only drink endless cups of coffee while she waited. What was Angela doing? Waiting as she was? She wished she could go to her, try to make her see sense, but she didn't want to leave the hotel before Ralph came back or a message reached her.

It came at last in the form of a note. She was still sitting in the coffee room when a waiter came in. "*Pour vous, Madame.*"

> Count Balakov dying, or may be dead. He has been taken to the Hôtel Dieu hospital. Get a *fiacre* and go to the Hotel Bernard on the Quai D'Orsay, collect Angela and take her there. The driver will know the place. Freddy unhurt. We are going to the British Embassy as this is an Embassy matter and no doubt will have to see the police. We will come to the Hôtel Dieu as soon as possible.
>
> R.D.

She laid it down, drawing a long shaking breath. At least Freddy was unhurt, but it seemed as if he had killed the Russian, as he said he would. She had never before personally known anyone who had fought a duel and the reality of it shocked her. She had thought men just tried to draw a little blood and that satisfied honour, but this! It was quite awful – the Russian, so full of gaiety and charm and so handsome, dying at Freddy's hands. What would happen now? Would Angela go home with him?

But it was no time for speculation and, hurrying upstairs, she put on her warm pelisse and bonnet and sent the porter for a fiacre. Crossing the river by the Pont Neuf, passing the statue of Henry IV, she saw ice floes on the Seine, remembering how she had been here in bright spring sunshine with Ralph on their honeymoon. Then they turned to the right and pulled up outside a building. She told the driver to wait and hurried in – but what did she call Angela?

"She said, uncertainly, "Monsieur – Count Balakov – Madame – *Je desire* –"

The proprietor, a massive woman in a black dress, standing by the reception desk, nodded, "Ah, Madame Balakov. *Attendez,* Madame *'s'il vous plaît.*" She summoned a maid who led Maeve upstairs and knocked at a door. Maeve went in.

Angela stood by the window. She looked very pale. Turning to see Maeve, she said hoarsely, "You! What has happened? For God's sake, tell me. Gregor – ?"

A spurt of anger shot through Maeve that it was not her

husband who was Angela's first thought. She said, "Freddy is unhurt."

Angela came to her and almost shook her arm. "But Gregor – oh, God, is he . . ."

"The Count is very badly wounded." There was no other way to say it. "I'm here to take you to him."

Angela gave a low moan and swayed for a moment.

"Come," Maeve said. It was impossible not to feel swift pity for the girl who had caused all this trouble. She found a cloak, for Angela was wearing a pretty but ridiculously thin dress. Maeve tied her bonnet strings and hurried her downstairs and out to the waiting fiacre, giving the driver orders for the Hôtel Dieu which he apparently knew well.

Angela said in a low, throbbing voice, "What happened?"

"I don't know. I've only had a note from Ralph which said little other than I've already told you. At least your husband is unhurt."

Angela burst into tears. "Oh, you are cruel. I'm glad Freddy's not hurt but it is Gregor I love. He will die and Freddy's killed him. I can't bear it, I can't."

"You must," Maeve said firmly. "Stop crying, Angela, we are here."

She helped the shattered girl out and paid the driver. They stood before a grey, forbidding-looking building with a solid door in which there was a grille. In response to Maeve's pulling at the bell chain, it was opened and a face appeared.

"*Mesdames?*"

In her very limited French, Maeve explained they were there to find out about Count Balakov. The grille closed, there was a drawing back of bolts and then the heavy door opened. The portress stood there, an old nun in black robes, her face half hidden under a huge winged coif.

She stood back in silence as the two visitors entered. "*Attendez, mesdames.*"

She went silently away on sandaled feet and Angela suddenly caught hold of Maeve's arm, holding it tightly. They were in a long corridor. It was cold and cheerless, only a statue of a female saint in nun's dress broke the monotony of its white walls. Angela shivered again and Maeve said, "It may not be as bad as Ralph thought."

Angela cast a scared look about her at the bleak white walls. "What an awful place. Oh, Maeve, what must you think?"

"What I think is neither here not there," she answered, "and this is not the time to talk of it." Aware she had sounded harsh, she put her hand over Angela's. "You must try to be brave, whatever has happened."

Another nun, summoned by the portress, came and inclined her head towards the visitors. She was the Reverend Mother, she told them, and if they would follow her, she would take them to the injured man. "You must know," she said gravely, "that he will not recover."

Maeve nodded, but Angela did not understand the language. The elderly nun looked at her in great sympathy. "*Madame* Balakov?" she said kindly. "Be brave, *madame*, we are all in the hands of the Most Merciful."

Maeve shook her head. "*Madame ne comprend pas,*" and she said that her own husband would be coming as soon as he could – she did not try to explain about Freddy.

The Reverend Mother nodded and led them the length of the cold corridor into another. It was silent, still, and to Maeve oppressive. Once a sister slid past, her eyes lowered. Then their escort opened a door and they went it.

The cell was stark. The Count lay on an iron bedstead under a white coverlet, bandages about his throat, blood seeping through them. His breath was hissing, bubbling through the torn gullet, his face colourless, his eyes shut. A black-coated doctor was bending over him, a hand on his pulse, but he glanced up as they came in. Meave held Angela's arm and felt real pity now, for she gave one anguished cry and threw herself on to the bed, clasping the limp hands, calling his name, begging him to speak. But he gave no sign of hearing. She was covering his hands with kisses, sobbing, calling again and again.

Shocked, Maeve hardly knew what to do. The nuns stood passively, hands folded, while Angela's cries turned to desperate sobbing. They have seen such things before, Maeve thought, but how can they bear it? The pain, the anguish?

The Count's breathing grew more and more shallow and painful. He did not seem conscious, but a cleft deepened in his brows. Once he opened his eyes and Angela cried out his name, but the lids fell again without recognition. Then, after how long Maeve did not know, the doctor straightened and looked compassionately at Angela. "*Madame, il est mort.*"

There was no need to understand the language to know what the few words meant. Angela gave one shriek and collapsed over him, crying hysterically, and Maeve, herself horribly shaken, came to her.

"Angela, my dear, come away. It's over." She and the Reverend Mother tried to help Angela off the bed, but suddenly with surprising strength, she pushed them both away, screaming "He's dead – dead! There's nothing for me now – *nothing*. Let me go!"

She wrenched herself free and fled out of the room, down the long white corridors. Maeve went after her, calling her name, but Angela was too swift. She pulled at the main door, somehow got it open, then she was out into the street and running blindly went down under the hooves and wheels of a passing carriage. There were shouts, horses rearing, a frantic driver struggling with them, the carriage out of control, people hurrying up.

They brought her in to the convent, two stalwart porters carrying her, the nuns fluttering about her as she was laid on a bed in the cell next to that where Count Balakov lay. But she was already dead.

Chapter 22

White walls all round, white head-dresses like great bird's wings, as Maeve slowly came back to her senses to find herself lying on an extremely uncomfortable sofa in the Reverend Mother's room where visitors were received. For a moment she was confused and then there came the memory of Angela being carried in, her bruised and battered body, clothes torn and muddied, the loosened fair hair red with blood.

"Oh – " she gave a little moan. She wanted Ralph. Where was he? If only he would come. He would know what to do.

The nuns hovered about her, full of sympathy. Used as they were to death, this twofold tragedy was out of the usual and they fussed over her, bringing her coffee. The hot drink steadied her. She tried to stand but her legs gave way and she sank down. "Rest," Reverend Mother said kindly, "I trust your husband will soon be here."

She was left alone for a while, the nun deeming a little quiet and solitude to be what she needed, and she was lying with her eyes closed when the door opened. Then Ralph was kneeling beside her, his face lined with anxiety.

"Maeve – my love, my darling, are you all right?"

With a gasp of relief, she flung her arms around his neck, shaken by a storm of weeping. But it relieved her. To be lying here against his chest, being held by him, was all that was needed to restore her, and presently she sat up and dried her tears.

"Oh, I wanted you," she said shakily. "You heard?"

"Yes," he said. "I'll take care of everything now."

"Where's Freddy?"

"With Angela. Poor fellow – poor fellow. It is ghastly for him. To kill a man and lose your wife in one morning is an appalling thing. And yet," Ralph looked down at her gravely, "I doubt if she would have come back to him. Or if she had, they would both have been wretched. Such a thing as she did can't be undone."

He got up from his knees and sat beside her, his arm about her, his other hand clasping hers. "I can't help thinking of Lady Hamilton and what happened to her after Nelson's death, poor woman."

She leaned her head on his shoulder. "What time is it?"

"Past four. I am sorry we were so long, but there was such a furore. The Russian Ambassador had to be summoned, and there were interviews, and the French police to be answered. Duelling is not as accepted as it once was."

"How did it happen? I'm sure at heart Freddy couldn't have set out to kill him."

"I don't think he did. He said he would in the heat of the moment, but I doubt he meant it. It was most unfortunate. The two of them were ready, the doctor in attendance, then as the Russian aide who was the other second dropped his handkerchief, a couple of horsemen dashed out of the trees. They were drunk, singing and laughing, obviously having made a night of it. Even though they were a way off, it startled us all. Balakov was standing sideways, as duellists do, you see, but he moved a little at the interruption and became a vulnerable target at the same time. Freddy's shot went into his throat while his own went wild." Ralph paused, thinking of Freddy Hollander standing in shirt and breeches in the dawn light, sweating despite the hard frost, staring as the Count went down, both hands at his throat.

Maeve asked, "What will happen now?"

"Two Russians are here to take Balakov's body away for burial, and we will have to arrange for Angela's. Do you think you're strong enough to come away? It's cold here. I don't know how these good women stand it."

With his help, she got shakily to her feet. "It's dreadful, isn't it? And they are so good."

He led her out into that corridor from where she had seen the distracted Angela fleeing to her death, and there found

Freddy sitting on a bench, a cup of coffee in his hand. He laid it down when he saw them. "The sisters are doing what is necessary," he said in a blank, emotionless voice.

"Come," Ralph said kindly. "We can safely leave her in their hands until tomorrow. We'll go back to the hotel."

"I can't leave her here. I can't – "

"Yes, you can, just for the moment. It is best. Come along."

Freddy got up submissively, seemingly incapable of decision. His face was entirely without colour. Ralph spoke to the Reverend Mother, went out and found a *fiacre*, and as the early winter darkness fell, the three of them were driven back to the hotel. There he said, "None of us has eaten all day," and ordered soup and bread to be brought to them in the coffee room which was fortunately empty. Freddy picked up his spoon, but his hand shook so much the soup spilled. He tried to smile and said, "I don't think I can."

"Try," Ralph said, "there's a good fellow. You need it. You too, Maeve."

Somehow he got them to eat, and then Freddy said. "I think I'll go to my room. Ralph – would you – would you come with me for a while if – if Maeve can spare you? Being alone is damnable".

She nodded at once, "Dear Freddy, Ralph will be all the help he can. You see, he has been through something like this himself."

Ralph gave her one swift glance, in wonderment at her new understanding, and then as Freddy murmured that he hadn't known, Ralph took his arm and said. "Come along, old fellow." At the door of Maeve's room he whispered, "I'll try not to be too long," before disappearing with Freddy.

She went inside. A fire had been lit and Gracie was there, drawing the curtains and turning down the bed. "Oh, ma'am! What can have happened?"

Maeve shuddered. "It's been a terrible day, Gracie, the worst I've ever lived through. I'll tell you tomorrow, but I want to be alone now, until Sir Ralph comes. He's with my cousin."

"Yes, ma'am." Gracie paused. "Dear ma'am, can't I get you something? Some hot wine?"

Maeve shook her head. "Nothing now, I've had some soup. I just want to sit by the fire."

The blaze was comforting, the warmth penetrating her chilled bones. She seemed incapable of thought and yet the scenes of the day passed through her head in a series of pictures. All her instinctive sympathy was with Freddy, and it seemed like a miracle that not only was he turning to Ralph for help and support, but Ralph was giving it. It was a long time before he came and she had fallen into a doze when at last the door opened.

"I've got him into bed," he said. "I managed to get some laudanum drops from the consierge and I hope they'll make him sleep. God knows, I pity him. Whatever one thinks of Angela's conduct, it was a terrible way to die."

He stood by the fire, holding his hands to the flames. "Thank God, at the end of it all, we're here together."

She jumped up and came to him, and then realised he was swaying. "Ralph! you're exhausted – come to bed."

He gave her an unsteady smile. "I thought this morning that tonight – but I've had no sleep, or very little for three days."

"Oh, my dearest, I didn't realise."

"Well, I left Dedham caring only to get back to you, and rode all night. I had to leave Centaur at an inn with a damned stupid landlord who I doubt could be trusted with a cart horse, let alone bloodstock – but he was done in, poor old chap – and I hired a wretched creature to get me to London. There I found you gone, as I thought, with Freddy, and I was frantic. I thought I'd lost you."

"Oh, no," she said softly, "not lost – found, I think."

He caught her hand and went on, "I took Jason and rode through that night to Dover and caught the first packet I could. The rest you know. I only got a few broken hours in my clothes on Freddy's bed last night."

He crashed rather than sat on the bed and Maeve pulled off his boots and stockings. "I'm afraid I didn't bring Bridges," he said with an apologetic smile. "I barely stopped at Bruton Street once I realised you'd gone."

She found his nightshirt, helped him off with his coat and shirt and threw it over his head. "I'm fit for nothing until I've slept," he murmured from the pillow.

"It doesn't matter," she said tenderly, "we've time now – oh, so much time." She bent to kiss him and within minutes he was fast asleep.

She sat for a long time watching him, the events of the day receding a little as a deep peace and happiness beyond expectation flowed into her. Once she got up and looked out of the window. The street lights were being extinguished, Paris settling for the night, an occasional horseman returning home passed by, once a party of revellers, and then it was quiet again.

Above the dark sky was clear, filled with stars, a sharp frost settling again. The peace of it seemed strange, eternal, with a permanence regardless of the stormy tragedy of the day.

With a deep sigh she undressed and crept in beside Ralph. The joy of lying with him close to her once more was overwhelming. She thought the tormenting pictures of the morning passing through her mind would keep her from any rest – Angela dead, Balakov dead, Freddy so broken she hardly knew him – yet the comfort of Ralph's sleeping body achieved the seemingly impossible and she fell asleep almost at once.

It was light when she woke, her first thought that yesterday, and many yesterdays, thank God, were in the past. Turning to look at Ralph, she saw he still slept and it was another hour before he stirred, threw one arm above his head and stretched his long limbs. At last his eyes opened and he saw she was smiling at him. "I've been waiting for you to wake," she said. "Lying here, looking at you. I didn't know I could be so happy. Is it dreadful of me – after yesterday?"

The question was not answered, did not need answering. He brought his arm down around her and she felt herself melting into his embrace.

"I dreamed of this," his voice was low, "ever since the day you walked down the aisle to me."

They lay close, touched, kissed. Desire leapt between them and she exulted in yielding to him, every sense responding, knowing at last the joy of giving and what it did for him. Deeply fulfilled and content, quiet after ecstasy, they were reluctant to move until, with a deep sigh, Ralph reached for his watch.

"Eight o'clock," he said. "I'm afraid we must get up. There's a great deal to be done today." He leaned over her and kissed her again. "Beloved girl, wife of my heart, I'm afraid I will look a pretty reprehesible fellow today. I brought only the barest minimum with me. Bridges would be quite ashamed of me."

At breakfast, Freddy was pale and hollow-eyed, but calm. He ate in silence until Ralph said, "We must make arrangement, you understand? If you like, I will see to it all. Perhaps the Père Lachaise cemetery?"

"No." Freddy was spurred into sudden, unexpected violence. "*No*! I won't leave her here among strangers. She's my wife and a Hollander. I must take her home to lie in our own place."

"It will be difficult," Ralph said, "and a tedious journey."

"I don't care." Freddy shook his head. "I'll arrange it. You two don't need to stay. You can go on home and tell them all."

"Certainly not," Ralph said firmly. "If this is what you wish, we'll set about it together."

"Of course," Maeve agreed. "As if we'd abandon you, dear Freddy." There was a new confidence in her now. She could be openly affectionate, as to a brother, and both would know that was all it was.

However, when it came to it, seeing Angela lying white and still at the convent and laid in a coffin, Freddy was so shaken and overcome that rational thought was difficult and Ralph undertook everything. He found a carter willing to drive to Calais, settled the expenses, and thus began a strange journey home.

The hired carriage followed the cart which was slow enough to keep the horses at walking pace. Everywhere they stopped, innkeepers and stable boys were curious but deferential. Ralph saw to that. Maeve felt she could not have borne it if he had not come. Freddy was, for the moment, quite changed. Gone was the ebullient, cheerful, easy-going, talkative Freddy; instead there was a man broken by shock and grief and remorse. He spoke little. Only once he said, "I don't think I ever really understood her. And I thought anyone would love Hollanders and Mama."

Maeve said gently, "You couldn't know how it would turn out." And he merely answered, "No," and lapsed into silence. He accepted Ralph taking charge and was almost pathetically grateful.

In the carriage, Ralph and Maeve sat close together, their hands often clasped, wrapped in their new discovery of each other, trying not to show it too much in the face of such tragedy. But once, when Ralph was paying the landlord and he and Maeve were waiting by the cart, Freddy said, "I'm glad about you and Ralph. I – I thought once that we – Angela and I – " He broke off, laid his hand for a moment on the black pall Ralph had managed to find to cover the coffin. "But I can see yours is no sham."

Her heart ached for him. The business of Angela's remains being carried aboard ship, carefully enough by four porters, was wretched, but Freddy stayed beside her, and Ralph's presence ensured proper respect. At Dover Ralph again organised a carter and a carriage, which took a little time. He also hired a messenger to ride to Hollanders with a letter of explanation to warn of their coming. Freddy was silently grateful. Only as they reached Hollanders he held out his hand and said, "Thank you, Ralph. I don't think I could have managed without you."

Ralph took it and gave it a strong clasp and it seemed to Maeve a healing of many wounds – to Ralph too, as he sat in his corner of the carriage. For the first time in the years since Alice's death, he was at peace with himself. It was as if winning the love of this woman beside him had exorcised all the old guilt which, rightly or wrongly, he had laid on himself. After fourteen occasionally stormy months she had at last become the wife of his heart, as he remembered dear old Prinny called Maria Fitzherbert, and for him, it was a new beginning. He was the same man – and he was not, for he knew now a mature happiness that was more blessed than he could have believed possible. She would fill the old emptiness, banish the restlessness, and perhaps, in due time, bring him the thing he wanted most. He watched Dymchurch slip away, wreaths of mist lying over the Marsh, the air dank and cold. The sky was leaden and he said he thought they were in for snow.

It came on the day of the funeral, the flakes falling lightly on the bier. Only the family were there and the Rokebys, Ellen tearfully holding Elizabeth Rokeby's hand, for of all of them, perhaps it was only Ellen who had really liked Angela. As an impressionable fifteen-year-old, she had admired Angela's beauty and been impressed by her, and the shock of the tragedy had appalled her young mind. Elizabeth too had tears running down her cheeks, but she was looking at the living bereaved husband rather than at Angela's grave. Well, Maeve thought, perhaps that would suit Freddy very well later, when the wounds were healed – and immediately wondered if she had become so much a happily married woman that she was starting to matchmake. If the moment hadn't been so tragic, she would have laughed at herself.

Freddy had asked Ralph to keep nothing back from his family in the letter that was sent ahead of the sad procession, but the home-coming was at least cheered a little by the recent and unexpected arrival of Lionel Hollander.

He was only a year younger than Freddy and they had been inseparable as boys, so his presence was the best possible support for his brother. Ralph liked the tall, immaculate naval officer at once and Maeve said to him, "Now you have seen a replica of my Uncle Tom."

Lionel's ship had docked only two weeks before and he had come alone to Hollanders, planning to bring his wife and young family in the summer. He was to command his sloop on a cruise to Naples after his leave and did not expect to be away as long as before. Everyone was glad of him and constantly referring to him, which was strange, considering he was the most silent member of the family.

Isabel was shocked by the change in her eldest son; his voice seemed several tones lower than usual, all his cheeriness gone.

"He will get over this," Ralph had said quietly to her last night after dinner. "I know, ma'am, for I've been through the same bereavement myself as a young man." Touched by his concern, she was learning to like Maeve's husband after all, for it was impossible not to see the change in their relationship, a fact that Maeve was unable, even in this time of sorrow, totally to hide.

She and Ralph had slept at the Vicarage last night and yesterday afternoon she had had a few moments alone with her stepfather in his study.

"You don't need to tell me," he said, smiling. "I can see that all is well with you."

But she did tell him almost the whole of it and when she left him, she felt that at least his sorrow for Angela and Freddy was mingled with thankfulness that his instinct for her had been right.

On her way up to change, she sat on the window sill on the half landing, glad to be in this dear old house again, and looking out at the path that led between the yews to the ancient church, thought of the quiet and peace there, of the Sundays sitting beneath the funeral hatchments of past Hollanders, the stone effigies of the first Hans Hollander and his wife lying side by side in Tudor ruffs, their six children carved along the side of the tomb. She was, she always had been, the girl from the vicarage, and gratitude welled up in her own heart for all that meant. Unthinkingly, Selena had spoken only the truth and, despite all the gaiety of Brighton, the excitement of moving in the highest society, meeting the King and the Duke of Wellington and so many others, this was where her roots lay. Only now experience had brought her a new maturity.

The next morning, standing by Ralph in her black bonnet and dress, she watched the gentle flakes settling on the coffin as it was lowered into the newly dug grave. Freddy cast a few of the first snowdrops on it and she remembered how his mother had done the same thing two years ago at the funeral of his father. He was quite composed now, in control of his grief and his feelings, and seemed to Maeve to have changed beyond recognition in the last few days. Gone for ever was the youth who had enjoyed the carefree life of a young officer in India that had suited his personality so well. As he stood with bowed head between his mother and brother, Maeve prayed that something of the old gaiety and charm would come back, when the time of mourning had passed.

The Monarchs were there too, Mary clinging to William's arm, her gentle nature shocked by what had happened, while William, who had idolised his eldest brother since they were boys, realised that once Lionel had gone back, Freddy would need him.

It was inevitable that memories of that other burial, more than two years ago, should come into Maeve's head, when Ralph had thundered down this very path and into her life. As they walked away, she whispered, "Do you remember?"

He gave her a quick smile. "To my shame! Did you want to kick my hat into the mud?"

"I admit that thought was in my head that day."

She gave him a quick smile and clung to his arm while he covered her hand with his other one. As they all turned to leave the sad place, she added, "Oh Ralph, take me home, as soon as we can leave. I want to go home."

And this time he had no doubt as to which place she meant.

Postscript

Spring came at last. The garden at Welford was filled with the daffodils Lady Digby had planted last autumn, and in May bluebells filled the nearby woods. Mellower days, the sharp spring winds yielding, the countryside turning soft green. Ralph threw himself into everything to do with the estate and set about forming a cricket eleven with which one day he hoped to challenge the Marquis of Dorset's famous side from East Grinstead.

One morning, having been out and about early, he went up the stairs three at a time to tell his wife that the peahen had laid two eggs. He found her still in bed, a tray of breakfast on her knee. Imparting his news, he then said, "Gracie said you were having a tray up here – tea and toast? Is that all you want? And you don't appear to have had much of that!"

She pushed away the tray and held out her hand. "I'm glad about the peahen."

"I must tell Ackroyd to see that the eggs are safeguarded from foxes. Are you sure you're all right?"

"Of course," she said, smiling. "I'm just feeling a little queasy." And then, as joy came bubbling up irrepressibly, she added, "I'm in the same condition as the peahen was."

"The same –?" And then, as realisation came, light flooded his face. For a moment he could find no words, crushing her fingers, putting them to his lips.

"My love, my love," he said at last. "Maeve, if it's a boy –"

"– you'll teach him to play cricket and fence and box," she finished, laughing. For a moment they stayed wrapped in each other's arms until suddenly the male peacock shrieked right beneath their window, so that she jumped.

"That damned bird!" Ralph said. "I swear that one day I'll shoot the wretched things. I don't know why I bought them."

"Yes, you do," she answered. "I wonder if, like the peahen, I shall have twins!"